EVERY TIME
I LOVE YOU

Also by Heather Graham
in Large Print:

Lord of the Wolves
Queen of Hearts
Quiet Walks the Tiger
A Season for Love
Spirit of the Season
Tempestuous Eden
Tender Taming
When Next We Love

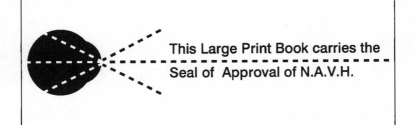

This Large Print Book carries the
Seal of Approval of N.A.V.H.

EVERY TIME
I LOVE YOU

HEATHER GRAHAM

Thorndike Press • Waterville, Maine

Published in 2002 by arrangement with Bantam Books, an imprint of the Bantam Dell Publishing Group, a division of Random House, Inc.

Thorndike Press Large Print Basic Series.

The tree indicium is a trademark of Thorndike Press.

The text of this Large Print edition is unabridged.
Other aspects of the book may vary from the original edition.

Set in 16 pt. Plantin.

Printed in the United States on permanent paper.

Library of Congress Cataloging-in-Publication Data

Graham, Heather.
　　Every time I love you / Heather Graham.
　　　　p. cm.
　　ISBN 0-7862-3514-4 (lg. print : hc : alk. paper)
　　1. Reincarnation — Fiction.　2. Large type books.
　　I. Title.
　　PS3557.R198 E94 2002
　　813′54—dc21　　　　　　　　　　　　2002018045

To Marian Davant,
my sister's mother-in-law,
a beautiful lady who has done lots of
beautiful things for me.
Thank you.

CHAPTER
1

"The ultimate. Exquisite. Brilliant. Well?" Geoffrey Sable hiked a curious brow, watching his assistant's face with interest. She was attempting to appear reserved, but a slight smile was curving her mouth. She was a tall woman, slim and sophisticated in appearance, whose fashionable wardrobe complemented her very fashionable figure. She was a capable, charming blonde with big innocent eyes. They were blue eyes, like the sky, wide and clear and beautiful beneath the startling contrast of very dark lashes and honey-colored brows.

"Interesting," she said slowly, carefully observing the canvas. "Interesting."

"That's all?" Geoff demanded.

Gayle Norman hesitated, still studying the oil painting hung on the stark white wall. Little shivers rippled up and down her spine, yet, for some reason, she wanted to deny the obvious and rare talent behind the painting.

"Well . . ." she murmured.

"Oh, come on, Gayle!" Geoffrey demanded gruffly at last. He was the owner of the renowned Sable Gallery in Richmond, Virginia, and had been her boss for the past four years. Even before that, they had been the best of friends and knew each other like open books. He prodded her impatiently. "Gayle — you know talent when you see it! And you know that somehow these paintings are the most evocative art either of us has seen in ages!"

Evocative . . . perhaps that was the word. Gayle had initially thought *erotic* — but perhaps that was too strong a word, for there was something in the muted colors, in the poses of the figures in the painting, in their almost mystical beauty, that transcended eroticism. In the particular oil she scrutinized, two lovers — a man and a woman — were entwined in an embrace. Gayle could feel the strength of the emotion there, the deep caring between the two. The painting was powerful because of the emotions it evoked. The intensity of the man's love for the woman, his strength, even his determination to protect her. And the woman's total trust in the man, her comfort in resting against him. The muted colors faded into misty grays at the edges of the canvas. It was beautiful and it made her ache with longing. She wanted to be loved, to know love as it was portrayed in this painting. She wasn't involved at the present time. Maybe that's why she felt a deep pang of loneliness when she looked at the canvas. But she wasn't involved because she didn't want to be involved — and besides this painting was about something far deeper than involvement. It spoke of deep love and tenderness and total commitment. The kind that came only once in a lifetime, and only then if a person were very lucky.

Gayle backed away quickly, drawing her eyes from the canvas to scan the others in the room. They were all nudes.

In art school, she'd spent hours sketching nude bodies: slim bodies, voluptuous bodies, muscular bodies — even some damned good bodies. She'd studied Rubens and Botticelli, and she'd been to the Louvre and most of the great art museums in the world.

Yet she'd never seen nudes quite like these. All these oils seemed to reach out and touch the senses and the emotions. *Evocative*. The word wasn't strong enough to describe these nudes, but she didn't know quite what to add to it.

"You're right, Geoffrey," she said at last.

"These are wonderful. McCauley is marvelously talented."

Geoffrey nodded, still studying one particular oil with satisfaction. "Have the RSVPs all been answered?"

"Every single one."

"And?"

"We'll have two hundred people — very illustrious people, that is! — strolling through here tomorrow night."

"Good, good." Geoffrey was pleased. Inordinately so. The grin that broke out across his pleasant features belied the dignity of his businesslike three-piece suit. Well, why not? she speculated affectionately. Geoff deserved to be pleased. A McCauley showing was a coup. McCauley was a recluse, Gayle had heard. His first painting had sold in Paris more than a decade ago for a ridiculously high sum, and the man hadn't consented to an interview since then. He never made personal appearances. Gayle imagined him to be a stoop-shouldered hermit with a beard down to his knees — a dirty-old-man type, perhaps, wheezing and chortling while he created works of spellbinding beauty.

She just couldn't help feeling a little negative about the artist. Organizing the showing had been pure torture. He wouldn't even speak with her personally. Every arrangement had been made through his personal manager, a man named Chad Bellows, who was charming and pleasant enough but still not the artist. Arranging each little detail had been an exercise in torture. Everything had to be checked and rechecked — no instant decisions were possible.

"What happens if your artist doesn't show up?" Gayle queried.

Geoffrey shot her a hostile glance, and though he seemed annoyed, she knew that he was nervous. He was still more her friend than her employer. They'd met at a café in Paris when they'd been art students with no real talent themselves, but with absolute admiration for those who did. They had become friends right away and business relations later. They'd never been lovers, although there had never really been a reason not to be — they'd both been young and — Gayle thought wryly — heterosexual. The friendship had just always been too important. Geoffrey had been simply wonderful to her. An orphan with a trust fund, she had clung to him like a marvelous new gift of an older brother. And in time, his dream of establishing an esteemed gallery had come true, and seven years after that fateful meeting in Paris, they were even hosting an exclusive showing of Brent McCauley oils.

Geoffrey grinned suddenly. "He'll show. If he doesn't, I'll send you after him."

"And what makes you think that I could do anything?" Gayle retorted to the threat.

"He likes bodies."

"I'm not sure how to take that!"

"Take it as a compliment. You might have been too skinny for Rubens, but in this day and age you've got a great arrangement of assets." She was staring at him, curious at the compliment. Geoffrey laughed. "Ah, come on! You mean to tell me that you wouldn't bare all for the sake of art?"

"No," Gayle said flatly. "And certainly not to that old hermit."

"Ah-ha! If he were young and handsome, it would be okay?"

"No! I didn't say that." She smiled. "I don't model. I sell art, remember? I'm the woman with all the hang-ups you love anyway."

He grinned. "But to model for Brent McCauley . . ."

"You know what I'll bet? I'll bet he's a real recluse. Seriously, I'll bet he has wild white hair and a beard to his knees and he never bathes because he's always in his studio painting. He probably has little beady eyes with a blazing light of insanity in them. And we'll probably spend tomorrow wishing that he hadn't shown up!"

Geoffrey chuckled, raising his brows curiously at the tone of her voice. "Making arrangements for the show has been that difficult?"

"It's been worse!" Gayle shrugged and turned away from the paintings on the wall to stride toward her desk, a richly polished Victorian secretary that added to the subdued richness of the gallery. She plucked up her shoulder bag. When she turned around, Geoffrey was still staring at her curiously.

She sighed. "He may be brilliant, Geoffrey, but he's also a royal pain. Nothing has gone smoothly. And I promise you, if he does appear tomorrow, he'll be changing all my arrangements."

"Maybe, maybe not," Geoffrey said simply. He was still smiling. Of course. He wasn't the one who'd had to struggle through a third party to reach the simplest agreements. "You're ready to go, I take it."

"Everything is as done as it can be."

"Yeah, but you're forgetting something. You can't leave without me. I drove you in this morning."

"Well . . . ? I'm ready. And I'm the work force."

"This is pathetic. I get absolutely no respect. All right. Come on. We'll lock up and get out of here."

In Geoffrey's silver-blue Maserati, which he had just been able to afford this year, he asked her about her plans for the evening. He glanced her way as he careened from the parking garage into Richmond's rush-hour traffic. "Are you still going to the Red Lion with the girls?"

"Yes, I'm still going to the Red Lion with the girls. It's Tina's birthday and she loves the place. It's really nice."

"The music is too loud, there's too much smoke, and it's too crowded."

"Want to come?"

"No."

"Ah — you've got another date with Boobs."

"Madelaine Courbier," Geoffrey countered good-naturedly.

"So you do have a date with her. With Boobs." Gayle smiled and quickly lowered her eyes. She couldn't help teasing him. Because Madelaine Courbier did have a hell of a chest, and Geoffrey was into heavy chests.

"Maybe. I do have an appointment."

"Well, don't smother yourself tonight, huh? Don't forget the showing tomorrow. Your dream of a lifetime. I can just see the headlines. 'Illustrious gallery owner found dead of asphyxiation in his lover's arms on eve of greatest achievement'!"

"Very funny, Ms. Norman. And I didn't say that I had a date with her; I said that I had an appointment. You watch yourself: big brother won't be around to protect you if you flirt yourself into an awkward situation."

"I never —"

"You do."

"I'm barely friendly."

"No — you smile and leave them drooling."

"Geoffrey, you're terrible!"

They drew up in front of her house. Geoffrey leaned over to open the car door. "Be kind to Boobs and I'll be kind in return. Besides, I'm not so sure that you should be going to the Red Lion. You should be going to a church social."

"Meaning?"

Lights flickered over Geoffrey's tanned features as a car passed by. He shrugged. "You should meet some nice guy and settle down. You're not getting any younger."

"I'm all of twenty-eight, Geoffrey."

"What was wrong with Tim Garrett?"

Gayle frowned, wondering where the conversation was going, uneasily aware that she had an idea of what he was getting at. "He hates art."

"Howard Green?"

"He pants all the time. Really. It's horrible. Like dating a large German shepherd."

"Bill Williamson? Does he pant too?"

"We just weren't suited to one another."

"He thought you were just fine. You never give anyone a chance."

"I date all the time —"

"Yeah. But I'll bet you haven't been to bed with a guy since Thane Johnson."

She stiffened. "That's none of your business, Geoffrey." She started to get out of the car. He caught her hand and offered her an apologetic grimace.

"I'm not trying to stick my nose where it doesn't belong. I just want to see you happy, Gayle."

With a sigh, she smiled and squeezed his hand. "I know, Geoff, but I am happy."

"You have a nickname, you know. Ice Princess. Howie was complaining in Duffy's at lunch the other day."

Gayle started laughing. "You were just calling me a flirt, now I'm an Ice Princess."

"I just don't want you to base all your assumptions about men on the one affair in your life. And I want you to be careful.

16

You're used to calling the shots. One day it won't work out that way. You'll hit one of the big boys, and it won't go your way."

"Geoff! I'm going out with the girls for Tina's birthday. I'll be good, I promise."

He was silent for a minute. "It may be more," he murmured curiously, but when she tried to question him, he shook his head.

"Have you been into Tarot cards lately?" she teased him.

"A Ouija board!" he retorted. "Now go on in. It's chilly out here. And maybe Boobs is waiting for me!"

"Is she?"

"I never kiss and tell."

Laughing, she got out of the car. A soft snow was falling and she wrapped her coat tightly to her chin to wave as he drove off into the coming night. When the taillights disappeared, she still paused. It was a beautiful night. There was no slush, just fresh, pure beautiful snow. The air was crisp and cool.

Gayle waved to one of her neighbors as she hurried up the path to her small house. She was in the middle of Monument Avenue, in a house way over a hundred years old, with a beautiful view of the park and several of the statues. She'd moved in her first year in Richmond, and she'd been furnishing it ever since. Once, it had been bare. Now she had two fine old Persian carpets on the hardwood dining room and parlor floors, and in her bedroom she had a canopied bed partially hidden by a Chinese silk screen, a set of high Victorian sofas and an Eastlake dressing table. She also had two Dalis, a Rauschenberg, and a set of seascapes by a budding young artist named Ralph Filberg. Those were her favorites. Geoffrey had talked her into the Rauschenberg as an investment; she had liked the Dalis and known she was getting a deal; but she loved the seascapes. No one had ever had to explain the talent to her — she had discovered it herself. It had been exciting to meet Ralph out on the Cape, a sullen young man with a wispy beard and a chip on his shoulder a mile wide. But when he had seen Gayle's enthusiasm, he had warmed to her; and when he had discovered she could actually help him, he'd become excited, eager, all too willing to please. Geoff had given him his first showing a little more than a year ago — and Ralph had given the paintings to Gayle.

The paintings always made her happy. Gayle nudged off her shoes with a little sigh. She left them in front of the paintings and padded on her stockinged feet to sit upon the sofa and glance through her mail. Among the junk mail and bills was a letter from Sally Johnson. Gayle felt her heart beat a little erratically; then she slit the envelope open. The little note didn't say much of anything. Sally was fine, her family was fine. She'd heard the gallery was showing Brent McCauley's work, and she was glad life seemed to be going so well for Gayle.

Gayle set the letter down and closed her eyes. She could still remember Thane. All too clearly. Tall, young, brash, exciting, so sure of himself. They'd lived together for almost two years, and she'd been deeply in love with him and so very happy. Every time he came home they met in the hallway and kissed. They shared candlelight dinners on the floor. They'd both been wild and young and impetuous and sometimes jealous, but they'd both been very happy . . . at the beginning.

But then Thane had started drinking heavily and taking drugs. He couldn't paint, so he drank; or something wasn't coming out just right, so he needed a snort of cocaine. Gayle had warned him that it was too much, that it was destroying him, that it was destroying them. Geoffrey had talked to Thane. In desperation Gayle had thought to call his parents and his twin sister Sally.

Nothing had meant anything to Thane. In an angry fit he had thrown Gayle across the room. That had been the end for her. She had walked out. One month later he'd overdosed on the alcohol and drugs. At the funeral she had been wrenched with guilt. Sally had tried to assure her she couldn't have done anything to prevent Thane's death. His mother had asked her hopefully if she were pregnant. Gayle had been forced to see his face in the open coffin, and something in those moments had assured her that she didn't want to love again. Not deeply. And certainly not another artist.

She was the only one of her group of friends and acquaintances who actually looked forward to an evening with an accountant or a banker. Too many of her emotions had died along with Thane. She liked her independence; she liked her life the way it was. At least she had liked it, she thought with a puzzled frown. Then she remembered the oil painting of the lovers and the feelings it had stirred within her. She smiled a little wistfully. Had she ever even loved Thane that deeply? As deeply as the lovers in the painting? Had Thane been capable of loving her that deeply?

"Maybe no one really loves that intensely," she murmured aloud. But instinctively she knew that they did. Very special people were surely privileged to love like that.

The phone rang. Before Gayle picked up the receiver she reminded herself to write back to Sally.

"Gayle! Good — you're home." It was Tina.

"Happy birthday, kid."

"Thanks. Are you ready?"

"Ready? I just got in. I thought we weren't going out until eight."

"No! We got reservations for dinner at the new club down by the Sheraton. Didn't Liz call you?"

"No, Liz didn't call me."

"Well, get dressed! Hurry! She's picking me up in twenty minutes. We'll be at your place in half an hour. And, oh, make it dressy, huh? It's coats and ties only for men, so we may as well use the opportunity, okay?"

"I haven't got anything —"

"You've more clothes than Macy's. It's my birthday! Find something!"

Gayle was about to say that she couldn't possibly be ready in thirty minutes, but a dull buzz assured her that Tina had already hung up. Muttering, she hurried to her bedroom and walked quickly over to her closet and began to flip through the hangers. She found a backless black silk, pushed past it, came back to it. She could swish her hair to the side with a barrette, wear the gold choker and her new black heels and be all set.

She should have hopped into the shower but decided that it had been a long day at the gallery and she deserved a decent bath. She filled the tub with bubbles, poured herself a glass of wine, and stepped in. The water was good and warm, the scent of the bubbles delicious. She closed her eyes and leaned back, then opened her eyes again and decided she even liked her bathroom. She'd decorated it in different shades of mauve. Her towels were monogrammed and her curtains were the sheerest gauze over a darker velvet. Tina once said that Gayle's bathroom reminded her of a powder room in a classy whorehouse. Gayle wasn't sure she liked the description, but her bathroom was nice and luxurious. Little Hummel figurines sat on the marble commode, a Lladró angel stood high above the brass towel rings. Gayle shrugged. She couldn't draw or paint, but the artist inside of her appreciated beautiful things. Not that she had to have them. When she and Thane had first met, they'd slept on comforters on the floor. They'd eaten bread and cheese and laughed over cheap wine.

She stood, ignoring the bubbles that clung to her. She hadn't thought about Thane in a long time, but today Geoffrey had mentioned his name and then she'd received the letter from Sally. It was probably natural that she was thinking about him. But it wasn't natural to be feeling quite so . . . disturbed.

She sipped her wine. It was the paintings, she thought. She couldn't get the image of those lovers out of her mind, and they were making her acutely unhappy with a life that had pleased her very well. No. She shook her head and swallowed down the rest of her wine, wincing as she did it too quickly. Everyone was unhappy once in a while, right? Married people wanted to be single; singles wanted to be married. Tall people wanted to be short. It was human nature.

Gayle wrapped a huge towel around herself and hurried back to her bedroom to dress; more time had gone by than she had planned. She dug quickly into her small nightstand for underwear and stockings, smiling ruefully at her weakness for pretty lingerie. The drawer was filled with soft, silky teddies and string-line panties in satin and lace.

Her doorbell rang just as she was fixing her long blond hair to one side. She yelled that she would be right down, hurriedly slipped into her heels, grabbed her coat, her purse, and the elegant negligee she had bought for Tina, and rushed out.

Out on the street, the night had become even more beautiful. The snow was silver beneath the moon. There seemed to be an air of expectation about it, something in the freshness that swirled around her. She gave herself a little shake. If she weren't careful, she'd start believing in destiny. But, damn, it had been a strange day! Not so much because of things that had happened but because of the way she had been feeling.

"Hey! Get in! It's a cold night, if you haven't noticed!"

Tina was the one speaking. The back door of Liz's little Volvo swung open and Gayle stepped in and slammed the door. Liz told her Hi through the rearview mirror, and Tina turned around to survey her in the shadows and glares of the streetlights.

"Happy birthday, kid," Gayle told her.

Tina grimaced. "Thirty-five. I'm almost middle-aged."

"You are middle-aged," Liz told her cheerfully.

"That's okay," Gayle assured her. "You're

aging better than Joan Collins."

"I hope so. She's twenty years younger than Joan Collins!" Liz supplied.

"Just drive, will you?"

Liz winked to Gayle in the back and turned her attention to the traffic. It was still bad. City traffic was always bad, Gayle decided. Tina quizzed her about the showing, and Gayle filled her in on how she'd rushed around to see that the pictures were hung to their advantage, watching Geoffrey become neurotic, fearing that McCauley would never show up. Tina, who managed the spa where they had all met a few years before, complained about an overweight man who thought she could make him look like Sly Stallone in two weeks.

"Shall we go for valet parking?" Liz asked. Then she answered her own question. "Oh, of course we should. We're dressed up to kill and Tina isn't getting any younger here."

Tina knocked her lightly against the nape. Liz howled softly and laughed as they drove up to the entrance. When the doors opened and Liz turned the key over to the young valet, Gayle mused that they were all dressed up to kill — and that they looked pretty damn good as a threesome. Tina was small and elegant in silver sequins and a white ermine, with midnight hair and eyes

25

that contrasted magnificently with her outfit. Liz — tall, lean, and statuesque — was in green velvet, which was a perfect match for her eyes and an emphasis for her deep auburn hair. Gayle was a tawny blonde in black, not as tall as Liz, not as built as Tina, but somewhere in between.

Someone on the street whistled at them. They all laughed at one another and went into the building, then up to the club on the twenty-fifth floor.

It was a perfect night for Tina, Gayle thought. They were seated by the window and had a beautiful view of Richmond. Their captain was extremely attentive. Liz, who had been taking classes, ordered the wine and it was just perfect. Tina and Gayle decided to have the rack of lamb for two, and Liz decided on the salmon. They ordered Caesar salads and crab cocktails, and everything that came to them seemed to taste ambrosial. Liz, the only divorcée among them, amused them with a tale about her new baby-sitter, and Tina talked about the cop with whom she'd had her last date, complaining that he had seemed to consider the night to be target practice.

"Yet here we are, on the prowl again," Liz said.

"We're not on the prowl!" Tina protested.

"We're having dinner."

"Ah-ha! But we're heading on to the Red Lion afterward," Liz reminded her.

"Does that necessarily mean we're out on the prowl?" Gayle asked her.

"Well, we certainly can't dance with one another," Tina stated. She grinned. "Face it, men are necessary."

"Yes, and you must quit going through them like toilet paper," Liz said.

"Would you shush! This is a very elegant place!"

Gayle laughed at the two of them and sipped her wine, marveling again that Liz had made such a good choice.

"Personally, I don't know what you're doing out anywhere," Liz told Gayle. "Geoffrey is so darling. All these years the two of you have been together! Has it always been platonic?"

"Always," Gayle said, smiling. "I love Geoffrey. But we're too important to each other as friends to be anything else." Her smile faded suddenly because she wondered if she and Geoff might have been something else if Thane hadn't come into their lives at the same time. Actually, Thane had been a friend of Geoff's.

There she was, thinking about Thane again. Not that she could really picture him anymore. She was seeing him as the man in the oil painting, as a different kind of lover.

"What's the matter?" Tina asked.

Gayle looked at her, startled. "Oh, nothing. I was just thinking."

"The deep, dark mysteries in life," Liz said sagely. "Gayle is in deep introspection."

"I'm not really. And I'm an open book. You both know about my one big affair. There's no mystery to it."

"Gayle's the one who goes through men like toilet paper," Tina reminded Liz.

"Yes, but darling, she doesn't even bother to use them!"

"Well, it's getting rough these days," Tina said. "You feel you need to see a man's health certificate before you kiss him. What is the world coming to?"

"Celibacy?"

"Heaven forbid!" Liz laughed. "Shall we order dessert?"

They did. They ordered cheese trays and amaretto cake — with a candle for Tina. The waiters sang "Happy Birthday" and the entire room clapped, and Tina promised Liz and Gayle that she would kill them both. They laughed and started on the cake, then complained that they'd be exercising for the next two weeks but enjoyed every mouthful anyway.

The check came and Liz and Gayle split the amount between them. As they drove to the Red Lion, Gayle scooted up in the middle of the seat so that she could watch while Tina opened her presents. From Liz, the gift was her favorite perfume, and from Gayle, the negligee. She thanked them both, oohing over the nightgown, then she was curiously silent.

"I just wish I had the right guy to use them on!" She sighed.

"You wanted to be single. You wanted your career," Liz reminded her.

"Oh, yeah, I did. But now I see time rushing past me, and I suddenly know that I want children, too. Time used to be my friend; now it's running out on me."

Liz and Gayle both assured her with stories they'd heard about plenty of women having their first babies at forty these days. Although Tina agreed with them, Gayle realized that they really were out on the prowl: Tina wanted a mate.

They reached the Red Lion. Again, Gayle thought about what a beautiful night it was. Fresh, clean air, snow-washed — that gave an expectancy to everything around her. She felt a cool tingle race along her spine, and she smiled. Something was going to happen tonight.

No, she was imagining things.

Maybe. Maybe not. She knew how Tina felt. She had almost said something while they had been talking. She had not been able to forget the lovers in McCauley's oil painting. The feeling captured there in paint was exactly what Tina was looking for. Perhaps it was what everyone looked for, what everyone ached for. That love so complete that it combined love and passion and the greatest tenderness.

"We are all mortals beneath the stars!" Liz said suddenly, tapping Gayle upon the back. "Shall we go in? These bright anti-crime lights are great, but I can almost guarantee a molestation if you stand there tempting fate much longer."

"It's just such a pretty night," Gayle murmured. "Spring is in the air."

"The stale smell of rotting fish is in the air. Come on, let's go in."

The Red Lion was alive with music and with smoke and with writhing bodies. A live group was playing a number by the Police, and couples were gyrating on the dance floor while people sat in small groups at dimly lit tables. Liz went to the bar and ordered a screwdriver for herself, a rusty nail for Tina, and Johnny Walker on the rocks for Gayle. Meanwhile, Tina found three seats together at the end of the bar, and the barmaid obligingly carried their drinks down that way.

"It's crowded tonight!" Gayle shouted over the din of the band.

"Very!"

"That's a group called Guts. They're good, huh?" Liz shouted.

"Hey!" Tina said. She straightened on her bar stool, trying to look over people's heads.

"Hey, what?" Liz demanded.

"Gayle — that's Geoffrey over there, isn't it?"

She frowned. Was Geoff here with Boobs? It wasn't really his type of place. People did come here to dance. Geoffrey liked to bring his steadies to his apartment. "Where?"

"Way over there, against the wall."

She sat up high on her stool, but it wasn't really necessary. It was Geoffrey and he had seen them. He murmured something to the other two men at the table and stood; one of the others did likewise; the third man remained seated. Geoffrey started to thread his way through the crowd.

"It's Geoff, all right," Gayle murmured curiously.

"Who are the other two?"

"I don't know. I can't really see them."

Geoff broke through. He caught Gayle's

31

hands, kissed her cheek, said hello to Liz and happy birthday to Tina. Gayle saw that the man behind him was Chad Bellows, Brent McCauley's personal manager. She leapt off her stool to take his hand with a smile. He was a tall, lean blonde with an aesthetic smile and an easy-going manner. She was glad to see him, especially since the show was tomorrow. Geoffrey had been nervous that something might go wrong, Gayle realized. She had actually been expecting something to go wrong.

"Hi, Gayle!" Chad said. Geoffrey was trying to introduce him to the others.

"Hi! It's nice to see you. It's a surprise to see you!"

"Geoff said we might run into you. It's your friend's birthday?"

"Yes."

"Tina!" Geoff announced, turning back. "Tina, Chad Bellows; Chad, Tina Martin, Elizabeth Dowell. Can we get you a drink?"

"Just ordered, thanks, Geoff," Gayle told him.

"Good. Come out and dance with me."

She didn't get a chance to protest. He led her out to the floor. It was a slow number then, and she'd danced with Geoff dozens of times over the years. They fit together easily.

She pulled back a bit to look questioningly at him. "What on earth are you doing here? Why didn't you tell me you were coming?"

"I wasn't sure that we were coming here."

"Aren't you being a little rude? There's another man with you. Why didn't you bring him over?"

"Oh, he's not the type you drag around. We'll go over to the table in a minute. And be on your best behavior, huh?"

"I'm always on my best behavior. What is this?"

The music ended. Couples began leaving the floor.

"The end of the song," Geoff laughed. "Come on —"

He broke off. Gayle was already looking toward the back, toward the table.

The third man was standing, leaning against the wall.

He was staring at Gayle. Across the length of the room. Through the crowd.

And Gayle felt it. Felt the power of his look, despite the distance. Felt his eyes, raking over her, piercing into her, searing through her . . .

He was tall, as tall as or taller than Chad or Geoffrey. His hair was nearly black; in the artificial light of the lounge, it appeared ebony, as pitch as the darkest night. The others were dressed in three-piece suits; he was wearing a light blue denim western shirt, a casual beige jacket, and blue jeans. He was broad-shouldered, well muscled, and dark-eyed, with handsome, thick brows. She judged him to be in his mid-thirties, with a well-sculpted face, nice firm jaw, high cheek bones, long, straight nose, and a firm, sensual mouth. He was shatteringly attractive, arresting in the most masculine, rough-and-tough sense. He wasn't smiling; he was just looking at her. Studying her, as if she were a portrait, a piece of art to be carefully evaluated and judged.

And it was so strange. So very, very strange. It was as if he had waited a long, long time to study her.

Her palms were wet, she realized. Her knees were weak, and a streak of white heat seemed to be searing along her spine. She knew that she had never met him before, and yet he looked strangely familiar to her, as if she had known him before.

She was dimly aware that she was staring at him as blatantly as he was staring at her. She felt as if mist swirled around her. For the most fleeting of seconds, she felt as if she had actually blacked out. As if something had . . . happened.

Between the two of them.

Gayle cleared her throat, gripping Geoffrey's arm. "Who-who is he?" she asked him.

"Who?" he said innocently.

"That man! The man with you. Who is he, Geoff?"

"Oh, him? The tall guy over there?" Geoff laughed. "Tall, dark, muscular, and handsome? Why that's just that scurvy old hermit with the dirty beard you've been dreading all week."

"What?"

"That's the old hermit. The artist — Brent McCauley. I think he's been waiting to meet you."

Waiting . . . yes.

Gayle shivered and swallowed. She had the most curious feeling that she had been waiting to meet him, too. Waiting . . . all of her life.

CHAPTER
2

Who is she?

Brent had voiced the question to Geoffrey several minutes ago. It still rang loudly in his mind. A ripple of heat and excitement knifed through him, settling in the pit of his gut. For a moment, it seemed to steal his breath away like a crippling blow. It was almost as if he had seen her before, and yet he knew that he hadn't. He wouldn't have forgotten her. The sensations that streaked into him at the first sight of her were so strong, almost painful. He hadn't been able to walk over to the women with Chad and Geoff. He had barely been able to move. He had forced out some kind of casual comment, and then he had played the eccentric artist with an "I'll-wait-here-you-bring-your-friends-to-me," type of comment.

And now she was coming.

If he had ever known her, he would have definitely remembered her. She was medium tall, slim, extremely shapely. What he'd noticed first was her hair — a head of long, lush, honey-blond hair, falling over one shoulder. What he'd noticed next had been her back — a gorgeous back, long, supple, graceful. As an artist, he'd been impatient with the swatch of black cloth that covered that elusive, flowing spine from the waist down. The temptation was to rush to her in the midst of the crowd and snatch away the offending fabric. It would, of course, be rather difficult to explain that he was undressing her in the name of art. She was the most elegantly sensual woman he had ever seen, from the flash in her eyes to the quiet, confident sway of her hips. She was the perfect, fascinating woman . . .

Brent told himself that surely that was it — the key to the violence of the emotion that swept through him at first sight of her. She was an artist's dream. The body magnificent. Not that he didn't appreciate most women; he did. And his adrenaline had certainly been sent into motion before.

But not to this extent. Not so strongly that it was almost overpowering. Not so much that time and music and the very pulse of life seemed to stand still — light and darkness and shadow to seep away just because she was walking toward him, because their eyes met and some shimmering chemistry was being awakened.

Her eyes were blue: sky blue, pure blue, innocent blue — a rather incongruous color when compared to the sophistication of her dress, her hair, even her easy smile. She knew that she was an attractive woman, that she appealed to men. Perhaps, Brent thought wryly, she even set herself slightly above the tongue-hanging appreciation she could surely accrue. Brent crossed his arms over his chest and a slow smile seeped into his own features. His eyes were still locked with hers, and hers with his. He felt definitely challenged. Alert, aware, tempted — excited. And more than ready to march to the fore. He smiled with a slow, sure assessment of the woman approaching him. You've met your match, sweetheart, he wanted to tell her. I'm the man who is going to call your bluff.

Geoffrey Sable had reached the table with her. Chad was coming over with two other women.

"Brent, this is Gayle Norman, my assistant, the lady who has been doing most of the work for the showing. Gayle, Brent McCauley. Oh, and these are two of Gayle's friends . . ."

Geoffrey was still talking. Brent didn't hear him. Gayle Norman's hand was in his.

Warm, electric. She was smiling at him, not a foot from him. Her smile had a haughty little curve to one side, as if she were longing to tell him that she wasn't in the least impressed by the fact that he was a great artist. It was all a lie, he thought. Or maybe she wasn't impressed with the fact that he was an artist. Still, she was affected. He could see her breasts rising and falling beneath the hugging black silk; he could feel the terror of her heart, the beat accelerated.

"Mr. McCauley," she said simply. Her voice was music. Cool, melodious. She was fighting it; she knew that it was there, that shattering chemistry, but she longed to deny it.

"Miss Norman," he returned. He seemed to be testing the sound of her voice, she thought. Tasting it . . .

He released her hand. He said something polite to the other two women. They all slid into the booth he had been sharing with Chad and Geoffrey Sable; conversation ensued. Easy laughter, easy chattering. It was a nice group, very relaxed. They were talking about the showing, about oils, about painting in general, about their expectations for tomorrow. He answered everything said to him; he replied — coherently — he believed.

But she was sitting across from him, and his eyes never left hers. She knew the intensity of his interest. She tried to ignore it. She talked too. Her voice was clear and feminine. He liked it.

And every once in a while, she would look back across the table to see if he was still watching her. When she discovered that he was, she would flush slightly despite herself, lower her eyes, and then jump back into the conversation.

The band began to play something by Robbie Nevill. She sweetly asked Chad to dance; Chad jumped at the chance.

Brent didn't mind. He sat back and watched. She was playing a game and he didn't mind it one bit. She was nervous.

He danced too, with the redhead, with the pretty brunette.

He always knew where she was. And he watched her still. He watched the curve and the sway of her back and, again, he convinced himself that his utter fascination was as an artist. He knew just how he would pose her, angled upon her derriere, legs flowing in a curve, her back rising gracefully high, her head tilted just slightly toward him, her eyes downcast, that rage of hair falling long over her shoulder so that its beauty was evident without hiding any of that glorious, elegant back.

The number ended; another began. A slow song, Lionel Ritchie. She had been dancing with Geoffrey. This time, when they started back for the table, Brent grabbed her hand.

"Want to dance this one with me?"

Those blue eyes hit him, clean and pure. They fell over his features, forehead to chin. Her lashes swept over them.

"I'm really rather tired —"

"Are you afraid of me?"

"Of course not."

"Want to pose for me, then?"

Her eyes opened again, full, honest. A ripple of laughter issued from her lips.

"Here?" She countered skeptically. Umm, she could be cool. Very superior when she chose.

"Anywhere." He could deal with it.

Her head rose high. "And just how would you want me to pose, Mr. McCauley?" She queried with weary sarcasm.

"Nude, of course."

Couples were moving around them. He slipped his arms around her and moved her onto the dance floor. She stiffened; she acquiesced. They swept along in circles. She fit wonderfully in his arms. Lights spun around them. Her eyes were on his.

"No," she told him. "I don't want to pose. Nude or otherwise."

"Want to sleep with me, then?"

She laughed. She had beautiful dimples. "No!"

He pulled her closer against him, resting his chin against her hair. He breathed in the scent of it; he let his fingers fall over the bareness of her back, and he felt her flesh, smooth as the silk, ripple and heat to his touch.

She leaned her head back and she stared at him, a brow arched in pure challenge. She wasn't about to do anything so gauche as shove against him nastily. She was going to tell him in eloquent silence that he was over-stepping his bounds.

He met that challenging stare . . . smiled slowly and pulled her closer, hard against his chest. She wasn't wearing a bra. He had known it, of course. Now he felt it. And she was either halfway frozen to death or feeling the same desperate ache he knew himself; her nipples were like hard, smooth marble. Her breasts were full and firm, flush against him. His arm was about her so tightly that even her hips were pressed against his, and everything he knew about her body, she had to know about his.

Desperate . . . that was the least of it.

Lightning might have jolted through him, hard, fast, searing. He burned throughout the length of him, experiencing another of those feelings that had seized him at first sight. It was shattering, as if he had been razed to the ground, body and soul. He almost seemed to black out; the world to disappear. And it left him simmering, seething, brewing . . .

Hungry.

She strained against his hold; he loosened it. Her arms were still about him, one resting lightly upon his shoulder, the other at his waist. There was something a bit frantic about the way she was staring at him.

"The music," she whispered urgently.

"What about it?"

"It's fast now! You have to — you have to let me go."

"Oh."

The music was fast; people were barely touching now as they danced. He'd been living in his own little sea, a place where the two of them had been dead tight against one another while life careened on around them.

He caught her hand, his fingers twining around hers. "Come on, let's sit out a few."

He didn't lead her back to the table, but out into the night. It was probably cold for her, but he felt that he had to have the air. He slipped off his coat and set it over her shoulders and when they had walked down the street a ways, he suddenly backed her against the wall, leaning over her, his palms flat on the concrete on either side of her head.

"Where have you been all of my life?"

She offered him a captivating, knowing grin.

"That's a hell of a line, if I've ever heard one."

"You have to sit for me."

"I most certainly do not."

"Please."

Everything seemed to echo sweetly in that single word. Gayle shivered slightly, not with the cold. He really wanted her to sit. She felt anew all the raw emotion she had sensed in his work. She felt the aching, the longing . . . the sense of something missing in her own life. He wanted her. It was a plea, but it wasn't exactly humble. It was probably the most humility she — or anyone else — would ever get from him. He was not a humble man.

It was crazy. She had no intention of posing for him. She didn't trust him. She didn't trust herself. He was beyond a doubt the most sexually alluring man she had ever met. The most self-assured, audacious, confident, and charming. He was absolutely fascinating.

"I don't — I can't see myself sitting there . . . the way that you want me."

"I'm an artist."

"I know. I've seen your work."

"I can be very professional."

She hesitated a moment. He was no old, bearded hermit. He was young, macho, and gorgeous. Ever since she had seen him, she had felt as if heated honey filled her veins, rushing through them. She wasn't terribly sure that she would have the strength to stand if he turned away. Her own palms were at her sides, braced against the wall.

"I — can't."

"But you will."

"You are quite sure of yourself."

"Yes, I am."

"Don't be, Mr. McCauley."

"Brent."

"I won't sit for you, and that's that. I've never been a model; I never intend to be."

He sighed softly, dropping his hands. He reached his left out to her, entwining his fingers with hers when she hesitated, then accepted his touch.

"You're giving up?" she asked.

"Disappointed?"

"No! No, I told you — I just don't sit."

They were nearing the door again. Gayle stopped, pulling back on his hand. "Mr. McCauley . . . Brent. I wanted to tell you, though, you are a wonderful artist. I've never seen paintings like yours. Your work is beautiful."

A slow, slow sensual curve caught one corner of his lip. He took a step back toward her, catching both of her hands, bringing them to his lips. She felt the brush of his kiss against her knuckles, very light. She might just as well have been branded, and her reactions started all over again. The palpitations of her heart, the gasping for breath, the spinning that tilted the world.

"Thanks." It was husky. He could have been a linebacker, a cowboy, Cool Hand Luke. But he was an artist. No — that was what he *did*. He was a man.

"You don't want to be painted — immortalized! — by one of the great masters of the century, huh?"

"I said you were good. I didn't quite say that you are Michelangelo."

He laughed, unoffended. "It was worth a try."

"Mr. McCauley, if you were me, would you consent to sitting in the nude for a man who was definitely coming on to you?"

"Now that would depend, wouldn't it?"

"On what?"

"What you intended your eventual response to be."

"That's something else that I just don't do, McCauley."

"What's that?"

"Respond — not the way I think you want me to. I don't just jump into bed with men. I'm sorry."

He was silent for several long minutes. He arched a midnight brow at her and spoke softly. "Did I ask you to jump right into bed with me?"

"Yes — the third time you spoke to me," Gayle told him dryly.

"Sorry — and I didn't say that we needed to jump right into bed. I've got all the time in the world. And a response, well . . . that remains to be seen, doesn't it? And anyway, I'd promise to play fair. Honest. I am an artist. Maybe I'm not a Michelangelo, but then maybe I am one of the great masters of this century. Only history will judge. I'd never come on to you until you had a chance to dress. If you wanted to put your clothes on, that is. You might discover that you really had no desire to do so."

"You really are something!" She forced anger and disdain into her voice. She didn't know what she really felt. He was so blatant. She'd never met anyone like him.

"Yes," he said simply.

"Tell me, do you do this with all your models?"

"I've never done it before in my life."

He spoke flatly; she sensed the honesty. Kinetic energy swept through her, and she couldn't deny the excitement he aroused in her. She couldn't wait to be away from him, just to see if it would be possible to think of anything besides him once they were apart. He was a total stranger. They'd exchanged a few words, rather crude words! — and she was feeling as if they were long-lost friends. No. *Lovers.* Maybe he was right. Maybe he was just honest enough to speak his feelings aloud. It was surely a streak of curious chemistry, nothing more. And she wasn't like that, she simply wasn't. Her values were a bit old-fashioned, maybe; and though she didn't consider herself a prude, she did believe in getting to know a man properly. A handshake on the first date was all she believed in offering. And she'd never in her life — not even with Thane — been tempted to anything more.

But this was different. This was frightening.

She felt an impulse to run her fingers

through his hair. To lean up and taste his lips. Oh, God, it was deeper than that. The impulse was to be with him. Bare, vulnerable, touching him, flush. Knowing him. Standing, just as the couple stood in his painting. Standing in a naked embrace that evoked every primitive feeling in a man and woman, passion and protection, lust and security, infinite tenderness, and a love that blocked out the rest of the world and stood tall before it.

She realized how intensely she was staring at him. And that he, in turn, was watching her with fascination.

She hugged his coat around her. "We should go in."

"I suppose we should."

But neither of them moved. Couples laughing and complaining about the cold, moved in and out of the doorway to the Red Lion. Occasionally, glances came their way. Neither of them noticed.

She smiled suddenly. She couldn't quite help it. She liked him, and she couldn't forget the feelings that his work had aroused in her.

"Have you ever been in love like that?" she asked him at last, rather wistfully.

"I beg your pardon?" He looked at her quizzically, an ebony brow arched high.

Gayle reddened, wondering if he were laughing at her sentimentality. She was thinking love, and he was thinking lust. "Never mind, I shouldn't —"

"No, no — I'm the one who is sorry. You're talking about the painting. 'Jim and Marie.' " He paused, then shrugged. "No, never. I've never been in love like that."

"Then how . . . how could you create such a thing?"

"Imagination. Hope. That's the way people should be in love, don't you think?"

"I don't know —"

"Surely you have an opinion."

"All right! Yes!"

"Do you know what it's like?" He asked her. She realized that he was still holding her hands.

"That's none of your business —"

His fingers tightened roughly around hers.

"Have you?"

She swallowed and shook her head. "I — uh — no," she murmured uneasily, not meeting his eyes. Then she added softly. "Not like that."

He smiled, then laughed, then whispered against her earlobe. "Good. You've saved yourself for me."

His teasing words broke the spell. "You

really are a pompous bastard, you know."

"*Pompous?* I object to the word. A little rough around the edges, perhaps, but *pompous?*"

"*Pompous.*"

"I prefer *arrogant.*"

"You would. It would fit the image. But trust me — *pompous* is correct."

He laughed and put his arm around her shoulders. His incredibly dark eyes held hers, yet she was laughing too. And it felt marvelous. She was so warmed by his touch.

"You really are freezing," he told her huskily. "I'm taking you back inside."

He held her close to his side as he opened the door, ushering her in. The crowds were upon them again. Gayle was vaguely aware that heads turned toward them, that they drew attention. There were so many people around them. She glanced up at his face, and she very much liked what she saw. There was a sense of strength to his jaw. Intelligence in his eyes. Warmth and laughter. And he was just a bit arrogant — not pompous.

Aware of her scrutiny, he gazed down at her with a questioning look in his eyes. She looked away quickly — she wasn't accustomed to being caught in the act of studying a man with such deliberation. But they were coming closer and closer to the table, and she knew that she was about to lose something. Him. Having him alone with her . . . and the unique intimacy they had shared.

"I'd really like to get to know you," she blurted out suddenly, and she prayed that it had sounded casual enough.

He stopped, catching her chin with his knuckle, raising it to meet her eyes.

"Isn't that supposed to be my line?" he teased.

"Ah, but you've had so many lines already."

"Pose for me," he demanded again heatedly.

"I —"

"You've the most beautiful back I've ever seen. I watched you, and I know exactly how I want you seated. It would be chaste, I swear it. No terribly intimate part of your body would have to show. My God," he swore passionately, "I've got to paint your back."

"My . . . back?" She couldn't help it; she felt a little disappointed. She'd wanted to imagine that he had fallen head over heels with her face, her eyes, her lips . . .

Her back? It didn't sound at all erotic.

"Think about it?" he said. He was very determined and very professional. She realized it wasn't at all a come-on. He wanted to paint her — her back.

"I'll bet it has dimples," he said suddenly.

"What?"

"Your back. Way down, on either side, just below the small of your back. Cute," he added with a grin. He lowered his voice. "Sexy. Do you?"

"You have the most incredible nerve," she charged him.

"It comes from being pompous. Do you?"

"Do I what?"

"Have dimples on your — rear."

"I really haven't the faintest idea."

He broke out laughing. "You haven't?"

"No! I'd hardly run around staring at my own —"

"Buttocks," he supplied. "Come, come, Ms. Norman! You were an art major. You've got to know something about anatomy. Enough to call a spade a spade and — a buttock a buttock. Or a rear or a derriere or an ass —"

"Enough!" Exasperated, Gayle stared at him. She tried to walk past him quickly, but he caught her arm and pulled her back. His warm breath caught her earlobe as he whispered, "I do believe you have dimples on your buttocks. I'm willing to bet on it. Has no lover ever mentioned such a thing, Ms. Norman?"

"No!"

"Then you have indeed been neglected. And I do intend to remedy such sad circumstances."

A flood of color washed over her and she pulled her arm away. She felt naked. She hadn't blushed in years and she had never felt at a loss for words with a man.

Especially with a man who possessed such an overwhelming magnetism. One who called to every need and longing inside of her.

Gayle slid his jacket from her shoulders and handed it to him. She walked on ahead of him to the table.

The group had been dancing. Chad and Liz and Geoff and Tina, then Geoff and Liz and Chad and Tina. No one seemed to have noticed that Gayle and Brent had disappeared for any length of time. Or maybe they did. As Gayle slid in beside Geoff she felt his scrutiny, sensing that he was just barely containing a snicker. Geoffrey knew she'd been outside.

She leaned back in the vinyl-padded booth and murmured, "No, the man isn't exactly a bearded hermit. When did you meet him, and how did all this come about?"

Geoffrey sipped something that looked like

54

a gimlet and raised his glass before his face.

"I met him this morning — you knew he was coming into town. And I came here because you always talk about it."

"You might have warned me."

"Why on earth would I want to do that?" he demanded, chuckling softly. "You were so intent on meeting a bearded hermit."

"All right! I've admitted he's not a bearded hermit."

"He doesn't seem to smell too bad, either. I'll bet that he even bathes."

"Geoffrey —"

"Gayle!" he protested innocently. "I did tell you —"

"Liar! You told me you had an appointment!"

"I did not lie. This is an appointment. You were so busy making fun of Madelaine —"

"Boobs!" Gayle interjected.

"I rest my point. Why should I have warned you that I might be out with a hermit?" He sipped his gimlet again and looked at her pensively over the rim of his glass. "Come to think of it, I did try to warn you. I wonder why. Can chemistry spark before two people meet?"

Gayle glanced across the table, but Brent McCauley was busy answering a question Tina had asked him about his work habits.

Chad laughed and broke in with something.

Gayle glanced back to Geoffrey. He was still watching her in a brooding appraisal.

"He wants you to sit for him, you know. It was the first thing he said when I pointed you out across the room. Before he even asked your name. He really thinks you'd be a fabulous subject."

"And you want to feed me to the wolf."

"I don't consider him a wolf. I think he's a nice guy. I like him a lot."

"A man's man?" Gayle taunted.

Geoffrey exhaled. "He's intelligent, interesting, and fun. Yeah, a man's man. I like him. He's a person first, then an artist."

"You do! You want me to do it! To sit for him! Nude."

"God, you're making me sound like a pimp."

"Well, I won't do it, boss."

"Hey — your choice. This whole thing is in your hands."

"There is no 'whole thing,'" Gayle snapped. Then she smiled. "Say that *he* was a *she*. Would you do it?"

"Sit in the buff?"

"Yes."

Geoff laughed. "I'll pose for you anytime, sweetie."

"Oh, you're an awful liar!"

"I'm not!"

"All right. Maybe you would. Maybe Boobs stands before an easel every night —"

"Don't you just wish you could be there!"

Gayle started to laugh, amused, and not at all sure what Geoffrey really would or wouldn't do.

"Hey . . ." Geoffrey lifted his hands with an exaggerated shrug, then turned from her to answer a question Chad had just asked about lighting in the gallery.

They were all talking around her. Someone had ordered her a new Scotch and Gayle quickly sipped at it. Once again she was seated across from Brent McCauley. When she tried to cross her legs she kicked him by mistake. He stopped speaking to Tina and looked at her, and his sexy arrogant smile slipped into place. He seemed to think she had kicked him on purpose to draw his attention.

"I didn't," she retorted, though he had said nothing out loud.

"Pose for me," he whispered.

"No," she mouthed in return.

She wanted to go home. While everyone else was having a good time, she was burning up inside. She was in panic. She needed things to go slowly, very slowly, with a man. She couldn't deal with this kind of emotional assault. Her head was pounding. She began to wish that Brent McCauley had been an old hermit with a mile-long beard. When would this party break up?

Not ever, or so it seemed. For a reclusive eccentric, Brent was friendly and funny. He had an ability to draw people out. He listened to stories about Liz's kids, and laughed about the foibles at Tina's spa. He and Chad seemed to be good friends, not just employer and employee. They all talked; they all had a nice time. And Gayle just couldn't bring herself to be the one to break it all up.

Liz finally suggested that it was time to go; she had to get the baby-sitter home. Brent McCauley went to retrieve their coats for them. While Chad and Geoffrey stayed inside, Brent walked the three of them out to Liz's car.

Gayle never entered it.

Before she could, he caught her hand again, pulling her back to his side.

"I'll drive Gayle home."

"You needn't —" Gayle began.

"Are you sure?" Liz interrupted.

"We've a few things to talk about. The show tomorrow, you know."

Gayle knew that she could have protested politely. She could have said that she was tired, that she would see him at the gallery. She could have said a dozen things. But she didn't. She stood there silently, her hand in his, as Liz and Tina and Brent talked.

They exchanged pleasantries. Brent Mc-Cauley was a star, of sorts. Maybe it was natural that Liz and Tina seemed a little awed as they told him good night.

But he was just as warm in return. He liked them, Gayle realized, and she was grateful without knowing why. He liked them as more than pretty women; he liked them as friends.

When Liz's car drove away, the parking lot seemed very empty. The air was cool. They were silent together, watching Liz's tail-lights disappear.

"Come on," Brent said after a moment. "I'll take you home."

"You came in your own car?" She asked him. She was nervous. She wanted to be with him; she wanted to lock a door a mile thick between them.

"We all brought our own cars."

"No one ever harasses you?"

"No one knows who I am."

"They will tomorrow."

"Yes. Still, not many people really notice

artists. But then again — maybe being there in person is a bad idea."

"Oh, no! You can't back out now! Geoffrey would be heartbroken."

"My work will be there, one way or another. It's already hung, isn't it?"

"Yes. But, you might not like the way I arranged the paintings."

"Trying to guarantee I'll make it, huh?"

"It's true. I'm sure you want your own more aesthetic eye upon it all."

"Pose for me. You'll have a royal guarantee."

"Sorry. I can't be bribed."

"Too bad."

Brent stopped next to an old Mach I Mustang. "This is yours?" Gayle demanded, looking at the big black air scoops and wondering just how old the vehicle was.

"It's mine."

He opened the passenger door for her. She sank into a nicely upholstered leather seat. He came around and sat down, quickly revving the engine, then looking at her.

"I don't know where you live."

She gave him her address. A silence fell between them as he shifted out into traffic. She was almost afraid to speak. She had to know something about him.

"Where do you live?" she asked.

"North, towards Fredricksburg," he answered shortly, then added, "a nice little house, with a big loft. I like it."

She nodded. It wasn't really what she wanted to ask him. She wanted to know if he was seeing anyone; she wanted to know just how many women he had had in his life. She wanted to know if he drank his coffee black, what he ate for breakfast, and if he slept in the nude or in pajama bottoms.

The car stopped. She realized that they had come to Monument Avenue and her house. He wasn't moving to let her out. He had shifted casually, watching her in the shadows of night.

She turned to him too. She didn't know if she should run or if she could possibly ask him in casually for coffee and brandy. She wanted to tell him that she was attracted to him but that he was moving way too fast for her. She didn't know what she really wanted at all, except that she didn't want him walking out of her life.

She didn't say anything. She didn't know what possessed her, but she felt as if she had to touch him. She shifted; she reached over and cupped her palm around his cheek, feeling the stubble of his beard. She felt the pattern of his jaw and a pulse against his throat. And somehow she knew that if she kissed him he would remain passive for a moment, then become the aggressor, nearly ravaging her mouth.

She brought her lips to his, lightly, and then she waited, but he didn't move. Some wonderful smell that was more pure male than cologne caused a riot of sensations to wash through her, and she hesitantly teased his lower lip with her tongue.

His arms wrapped around her, strong and sure. And his mouth covered hers, his tongue plunged deeply and erotically into the recesses of her mouth. Odd, that he touched her lips and the excitement swept to her abdomen. It was wonderful. It filled a void; it began an aching.

His fingers shoved at her coat, parting it. She felt his hand on her breast, thumbs teasing her nipples beneath the material. He wasn't still. His hand was on her thigh in record time.

It was too fast, yet it was incredibly natural. She barely pulled back in time and when she did, she was flushed and felt ashamed. It was her own fault. She had led him on. She wanted him, she wanted everything. It was still wrong, and she had never acted this way before in her life. Like a tease.

"What's the matter?" he asked.

"I'm sorry." She wrapped her coat around

her shoulders. She couldn't look at him. "I'm sorry, really. It's my fault. I — uh — I don't do things like this. Not until I've known someone for a long, long time."

He didn't say anything for a while. At last he opened the car door and came around for her.

"You don't have to walk me in," Gayle said miserably.

"Yes, I do."

She fell silent. He led her along the walk and to her door. He didn't try to come in. She stood there, awkward, ready to cry. In the hall light, he seemed very mature, very much the man. She thought again that he was striking, that he had everything, that he was fascinating, and that she longed to rest her head against his shoulder. She didn't dare.

He touched her cheek.

"Next time, my love, be ready to finish what you start."

"I'm sorry, I didn't mean —"

"Then don't kiss me again — until you do mean it."

"You don't understand. I said that I was sorry."

"I do understand. And I know that you're sorry. I'm just telling you — be sure that you do mean all of your actions in the future."

"You needn't worry," she promised him softly as she twisted her key in the lock. "There really isn't going to be a future."

"Yes, there is. We both know that."

She raised her head to protest. The moonlight was falling down upon his dark hair, upon his wide shoulders. Gayle trembled, aware of the shadows that played across his face. She parted her lips to speak, but no words would come.

"Good night, Gayle," he said politely. "I'll see you at the gallery tomorrow."

He turned and walked back down the path to his car. Gayle stepped into the house and locked the door, still trembling.

She kicked her shoes off and pulled out her oldest flannel nightgown. She washed her face and brushed her teeth and tried to go to sleep.

"He's the most obnoxious man I've ever met," she assured the ceiling. Tomorrow would come, the showing would take place, and then he would leave and she would never have to see him again.

Her heart began to thunder painfully. No . . .

She tossed and turned in bed. She touched her lips and remembered how his had felt there, and then she started to burn, realizing that she was wondering how he would look naked.

And how he would feel naked, lying beside her. Here, in this bed.

It was a strange night for Gayle. She continued to toss and turn for hours, and when she did sleep she fell into a realm of deep, deep dreams.

CHAPTER

3

PERCY

WILLIAMSBURG, VIRGINIA
MAY 1774

The first time he saw her — the very first time
— he knew that he would move heaven and
earth to have her.

And he learned quickly that such a miracle might very well be required.

It was a beautiful day in May. The sun had
just dried the dew on the grass and cleared
away the mist as Percy at long last reached
the road into Williamsburg. Although the
journey had been long, he smiled, enjoying
the simple beauty of the day. It was almost
as if life were just beginning; there was so
much splendor in nature all around him.

The roads were slushy that May. As he
rode into town, Percy ruefully acknowledged the fact that he was covered with mud

from his boots to his tricorn. His neat cream breeches were spotted in several places, and even his navy coat betrayed soiled spots. Well, it couldn't be helped. Once he'd had Goliath shod at the blacksmith's, he'd head straight for Mr. Griffith's tavern and see about his own appearance. He was much more accustomed to buckskins and un-bleached cotton, but Colonel Washington had warned him that maintaining an elegant appearance might well help him sway citizens to the rebels' position.

"What, whoa there, Percy!"

The cry came from the green before the tavern, just down the road from the Governor's house. "James!" Percy smiled and called the greeting, sliding from Goliath's back. James Whitstead, his friend from the next county, came hurrying toward him, his hand outstretched in greeting. Percy accepted it with enthusiasm.

"Why, Percy, look at you, will you!" James demanded, standing back to survey him. "Where's my country clod, eh? You're looking fine, man, I tell you, with or without the buckskin!" He tapped his knuckles against Percy's shoulder. "No wig though. Alas! How gauche. We'll work on appearance."

"We'll work on nothing," Percy promised,

absently pulling upon the dark queue of his own hair. He looked past James and saw that an older man was approaching them, a pleasant smile on his face.

"He'll not need a wig, I daresay," the man observed, shaking Percy's hand firmly. "I daresay he'll do quite well with our ladies, eh? From what I've seen, a fine pair of shoulders and a gleam in the eye, such as this lad's, do greater wonders upon the, ahem — soul — than any flight of fashion."

"I thank you, sir!" Percy laughed and eagerly surveyed the gentleman. He was Patrick Henry, the great orator who had first filled him with revolutionary fervor. Henry was not an old man — on the contrary, he was not yet forty. But James and Percy had both just passed their twentieth birthdays, and Henry appeared very mature to them. He also was a man of formidable presence. When he spoke, the walls seemed to shake and shiver.

"Will you have a pint with us, Percy?" young James demanded.

"Aye, I will. Goliath has shed a shoe and as soon as I've had him tended to, I'll be glad of a pint. If —"

He broke off because he was forced to do so. A carriage came sweeping along so quickly that Goliath reared and shied. More mud came sloshing over his clothing, his boots, his breeches — and even Goliath.

"God's blood!" Percy swore, then he laughed with a fair share of hostility for the speeding carriage, for its haste caused sure disaster as the axle cracked, the wheel flew off, and the frame crashed neatly to the ground.

"Ah, sir! See what your rudeness has accomplished!" Patrick called.

The coachman, a slim, dour-faced fellow in the Governor's livery, cast an evil glare their way. He hopped to the ground, eager to reach the doors. Yet when he stood, he began to walk dizzily in a circle and then fell to the ground.

Percy raced over to him, ducking down to seek a pulse. He looked up at the other two. "He is alive."

They'd attracted a gathering then. A hostile one, so it seemed, for in these grievous days no one could quite decide who was friend or foe.

"Dazed, I suppose," called someone.

"Racing through here like a hellion, 'tis what he deserved."

"On the damned Governor's business!" someone else swore.

"Give the poor man aid!" cried one goodwife, and she hurried to the crowd, smiling at Percy before she knelt by the fellow, a cool cloth in her hand to bathe his face.

Percy turned to the carriage then, aware that someone must be inside it. He stood and started to walk toward it and then started to run. He reached the doors just as they flew open, and the woman appeared. Actually, she was little more than a girl. A bit of a thing, scrambling from the cockeyed angle of the coach to gain her balance and jump down, her voluminous skirts and petticoats hindering her progress. She caught hold of the door and saw Percy's eyes upon her and the laughter deep within them.

He did not know if she was so much beautiful as she was breathtaking. She was dressed in a gown of royal blue velvet, a color that matched her eyes, with all the fire of daylight streaming from them. Tendrils of hair, golden and rich, escaped her cap to curl about her nape and throat and bosom. She was deeply agitated, he saw, and outraged at his laughter. He scanned the riot of her petticoats and the rapid rise and fall of her breasts with bold speculation, his own breath quickening as he reached for her hand to help her.

"Knave!" she snapped. "A gentleman would not —"

"I know not what a gentleman would do, milady," Percy said, swiftly reaching for her and lifting her from the floor of the coach, and holding her against himself for those few seconds before her feet could touch the ground. Her body, next to his. Her eyes, burning deep into his very soul. He inhaled, and she filled him. He would never forget her eyes, her fingers, delicate but strong upon his shoulders. Looking into her eyes, he smiled slowly and continued to speak. "But a man? A plain and simple man, milady, could not help but be eager to hold you."

She did not respond. For aeons she stared into his eyes. And for aeons he returned that stare, his eyes narrowing as he made a silent promise.

"Percy, is she well?" Mr. Henry called to him.

He saw her eyes widen; he saw the horror and then the fury within them.

"Percy! Percy Ainsworth." She struggled furiously to free herself from his grasp. "The traitor!"

He laughed dryly and set her down, then swept his tricorn from his head. "Traitor? Nay, lady. Just a patriot, and no other."

"A traitor!" she spat back. "A backwoods traitor. Step aside, sir, and let me pass."

He grit his teeth and maintained his smile. "So soon? Why I had thought we were just coming to know each other."

"Let me by!" When she tried to move past him, her elegant skirt caught upon the footstep of the carriage and she was thrown toward him. He caught her within his arms, lest she topple into the mud in the road. "Oh!" She cried in furious distress. "Let me go, I say!"

He laughed, and then it seemed that something caught in his throat and he heard himself whispering to her.

"Lady, I do believe you're eager to be in my arms."

"I do believe you are rude as well as brash!"

"Am I, then?" He felt her shiver, just as it seemed lightning streaked a burning path throughout him. His smile faded and his laughter disappeared.

Who was she?

"Lady," he promised her softly. "You will be mine."

"You are mad! Do you know who I am, bumpkin?"

"Nay, lady, tell me, for I have to know."

"Katrina Seymour," she informed him with a quiet dignity. "I am the sister of Lord Seymour!"

Seymour. The fiercest of the Tory advocates. His Lordship.

He smiled bitterly. "You will be mine. But lady, I do beg you. Please, you mustn't fall into my arms so openly. We are making a public display."

"Oh!" She strangled out the sound, struggling again for balance, so eager to quit herself of him. He worked to free her skirts to release her. He felt the rush of her breath against his cheek and the tremors that raged through her.

He laughed softly, able to release her at last, meeting her eyes once more before she could escape. "Tonight, Lady Seymour?" His eyes teased her, as did his voice. "Just south of town —"

Her delicate palm nearly cracked against his face. He caught it and pulled her close. "I will see you again."

She pushed from him. "You insolent —"

"Yankee bastard?"

She hesitated and smiled, unable to resist the humor of the situation. "That will do quite well, thank you!"

He freed her skirt and steadied her. "You do need a man, milady."

"And you think you're that man?" She had a wonderful laugh. High, flushed cheekbones, and an impudent chin that raised high with her laughter.

"I know it."

"You're insane."

"The time will come when I'll need but lift a hand, and you will run to me."

"Nay, sir, for I do believe you'll soon be hanging from a tree!" She flounced past him, bending down to see to her coachman. Percy noticed that she said soft words to him and that when he stood she slipped an arm about him to assist him.

James came over to stand beside him.

"I have to see her again," Percy murmured.

"Are you daft? Do you know who she is?"

"Aye," Percy murmured distractedly.

"She's Seymour's sister. Seymour wouldn't wipe his boots on the likes of us. And she's as outspoken as he, a Tory to the heart, that's what she is."

Percy shook his head slowly. "Nay. Tory . . . that is what she believes. What she is —"

"Percy, my friend, you are worrying me. The world is about to be split assunder, and you are behaving like a madman."

Percy ignored him, his grin deepening. "She is a woman, my friend. The only woman in this world — or any other — for me." He offered James another grin, then clapped him on the shoulder. "Let's hie to the blacksmith's man, shall we? Then we can drag Mr. Henry into the tavern, close the doors to all but the brave, and hear what he'll be saying at the next convention!"

CHAPTER

4

The gallery was filled to capacity. Small tables covered with velvet and white lace tablecloths held chilled bottles of Dom Perignon in silver buckets and subtly decorated trays offering the finest in pâtés, red and black Russian caviar, smoked Nova, Brie, Camembert, and delicate rye and wheat crackers.

Every painting on display had been sold within an hour after the first guest had arrived. The patrons who had not made purchases now wished they had, and those who now owned McCauleys were gloating over their newly acquired treasures.

Dressed in a long blue velvet gown designed by Oleg Cassini, Gayle idly twirled her strand of cultured pearls as she leaned against her desk and listened to Sylvia Guteledge, the art critic for the prestigious *Richmond Mirror*, rave about the eroticism of McCauley's paintings. Gayle nodded politely now and then, but she couldn't really keep her eyes off the man of the hour.

He was actually in a tuxedo, of course an unconventional one. The coat wasn't exactly tailed, nor was it short, but made more to resemble the coats of an earlier era, perhaps a Civil War frock coat. His shirt was pink — which she had never imagined as a proper color on a man, but appeared exceptionally masculine on Brent. He'd consented politely to photographs throughout the evening. He hadn't behaved at all like an eccentric recluse. He'd been completely charming to everyone.

Gayle hadn't known what to expect earlier in the day. He had appeared at the gallery that morning in a pair of worn jeans and a T-shirt that advertised a heavy metal band. Artists were strange people — Gayle knew that from experience. She had wondered if Brent McCauley did not only mean to make an appearance, but to make such an appearance that the art world would gossip about it for the next ten years.

To her surprise, he hadn't chosen to move a single painting; he had approved all of her arrangements. She grew nervous showing him around, explaining her use of light and space within the gallery. And when they'd stood before his painting of the entwined lovers, she had found herself growing very warm.

Something bothered her. Haphazard snatches of her strange dreams came to mind. She tried to remember her dreams, but she couldn't seem to hold on to the memories. She caught her breath sharply, realizing that her dreams had left her with the same curious feelings as the painting . . . a yearning to be loved that way.

McCauley was watching her. Stuttering, she praised the painting's unique beauty. It deserved to stand alone upon the divider wall, singularly lighted, she explained, because it was the star piece of the show.

"You really do like it?" he had asked her.

"Yes. It's your finest piece." She couldn't help it; she looked at the painting and realized that she was blushing again. Evocative, yes. With Brent McCauley standing beside her, it also seemed to be very, very erotic. She couldn't look at that painting now without imagining the two of them in such a pose.

It was embarrassing. She was flushing a deep shade of red. Because she knew . . . he was imagining the same thing. The two of them, entwined. Lovers for all time.

"It's strange, isn't it?" he murmured. She felt him behind her, looking over her head. If she were to lean back, her head would rest against his chest and her hair would tease his chin.

"What?" She asked him in a whisper.

"The feeling. Don't you see it? Can't you imagine it? As if it has happened a thousand times before."

"I don't know what you're talking about."

"Yes, you do. You and me. I saw it, in your eyes. The two of us. There. In the painting. You've imagined the two of us as lovers. In the mist and shadow and light of the canvas." He paused a moment. "A hundred times before."

"I barely know you," she said weakly, waving her hand dismissively.

"Last night you kissed me as if you knew me very well."

"Oh, God, that again!" She moaned softly. "Brent, please, I just — I'm sorry. I don't pose — nude or otherwise — and it was very wrong of me to kiss you last night because I just don't — move that quickly. And now you're giving me a new line because of this painting —"

"It isn't a line and you know it. I see it in your face. In your eyes . . . in that marvelous color."

"Brent —"

He interrupted her, brusque and businesslike. "I do agree; this wall is best. The lighting is very good."

Gayle stiffened, her feelings somewhat

hurt. She stepped away from him and surveyed his clothing. "Are you —" She broke off, hesitating.

"Am I what?"

"Are you going to change for the opening?"

He looked at her, looked at the Jolly Roger on his T-shirt, and laughed. "You think I should?"

"Well, I'm sure that Geoffrey would appreciate the effort."

"You don't like what I'm wearing?"

"It's just lovely — if you are digging a new septic tank."

He grinned, crossed his arms stubbornly over his chest, and stared at her. "If you were to ask, I'd come in nothing at all," he murmured. There was a smile on his face and a challenge in the sensual amusement that lit up his eyes.

"A suit would suffice," Gayle murmured. But, damn, she was imagining him naked again. Naked, walking toward her . . .

She turned around to flee into her office. "I'll see you this evening," she called over her shoulder. At that moment, she didn't have the nerve to rise to his challenge.

The next time she saw Brent McCauley it was early evening, and the show was open. He was decked out in the intriguing tux, looking devastatingly handsome and com-

pletely at ease. He was so gracious and ac-
commodating that Sylvia remarked to
Gayle, "He can't be the artist! I do believe
that Geoffrey has pulled a fast one here. He
has dragged in this charming young man off
the street to impersonate McCauley, that's
what this is. A sham."

"Sylvia, I assure you, that is the real Brent
McCauley."

"Well, where has he been all these years?"

"Painting, I suppose."

"Actually, I knew a girl who modeled for
him once, oh, three, four years ago. I believe
he was living in Rome then. She told me that
he was young and very good-looking, but
then, one can never really trust these girls.
So young! And the poor dear seemed simply
brokenhearted that the man was entirely
professional. So detached. But then, it must
be unnerving, don't you think?"

"Pardon?"

"Oh, sitting there in one's birthday suit
while the artist looks on as if the model is a
vase of flowers."

Gayle shrugged. "I don't know, Sylvia. I
remember art school. Most of our models
were students. It was one way to get through
school."

"It's one way to make a great deal of
money, should a model become hot," Sylvia

said flatly. She adjusted her little pillbox hat — askew on her head; Sylvia seemed to be enjoying the champagne too. "I should have believed that young lady. And you!" — she wagged a finger at Gayle — "you might have given me a call, Gayle. I could have had a jump on all these others."

"I didn't meet the man myself until last night," Gayle told Sylvia. She sipped her champagne. Her sixth glass? She wasn't sure. She was certain that she'd have a miserable headache the next morning. Brent was talking with Riva Chen from the New York newspaper. Gayle knew Riva well, and she liked and respected her. She was of Oriental descent, a gorgeous girl, tall, with sleek ebony hair that fell to her buttocks. She and Brent were laughing. Gayle was appalled at the jealousy the sight of them together aroused inside of her. She had no right to feel anything that even resembled jealousy. Logic didn't help her any; she wondered if he were asking Riva to pose for him. She wondered if Riva might be saying yes. Riva probably had a glorious back, she was so slim and sleek.

Riva must have said something very softly because Brent leaned down to catch her words. He laughed. His face seemed to be very close to Riva's.

Sylvia sighed, interrupting Gayle's train of thought. "The painting I really wanted I couldn't buy. Someone beat me to it."

"Oh?" Gayle smiled, forcing herself to pay attention to Sylvia. "Which was that?"

"The lovers. Oh, what a glorious painting!"

"Who did buy it?"

"Why, I don't know, dear. A very savvy collector moved quickly. It was sold almost as soon as Geoff opened the doors." She sighed again. "Such a wonderful, wonderful piece. I shall write a column about it!"

"I'm glad, Sylvia."

Who had bought the lovers, Gayle wondered? She felt a little pang. She would have loved to have owned that painting. She would have loved to have studied it until she had discovered its secret, understood just why two figures embracing could eat away at her heart.

A lightbulb flashed brilliantly; Brent was being photographed with Riva Chen at his side. They made a beautiful couple, both so dark, graceful, and sleek. Riva was smiling and laughing. There was no doubt that there was a certain amount of chemistry between the two of them.

"Gayle?"

She turned around. Her head was already

beginning to ache. It was Geoffrey. "Excuse me, Sylvia. Gayle, phone. Would you care to take it in my office?"

"Run along, dear, run along," Sylvia said, adjusting her little hat again. "I see that Chad Bellows is all by himself over there. Perhaps I can pry a few secrets from him!"

She moved off, intent on her prey. Geoff smiled at Gayle and she shrugged. "Oh, the phone! Who is it?"

"Tina. She called to wish us luck. I told her to come on over, but she can't get away. Go take it in my office."

"I really shouldn't —"

"You've been the perfect hostess. The opening has gone flawlessly. You deserve a reprieve."

Gayle slipped off the corner of her desk and excused herself through the crowd of people to reach Geoff's office in the back. She sank into Geoff's leather chair and picked up the line.

"Congratulations!" Tina said. "Geoff said it's all been a smashing success."

"Smashing," Gayle agreed, twirling the phone wire.

"How's McCauley taking it all?"

"The perfect picture of charm."

"You sound funny. Has he been rude? Bristling at criticism? He seemed like such a nice guy. And he's glorious to look at! Oh, well, a tiger when he's cornered, huh?"

"No. I mean it — he has been completely charming."

"Then what's wrong?"

"He's out there with the Dragon Lady," Gayle muttered.

"What?"

"Oh, nothing. Forget I said that."

"Dragon Lady?"

Gayle inhaled, shaking her head ruefully. "Riva Chen. And I don't mean it. I think very highly of her. It's just that she's . . . I don't know. She's beautiful, I guess that's what I'm saying."

"The green eyes of jealousy."

"I can't be jealous. I barely know the man."

"No one would have guessed that last night."

"Oh, he's full of lines. He's probably asking her to pose for him right now."

"He asked you?"

"Yes."

"What did you do?"

"I refused!"

"Well, well, well! Then he's free to be looking for another model, isn't he?"

Gayle bit into her lower lip pensively. She couldn't help it. She just really didn't do things like casually undressing in front of virtual strangers.

"You still there?"

"Yes."

"You sound funny."

"Six glasses of champagne funny," she agreed.

"Can you see him now?"

"No. I'm in Geoff's office."

"Maybe you had better get back out there. Protect him from the Dragon Lady."

"He probably doesn't want to be protected."

"No! I meant that you should protect him for yourself."

"I can't —"

"Well, I sure as hell could! Damnation!" Tina swore on a note of laughter. "Just once in my life — just once! — I'd like to sleep with a guy like that. A one-night stand would be fine. I work in a health spa — and I haven't met a guy yet who's ninety-five percent fat-free."

"Tina! That's awful!"

"That's truthful. Go get him, sweetie."

And do what with him? Gayle wondered. But she straightened suddenly, uncoiling the wire, determined. The champagne was giving her a headache; it was also suddenly giving her bravado.

"I've got to go, Tina. Talk to you soon."

"I want details," Tina warned her.

"There's not going to be anything to give details about, I promise you!" She hung up the phone. She felt breathless. Her heart was pounding too quickly, and shivers of anticipation were racing along her spine again. She hurried out of the office and back to the main salon.

Brent McCauley was at one of the little round hors d'oeuvres tables — pouring out two glasses of champagne. He arched a brow at Gayle. She was still breathless. She noted the champagne; she saw Riva, talking with Chad and a bearded art buyer in front of the painting of the lovers.

"Well, Ms. Norman, how am I doing? Should I still be cleaning sewers? I've done my very best to be on good behavior."

She ignored his question. She looked straight into the black depths of his eyes.

"Do you still want me to pose for you?"

He was motionless for a moment, as if he were analyzing her question. His brow arched higher and his gaze raked over her curiously. "You've had a change of heart? Last night, I couldn't even bribe you. You've suddenly decided to bare it all?"

"Do you want me to pose or not?"

Looking amused and skeptical, he hesitated just a second longer.

"Yes, I do."

"All right."

"That simple?"

Why was he making it so painful now? "Yes."

He extended a hand to her. She took it and felt the warmth spread into her chilled fingers. "It's a deal then, Ms. Norman."

She wet her lips. "When?"

"No time better than the present."

"What?"

"Tonight. I'd like to start tonight."

Gayle heard the enthusiasm in his voice. He told her again how he intended to pose her, and she knew that he meant it — there was no time like the present. He could have started right then and there in the gallery. He said something about color and lights, angle and slope, and she felt shivers again. What had she promised?

"Brent?"

Riva had come to the table.

"Oh, excuse me," Brent apologized. "Champagne, Riva. I am sorry. I got sidetracked. I didn't mean to take so long." He handed Riva a glass of champagne and she smiled as she accepted it. She complimented Gayle on the arrangements; Gayle thanked her.

The three of them talked a moment longer. Riva watched Gayle and she watched Brent McCauley. Then she excused herself and left them.

"Did you . . . make previous plans?" Gayle asked him.

He shook his head.

"Oh, I thought —"

"She's a nice woman."

"Very," Gayle agreed. Exotic, beautiful, Gayle added in silence to herself.

Brent stepped a little closer to her, picking up a cracker, piling black caviar on it.

"She knows."

"She knows what?"

"She's a savvy lady."

"Meaning?"

"She knows that she's attractive and very, very sexy. She's a sensual, generous woman. And ordinarily I would have been very receptive to everything she could wish to give."

"You are terribly obnoxious, you know."

"You think so? I think I'm honest."

"I said, if you've made previous plans —"

"No, no. You don't listen, Ms. Norman. I didn't make any plans. Although I might have done so. Riva is beautiful. She just isn't — you. She's charming and sophisticated and — she knew. She stood here and saw that I had made a previous commitment."

"You've no commitment to me."

"But I do." He smiled and sipped his champagne. She wasn't sure she liked his smug look. Like the cat that had eaten the canary. "Did you have previous plans for the evening?"

"Yes. No. What difference would it really make? We don't have to start tonight. I rather thought you might like to work in the daytime. Don't artists prefer natural light?"

"It depends on what they have in mind." It could have been an innuendo; it wasn't. He told her how he wanted the painting to have a hazy dreamlike quality. "False light, a soft beacon in the night, that's exactly what I have in mind."

"I don't know," Gayle murmured. "It's been a long day. Maybe tomorrow would be better —"

"Tomorrow is a Saturday. Geoff won't be opening the gallery. We should start tonight. It's only about eight fifteen, and the reception seems to be winding down."

"But —"

"Are you trying to back out on me? My house isn't even an hour's drive from the city. We'll leave soon."

He picked up one of the fine crystal champagne glasses and pulled a bottle of the Dom Perignon from the ice. He poured, then thrust the glass into her hand. He picked up his own glass and touched it to hers with a little clink.

"The deal is made, Ms. Norman."

A half hour later, she was in his old Mach I, watching as the city flew by her, silently promising herself that she would never drink champagne again. It was a very dark night on the highway, and very cold. She wasn't even able to talk to him; she sat huddled in the bucket seat, her arms wrapped tightly around herself. He didn't seem to notice. He was carrying on a conversation by himself, explaining that he wanted to start with a preliminary sketch and, once he did, she would understand what he had in mind, and be pleased.

"I'm . . . sure," Gayle murmured uneasily. She glanced his way, watching the night lights play over the contours of his face.

"Riva probably would have gone just to be with you, you know," she heard herself tell him.

"What?" Amused, he glanced her way quickly. He was still smiling as he looked ahead at the road again. "Yeah, I think that you're right. I think that she and I might have had the same finale in mind."

"I — I've warned you. I don't. Maybe I

didn't play fair. We could turn around. Maybe you could still catch Riva."

He shook his head in the darkness. His smile remained in place. "A smile from you," he teased, "is worth total ecstasy from another woman."

"Oh, please, don't laugh at me. I have a god-awful headache."

"Do you? Poor baby. You can't just guzzle down champagne that way."

Eventually they left the highway and started down a rural route that was even darker. It seemed to Gayle that they twisted and turned endlessly before they came to a walled estate, the brick of the wall nearly hidden by a profusion of skeletal trees. Brent used a little plastic card to cause the wrought-iron gate to open, and they started along a curving, ebony ribbon of driveway. When they came to the entrance of the house and parked beneath the massive portico, Gayle realized that the house wasn't old at all, as the brick wall had seemed to imply. It was a contemporary dwelling. From the portico she could see the living room through massive plate-glass windows. There was an immense granite mantle at the far wall before which were leather sofas and chairs in soft grayish-beige to complement the stone.

"You like it?"

He hadn't stepped out of the car. He was surveying her in the dim light beneath the portico.

"Yes."

"No, you don't."

"I'd imagined you in something different. A real Colonial, something with more . . . character, I suppose."

He laughed. "Yeah, I do like old places. We've one in the family, though, already. I like this house because it gives me the privacy I need; I loved the woods here." He opened the door and stepped out of the car at last, walking around to open her door. Her knees were a little shaky. He kept a hand on her elbow and led her to the front door. He rang the bell and she frowned at him curiously. He grinned.

"My housekeeper should be here. She and her husband live on the grounds."

"Oh." Gayle was certain that she blushed again. She'd been so convinced he wanted to seduce her.

"You thought I meant to steal you away and ravish you."

"No. Of course not."

"Oh." She felt his eyes on her and pretended to study the house through the windows.

No one came to the door. Brent swore slightly and searched through various pockets in his trousers and coat until he found his keys. He opened the door, and ushered her in.

It was really magnificent. Wide-open space met her gaze. The living room stretched from one side of the house to the other, with soft cream carpeting subtly switching to cool tan Mexican tiles. There was a long stairway at the rear of the room.

"Mary!" Brent called out. There was no answer. He glanced at Gayle and shrugged. "She must be in the kitchen. Excuse me."

He disappeared to the right of the room through a multipaned doorway. Gayle felt so nervous about being alone with Brent that she couldn't quite leave the entryway, raised about a foot over the even level of the floor.

He came back with a slip of paper in his hand and a rueful shrug. "Her grandson broke an arm playing football. She's in town with the little boy. Ralph must be with her."

"Oh." Gayle still couldn't leave the entryway. He smiled. She gazed at him, thinking that he was a very handsome man who looked like a gallant from the past.

"Well, come in," he said a bit impatiently. "I won't bite you."

She stepped into the room. He came to take her coat, not hanging it up but tossing it over the back of one of the leather chairs. "Can I get you anything? A glass of wine, a soda?"

She shook her head, sliding nervously into one of the leather couches. If he was aware of the panic streaking through her, he gave her no sign. He began to pull his tie from his neck, struggling slightly with the knot.

"I'll show you the studio and the dressing room." He reached for her hand, found it, and pulled her to her feet. He led her up the stairs to the top landing.

The studio was located directly above the living room. Stacks and stacks of canvases lined the walls, some with pencil sketches, some with dabs of paint. A large table held tubes and bottles of paints and remover and brushes. His easel stood near the table. A massive skylight practically filled the ceiling and the room was surrounded by windows.

He left her standing in the middle of the room and selected a canvas and fit it upon the easel. "You needn't worry about the windows; we're surrounded by woods. Completely private." He paused at last, looking at her. "You're all right?"

She nodded, even though she wasn't all

right at all. She was very nervous, freezing one moment, hot the next. She wondered why she was there but, even then, as she watched him, she knew that she had come because she hadn't been able to let him leave without her. He had fascinated her, excited her — compelled her.

"Good, good," he murmured to her. He brusquely led her to a small section of the room in the corner and pulled back a heavy curtain. "This is the dressing room. Select a robe. I'm going to change. I'll be right back."

Then he was gone, and she was left standing there alone. She looked around the little corner; there were hangers and wall hooks. She saw a thick white terry robe and reached for it, but it slipped from her hand. She couldn't do it. She couldn't.

No! She had to — she was here. She would do it. It was no big deal. She thought of all the nudes she had sketched in art school. The model was just a body. The artist was completely detached. She could do it. Brent McCauley had, certainly, in his day, sketched hundreds of nude bodies.

She slipped off her shoes and wondered why she still didn't feel quite real. Maybe that was a bonus too. It wasn't really *her* here, it was the strange woman who had drunk too much champagne this evening and too impulsively volunteered.

Reluctantly, she took off her panty hose. She bit her lower lip and felt chills sweep through her. She couldn't do it. No, she had said that she would. She fumbled for the zipper at the back of her velvet dress and then hastily pulled the garment over her head. She hugged it to her, then slipped it onto one of the garment hooks. She quickly unfastened her bra, then hid it beneath the dress.

Then she realized that she was standing on a cold floor in an open room in nothing but peach string panties with see-through lace panels. She hugged her arms around her bare breasts and shivered and had to swallow down her sense of panic. She couldn't do it. She knew now for a fact that she just couldn't do it. When Brent came back, she would apologize profusely for leading him on in this manner. She wouldn't have him drive her back; she would call a cab.

She pressed her hands against her cheeks. What would he think of her? First last night . . . and now this. She could never accuse him of dishonesty, so there was no excuse for her own behavior.

"Gayle? I'm going to have you —"

She spun around, startled at first, then horrified to realize that she hadn't pulled the curtain closed. She was just standing there, practically naked. And Brent McCauley was back in the studio. He had changed into jeans and a denim work shirt. He was standing a mere few feet away from her, staring at her.

He was silent for the longest time. She couldn't move. She stared into his eyes, ebony-dark eyes with a slow-burning flame in them.

"My God," he breathed out at last, and the desire in his eyes seemed to touch her like a caress. She still could not move; she could barely breathe. She remembered vaguely that she had intended to apologize to him and leave. Her intention meant nothing now. Nothing had meaning, except for the touch of his eyes upon her.

"Come here. Come to me," he whispered to her.

And she knew that they were not talking about art anymore, that this had nothing to do with modeling or posing.

But, God help her, she was responding. She couldn't have denied his demand, not if her life had depended upon it.

The distance between them seemed to be incredibly long. She moved slowly, as if a compelling force were drawing her ever closer to him. All the while she felt his eyes locked upon hers. She could not look away from him. Her arms fell to her sides; her fingers clenched and unclenched; she felt the cold of the floor with each step. And then she was before him. Not touching him, a breath away. She saw the clean-shaven texture of his chin and the little nick where he had caught himself with his razor. She saw a blue vein in his throat, throbbing. She felt his scent all around her, heavily male, and then she saw his eyes again, so deathly dark, so fascinating.

His hands cupped her cheeks. Then his long fingers stroked and caressed her face. It was an artist's touch. A lover's touch.

She didn't move. She couldn't move. Tremors seized her, and still she could not tear her eyes from the fascinating darkness of his. His touch, so light, left her face. His hands slid down the slope of her shoulders, caressed the outward curves of her breasts, and settled upon her waist.

Then he knelt before her.

She first felt the heat of his breath, then shatteringly, the warmth of his tongue creating patterns over and through the lace panties that covered her. She cried out softly, gripping his shoulders lest she fall, stunned by the sensation that ripped through her. Nothing had ever been so keen in her life; nothing had ever left her so bereft of thought or reason. Nothing had ever been so blindingly intense as his touch, so blatantly intimate, so sensual, so stirring, so exciting.

The friction, the heat, the wetness, the probe and stroke of his tongue against her . . . the feelings washed through her with the force of a storm. Sweetness like honey flooded her; she shook and trembled and could barely stand, and only when it was so good that it was painful, that she could bear no more, did she begin to think to protest. To no avail. Frantically she whispered words, incoherent words, to which he paid no mind. His hand rounded her buttocks, his fingers played within the lace, and with a snap it was gone. Nothing stood between them and he knew no mercy. He played upon her leisurely but surely, like a master who knew her most erogenous zones. First he touched her lightly, then deeply, tormenting her with pleasure.

She screamed as she reached a delicious release. Then so utterly weak in her limbs that she could not stand, she collapsed, falling upon him. Then, just as intense as her pleasure had been, she felt shame. She curled into herself, away from him, then sprang to her feet, sobbing. She lurched for the dressing room, desperate for something, anything, to cover herself.

"Gayle!"

She heard his command, loud and ringing and harsh. She stood still, then felt his hands upon her shoulders, firm and tender. "Gayle, Gayle, Gayle . . ." Just her name whispered so gently.

"Oh, my God, I said that I didn't . . . and then I just stood there while you — and I don't do this kind of thing with a stranger, and, oh, my God! I've never done this type of thing, ever . . . I don't —"

"Look at me."

"No!" She spoke in fervent horror.

"Sweetheart." His kiss grazed her hair. He turned her into his arms and she buried her face against his chest. "I know that you don't because I don't. I swear to you, I never meant it to happen. Not here. Not now. I never meant to take such an advantage. Look at me, dammit, will you?"

She really had no choice because his fingers were in her hair, and her head was arching back. She was astounded by the emotion betrayed in his eyes.

"This is special. We're special. Good God, can't you see that yet? Can't you feel it, can't you admit that you feel it?" He demanded ardently.

"I —"

"Tell me that you want me."

"I . . ."

He leaned down and kissed her full on the mouth. The salt of her tears mingled with the taste of his mouth. She came closer and closer to him until he had lifted her against him.

"Tell me," he whispered the words, his lips hovering just above her own. She stared into his eyes, feeling weak. She clung to him for support.

"Tell me!" he insisted.

"I . . . want you."

He swept her into his arms and gave her a ravaging kiss as he strode from the studio. She didn't know where they were going; she didn't really care.

He moved quickly with long, strong steps. He paused, kicking open a door with the toe of his shoe.

They came into his bedroom. Gayle never saw what it looked like that night. They entered in darkness and he laid her on the bed and all she knew then was sound. The thud of his shoes, the rasp of his zipper, the whispery noise as he cast his shirt and briefs aside. Then he was back beside her.

She was able to touch him; to feel his shoulders, run her fingers over his cheeks. Run her hands along his muscular body. He groaned. She felt him shift his weight so that he was on top of her. He nudged her thigh with his knee, and she felt his breath and heard the anguish of his whisper.

"I am dying for you."

"I know." She caught his face between her hands and kissed him, arching against him. "Please!"

He thrust and she felt him then, deep inside of her, hard and sleek. To her amazement, it all came to her again, every sensation of riveting excitement. She felt filled to the point where she would shatter, but she did not. She soared. He was like heat and lightning. There was no subtlety, no finesse, just raw hunger, yet she was ready for nothing less. She loved the rough power of him, the sleek sweat upon his gleaming flesh, the hardness that coiled and tightened his features and body.

She had not thought it possible to climax again so quickly on such a high note; she had never known it could feel so good to simply feel a man's explosion inside of her.

They didn't talk. They breathed and lay still, entwined. He didn't seem to think that they needed to rise. She couldn't begin to imagine that they should do so. Thinking would be dangerous altogether. It was better to savor the moment. His leg cast over hers, his fingers entwined in her hair, her cheek against the rough hair on his chest. It should never have happened but it had and, whatever else, she knew that nothing would ever be like it again in life. She should have been in panic once again; she should have been analyzing, trying to explain it all to him, to herself . . .

A portion of her mind was simply blank. To her amazement, she began to drowse in a delicious lethargy.

Moments later, hours later, she felt him, hard again, prodding against her rear.

"No," she moaned softly, barely awake. A smile curled the corner of her mouth.

He pulled her against him. "Thank God for that underwear," he muttered.

"What?"

"I'd thought that this would take weeks. Months. Those damn panties you wear are so erotic that I was barely able to breathe, to think — much less restrain myself."

"Were," Gayle said. His hands curled over her hips, fitting her snugly against him.

"Were?"

"You ripped them off me," she murmured.

"I'm sorry."

"It's really all right."

His arms were around her, wrapping her to him. She smiled, feeling the determined probe against her, the stroke of his hand along her back.

"You do have them," he stated, very self-satisfied.

"What?"

"Dimples. You have these glorious dimples right at the base of your spine. Right here." He bent to kiss the little indentations. "Right here, and right here."

"Brent . . ." she protested breathlessly.

"Gayle."

"Brent!"

She laughed, then she was shuddering, and then she was beneath him again, twisting in his arms, parting her lips to meet the wet heat of his kiss.

CHAPTER
5

Gayle felt as if she were in some deep, deep nether region when she heard the shrill and horrible sound of the phone ringing. At first she thought that she was home, and she stretched in the right direction to catch the phone and stop the noise. She hit a muscular male body instead and remembered where she was.

Brent groped blindly for the phone, caught it, and swung his legs over the side of the bed to answer it. It was still pitch-dark outside. Only the light from the studio down the hall and the entryway downstairs filtered into the room. Gayle tried to watch the planes of his face as he frowned and muttered a few monosyllabic words, and she drew the sheets around her.

Brent was laughing now at whatever was being said over the phone. He turned to her and, even in the shadows, she could see the amusement and tenderness that softened the clean masculine lines of his features. He reached out his free hand, rubbing it over the rise of her sheet-covered hip and rump as he said into the phone, "She's here, she's fine, and she's under no coercion, I promise you. Here, talk to her yourself."

Gayle sat up, frowning at Brent. She covered the mouthpiece with her hand.

"Who is it?"

"Geoff."

"Geoffrey Sable?"

He grinned. "Yeah, go ahead, talk to him."

"But —"

"Go ahead, talk."

Gayle uncovered the mouthpiece and brought the receiver to her ear. "Geoff?"

"Hi, kid."

"Uh . . . Geoff, hi. What time is it?"

"Three-thirty A.M., Eastern Standard Time."

"Then —"

"Why am I calling? Sorry, kid. But Tina tried to call you at your house; then Liz tried to call you at your house; and then they both went over there. Then they came over here."

"Oh!"

"We all voted on the possibility that you might be at Brent's, but we couldn't quite convince ourselves, due to your customary wave and a handshake. Personally, I was convinced that you were at McCauley's place. But we didn't know if we should call the police or break into your house, and these two ladies here were beside themselves over your safety. They didn't know if you were stabbed, robbed, raped — or having the time of your life. Well, I figured it might prove a little uncomfortable, but we had to call. You were either with McCauley or we needed to call out the National Guard. Can you understand?"

"I — uh — of course. Thanks, Geoff. And say the same to Liz and Tina."

She knew her face was flaming with color. She appreciated her friends' concern very much, but she felt uncomfortable. What was Brent thinking? What was he feeling? He'd been awakened at three-thirty A.M. by people checking up on her.

Brent took the phone back from her, offering her a fleeting smile. Or was it grim? Perhaps he was thinking that he had bitten off more than he really wanted to chew, that he wasn't really dealing with an independent woman at all, that this intrusion into his life wasn't worth the sex, no matter how good that sex was . . .

"Geoff, tell those two that we're sorry they lost the night's sleep worrying, and thanks for caring. Talk to you soon."

He hung up the phone. She felt him looking at her.

"I'm — uh — sorry," she murmured.

"Why?"

"Well, for . . . interrupting your sleep," she murmured awkwardly.

He laughed, leapt over her like a gazelle, and caught her face between his palms.

"I thought it was very nice."

"You did?"

"Tina was cute."

"Tina?"

"She was talking first. That's what took me so long to figure out what was going on. She was very apologetic, but she told me that you just don't sleep with people."

"Oh, God," Gayle groaned softly, silently cursing Tina's way with words. She didn't want him to think she was a complete babe in the woods. It was difficult enough to deal with a man like McCauley. She needed some mystique if she were going to keep up with him.

"Is that true?" He was grinning like a wolf.

She did her best to sound worldly. "Well, obviously, Mr. McCauley, you're not the first man in my life."

His smile faded, but his eyes remained fixed upon her. "So tell me about it," he said softly. "Geoff warns me that you blow hot and cold —"

"Geoff said that?"

"Geoff said that. Nicely, of course. He's crazy about you. And your best friends tell me that you don't sleep with men." He stroked his thumbs over her cheekbones. "So, what was it? One great love in your life?"

She inhaled, remembering that she had met him less than forty-eight hours ago. "Want to tell me all about the romantic relationships in your life?"

He shook his head and smiled again. "Not one of them would matter. Not a single one. The romance in my life started tonight."

"Oh!" Gayle said softly. Again, there was that ring of honesty to his words. It could have been a line, but that clear-sighted honesty was there, and it touched her so deeply that she trembled.

"That was really nice," she told him. "An artist with a way with words. But you have had affairs," she accused him, determined not to give away too much emotion.

"Lots of them," he agreed. "But I've been waiting — for you."

She laughed, but then her breath caught in her throat again. He leaned down to kiss her, his hands moving feather-light along her thighs. Then he broke away and his words were muffled against her breast. "I can't seem to get enough of you."

It was different this time when they made love. Somewhat blunt and rough. He had incredible energy and stamina. A dozen times she would have gasped and fallen; a dozen times he held and shifted and manipulated her body. Sweat beaded upon his brow and little droplets fell upon her, and in moments they both glistened. Gayle wondered if she didn't black out for seconds now and then. She alternately marveled and trembled, soared, flew and fell, and started all over again.

When it was over, they were both panting. He fell back beside her, inhaled and exhaled, and cast one hand over his damp brow while the other rested casually on her thigh. Gayle was taken with the comfortable intimacy of his touch. It was as if they had been together forever.

"Want to raid the refrigerator?"

"Sure."

"Come on, let's take a shower first."

He was up, pulling her to her feet. Light cascaded all around them as they entered the bathroom and Brent hit the switch. Gayle blinked against the sudden brightness and surveyed the bath. It was spacious and very modern, like the rest of the house. It contained a black sink and a black commode and a huge black circular tub on bronze clawed feet with a bronze ring overhead to hold the inner and outer curtains. Brent reached for her again, leading her into the tub, then pulling the curtains around them with a swift motion. He turned on the water and Gayle gasped as it poured down on them, cold at first. She stepped back, winding up her hair. Brent stuck his head beneath the spray and grabbed a bar of soap. He scrubbed himself vigorously, working up a lather, then rinsed and turned to Gayle. A light immediately touched his eyes, like a little kindle of flame freshly set. He brought the soap to her shoulders, creating a rich lather, then he swirled and circled it lower over her breasts. Gayle gripped his biceps and narrowed her eyes, swallowing and watching him suspiciously as he surveyed not her face but his hands and the way they moved over her. He rinsed away the soap from her breast and lowered his head to it, slowly, leisurely, sucking it.

"Brent . . ."

His soapy hand slipped between her legs.

"Brent . . . didn't we just make love several times — ?"

"Mmm, " he murmured. "And maybe in

time, after we've been lovers for years, maybe some of it will be old hat."

"Old hat!"

"Maybe. But I doubt it. I suppose that things do calm down somewhat, though. But right now, I can't think of anything I'd rather do. Over and over. Every time I look at you, it starts all over. And isn't that part of it? Isn't that the way it works? I'm falling in love with you."

She stared at him a little helplessly. His fingers were inside her, and she felt hopelessly weak, brimming again with the erratic little liquid flames that could shoot through her body with sweet desire.

"Well?" His stroke touched deep, deep inside of her. "A shower is the best place in the world to fool around. Honest."

"Why?" She let out a soft little sound and went on tiptoe to kiss him and press hard against him. He lifted her, straddling her legs around him while he balanced himself slowly down to his knees, sliding her over himself.

So this was it . . . new lovers, in love with being in love, in love with making love. Gayle kissed him while the water fell down upon them, soaking their faces, while he led her in a fast, staccato rhythm above him. This was it . . . this was the wonder of falling in love, of being together, of taking the time to think of nothing but each other, to touch, explore, and know one another, inside and out.

When she fell against him, the water was still shooting down upon him. Gayle's hair was drenched. She smoothed it from her face. Brent smiled as smoothly and laconically as the old king of the beasts, stretched, and curled his fingers around her wrists to help her balance back to her feet. He followed her up. "See?"

"See what?"

"A shower is a fabulous place to make love. When you're done, you're already in the right place to rinse off."

"Umm. And since I'm here and my hair is soaked, have you got any shampoo?"

"Your slightest wish . . ." he murmured.

A moment later he was back. Gayle was about to protest when he squeezed shampoo into her hair — she didn't like anyone else doing her hair. But her protest died on her lips. It felt good. His fingers massaging her scalp were like magic, and it was a nice, nice feeling, intimate and domestic.

He gave her a slight tap on the rear and left her to rinse it out herself as he stepped out of the tub. He was back by the time she pulled the curtain to get out herself, dressed comfortably in a pair of cut-offs himself, and offering her a towel and a model's robe. "Hope you don't mind bare feet," he told her. "I haven't got any women's slippers."

Gayle slipped into the robe, smiling. "Be glad that you don't."

He adjusted the collar for her. "I've never had anyone sleep here before."

"We've done very little sleeping."

"Okay. I've never had anyone sleep at all — even for two minutes — here before."

Gayle smiled, meeting his eyes, biting her lower lip, just a little bit shyly.

"Hurry up and come down, huh? I'm starving. We can scramble eggs or — no, never mind — I've got steaks in the freezer. Microwaves defrost things, don't they?"

"Most of them."

"Hurry."

In ten minutes she was downstairs in his big gourmet kitchen. Brent made salad; she fixed steaks. She sat on a stool at the kitchen counter, and they both ate ravenously in silence for several moments. Then he smiled suddenly and said, "So tell me about yourself."

"Tell you what?"

"Where were you born, where do your folks live, siblings? All that type of stuff."

She smiled slightly, lowering her eyes. "I

was born outside of Philadelphia, an only child, and my folks are dead."

He glanced at her quickly. "Sorry," he said softly.

She shrugged, offering him a smile that said, It's okay. "It was over ten years ago now. There was a fire on a cruise ship. Seven people were killed, and my parents were among them."

"That must have been hard."

"It was. They were wonderful people. But we had a great priest up there. Father Tom. He had a way of making me feel that they had been so very special that seventeen years with them was better than having anyone else for a lifetime."

"What then?"

"I went to school. My parents had left a fair amount of money. I didn't want to keep living where I had lived with my folks, so I finished high school in England. I had always wanted to travel, so I spent college all over the place — ending up in Paris. That's where I met Geoff."

He looked up now, arching a brow her way. "Geoff wasn't that one great love of your life, was he?"

She smiled. "No."

"Good."

"Why?"

"I don't know. I'm just glad. I mean, love does transcend all, but it's got to be uncomfortable to wonder what two people are thinking at times if they did sleep together somewhere in life."

"What makes you think there was just this one great love in my life? Maybe I've had a dozen."

"Uh-uh. You're not the type."

"I'm not?"

He studied her carefully and shook his head with a slow smile. "No, you're not." His voice was husky as he touched her cheek tenderly. "You're the type for one great love in your life, a deep, passionate love to last forever and forever."

"You're certain about that?" she whispered softly.

"I am."

Gayle searched out his eyes. "And you?"

"I've been searching," he said lightly. "For you. All of my life. Nothing else mattered."

She started to laugh, but then his eyes touched hers, and the laughter died. He was speaking lightly, teasingly, and yet it was there again, that grain of truth.

Gayle hesitated just a second, looking away from him. "He's dead," she said quietly.

"What?"

"He's dead. That one lover."

"What happened?"

"He — uh — he overdosed."

"And you were there?"

She shook her head. "No. I'd walked out on him. He —" She paused again, then looked up at him a little guiltily, and not sure why. "He was an artist. A good one. A friend of Geoff's. I lived with him those years in Paris. All of a sudden he couldn't paint. He started drinking. Then he started on 'ludes, cocaine, anything he could get his hands on. I told him that he was self-destructive. I did care about him, though. I stayed and I tried. Geoff tried."

"Why did you leave him? You said that you cared, that you tried and tried."

"One night I poured his Scotch down the drain. I didn't have the sense to know that it wouldn't do any good. We got into a horrible fight."

"Fist fight?"

"Yeah, I suppose. He slapped me so hard that I landed against the wall. So . . . I left him. A few weeks later, he was dead."

Brent reached for her, pulling her into his arms. "You poor baby," he murmured.

"It's not that bad," she murmured.

He pulled away the towel she'd wrapped about her hair and let all the damp strands fall about her shoulders. He smoothed back the drying tendrils. "It's affected you so deeply."

"Well, it was traumatic." She smiled ruefully. "I swore after that I'd never get involved with an artist again."

"Well, you are involved now, you know."

"Am I?"

"Completely. Come here . . ."

He caught the lapels of her robe and pulled her against him, kissing her. His mouth hovered just over hers. "I'll never let anyone hurt you again, Gayle. Anyone . . . or . . . anything."

His lips touched hers again. Then he smiled down at her, and she noticed that the intensity with which he had been gazing at her had changed. It hadn't dimmed; it had just changed.

"Are you tired? Think you could sit for a while now? I wouldn't make it long, I promise. Just long enough for a preliminary sketch. Would you?"

She'd forgotten all about posing. It was probably just about five A.M.

She had come over here to pose for him, she reminded herself. And she had been so very unsure about it all.

But she didn't feel in the least uncomfortable with him anymore. She could still feel a

119

little shy with him, awed perhaps. But she had enjoyed everything that had happened between them. First she had been fascinated by Brent, then she had been drawn to him, and now she was falling in love with him. She felt awake and alive with the sweet excitement of falling in love. If he wanted her to pose, she would gladly do so.

"Sure."

"Wonderful! Come on."

He took her hand and led her back through the living room to the stairs. She panted by the time they reached the upper landing, but he didn't seem to notice. He led her straight to the studio, where he released her to set up a table. He hesitated for a fraction of a second, then chose a royal blue velvet throw to place over it. Then he looked to her, reaching out for her hand.

"I want your back, seriously —"

"You could have fooled me."

"Funny, sweetheart, funny. Now, if you'd bring your — buttocks — right here, curl your toes beneath you, then just look over your shoulder . . ."

He slipped the robe from her and swept her up, lifting her to the table. Gayle glanced at him, a little lost, then tried for the pose. "Toes under . . . now twist, just slightly. Perfect! Now wait — wait just a second."

She did so, barely daring to breathe. This wasn't easy. She had barely arranged her body, and already she was feeling stiff and sore.

He came bursting back into the room, a brush in his hands. "No, stay, stay, I'll take care of it," he told her.

She held still, lowering her eyes, smiling to herself. Well, there might have been a great deal of passion between them at the beginning of the evening, but now she was just a body to him. He was quick and deft with her hair; he knew just what he wanted done with the drying tendrils.

"You okay?" he asked her.

"I *have* been better."

"Good, good," he muttered.

From her position it wasn't easy to see him once he'd gone back to his easel. All she could do was sense his motion. He called out a few more instructions to her — lower her head, raise her chin — then he was silent.

The sketch seemed to take forever. Her toes began to cramp, and then her lower back. Her neck was stiff. When would he call it quits?

She realized somewhere along the line that the light around her was no longer all artificial. Dawn was breaking, breaking beautifully. The sun was playing patterns over the room, over her. It sent out little rays of warmth that touched her flesh and danced upon it.

"Cramped?"

She nearly jumped at the question. "Yes."

He was coming toward her. He didn't give her permission to move, and so she didn't. He stopped behind her. And then she felt a touch of true warmth. His lips against her nape. His kiss there. A kiss that fell and departed and came again. Upon her nape, upon the next vertebra, and then the next. Down the entire length of her back.

She turned to him, moving at last, circling her arms around his shoulders.

"It's day," he murmured.

"Yes," she buried her face against his neck. He ran his hands along her torso, encircling her breasts.

"Feel the sun."

"I do."

He lowered her down to the floor. The patterns of the sun slashed gold and crimson over her flesh and his. She closed her eyes, smiling as she heard the rasp of his zipper. She shielded her eyes, then stared up at his form, loving the way the light fell over him too, an artist's light, the crimson of dawn against the bronze of his flesh, the dark hair on his chest, and the fullness of his arousal, hard as a shaft, fascinating . . .

This was falling in love.

She smiled and opened her arms to him and he came to her, there on the floor. She locked her arms around him, and she marveled again at the impetus and the urgency and the energy. She barely noted the hard floor beneath her. All she felt was the piercing warmth of the sun, and it seemed that it was the sun itself that throbbed and pulsed inside of her, making her feel delicious.

Taut and strained, he lay over her, hands at the sides of her head, the muscles on his arms like cords. She slid her fingers along his back.

"Love me!" He urged her.

"I am," she whispered, moistening her lips for they were dry, shuddering, for he rammed deep.

"Love me!" he repeated.

"I do!"

Perhaps that was the right answer. His face tensed further in exquisite passion; she cried out something; and he fell against her.

Then she felt the floor. The hardness of the wood beneath her. She felt his weight and the thrust of his kneecap against her ribs.

"Brent," she whispered, stroking his hair.
"Hmm?"

"You're — you're killing me," she told him as sweetly as she could.

"What? Oh?" And then he laughed and shifted and pulled her against him and stroked her back carefully. He touched the two little dimples. "Wouldn't want anything to happen to these," he muttered. She smiled.

"They're really there, huh?"

"Want to see them?"

"What?"

He stood and lifted her against his chest. She threw her arms around him. "I could walk."

"Sure. Ruin my image," he said. He strode over to the easel, turning so that she could see the sketch. She gasped softly, amazed at the image he had created with his pencil.

It was beautiful. She was beautiful in it. The long line of her back had been made achingly graceful; her hair just fell to the side, over one shoulder, like rays of sunlight. Her head was bowed to the right, her profile just caught, her lips just parted, her lashes rich and long on her cheek. Just the hint of the swell of her breast appeared, peeking out from the smooth line of her arm. She couldn't have completely described this image any more than she could have described the painting of the entwined lovers.

Maybe that was it. He had caught her inner feelings. He had caught everything in her heart. The feelings of being entirely feminine, of needing him, of being . . . in love.

There seemed to be a flush on her face, a special sensuality to the curve of her back, to her look. She was a woman who waited for her lover. She was completely beautiful.

"Like it?"

"It's . . . lovely."

"It's just the sketch."

"Is that really how you see me?"

He stared down at her. He smiled slowly, ruefully.

"No. No, I could never paint or draw everything that I see in you. I can try. But it's far deeper than anything visual."

He kept smiling. She didn't reply but reached up to touch his cheek, awed.

For the second time since they had come, he carried her from the studio. They came to the bedroom and he allowed her to slide down against him, her breasts raking his chest. She wrapped her arms around him and she trembled, wondering if she had always known.

They were entwined themselves, embracing, sexual, sensual, and desperately in love . . .

The very image of the painting that had attracted her from the very first.

CHAPTER
6

KATRINA

WILLIAMSBURG, VIRGINIA
JUNE 1774

She slipped quietly into the entryway of her brother's townhouse and set her hat upon the tree. She could hear her sister-in-law in the parlor with her friends, laughing softly over tea. Katrina didn't want to see anyone yet. She was trembling from head to toe, dizzy. Inside of her it seemed that her very blood was racing through her body.

And it was just from the sight of him.

She had seen him today on Duke of Gloucester Street. He hadn't made way for her, and when she had tried to walk around him he had touched her, holding her. He had stared down at her with his laughing eyes and bid her a good day.

Oh! She could remember his smile and

she could remember his laughter. She could remember every plane and ridge of his handsome young sun-bronzed face. She could remember the strength of him, the scent of him . . .

She leaned against the fine French grass paper that covered the walls and brought her hand to her heart, willing it to calm its frantic beat. Her breast rose and fell — so quickly! Surely this was no way for a decent woman to behave. But then, she mused with quick inspiration, how could something natural be indecent? She could not control her heart's beating, nor could she control these feelings from raging inside of her like a hot and furious summer storm.

She pushed away from the wall and pursued an opposite train of thought. The nerve of him, the very nerve of him! She went to the glass in the hallway and she turned to survey her reflection. Her cheeks were very red — she was blushing shamefully — and her eyes were brilliant. She touched her midriff and felt the bone of her corset and remembered how he had held her, and she burned anew. Brash, uncivilized Yank! Backwoodsman, that was what he was. At the Governor's mansion she had learned that he was a landowner with a vast spread near the Washington residence,

Mount Vernon, a manor in the Tidewater region, also near the lands belonging to Lord Fairfax. In fact, it was said, young Percy Ainsworth was something of a protégé to the distinguished gentleman.

Katrina's brother, Lord Henry Seymour, despised Washington — "a yokel who thought himself an army man" — but he was fond of Fairfax, who was avidly loyal to the Crown of England above all else. Katrina was personally bored with the subjects of states' rights, independence, and war. Men — they all tended to be little boys who wished to play soldier; wasn't Patrick Henry himself such a one? Hadn't the Boston colonists dressed up like Indians just to throw a bunch of tea into the water? It all seemed very silly to Katrina. She was an Englishwoman; she was loyal to the King, and though she sympathized with many of the colonists' complaints, she could not imagine anyone really wanting to break away from the mother country. She tried to understand the Stamp Act that had seemed to start it all so many years ago, and she did believe that taxation should be linked with representation. But they were all behaving so badly! If they would just negotiate and compromise, surely it would all work out.

Men like Percy Ainsworth were the hotheads causing the problems, she knew.

And yet, she thought, her breath catching in her throat even as she gazed without seeing at her own image, she was quite fascinated by the passions elicited by all the talk. Nay, she was fascinated by the man. Percy.

"Percy . . ." She said it aloud, then smiled, seeing her image again. She smoothed back a lock of her hair and wondered what he had seen. She was sixteen last fall, surely a woman, yet had he seen a woman or a child? Henry had nearly promised her in marriage to that stuffy old General Olmsby, so surely she was old enough . . .

Percy. She bit into her lower lip and smiled again and dreamily dipped to pick up the front of her spring-flowered blue muslin skirt. Dreams danced in her head along with her feet as she moved, imagining herself with Percy.

He would want her; he would burn for her! Alas! She would be so cool, so disdainful. She would break his heart surely, for he must pine for her romantically.

Ah, she could see it so clearly! She could hear the musicians playing in the ballroom. She could see Percy. His breeches would be taut doeskin, his boots high and buckled. He would wear an elegant white waistcoat beneath a very fashionable frock coat, and the ruffles on his cambric shirt would be the height of elegance. He would be ladling himself punch from the bowl when his eyes would catch hers across the room.

All thoughts of punch would vanish. He would set down his glass, nearly tossing it aside. He would stride across the room to her, giving heed to no other.

And of course she, well . . .

She would play with her fan. She would laugh melodiously and answer the question of another young beau. Then he would touch her. He would turn her into his arms and demand the dance.

And while they were on the floor, he would worship her. He would tell her that he could not live without her. He would say that she had filled his moments, waking and sleeping, since he had first set eyes upon her.

"Why, Mr. Ainsworth," she would say coolly, "please! Such behavior is quite unseemly. Do cease, sir, so that we might enjoy the dance — and nothing more."

"I must have more!" He had the darkest eyes and they would flash, full of passion. His voice would be deep and raw with emotion. "A token, something, let me hold to the dream of thee, dear lady!"

Katrina turned to dance into the hallway

and crashed straight into her sister-in-law, Elizabeth. "Oh! Excuse me!"

Elizabeth was a plain girl with brown hair and a wide mouth, but when she smiled she seemed to light up a room. Katrina loved her. She was sweet and gentle — and Henry was not. Henry had married Elizabeth for her money. The Seymours might have a title and social prestige, but the Barringtons had supplied the gold for Henry to live in the style to which he had quickly become accustomed. Katrina was not terribly fond of her own brother. He was fifteen years her senior and far more severe with her than any natural father would have been, she was sure, but alas, hers had been dead — along with her saintly mother — for the last ten years, and therefore, Henry was her guardian. She knew that he frequently saw her as nothing more than a pawn in his power game, but thanks to Elizabeth, he had not been able as yet to marry her off to any rich old gentleman.

"Did I not know better, Katrina," Elizabeth teased, "I would say that you are in love." She smiled. "Come into the parlor, my dear. Lady Walthingham and Mistress Tether are here, and they have brought the latest fashion dolls from France."

"I'm rather tired, Elizabeth," Katrina

tried to excuse herself. "I've been busy running errands all day." She realized that her sister-in-law's friends — the very portly and proper Mistress Tether and the very lovely and terribly sly Lady Walthingham — could hear her, and not wishing to show Elizabeth any disrespect, she came into the room and quickly acknowledged the women. Mistress Tether was quick to ask about her health; Lady Walthingham asked no questions but assessed her carefully.

"You must see the newest fashions!" Mistress Tether insisted, and though she attempted to demur, Lady Walthingham was up, taking her arm and leading her into the room.

"My goodness! Look at the hair!" Katrina said and then laughed. The French were known for being terribly ostentatious, but really! It was quite absurd. "Why, a whole flock of crows could nest in that wig, it rises so very high!" Katrina marveled.

Even Lady Walthingham laughed, but then she sighed. "Katrina, God knows, only the French would dream of such an absurdly high hair style, but look at the dress, child, look at the dress! It's quite, quite lovely."

Katrina could see that the hoops were very full, arching high at the waistline; the neckline was excessively low. The gown itself was beautiful, though, rich in color, a sky-blue overskirt covering a white, frill-trimmed underskirt. The little doll carried a reticule and a green silk fan, and she was indeed lovely with her half-length laced sleeves and white lace cap with ribbons and feathers.

"It is indeed lovely," Katrina murmured, but at that moment, even as they chatted so inanely over the current state of costume, there came to them a loud ruckus from the street.

" 'Tis the home of Lord Seymour, gents, 'tis, 'tis! The home of Lord Tory!" men cried out loudly. Then something flew and the window shattered, spraying glass into the very room where they sat. Mistress Tether screamed; Elizabeth gasped. Katrina ran to the window, heedless of the danger, her cheeks turning pink.

"Cowards!" she screamed. "Sniveling cowards! To seek to harm women!"

But the men were already gone — boys, surely, Katrina thought, behaving like drunken cowards in truth and then realizing that they had really wrought violence. But then, violence was in the air these days. The Commonwealth of Massachusetts was already in revolt, and it seemed highly likely that Virginia would follow. Everyone spoke of war, and Katrina was aware of the great events that whirled around her. Patrick Henry spoke here, and when he spoke, the House of Burgesses grew agitated. Some men claimed that they longed merely to make the King see to their rights and their needs; others claimed that things had gone too far now, that all that remained was the inevitability of war. Henry laughed at such things. The colonists were backwoodsmen, he claimed. Barely literate. The King had trained soldiers. There could be no real revolution, but life could become unpleasant.

"Come away from the window, Katrina," Elizabeth begged her. "Please come! You shall get hurt there!"

Katrina pulled her head in but told Elizabeth contemptuously, "They are gone. They are afraid to face their deeds." She started for the hallway. "Elizabeth, I will go and see Mr. Rothenberry and tell him that we must have new panes made for the window."

"Katrina! You should not go out —"

"I'll be back soon, Elizabeth!" Katrina promised.

She could hear them talking about her as she left. Lady Walthingham warned Elizabeth that Katrina was trouble and that she should be married off quickly. Elizabeth demurred. Mistress Tether commented on her youth. Katrina smiled as she carefully picked up her skirts to avoid the mud and walked toward the green. Lady Walthingham was very eager for Katrina to be married off to Lord Olmsby, an officer in the King's dragoons. He was very short and very portly and three times Katrina's age. Katrina thought grimly that Lady Walthingham was anxious for the match only because of Lord Charles Palmer, a much younger man, a peer of the realm. Lord Palmer had been coming to the Williamsburg townhouse more and more frequently over the last months. He was a tall man, well muscled, blonde and handsome. Yet Lady Walthingham had little to fear from Katrina as far as competition went; Katrina despised the man. He had a way of smiling that was frightening, as if an evil lived in his heart. Katrina did not like him to so much as kiss her hand.

She sighed, walking along, because she was smiling herself and her mind was on Percy again. He was so very audacious. He deserved a good switching, she told herself. But there seemed to be a lump in her throat and that drastic beating of her heart had begun all over again. She did not care about the broken glass. Or perhaps she did, but that was not why she had left the house.

She wanted to see him again.

It was wrong. He could very well be labeled a traitor, for he was a traitor to the Crown. Her anger rose as she thought of the window breaking — he had sided with the riffraff who would sink so low. She wanted to find him; she wanted to tell him what had happened, that it was his kind who would do such things!

Yet . . . how?

She could quite properly visit the shoemaker or pause at the blacksmith's or even stop at the candlemaker's or the tailor's or seek any type of merchandise. But Percy Ainsworth would not be here in Williamsburg to shop. He was here to plot new treachery with his friends. Where would he be? Inside one of the taverns, and she could not simply step inside alone and unescorted and . . .

"Milady Seymour!"

Her name was shouted. A pair of strong, deft arms lifted her high and swept her around, pulling her from the muddy street just as a milk wagon swept by.

"Oh!" she gasped.

She had no need to find him, for he was there. The devil's own dark laughing eyes

137

stared down into hers beneath the shadows of his tricorn. He held her still, against his body. She felt incredible warmth; she felt the beat of his heart.

She felt her own heart take flight.

"Mr. Ainsworth, sir! Put me down!"

"Why, milady! You were about to have been run down there. My stars, mistress, but you've a knack for dangerous positions, and an even greater knack for ingratitude."

"Ingratitude! Why the cart was nowhere near me —"

"It had just about knocked you solid!"

Her feet were upon the ground. Her hands were still upon his shoulders and his were about her waist. She flushed furiously. "Mr. Ainsworth!" She cried. "Ingratitude, you say! Why I'd not be out and about now were it not for the despicable likes of yourself!"

His eyes narrowed sharply. "Aye? And why is that?"

"A horde of your fellows just broke a window at our home, when all who abided there then were four defenseless ladies."

"Defenseless!" He laughed and, before she knew it, she was swept off her feet, whirled around, and set upon higher, greener ground.

"Damn you —"

"You're beautiful, you know," he told her.

It seemed that her heart stopped, dead stopped, then thundered onward again. Why, she wondered, wasn't he Lord so-and-so or Lieutenant so-and-so or someone of whom her family might approve?

Why wasn't he somebody she could love?

"Let me go!" she demanded.

But he did not. His laughter left him, and his smile faded and he continued to stare at her. "You're very beautiful," he repeated softly. "You should run away with me. The world is about to explode, you know. I would keep you safe. I would guard you with my life."

It was her turn to erupt in laughter. "You, Mr. Ainsworth? You would protect me? You, sir, will most probably hang. That is the fate of traitors."

"Trust me, milady, the Tories shall be evicted soon. Can't you feel it? There is rebellion in the air. People crave freedom. Soon no man shall claim the rights of another. No man shall claim superiority to another. It will come. It will come, a rising wind that cannot be stopped. Come with me. Feel that wind."

"Come with you where?" she taunted him.

And he smiled again, slowly. "Wherever I

go, milady. I promise you, I can make you die for my touch, for my soft whisper."

She laughed again, but the sound was breathless and she had to jerk away from his hold. "You are mad! Even to speak to me so! You are rude and discourteous, and I can tell you, Mr. Ainsworth, that I shall never long for an unwashed, backwoods bumpkin —"

"Backwoods, yes. But I do beg to differ, milady. I wash most frequently. Bumpkin? Perhaps. But a man, milady. Not a silly fop like that aging crustacean they would wed you to —"

"What do you know of it?" Katrina demanded.

"Alas, only what a man hears in the taverns. But see, then? You should come with me now. You should know a man, before being sold to a crustacean."

She struck out, slapping his cheek as fast as she could, her own growing crimson. He caught her wrist while the harsh sound of her slap seemed to resound in the air. He held her while he rubbed his cheek ruefully, and neither of them was aware of a thing that went on around them. Horses, carriages, and wagons continued to traverse the streets. Down along the green, someone was speaking and drawing an audience. The soldiers could be seen, and the men of the Commonwealth, barely civil now to one another as events tightened around them. Birds chirped; the sky remained a glorious blue.

And neither of them saw it, for they saw only each other.

"I am in love with you," he told her.

"You are crude!" she cried.

"Only because I am in love with you," he said very, very softly, "and because I cannot bear to hear the rumors. That you will soon be wed to one of these lobsterbacks two or three times your own age. Only because I cannot bear that he should touch you. Only because I must have you . . ."

She heard his words and his whisper seemed to fade. He shouldn't be talking to her so, as if she were a common . . . whore. It showed a horrendous lack of respect. Men did not marry women with whom they so teased and played . . .

She could never marry him. The whole idea was mad. If violence did indeed break out in earnest, she would most probably leave the country. She would never see him again.

She lowered her head and moistened her lips and nearly cried out and reached for him, so weakened was she by the sudden heat that shot through her. She wanted to touch him. To feel his cheek, fresh shaven now, to run her hands over his shoulders and feel the muscles beneath his coat.

She wanted things that she dared not speak of; she wanted to know what was forbidden, what she had only heard whispered about, what was hot and sweet and carnal . . .

"I cannot stand here!" she cried suddenly. "Henry, my brother, would kill one of us, were he to see us."

Percy looked up and realized that there was a world around them. They were in the center of the green, near the blacksmith's. Williamsburg was not so large a place that they would not be noticed, and all that he had been saying was true. Tension was in the air. Fights and riots broke out constantly these days, and in Massachusetts many a man had been tarred and feathered for one belief or another. Percy was aware that Lord Henry Seymour would just as soon see his sister with a raw savage as he would see her with himself.

He did not hesitate though; he took her hand. "Come with me."

"What? Are you mad!" Katrina stared at him, trying to wrench her hand from his. "Let me go this instant!"

142

He smiled, tightening his grip. She was flushed and her breasts were heaving, and she was determined to fight him. The challenge was clear, and through fair means or foul, Percy was determined that he would not lose.

"Let you go, love? Never!" He jerked her hard against him, staring down at her. Her eyes, afire, met his. She couldn't combat his strength.

"I'll scream!" she threatened.

"Will you?" He laughed. "Nay, lady, you will not!" With that, he clamped a hand down hard upon her mouth and swept her off her feet. Long strides brought them quickly across the road, behind a tavern, and into a barn.

He closed the door and set her down. Katrina swore and she kicked him and he laughed, but then he threaded his fingers through her hair and forced back her head. He stroked her throat with the pad of his thumb, and then he kissed her. She held her lips still to his assault, and then she tried to bite him. But he held firm. Eventually her struggles ceased. Her lips parted to the pressure of his, and he drank deeply of her sweetness, offering her no quarter. She fell limp against him.

"Bastard!" Shaking, she managed to push

away from him at last. She threw open the door and entered into the light. He followed, catching up with her.

"You won't leave me! We need to talk."

Katrina lifted her head, trembling. She could still feel the pressure of his lips against hers. She knew that he was right. No matter how much she desired to, she could not run away.

She walked down to the gate to the corral and turned around disdainfully to survey the tavern in front. This was not a place that Henry would frequent. He would not come where any of the wild Yankee ruffians might imbibe a pint. Henry did not often frequent taverns; he preferred to spend his leisure time in the Governor's mansion.

Beneath the shade of a giant elm, Katrina turned her back on Percy and stared out at the corral and at the group of horses that played all along the length of the white picket fencing. The horses were beautiful; they ran wild and free. Katrina noted that a sleek black stallion nipped the neck of a snow-white mare. The mare, in return, tossed her head and began to race the very wind again, leaving him to trail in her wake.

"How she teases him!" Percy observed.

Katrina lowered her head quickly, flushing. Then she looked up and she caught Percy's dark eyes upon her. She wondered if he was speaking about the horses, or perhaps his words were a taunt, more personal. She had already gravely compromised her position. A young lady simply did not even see a man in private. She did not follow where he led her so easily. She did not shiver at his touch, then tremble in heat.

"I have to go. I don't know why I am here —" She began.

"You are a liar. You came out to find me. And you have found me, love!" He caught her hand again.

"Percy!" She cried out in dismay, for he pulled her back to the barn. "Stop!" She pleaded.

He was determined. He swung her around as they reentered the cool darkness, fragrant with the scent of fresh hay.

"Percy!" She backed against the paneling of the tack room and his hands fell upon her cheeks, either side. She felt the spellbinding dark heat of his eyes and she tried to speak again. "I should not have come. I'm sorry. I do not know why —"

"I think that you do know why," he whispered to her softly and stepped against her. His arms swept around her, and his body came flush with hers, their hips pressed together, her breasts forced high and taut and firm against the breadth of his chest. His fingers massaged and cradled her nape, drawing her closer, and his lips came down upon hers once again, forceful still, but tender.

She had been kissed once before today. A silly, awkward kiss from a silly, fat man, that boor whom Henry so admired. She had demurred; she had escaped; she had felt nothing.

Nothing . . .

And now she felt everything. She felt the warmth of the day, the blaze of the springtime sun. She felt the wet fire of the sure, insinuating sweep of his tongue; and she felt the scent of him entering her body and her memory; and she felt the sheer masculine force of him, of his lips and his form and his dark and forbidden and very bold desire. She knew that she had to pull away from him again. She knew that what she did — this kiss — was wanton and decadent and that her sheer enjoyment of it labeled her less than a lady. But she could not deny it. She clung to him while he kissed her, on and on. She dug her fingers into his shoulders to hold him, to stay straight. She felt his tongue against her teeth, then deep inside her mouth. She felt the savage desire and she felt the tenderness and she shivered and trembled, feeling the raw, desperate excitement.

It was madness. Some logic remained with her in a distant but demanding section of her mind. It was sheer lunacy. Not only would Henry kill her but wasn't she loyal to the Crown herself? She was English, not American. She had grown up in London, and she had come here only because Henry was her guardian and because he had been given vast stretches of land in the colonies. Because of the townhouse here and the acreage in the Carolinas and the beautiful white-pillared mansion in Philadelphia. She herself was English, and here she stood, locked in this debasing embrace with one of the greatest blackguards of the time. A man who brazenly and crudely stated that he wanted her. He loved her . . . ah, yes, love! she told herself bitterly. He did not court her; he whisked her away. He did not mention the honorable state of marriage; he just promised to sweep her away. Men did not take as wives the women with whom they so rakishly played . . .

Surely, he laughed at her. He made a fool, a trollop, of her, and he would laugh tonight in the tavern and tell his revolutionary friends of how he petted and mauled Lord

Seymour's haughty sister, and left her languishing for more.

"No!"

She wrenched her lips from his and beat her fists against his coat, pushing away from him in horror. She brought her fingers to her swollen lips and stared at him, furious, dismayed.

"No!" she cried again.

"Katrina?"

He set his hands upon her shoulders to pull her close once again. She shoved against him. "Fool, oaf, traitor! You'll leave me be!"

She turned blindly to run. He reached out for her, catching her hair, entwining his fingers there. "Katrina!"

She tried to turn on him with a vengeance and she cried out instead, tripping over her skirts. Her heart thundered furiously as she fell, her breath coming in ragged gasps. She heard his laughter; then he fell down beside her. He straddled her, pinning her down.

"Get off me!" she cried.

"Katrina, listen to me —"

"No! I hate you. I don't want you touching me. I want them to hang you —"

He flushed darkly and his eyes glittered with fury. "Don't be a fool, Katrina."

"Let me up —"

"You are like the mare, my love. A tease until the very end."

"You are a traitor!"

"And you, love, must realize that you are a woman before you are a Tory." He caught her hands; his fingers entwined with hers and he pulled them high over her head, then he lowered himself over her. She continued to gasp for breath, but she did not cry out. She stared at him with hatred.

And with fascination.

"You quiver!" he whispered to her. "And your lips are parted. Is that anticipation?"

"That is my desperation to breathe!" she spat out. "You are a heavy traitor."

Percy laughed with pure pleasure. She trembled anew, for his lashes swept over the shadows of his cheeks and he kissed her forehead. She twisted and he caught her lips.

She felt it again, the sweetness, the rising passion, the magic. She breathed in the sweet fresh hay and the man and, hysterically, she thought that she could so easily yield all. He touched her. He caressed her face. His hands swept over her breasts, along her waist . . .

With deep chagrin she realized that he was no longer holding her down. She was yielding far more than she had ever imagined.

She twisted from his lips at last. "Percy!" There was a note of anguish in her cry.

"What?" he demanded angrily. "Do I hurt you, lady? Or are you so determined to ignore what wages here between us?"

"Yes, yes! Let me up!"

"Let you run!" he corrected her with quiet derision. "Yes, run, Katrina. You will come back."

"Percy!"

"There! There!" Swift, agile, he rose, reaching for her hand and wrenching her to her feet. "Go!"

She stared at him, her breasts rising and falling with each of her desperate breaths. She inched away, backward, wary lest he should move again.

He opened the barn door himself. He followed her out into the sunlight. She walked by him, absently touching her moist and swollen lips, warily keeping an eye upon him.

He laughed and leaned against the picket fence. The sunlight caught his eyes and his hair. He inclined his head slightly toward the fence.

"You'll be back, my love, I promise."

"Never!" she spat.

He turned around, resting a booted foot upon the fence. "My, my," he murmured.

150

"Seems the lady has been caught."

Katrina could not help but follow his gaze to the corral, and then she gasped in dismay, for the mare was no longer teasing the stallion, but bearing the full brunt of him, caught, his creature.

"Oh!"

"Come, Katrina, you cannot be so shocked!"

She did not dignify his comment with an answer. Tears stung her eyes again. What did he think of her? No gently born woman would not be shocked at such a sight! How she hated him.

How she hated his effect upon her . . .

She started to run. She heard his laughter following her. "Come to me, my love! Anytime."

Her cheeks burned. She forgot that she had come out to see about glass for the window. She ignored the mud in the road and kept running. The bone stays of her corset tightened around her, threatening to rob her of all breath.

She came back to the house at last, and then she knew that she could not enter it. Not then. Not until she could breathe again, not until the color left her cheeks. Her brother was back. His carriage, with the gilded initials on the door, stood in front.

Katrina walked around to the back and entered the carriage house. She leaned against the wall, then sank to sit upon a pile of red bricks. She heard the motion from the cool darkness in the back and jumped to her feet once again.

"Henry?"

"Aye, Katrina, it's me."

He walked toward her. He was a striking man with a neatly queued and fashionable white wig and tight fawn breeches that he wore very well. He was smiling as he approached her. Smiling and tapping a riding crop against the palm of his hand. She realized then that someone was behind Henry. It was Lord Charles Palmer, tall and elegant in a blue satin waistcoat and white breeches. Like Henry, he was smiling, and she did not like his smile.

She tried very hard to calm her breathing, knotting her fingers together behind her back. Henry came closer and closer, until he smiled down at her.

"Say good day to Lord Palmer, Katrina."

She offered up a small curtsy and murmured a proper greeting to the man. He returned it very pleasantly.

"You're out of breath," Henry commented.

"Am I?"

"And alas! You've mud spattered all over your skirts and upon your new slippers."

"Have I? Well, it is spring, you know. And the roads are so very bad with all the rain."

"Where have you been?"

"I was — looking for ribbons."

"Elizabeth said you went to see about replacing the panes of glass."

"Um, yes, well, I intended to do so." She looked past her brother and offered Lord Palmer one of her most dazzling smiles. "I am afraid I was waylaid, looking for ribbon."

"Liar!"

Katrina screamed, stunned by the force of her brother's attack as he raised the crop high and brought it down viciously upon her shoulder. She fell to her knees and stared up at him, blinded by her tears.

"You were with that piece of odious rabble, Percy Ainsworth."

She tried to rise. He struck her again. "Henry!" she screamed in dismay, placing her hands before her to defend herself, seeking help from the man who stood behind him. She could not believe that Henry would treat her so before anyone else, especially Charles Palmer.

But then she saw that Lord Palmer was smiling more fully, that his breath now came more quickly than her own and that his eyes held a curious excitement. He was enjoying it, she thought bleakly; he would love to be the one beating her himself. He would not help her.

"You were with him!"

"Henry, please!"

Katrina swallowed quickly and lowered her head, thinking desperately. Elizabeth would help her. Elizabeth would help her if she could. But she had to get to Elizabeth first.

"Henry, I saw the man in the street. He spoke to me; I spoke back. That is all."

"Nay, that is not all! You followed him. You went with him, alone, like a bitch in heat."

"No!"

The crop fell upon her once again. Her back stung as if a thousand needles were embedded in it. "Please, Henry!" Prone upon the floor, she bit her lower lip so that she would not cry. He reached for her, wrenching her to her feet. He pulled her close to him, glanced at Lord Palmer, and then smiled.

"Katrina . . ." Softly, he stroked her cheek. "Katrina, my dear sister. At last, long last, I think I have found a use for you."

CHAPTER

7

"Details!" Tina insisted. "I want details!"

"Come on!" Liz pushed.

Gayle sat back, stretching slightly, a slow, lazy smile curling her lips automatically. She couldn't help it. The mere mention of his name made her smile, made her blush, made her feel warm and delicious all over.

The three women were having dinner together seated at a little booth at Trader Vic's, an establishment not far from the Confederate White House. Gayle hadn't talked to either of them in two weeks, but then she hadn't really talked to anyone in two weeks. Brent had wanted time alone together, and she had wanted time alone together. She had barely met Brent's charming, motherly housekeeper before the woman had been sent off for a vacation to help her daughter and grandchildren. Mary Richardson had been delighted with the unexpected holiday, if a little bit startled by the suddenness of it all. Geoffrey, on the other hand, hadn't seemed surprised when she had called to ask for some time off. "Just so long as we all know where you are, kid, huh?"

Gayle swirled her swizzle stick against the salt that rimmed her margarita glass.

"Come on!" Liz repeated. A glass of white wine sat untouched before her. Gayle shrugged, sitting comfortably back in her seat. She licked her swizzle stick, grinning at Liz. "Okay. Okay. It was the best time I've ever had in my entire life. He is the best thing to have ever touched my life."

"Oh . . ." Liz breathed, smiling. "That's so romantic."

"Romantic," Tina agreed, complaining. "But there's not one lousy detail in it. I want the whole story — from the beginning."

Unperturbed, Gayle leaned back again, sliding against the seat. Her eyes were vague, as if she relived her dreams. "That's like starting with the beginning of — life!" she murmured.

Tina glanced at Liz. This was bad. This was so much more than a crush. Gayle — dependable, practical Gayle — seemed star struck.

"Two full weeks," Liz said dryly.

Gayle focused her eyes upon them both. "I'm going to marry him, you know."

Liz choked on a sip of wine, exchanging a

shooting glance with Tina one more time.

"You — ah — you mean in the future."

Gayle laughed, the sound delightful, her eyes radiant. "Well, of course, in the future. I'm having dinner with you two here in the present."

"No, no —" Tina began.

Gayle leaned forward. "He's built just like an Adonis."

"All over?" Liz interrupted mischievously.

"Liz!" Tina protested.

"Hey — you're the one who asked for the details. All the heavenly little intimate details."

Gayle smiled, completely serene, and then she was halfway laughing again and very excited. Her smile deepened and she told Liz in a low, husky voice, "All of him. Oh, Liz, he's gorgeous. From head to toe and in between."

"Oh . . ." Liz said on a soft note again. "How romantic."

A waitress appeared with their dinners. Gayle played with her food, and the dream quality was back in her eyes.

Tina sat back uneasily. "It's nice to be in love with being in love," she murmured. "But Gayle, honey, you've got me worried."

"Why?"

"I don't want you to get hurt, that's why."

"You wanted me to date him."

"Date, yes! Dates are things that you have on Saturday nights. He takes you out — dinner, dancing, maybe a movie. Then he takes you home. Sometimes it's a handshake and sometimes it's a kiss and sometimes, it's a night in the hay. But you left one night and disappeared for two full weeks! With Liz and me in a dither, I might add."

"I'm so sorry about that —"

"I'm more worried now!" Tina proclaimed.

"Oh? Why? You shouldn't be. Details, huh . . . ?" Gayle curled some linguini around her fork and looked at Tina innocently. She set down her fork, and she was like an excited child all over again. She leaned forward, speaking in a hush.

"When we got out there, it just happened that his housekeeper had been called away —"

"Now that figures," Liz stated dryly.

"Uh-huh," Tina agreed.

"And I almost chickened out," Gayle continued as if she hadn't heard them. "I wasn't going to do it."

"Do what?"

"Model!"

"Hmph! And I'll bet you never did!" Liz stated.

"Cynical, cynical!" Gayle chastised. Then she sighed again, lost in the rose-tinted mists of memory. "Brent . . . he didn't intend what happened —"

"Of course, he didn't!" Tina murmured with sweet sarcasm.

"Surely, he wouldn't," Liz agreed, and they both rolled their eyes.

"Oh, you doubting Thomases!" Gayle laughed happily, her eyes flashing with brilliant amusement. "He didn't. He really didn't. But I was standing there and he was standing there —"

"Right there in his studio? Did you ever pose?"

Gayle flushed. "Tina! Yes! I mean — no, not that first night. We started in the studio. You two are terrible! And then he carried me into his bedroom —"

"Oh, man!" Liz murmured. "All that time, huh?"

"No, of course not." Gayle grinned. "A lot, though. I've never — I've never had such a wonderful time in all my life."

"What did you do?"

"We didn't really do anything —"

"Oh, is that romantic!" Liz interrupted. "You walked around in robes and you sat before the fire and he filled your wineglass and then his eyes would touch yours —"

"Liz! I want to hear this from Gayle. Remember? The girl who was actually there?"

"I did pose for him," Gayle said. She was smiling again. "I posed for him and" — she paused to offer Liz a special smile — "we did sit before the fire and we did walk around in robes. We went out a few times, into the forest around his house. We cooked some wonderful meals and we sent out for pizza and Chinese. And we talked. We talked and talked." She hesitated. "I told you, I'm going to marry him." They both stared at her, stunned. Gayle looked from one stunned face to the other and laughed again, reaching out across the table to squeeze their hands. "I thought you both liked him."

"We do," Liz said automatically.

Gayle smiled at Tina. "You're the one who told me to go out and get him."

"I know. I did. But —" she broke off, looking at Liz helplessly. Liz didn't give her any help. "I think that he's fabulous. But —" She paused again, then plunged in. "Gayle, I really think that a good relationship in bed is very, very important in a marriage."

"But it isn't everything," Liz plunged in too, finally determined to give Tina some assistance. But now she looked at Tina helplessly. "You're kidding, aren't you?" She asked Gayle. "I mean, about this marrying bit?"

"Oh, no. I'm going to marry him."

"But you mean in a year or so, right?"

"No. I mean in one month."

Tina gasped. Liz choked on her wine again. "Gayle, you're not listening. You have to *think* about marriage. I mean, you can be — you can be —"

"Passionately involved?" Liz tried.

"Sure, sure, passionate, in a matter of two weeks. But Gayle, how can you be sure that you want to marry someone?"

"And him! It's Brent McCauley," Tina reminded Liz. She curled her fingers around Gayle's this time. "Honey, are you sure? Maybe he wasn't serious."

"Why don't you ask him?" Gayle suggested.

"Ask him?" Liz murmured.

Gayle smiled serenely at them, gazing past them. Liz and Tina turned to see that McCauley was coming toward them, sleek, bronzed, and handsome in a navy Izod and jeans. He wore that same silly, dream-quality grin that seemed to be permanently affixed to Gayle's features.

Gayle stood. "Brent!" She whispered his name so softly. In the mere voicing of it, she spoke volumes of love with such a force of tender sensuality that it was almost like watching the two of them in bed. Liz cleared her throat and stared down at her food. Tina still stared at them, caught by the emotion.

"Hi, sweetheart."

Brent reached her. He did nothing more overtly sexual than kiss her hand and stare into her eyes, but Tina felt herself grow hot all over. They were beautiful, she thought. Beautiful together. She was so blond; he was so dark. She was tall and shapely, and he was tall and muscular.

It couldn't have gone on forever, just the two of them standing there, staring at each other. Brent was too polite a man for that, pleasantly sensitive to those around him. He and Gayle broke eye contact. She slid into the booth, moving in far enough to give him room, and Brent smiled at Tina and Liz. "Tina, Liz, how are you? Has Gayle told you about the wedding yet?"

He laughed. Their mouths fell open, quite literally open. Brent looked at Gayle and she shrugged, circling her fingers over his hand, and then they both stared at Tina and Liz like a pair of Cheshire cats.

Gayle reached across the table and tapped Tina's chin, shutting it. "I did tell you," she said reproachfully. Tina swallowed and stared at Brent. He was every woman's dream of a lover. She liked him very much; she had encouraged Gayle to go after him. It was just too soon for the two of them to be talking marriage.

"It's okay," Brent told them softly. His eyes fell adoringly on Gayle. "It's okay. I'm not marrying her for her money, you know. I have plenty of my own."

He was rich. That much was true.

Tina shook her head. "Ah, Brent, you know how much I like you. We like you. Liz and I — we both do." Her words didn't seem to be coming out right, but Brent McCauley didn't notice. He was watching Gayle again. She had never seen a gaze of such fierce and protective tenderness. "And not that it is any of our business — but I really want both of you to think about what you're doing —"

The waitress came by, interrupting their conversation for a moment. Even though the table was full of food that no one seemed to be touching, Brent ordered a cheeseburger and fries and a large Coke, and when the waitress was gone he slipped an arm around Gayle and she lay back against him as sleek as a Persian cat.

"You two are so happy that it's — disgusting!" Liz blurted out. "And it's soooo romantic."

"Liz, you know, you're no help! This is serious!" Tina wailed.

"Yes, it is. Very," Brent agreed. "I love Gayle; she loves me. We're going to be married in about a month — three Saturdays from last and you're the first to know. Well, other than my parents and my great-uncle Frank."

"And Geoff," Gayle reminded him softly.

"Oh, yeah, and Chad."

"It was nice to be right at the top of the list!" Tina laughed.

"I meant you to be!" Gayle cried, stricken.

"It's okay, it's okay," Liz assured them.

"You are going to be my attendants, though."

Liz clapped her hands. "Oh! You're having a real wedding?"

"If they're legal, they're real," Brent reminded them, but Liz shook her head impatiently.

"How perfect! How romantic. A traditional wedding?"

Gayle smiled happily. "Neither of us has been married before. We talked about it. I want a church wedding and I want to wear white. I want to throw a bouquet, and I want lots and lots of rice thrown at us. Will you congratulate us, please?"

"Of course!" Tina murmured. She and Liz jumped up and they came around to kiss them both.

"You do like the idea of the Bahamas?" Brent asked after Tina and Liz had left.

Gayle, leaning against his shoulder while he finished his cheeseburger, smiled. "I love the idea of the Bahamas. I love the idea of the Out Islands. Sand, sea — and the two of us."

"We can go anywhere you want."

"I know," she said softly. "Thank you."

They both fell silent. Gayle stretched and moved away from him to take a sip of the coffee the waitress had just brought her. She smiled again affectionately, thinking of Liz and Tina and how much fun it had been to tell them this way. Then she frowned because, with the two of them gone, the conversation at the next booth began to come to their table, painfully loud.

A woman was talking to a man. She was very attractive, thin, svelte, dark. Gayle couldn't see the man's face; he seemed older, with graying hair.

"I don't want anything," the woman said. "Nothing at all."

"That's commendable, Mrs. Willows, but you want to be realistic too. If there is anything that you do want, we need to list it so that the papers are entirely clear when they are served."

"Oh, I don't want anything — just out."

The beautiful woman brought her napkin to her lips and her eyes grew damp. "Well, maybe I do need a few things."

"Fine. I'll list them."

"Well, the house, I suppose. I should have the house. And the Ferrari. I do drive it most of the time. The house, the car — oh, the little beach bungalow out on the Cape. My jewelry, of course. And the van and the furniture and . . ."

She kept on going. Finally the man — her lawyer, obviously — interrupted her. "Mrs. Willows, ahem, maybe we should do this differently. Let me rephrase the question: Is there anything that you intend to leave him?"

"Well, his personal possessions, of course."

"Good," the lawyer sighed. "The man gets to keep his underwear."

Gayle realized that she had been actively eavesdropping on the conversation. She glanced guiltily at Brent, then swallowed. He knew what she had heard; he had heard it too. He caught her hand and squeezed it. "All she wants is blood, huh?"

"Oh, Brent! It's awful, isn't it? Just awful. They must have loved each other somewhere along the line. They married one another and now look . . ."

He shook his head impatiently. "Gayle, face it, some people are greedier than others. Some are into vengeance. We're not like that. We love each other. Don't worry. It's never, never going to be like that between us."

"Oh, Brent! Maybe you should be frightened. Of me. Maybe you should call your lawyers —"

"Gayle, it is never, never going to be like that between us."

She smiled, and stroked the plane of his cheek. "It never will be, will it?"

"Never. Come on. Let's stroll for a while, then drive back out to the house."

"It's the first day we've been out of it."

"I had to let you go back to work sometime. It wouldn't have been fair to Geoff otherwise."

"And you're so fair."

"Yes, but the strain is beginning to tell now."

He lifted his hand for the check, then left the money on the table. He led her outside and they began to walk, hand in hand. In the near distance, they could see the Confederate White House and the Museum of the Confederacy.

"Can you imagine," Gayle murmured. "Poor Jeff Davis. He lost a son in that house. A child of his fell from the porch and died."

Brent paused, wrapping his arms around her and resting his chin on top of her head. "History tells many tragic tales."

"I suppose," Gayle murmured. Then she turned in his arms, looking up at him. "How strange!"

"What?"

"I just realized I don't even know where you're from."

"Virginia, m'am," he teased with an accent. "I'm a Virginian, born and bred."

"I love you!" She laughed. "I'm going to marry you — and I hadn't even known that, not until this minute."

He stopped for a minute and wrapped his arms around her again and kissed her beneath the moon. "That's what marriage is, sweetheart. A lifetime of finding out all the little things."

He caught her hand and they started to walk.

"You love old things," she murmured suddenly.

He glanced her way. "Like houses?"

"Houses and history."

"Yes, I do. But do you know what else I love?"

"What?"

"You. And do you know what I love about you in particular?"

"What?"

"Well . . ." He lowered his lips to her ear. With an artist's graphic detail, he described what he loved.

"We've barely been away —"

"We've been away too long. Come on; let's get to the car."

In an hour they were home. It was strange, Gayle thought, that she could already think so easily of Brent's house as "home." Sometimes she thought that it was presumptuous — they weren't married yet. But it wasn't the house that she was thinking of as home — she had her own perfectly good house, and she liked it very well and Brent liked it very well too. Where Brent was — that was home, Gayle realized. And maybe that was a little frightening too. It had come fast, very fast. They were so dependent upon one another. Not in the sense of needing crutches — they were both by nature very independent people, capable and confident. She didn't need to know where he was every second — but when he was gone for too many seconds, she simply longed to see him again, to touch him, to be with him.

As they stepped into the entryway Brent swept her off her feet and into his arms.

"Hey!" She protested. But her arms twined around him.

"Hey!" Long, long strides took them to the stairway; he seemed to take the steps two at a time.

"We really haven't been away that long," she teased him softly, playing with a strand of his hair.

"It seems like forever."

In minutes they were in his bedroom. In seconds they had fumbled out of their clothing. Gayle caught his face between her hands when he rose, taut and hard, above her.

"Do you think that we could ever grow tired of each other?"

"Never."

"Really?"

"Gayle!"

"What?"

"Could we discuss this later?"

She convulsed into a spate of giggles, but then the laughter faded and the heat began to rise. No, she could never, never grow tired of him. Never grow tired of loving him, of waking to his face, handsome or gaunt, young or old, beside hers. With his touch, she flew. She soared. She touched the heavens.

They made love and then relaxed against each other. And then more slowly he began to make love to her again. Instinct had taught him her erogenous zones; practice had made him such a lover that she could not resist, and he never failed to arouse her again at will. He knew where to kiss and where to stroke, and to kiss and stroke at once, and he could read every slight nuance of her movement. He left her exhausted and yet exhilarated, and when she drifted to sleep she would think of the little things that she loved so much, the feel of his body touching hers, wet and slick, still, sometimes, within her. She would smile at the thought of his hands, big hands, rough in a way, betraying emotion when he worked, betraying it in his slightest touch upon her.

That night was no different. She drifted to sleep feeling loved, feeling contented, feeling deeply, sweetly sated. His hand lay upon her hip; she was curled to his chest. She fell asleep, imagining, dreaming, his face, his smile, his laughter. She was at peace. All was incredibly right with the world.

That made the nightmare all the worse.

She was drifting off so pleasantly. She could see the wedding, her gown, white, as she wanted it. Chad, Geoff, Liz, and Tina were there, and of course Brent was there. He was wonderfully handsome, so tall and so sure . . . his words were so strong as he gave his vows. His lips were so warm when they touched hers . . .

It began with the woman in the aisle. She blocked them when they would have walked down it together. At first Gayle was merely puzzled, and then she was concerned. "I don't want anything!" She shouted. "Just the house and the car and blood. I want blood, I want blood, I want blood . . ."

Mist filled the room. It wasn't a pretty mist like a spring fog. It was evil. Evil and foul-smelling. It began to color things, and Gayle was very afraid that she would pass out from the smell of it. She reached for Brent's hand, but he was no longer there. She looked and then she realized that he had withdrawn from her, that he was staring at her furiously, that he was screaming at her.

"Traitor!" His face was taut with hatred and passion. "Traitorous — bitch!"

He struck her. He slapped her so hard that she fell to the ground. She clutched her cheek, and blood ran down her beautiful, pure white wedding gown. "No!" She shrieked in return, bewildered and hurt. "No! I don't want the house. I'd never take the house or the car or —"

"My soul, you whore, you stole my soul!"

The mist was green, swirling and swirling around her. It grew darker and darker as Brent came closer and closer to her. She was terrified of him, absolutely terrified.

"No!"

"Bitch. Lying, traitorous bitch!"

The mist grew blacker by the instant. Desperately, she tried to crawl away from him. It was Brent. She shouldn't be so afraid.

But it was Brent as she had never known him, and she was in mortal fear.

"No!"

It became black, completely black. She screamed with all of her heart, and then there was no more.

"Gayle!"

When she awoke, she was soaked in sweat. She was shaking and trembling. His arms were around her tightly. "Gayle! Sweetheart, what is it, what is it?"

Mist and blackness faded away. Brent flicked on the bedside light. She saw his face. She had been terrified, but when she saw his face the fear began to slide away.

"I'll get you some water —" he began.

"No!" She reached out for him, burying her face against his chest, seeking the shelter of his arms. "No, no, no, don't leave me!"

"Gayle —"

"Oh!"

He stroked her hair and he held her very close. "You had a nightmare. It's over now."

"Yes."

"You're still trembling. I'm here. I love you. It's over. It's all right."

"Oh . . . I know. I was just — so frightened."

"Of what?"

Of what . . . ? She thought and thought, but she didn't know. She shook her head.

"Sweetheart, talk about it. That can make it better. Bring it out into the open."

"I — can't remember." She laughed, nervously at first, and then more easily. She was able to sit up at last and smile at him ruefully. "Oh, Brent, I woke you up. I'm so sorry. I woke you up because I had a nightmare — and, I swear, I can't remember a second of it. Isn't that crazy?"

He smiled and pulled her back against him, ruffling her hair. "Absolutely crazy. You're a Looney Tunes, but I love you anyway."

"I love you," she promised him and then,

absurdly, she fought the urge to cry. To cry, to mourn, for something that had come and gone, for something that had been . . . lost.

"You okay now?"

"Yes. Just hold me."

He looked at her for a moment. He offered her an encouraging smile, then reached over and turned off the light. "If I hold you, am I allowed to get carried away?"

"You can't possibly —"

"But I can. More than possibly. Really. Want to check it out? Here — feel."

He led her hand to him and he had her laughing again. He said he was really, really sorry, but she did have this unique ability to keep him constantly horny. She told him it was a horrible word and he said he thought it was a damned good one, and when it was all over again, she was thinking once more about how much she loved him. By the time he had finished with her, she had forgotten that she had ever been frightened. She remembered only that she was very, very much in love and deeply, intimately, loved in return.

It was only when she slept again that fragments of her dream returned to haunt her.

CHAPTER
8

THE BALL

WILLIAMSBURG, VIRGINIA
JUNE 1774

Lady Dearling was having a ball. A costume ball.

The carriages lining the street were fine; the apparel of the guests was even finer.

Katrina seldom had anything to say to her brother these days. As they made their way to the ball, Elizabeth attempted to chat gaily. Henry grunted now and then; Katrina attempted to smile. When they reached Lady Dearling's at last, Henry took hold of her elbow. "Take care, my lovely!" he whispered to her in warning.

Katrina wrenched her arm away and hurried down the walkway bordered by Lady Dearling's spring daisies. She prayed that Percy would not make an appearance here, but it was rumored that Lady Dearling refused to believe that Williamsburg could become embroiled in political conflict. Politics were not to be discussed in her home. She welcomed her friends, and that was it.

It was very likely that Percy would be in attendance here. And Colonel Washington might well come, and any number of other dissidents. Only Lady Dearling would be so brash as to throw such a party. But she was a very gracious woman, and it was doubtful that any man would be so rude as to brawl in her home.

Katrina wore a bird mask, an elegant and elaborate creation of cobalt blue. The feathers fluffed out about her face, and the collar caught the brocade pattern of her petticoat. Her dress was soft white, caught in flowers above her knees to display the beautiful fabric of her petticoat.

"Elizabeth!" Lady Dearling greeted her sister-in-law first, and the two women — masked alike in ostrich feathers — hugged one another as they laughed. Katrina noted that Lady Dearling was not so quick to hug Henry.

"And dear Katrina! How you are growing, child!"

Behind her mask, Lady Dearling winked at Katrina as if they shared some wonderful secret. Katrina stared at Lady Dearling, her eyes widening. But other guests were arriving and Katrina had to move through the breezeway to the ballroom on the right. There, musicians played and couples danced in elegant splendor. She heard the spinet and the flute and the sweet sad cry of a fiddler. To her left was a buffet table piled high with delicacies. To her right was a snowy-clothed table with a crystal punch bowl and an assortment of fine glasses.

"Ah, Katrina! The night is now alight with radiance! You are here. Shall we dance?"

Charles Palmer, wearing a lion's mask, came to her, claiming her hand. She clenched her teeth. "I think not," she murmured to him.

"Nonsense. Katrina would love to dance." Henry pressed her forward into the man's arms. Perhaps she did prefer to dance, she thought. The alternative was a walk in the gardens. Lord Palmer would try to kiss her and pretend that nothing horrible and ugly had ever been forced upon her.

He swept her out onto the floor. He was an adequate dancer and Katrina set her mind to listen to the music. People greeted them on the floor. Katrina tried to smile and answer.

Across the hall, she saw a tall, broad-shouldered man moving fleetly toward her. He was dressed in fine white breeches with a blue brocade coat and a lace-trimmed shirt. He wore no wig, but his hair was queued at his nape. He wore the beaked mask of a hawk, with brown feathers completely concealing his features.

But Katrina's heart began to pound so loudly she thought others around her might hear it.

It was Percy. She recognized the breadth of his shoulders, and she recognized the confident, cocky sway of his walk. Just beneath the edge of the mask she could see his mouth, the sensuous lips forming a devilish smile as he approached her.

No! She thought, and she could barely breathe. Don't come to me now, while Lord Palmer is here to see us both!

But he did come to her. Audaciously, determined, he stepped up to them. With perfect courtesy, he tapped upon Lord Palmer's shoulder and then he bowed low before them both.

"Sir, I beg your permission to dance with the lady!"

Palmer smiled stiffly, then gave way to protocol. He bowed, handing Katrina's hand to the stranger. "My dear . . ."

He hadn't recognized Percy, she realized. She curtsied back to him with relish and, as soon as his back was turned, she allowed her amusement to show in her smile and the sparkle in her eyes.

"Alas! The poor man is not aware that he has turned a devoted Tory over to a most disreputable Yank!"

Percy did not reply at first. He swept her across the floor. The sweet tone of the flute seemed to enter into her then, a sensation of liquid pleasure. The music was more beautiful now that she had changed partners.

"Alas," Percy murmured dryly in return. "The man does not know that he wishes to wed a vixen!"

"Oh! Is that your opinion of me, sir? Perhaps I should dance with another."

"Nay." His eyes, behind the mask, seared into her. "Nay, love, you are, in truth, intended to dance with no one else at all, ever again."

She cast back her head, laughing. It was delicious to flirt with him. Her mind was spinning, her heart reeled. It was madness! She was afraid, and yet she was delighted. She hadn't wanted to see him because she hadn't wanted to play the spy. But he was here now, and she could not deny that she had longed for him, no matter what. She could not do as Henry ordered her — she couldn't. But neither could she pull away from this man. No, she could not deny Percy's touch.

"Sir, you are a braggart. Far too confident of yourself."

"Nay, Katrina, I but see the truth."

With those words, he swept her toward the terrace doors, which were open to the pleasant spring evening. The moon rode high overhead, and the intoxicating scent of Lady Dearling's first roses wafted around them. She had hated him many times, Katrina reminded herself. He had dragged her into a barn once, and now he was dragging her beneath the trellis where the vines would hide them from all eyes.

He stripped away their masks, and for a moment they stared at one another.

"I think, sir, that you forget who I am," Katrina said haughtily.

"Oh, no, Katrina, I never forget who you are. Not for a minute."

He was laughing at her! She swept past him, but he hurried along beside her, down the trellised garden path.

"You've no right to snatch me from the ball."

"It seems you are the one walking away from it."

Katrina stopped abruptly, indignantly turning around to face him. He laughed openly, capturing her arms and pulling her close to him.

Henry had ordered her to see him, she remembered bitterly.

As a loyalist, she prayed that she could sway him to her cause. If she didn't, the Tories would kill them. But in their treachery they at least gave her time, for they wanted Percy Ainsworth to be among the rebels now; they wanted his information.

It was strange that none of it seemed to matter, none of it at all, at this moment with the moon so high above them, the spring night so very sweet and fragrant.

His arms about her and his taunting smile warm. Warm, and yet still so assured. He smiled, leaning toward her as if he would kiss her. Katrina swiftly eluded his arms, trembling inwardly but offering him an innocent smile. She tapped her foot against the ground. "Why, listen!" she exclaimed. " 'Tis an Irish tune they play."

"And you long to dance?" There was skepticism in his voice. He leaned easily against the trellis, a fine figure with his broad shoulders and tight breeches.

He was teasing her still, she thought. And she wanted to see him pine desperately for her! He was far too relaxed. Katrina fought to maintain her smile. "But of course. It is a ball."

"An elegant ball."

"A beautiful ball," she agreed.

A smile tugged at his lips. "Yes, but no more beautiful than the moon or Lady Dearling's summer roses. Or the lady who stands beneath the one and amongst the other."

Katrina couldn't prevent the laughter that came to her then, or the delight. He pushed away from the trellis suddenly and caught her elbow, hurrying toward the heavily ivied arbor. She was glad of the tension about him, of the urgency with which he touched her.

"Percy! Really! We're within public view —"

"Nay, lady, we are not!"

They were deep in the arbor. She leaned against a trellis, breathless. She felt his eyes upon her and his movement against her. She knew then that he was going to kiss her.

"Percy, no!"

She tried to elude him again, but she could not. His lips fell against hers lightly, and she struggled to free herself from his arms. But his warmth and fever filled her. Weakly, she shoved against him. She tried to twist her face away from his. "Percy, no!"

"Katrina, yes." His eyes were upon her. They carried all the desperation and hunger she had longed to see. He moved toward her and, this time, she stood still. She awaited his lips with sweet anticipation. His mouth fused hungrily against hers and she freely wrapped her arms around his neck. Her fingers played against his nape and she held him close while she savored his manly scent and the strength of his touch and the caress of his lips, the stroke of his tongue.

She had meant to ask him all kinds of things. Where would the rebels meet again? What were they planning? But when he drew away from her at last, she could barely stand. She closed her eyes and swallowed, and when she gazed at him again it was with a rueful smile. Tease, he had called her. Well, it must be true, for it was the role cast upon her.

"Lady, I have missed you."

"Have you? I would have thought you were much too busily involved in your plotting and disloyalty to miss me."

"Disloyalty? Lady, I am a member of the House of Burgesses. I come when we are in session."

"And you do not do all your talking in the House."

He smiled. "Minx! Ah, you want to know what we are up to, eh, love?" She flushed and attempted to pull away. He held her close. "My love, I assure you there is no treachery afoot. We are gentlemen who enjoy our ale and our port, and that is all. I promise, it is all that anyone can prove."

He kissed her, lightly, provocatively, upon the cheek, then upon the throat. She turned away, her flesh burning. She fought hard to remember her purpose in coming here.

"And when else do you gentlemen meet?"

"Whenever we can."

"And where —"

"Try the Raleigh," he laughed. Katrina bit her lip. He was so bold and reckless, she feared for him. He caught her elbow and he pulled her back into his arms. He bent to kiss her again, and the kiss deepened until she felt that a flame burned between them and about them. And when he pulled away from her that time, neither of them was laughing. His eyes were fire when they lit upon her, and his words were rough and husky. "I must have you. I must! I love you, Katrina. I swear by all that is holy, I love you. I will love you forever."

Suddenly he swept her about, setting her upon one of the whitewashed wrought-iron garden benches.

"Katrina, I love you."

She shook her head, suddenly frightened. Things moved so very quickly. He fell upon one knee before her. She gasped when his hands slipped beneath her skirt, beneath her petticoat.

"Percy, stop!"

"Nay, I will not!"

His fingers skimmed along her flesh. Stunned and confused, she was aware only of the raw sensation that ripped into her.

"Percy, cease! Are you mad? What are you doing?"

His fingers deftly moved along her stockinged thigh and curled around her garter. "Percy!" She cried, holding his shoulders to stand, wondering desperately at his intention. He could not mean to continue this assault, not here in the garden, with the strains of the flute still coming to them and the full moon floating over the fragrant roses and the daises and the night . . .

"Percy! Please God, sir, for the very life of us both!"

He laughed with a hint of bitterness. His hand slid back to her ankle. He lifted it, kissing her foot. Then he removed his hands, and she saw that he had stolen her garter.

"Percy —"

"A memento, love. For when I face the future. For when I lie awake at night and imagine the time when you will give in to your heart and senses and come to me. Alas, now I am alone. So I will hold this piece of lace and silk while I sleep and I will hold you close to my heart and my dreams will be as sweet as the fragrance of roses."

"Katrina!"

It was Henry calling her. She stared at Percy and her fear was naked in her eyes. She was supposed to be flirting with him and gaining information. Yet she had not obtained the information Henry wanted, and she was in a most compromising position.

"Percy —"

"What does he do to you?" Percy demanded harshly.

"What?"

"Why is there such fear upon your face?"

Terrified of a confrontation between Percy and her brother, Katrina touched his face, taking it between her palms. She kissed his lips quickly. "Nothing! I am afraid for you, Percy. Please —"

"I will meet him, Katrina, this brother of yours —"

"No! For God's sake, no!"

"Katrina —"

"Please, Percy. He will stop us! He will ship me back to England. He will do something terrible. He will trump up charges against you. Please, do nothing now!"

"I cannot leave you so."

"You must!" She stood, swirling away from him. "You fool!" She denounced him furiously. "I want nothing from you, I have been triffing, and that is all. Leave me now!"

He shook his head. Watching her, he stood, heedless that he might be seen.

"Please!" Katrina begged him. He wasn't going to move, she saw. Her heart breaking, she said, "I despise you! You thought that you could drag me about and force me down! Well, I have but teased you in return, you foolish, strutting cock! I don't ever want to see you again!"

She turned then, tears stinging her eyes. She fled toward the house. The evening was over for her.

Just before she reached the glow of candlelight that spilled onto the terrace, she remembered to slide her mask back into place. Even as she did so, Henry caught up with her.

"Well?"

"Well what?"

He wrenched hard upon her elbow. "What have you learned?"

"That he is a member of the House of Burgesses, brother," Katrina spat out sarcastically.

He grit his teeth and spun her around. "You will find out what I want, Katrina. And I do not give a damn how you come about your information."

CHAPTER
9

Gayle and Brent were married at two in the afternoon on the thirtieth of April.

It was a big, beautiful ceremony celebrated in St. Stephen's. Gayle wore a white gown with a massive train and a million tiny seed pearls, which she and Liz and Tina and Mary Richardson — Brent's housekeeper — had spent half the night sewing onto it. Brent wore a tailed tux and a ruffled blue shirt that emphasized his dark good looks wonderfully.

Mary Richardson's grandchildren were a big part of the ceremony: Alexandra, her six-year-old granddaughter, was the flower girl, darling in pastel lavender satin and off-white lace, and Jason, ten — who had broken his arm on Gayle's first night visiting Brent — was a handsome ring boy in a ruffled blue shirt and tux. Chad and Brent's cousin, Gary, were the ushers; and naturally, Tina and Liz served as maids of honor.

It was beautiful, Gayle thought. It was

more than she had ever dreamed, more than she could have ever hoped might come true. The organist played "We've Only Just Begun" as Geoff escorted her down the long aisle to give her away. Brent, she thought fondly, watching him through the lace of her veil, had never looked more striking. Never more the heartbreaker. And it hadn't mattered to him, she knew. He hadn't cared about ceremony — a wedding before a notary would have served him fine. This was for her.

The aisle seemed very long. Gayle could see Tina and Liz ahead, both looking pretty in their mauve dresses. To the right she could see her friends and acquaintances from the art world — Sylvia was there, sniffling away into a handkerchief. To the left was Brent's family; they were a large group. His mother, Ria, as slim and dark and striking as Brent was himself, gave her a happy, encouraging smile that seemed to make her heart swell, and his dad, Jonathan McCauley, so straight and dignified, gave her a grin and an admiring okay sign.

It was a fairy tale. She was living a fairy tale. She hadn't exactly lived in the cinders, but Brent was truly like a prince who had come along on some kind of magnificent charger and swept her away into the land of "happily ever after." His dad was as welcoming to her as his mother, and his entire array of aunts and uncles and cousins were pleasant and pleased to welcome her. So far, that is! she reminded herself, but then she smiled. Honeymoons could not last forever, but she didn't believe that they could ever fall out of love. It had come to them so passionately, so overwhelmingly. It was total and absorbing. Bad times were bound to come, she knew, but with her whole heart she believed that they could see their way through anything.

Liz was crying too, Gayle saw. Sniffling, dabbing carefully at her eyes, then smiling — and sniffling all over again.

"You sure?" Geoff whispered to her. "Absolutely sure about this?"

"Yes!" Gayle whispered back vehemently.

"Ah-ha! The press is here too, you know. Flashbulbs will be popping all over the place in a minute. You'll be Mrs. Artist, you know. Mrs. Genius. Ready for it?"

"Yes! And shush, will you, Geoff?"

"I just don't want you passing out on me or bawling all over the place on me, huh?"

"I won't," Gayle promised; but she was afraid that she was going to start to laugh, she was suddenly so nervous. She was happy — thrilled — but she felt a lump growing in her throat. Her parents should have been here. For one moment, she missed them terribly. They had died so very long ago that she had adapted to their loss until this moment, and suddenly she wanted Doris and Ted Norman to be here so badly that she almost doubled over with the pain.

You would have loved him, Mom! She thought. Honest, you would have loved him. Daddy, he's rich, but that's the very least of it; he's wonderful, he's a man's man, he's —

Geoff squeezed her arm. "I think that they can see this; I really do."

"Oh, Geoff!" She whispered. "How did you know what I was thinking about?"

"Your face, princess. No sweet smile. And every girl thinks of her mother on her wedding day. But look ahead. Brent is there. The future. Look at him frown. No — it's a scowl. And all because he can tell that there is something wrong."

Gayle gave herself a serious mental shake. Why was she being so morbid at such a moment? They were coming closer and closer to the altar. To the priest in his robes, to Liz and Tina sniffling away, to Brent and Chad and Gary, all awaiting her. She saw Brent's eyes, dark and puzzled and confused, and all her love for him seemed to swell to the fore, and the smile she gave him was radiant.

"This is it." Geoff squeezed her arm again.

"Have I ever told you how much I love you?"

"Gayle, really! Right in front of the muscular hunk you're about to marry. Couldn't we have had this discussion before?"

"You're a nut."

"I love you too."

Finally, finally, they'd traveled the length of the aisle. He squeezed her hand one more time; the priest was already talking, demanding to know who gave this woman in holy matrimony, and Geoff was standing forward to give her hand to Brent, his voice clear, with no hesitation.

Liz sobbed loudly, Chad laughed nervously, and Liz hiccuped. Gayle noticed it all while she felt Brent's fingers twine around hers.

The service was beautiful. She heard the words, each and every one. They promised to love and to cherish until death did them part, and she knew that to each of them the vows were real, spoken from the depths of the heart. Her hand trembled when he slipped the wedding band upon her finger; she noted that his hand was firm and steady. The priest proclaimed them man and wife, and the pleasure that rushed through her with the words was almost too much to bear.

Brent lifted her veil and took her into his arms and kissed her soundly. She hugged him fiercely, returning his kiss with her whole heart. Gary McCauley let out a loud whoop — which somehow seemed appropriate despite the solemnity of the church. She and Brent parted breathlessly, stared into each other's eyes, and turned to travel back up the aisle to the laughter that followed Gary's irreverent sound and to a triumphant burst from the organ. She loved organs, she realized. She loved the sound that rushed around her and engulfed her.

Brent's fingers tightened around hers; she glanced up to see him smiling down at her as they seemed to race by the people in the pews, with Chad, Gary, Geoff, Tina, Liz, Jason, and Alexandra following behind them.

"Mrs. McCauley," Brent murmured to her, rolling it on his tongue. "I like the sound of it."

"Mrs. Brent McCauley. Be specific when you address me, will you please, sir?" She laughed, delighted with the new feelings. She was actually married to him; they were husband and wife. He was splendid. He was so gorgeous in the ruffled blue shirt and the vest and the tails. This was her moment. She luxuriated in it. She was happy just to study his face, to see the darkness of his eyes, the cleft in his chin, the structure of his jaw. She felt loved and cherished just having his fingers curl around hers. Just hearing the organ and the laughter and chatter that followed them then.

She didn't know quite what happened then; she never understood it; she could never describe it. It seemed that sound faded and paled and that mist fell around her to block out sight and sound. They were still there, the people, her friends. The church remained, and that never-ending aisle.

But the man holding her hand was suddenly not Brent. Not her husband. Or else it was him, and that was what was so frightening. He was different. His hair was very long, as if he were a wild man, and he was dressed differently — she couldn't even understand exactly what he was wearing because she was so very frightened. It was him, and it wasn't him; and he still had her hand, and they were still rushing along.

Then he looked down at her and she caught her breath, fighting not to scream. The look in his eyes was . . . awful. Ungodly. There was so much reproach, so much hatred there! She burned where he touched her and she felt his fury. It was as if he wanted to kill her. As if he really, truly wanted to kill her, as if he were dragging her toward her death and hell itself and every damnation . . .

She stopped still. She wanted to scream. No sound would come to her lips. The mist closed around her and she gasped, and suddenly Brent wasn't there at all anymore, nor was the church, nor the sound of laughter or music, nor the smell of sweet, fresh flowers . . .

There was only blackness. Silently, she closed her eyes and she fell to the floor, a pool of white against the crimson carpet of the aisle.

"Gayle!" He cried out her name, and it was Brent again; she vaguely knew it was Brent. But she could not answer him, for the blackness had claimed her.

Naturally there were a few screams. Brent ignored the sounds as he bent swiftly, plucked his bride of two minutes into his arms, and strode with her quickly from the church. Out on the steps to the street, the sun touched her face. He wasn't so startled or terribly alarmed that she had passed out — she'd barely slept in the last week, finishing up the arrangements with his mother, staying up half the night to sew embroidery with Tina and Liz, and laughing and fooling around all the while. She hadn't really been eating or sleeping properly, and she'd had natural shakes on top of all that. She'd lost a few pounds in the last few weeks too.

No, it wasn't so startling that she had passed out. In itself, it didn't really upset him.

What had bothered him, what had caused his heart to skip a moment's beat, was the way that she had looked at him.

One moment she had been the most beautiful bride in the world, bar none. A fairy-tale princess in white satin and lace, her hair a mass of golden tendrils and curls like a halo, her eyes bluer than the sky. She'd been regal, with the clean lines of her gown and the elegant train. He'd never loved her more than that moment when he'd seen her at the end of the aisle, looking across that vast space to him, coming to him on Geoff's arm, as if she walked on clouds.

And laughter became her too. As they had walked away, man and wife at last, she had given him that smile that dazzled, then laughed, and radiance in her gaze had all but caused him to explode with elation. She was his wife . . .

But then that gaze had changed. Slowly, as if a mist had descended. As if all that was real in life had receded. Her mouth formed into an O of horror, and her eyes mirrored a terrible, desperate fear. He had wanted to shout to her, to demand to know what was wrong, but he was so stunned by the depth of emotion in that gaze that he had not been able to whisper or make any sound at all.

And then she had fallen.

The sun lay against the softness of her cheeks. On the street below, a car went by, heading toward the Capitol building. Brent could feel the people rushing out around him, with all their cries of dismay and concern.

"She needs air! Stay back!" someone shouted. Brent dimly realized that it was Geoff keeping control.

Her eyes opened. She blinked at first, then her eyes opened full and wide and stared up into his with all the innocence and trust and purity of a child's.

"Brent?" She demanded quizzically.

"I have you," he told her. "Are you all right?"

Her arms entwined around his neck and she smiled, weakly now, but with a sweet and dazzling beauty again. "I'm so sorry," she murmured ruefully, realizing that people were milling all around them. "Oh, Brent! What a fool I've made of myself!"

Nothing seemed to be wrong — absolutely nothing. That strange look of terror she had given him was clean washed away as if the sunlight had erased it. *Poof.* Vanished. Never been.

His arms tightened around her; his features remained drawn and tense. "Are you all right?"

"I'm fine now," she replied, puzzled by the tone of his voice. "I am sorry —"

"Ah, yes! She does appear to be fine now!" With pleasant ease, Brent's mother stepped up to them and made the announcement. She winked cheerfully to Gayle and inclined her head toward a group of photographers just as a dozen cameras started to click. "Perfectly fine! Brent, Gayle, I'm sure that the reporters will have a fine selection of poses, but if you want a wedding album, you've got to get back into the church for your hired photographer to do the job. Gayle, are you up to it?"

Brent's arms were still tight around her. She had to strain against him to get him to release her. His arms constricted, fighting her efforts for a moment. "Brent!" His mother hissed softly. Then he let her go.

Tina hurried around her to straighten out

her gown and train. "Come on, you two!" Chad called cheerfully.

Gayle reached for Brent's hand, dismayed by the dark confusion in his eyes. He looked at her. He looked at her hand, so delicate in its white lace, upon his arm. He gave himself a mental shake. He smiled at her tenderly, lifted her chin, and lightly kissed her lips. "You're sure you're fine?"

"Absolutely," she vowed, her eyes on his, wide and clear.

They started back into the church, Gayle waving and smiling to their friends, relatives — and especially the press — to prove that she was really alive, well, and mobile. Once they had reentered the church, only Brent's immediate family were still with them, and of course Tina and Liz and Chad and Geoff, the children, and Mary Richardson.

"I know that marriage is supposed to be a scary step," Tina teased, "but weren't you overdoing it a bit, Gayle?"

"It was the man she was marrying," Chad said solemnly. *"Muy hombre!"* His eyes went wide and they all laughed.

"Oh, yeah, sure, but she already knew that," Liz said innocently; then she clamped her hand over her mouth, realizing that Brent's parents were standing right behind her, as well as Alexandra and Jason. Everyone laughed again, and Brent's mother assured her that since Brent and Gayle were over twenty-one, she couldn't really have much to say about it.

"Besides which," Brent's dad, as tall as his son, slim though, now, with a nice head of white hair and very distinguished features, cut in, "he's made an honest woman of her now. Or she's made an honest man of him. One or the other. We're just delighted." He took Gayle's hands and kissed her knuckles, and Gayle gave him a quick thank-you hug. Then the photographer cleared his throat, and they spent the next thirty minutes posing for pictures.

When they were done, they came back out into the light of day. Most of the guests had gone on to the reception hall, but enough remained to shower the bridal couple with rice as they laughed and ran to enter the limousine that awaited them at the curb.

They were alone then. Alone for the first time since the ceremony, for the first time since Gayle had fallen to the floor in a pool of ethereal white.

"Hello, Mr. McCauley," Gayle said softly, leaning against him.

But he didn't smile in return. His eyes were serious again, his jaw set and somber. He stroked her chin with his thumb, staring down into her face. "What happened, Gayle?"

She frowned, pulling away from him. "Brent, I don't understand you. I'm sorry, I certainly didn't mean to pass out in the aisle — I mean it isn't like 'something borrowed and something blue,' or anything like that. I told you that I was sorry —"

"That's not what I mean." He caught her hand, nearly grinding it between his own. "Why were you looking at me like that?"

"Like what?"

"As if you hated me. As if you were terrified of me."

She shook her head, staring at him incredulously. "Brent, I swear, I don't know what you're talking about."

"You don't remember?"

She felt like bursting into tears. Here was this beautiful Cinderella wedding; here lay her "happily ever after" — here lay their futures and their lives. Why was he doing this?

"Brent, there is nothing to remember. I swear to you, I did not look at you in any peculiar way. I love you with all of my heart and we were married today because — I thought — you feel the same way about me. Because we want to grow old together, share our lives. Because we can't stand being away from each other. Because —"

He laughed. He swept an arm around her

and pulled her tight against him, and when his dark, striking eyes fell on her again they were full of tenderness and love and amusement, and she felt deliciously secure in their love again and awed that such a man as he could love her as he did.

"I'm sorry," he murmured, and he delicately touched her chin, thumbing her lower lip, stroking her flesh. "I'm sorry. I married you today, Mrs. Brent McCauley, because I do want to share my life with you. I want you to have my children —"

"How many of them?"

"A dozen? No? Well, that point is entirely debatable, completely up to you, I should say. I love you. I was just very, very — worried."

She shook her head, searching out his eyes, entranced, her eyes brimming with tears again, of total happiness.

"Oh, Brent, I do love you so much."

"I adore you."

He bent and kissed her. She kissed him back, heedless of her gown, heedless of the car, heedless of anything but the feel and heat and scent of him and the way his heart beat beneath her fingertips.

The limousine came to a halt. Brent heard the driver coming around. He grinned at Gayle sheepishly. "I ordered champagne for back here. I forgot all about it. I even thought about sipping it out of your shoe."

She wrinkled up her nose. "Very unhygienic."

"Well, I'm not going to forget to sip it out of a few other things."

She arched a brow. "Really?"

He winked. "I'll do it hygienically, of course. An alcohol scrub on your navel."

"That's unromantic," she charged him.

"All right — I'll head straight for the raw flesh."

She laughed. "Now you sound like a cannibal."

"I can't seem to win. Come on, Mrs. McCauley. The reception is awaiting us. And when it's over, we're on our way —"

He broke off because, as the door had opened, another shower of rice came flying at them. "Hey!" Brent protested with a laugh. "We're not leaving yet — we just got here."

They discovered that Chad and Gary had been behind the rice incident as they were ushered through the hotel to the ballroom. Ria and Jonathan were already there, ready to form the reception line. Brent and Gayle slipped into place. For forty-five minutes she received handshakes and kisses, welcomed friends, and quickly met strangers.

Gayle was just a little bit nervous. Every once in a while one of Brent's old friends came through the line, and another teasing comment would be made. "She's a beauty, Brent. Nice to meet you, Mrs. McCauley, are you really all right? Passed out 'cause you realized you really married the old bugger, huh?"

His smile only slipped once though, Gayle noticed, and she was glad. She felt at a complete loss. She couldn't remember anything at all; she knew that their fingers had been entwined; she knew that they had been hurrying down the aisle, breathless and elated and smiling at each other in that sheepish, silly way that only newlyweds could. Yes, we've done it. We're man and wife. We've been living together for six weeks now, but this is it, this is different. We're man and wife. And for the magical beginning of it all, it was almost like being children again. Little kids. We've done this thing; we've played doctor, so now we can play house. *Father Knows Best* and *Donna Reed*. They were united; they were a family. Times had changed; she wouldn't be doing housework in a dress, and she wouldn't be saying good-bye to him with a kiss each morning at the door. He was an artist and he worked at home and she imagined that in the near future, on the days when she did not go to the gallery, she would work with Brent. He still had to do the finishing touches on his first oil of her; he had said that he wanted to do others. He was rich, but he liked to spend money, and so he had to keep making it. He wanted to keep that first oil for himself, for them, for their children. He wanted to do others, perhaps a series, to sell.

And she wanted whatever he did. She would sit for him from now until doomsday — she had that much trust in him.

At last it seemed that the final guest had passed by them. Ria McCauley turned to her new daughter-in-law and gave her a big hug. "Did I get a chance to tell you just how very happy we are to have you in the family?" She stepped back, still holding Gayle's arms, and grinning warmly.

Gayle smiled. "Thank you. You've been wonderful." Ria had a way of smiling with just a touch of mischief that reminded Gayle of Brent. Actually, of course, Brent had inherited the smile from his mother. It was a wonderful smile. It promised a hint of devilment, with lots of laughter and tenderness.

Ria looked past Gayle's shoulder. "Brent, may I steal your bride for a moment? She didn't get a chance to meet Uncle Hick. He's over in the corner."

Brent nodded. Someone was pulling at his arm and people were already milling between them. "Tell Uncle Hick I'll be over myself in a moment, huh?"

"Will do," his mother promised.

It took them a while to reach Uncle Hick; it was one heck of a reception, with free-flowing champagne and an open bar, so by now, most of the congratulations Gayle kept receiving were on the sloppy side. Happy — but sloppy. She received lots of hugs, when handshakes would have done just as well, and a few stories about I-knew-Brent-when, but she kept smiling through it all because everyone really meant to be very kind.

"Who is Uncle Hick?" Gayle asked. Ria was holding on to her hand to lead her through the crowd and save her when she was stopped too long.

"Brent hasn't mentioned him? Funny. He adores him." Ria grinned. "He's Jonathan's great-uncle on his father's side — he's over one hundred years old, though nobody knows by how much. He's a wonderful old man. As I said, Brent adores him. I'm sure you'll like him yourself."

Ria stopped suddenly; Gayle nearly crashed into her back. "Uncle Hick! I brought you the bride." Ria pulled Gayle around.

He was a small man, although he had once been a very tall man. Perhaps it was the way he had been sitting, hunched and shriveled over, leaning on a cane. When Gayle appeared, he stood. She started to protest, but he gave her a grin and kept standing anyway.

His face was like leather, brown and crisscrossed by dozens and dozens of wrinkles. His eyes were nearly colorless, a blue so light that it was almost translucent. But he had a mouthful of fine looking teeth — all false, he would tell her later — and a head full of fine white hair — all quite honestly his, as he would also tell her later.

"Welcome, Gayle McCauley! May I kiss your cheek?"

"Of course!" she promised, stepping forward. She was afraid to embrace him, but he proved to be very sturdy. He patted the chair beside him then and asked if she would mind sitting for a moment, which she did. He asked her about how they had met, and she told him about Brent's show at the gallery, and by the way he listened and smiled, it seemed that he had heard a fair amount about the quick progression of the affair. She decided to change the subject, asking him about himself. "Do you live near here?"

"Born and bred Virginian," he told her, and the way that he said it reminded her of Brent. These people were going to resemble him, she told herself with silent humor. They were his relatives. "Yep. I've got an old home out in the Tidewater area. Not too far from Williamsburg. Closer to Yorktown. Real old home. Older than the country."

"How wonderful!" Gayle told him enthusiastically. She mentioned her own house, circa 1850, on Monument Avenue. He described his home, telling her about the big deep porch, where summers were more beautiful than one could imagine, and the tall, beautiful Georgian columns.

"You ever seen Mount Vernon, young lady?"

"Yes, I have."

"Well, the house is just like that one. Built by a lad who was fond of the General and admired him greatly. Course, it's not just the same. Washington made all kind of changes during and after the war. And the lad died in the war."

"That's tragic."

"Lot of tragedy in warfare, young woman. Your husband could tell you that."

"Brent?"

Uncle Hick nodded, his rheumy eyes on his great-great-nephew, who stood across the hall, pouring champagne. Gayle smiled briefly. Sylvia had her hooks on him. Poor Brent. But then, better Sylvia than some of his beautiful ex-models, a few of whom had been invited. Gayle wondered if they had come out of curiosity. Then she felt guilty because she had met a few who were very nice girls and seemed genuinely fond of Brent and happy for her.

"Brent spent six months in 'Nam. He could tell you about war. It gets worse, so they say. I myself can remember what it was like being a kid, with the War between the States barely ended a decade or two before. And then there was the Great War — the war to end all wars — and then the war that came after it. You'd think we'd learn to get along, huh?"

"Yes," Gayle murmured, "you would think so."

She felt a little uncomfortable. She hadn't known that Brent had gone to Viet Nam. Maybe it wasn't such a big thing. There was probably a lot that she didn't know.

No. 'Nam was a big thing. She should have known it.

"It don't matter none, now." Uncle Hick patted her knee and she looked at him, startled. He had read her mind. "What matters is that you're a fine young lady and that the

211

two of you love each other very much. Anything else can come later. You just keep believing that, huh? You believe in love and in nothing else, and everything else can come good and right. You remember that now, all right?"

Impulsively, Gayle kissed him.

"You'll come to visit us?" She asked.

"I'll be delighted to. Can't eat too much of anything, though. These teeth look good, but I'll be damned if I can chew with the things. Hair's mine, but the teeth went early. But you make up some chicken soup, and I'll be happy to come to dinner."

"It's a deal."

"And you get Brent to bring you out to the farm, you hear?"

"It's a farm?"

"Sure. Not much of one anymore. I've a few horses, some vegetables — that's about it these days. But it's private and pretty, and I'm sure you'll like it."

"I'm sure I'll love it."

She squeezed his hand and murmured that she needed to get back to her other guests. He told her that she must go ahead.

She had barely gotten anywhere before Brent caught her, sweeping her into his arms and out onto the dance floor. They were alone, and the band had just begun to play. Brent smiled down at her.

"Tradition. Well, the bride is supposed to dance with her dad. Since he's not here . . ."

"He'd be so happy, Brent."

"You think so?"

"Yeah. I know so."

He whirled her around and around. "We dance well together, don't you think?" He asked.

"Beyond the shadow of a doubt."

She hadn't had a drop to drink yet, but she couldn't help smiling like a silly drunkard. It was so beautiful. The lights were falling down upon them like sunrays, and she was dizzy and flushed and it seemed that her feet barely touched the floor. She could vaguely hear people whispering, and she knew what they were saying — that she and Brent were beautiful together, that it was magical —

"It will never last. It can't last."

At the head table with Liz, Chad, Geoff, Gary McCauley, and his girlfriend Trish, Tina sighed and made the comment. Liz swallowed another sip of champagne, and shook her head woefully at Tina.

"What on earth are you talking about? They're gorgeous out there. I'm green with envy." She sighed softly, resting her chin upon her hands and staring out at the floor.

"Know what they remind me of? The end of *Sleeping Beauty* when Aurora and the Prince are just dancing and dancing and two of the good fairies keep zapping her gown from blue to pink. And she's just oblivious to it all because she's dancing with her prince . . ."

Geoff laughed at Liz and Liz flushed and Tina admitted that they were beautiful. "But it's too soon! They barely know each other."

"I think they know each other very well," Geoff stated firmly. "And Liz, you're either a great romantic or a complete nut case. Come on, let's dance."

The floor began to fill with people. Jonathan McCauley cut in on his son, and Brent danced with his mother. The band played waltzes and ballads at first, then it showed its versatility by switching to numbers by the Police and Crowded House, before settling down to a series of Beatles tunes. Brent and Gayle danced and ate roast filet of beef and sautéed asparagus tips and wild rice and sipped champagne and laughed and talked with friends.

Suddenly Brent swept her dramatically off her feet. She laughed, staring into his eyes. "What's this?" she whispered.

"Your garter," he said, shrugging with a

lopsided smile. "We might as well do it up right."

She was still laughing when he sat her down on a chair in the center of the room. The drummer let out a roll, and all eyes turned to them. Geoffrey called out something; then a riot of ribald shouts and wolf whistles followed.

Brent bowed and knelt down before her.

She had been laughing, right until that moment.

Then, as she stared down at his bowed head, it seemed that the room began to spin again.

No! She cried in silent anguish. No, not again . . .

Gayle gripped the rim of the chair. Behind her smile she clenched her teeth as tightly as she could.

But something was wrong; something was very wrong. She could have sworn that they had done this before. That she had been frightened, terribly frightened. And he had touched her like this. There had been no drumroll and there had been no laughter. But he had touched her. She had felt his fingers moving up her leg; she had heard his heated whispers . . .

The blackness was starting to surround

her again. She closed her eyes briefly and prayed. No, please God, no, please don't let me pass out again. This is my wedding day. Please . . .

"Gayle?"

She opened her eyes, and she swallowed. People were laughing. It seemed that Geoffrey had caught the garter with absolutely no effort. It had landed around his champagne glass.

"Gayle, are you all right?" Brent asked, holding both her hands.

"I'm fine." No one else had seen it this time. He had spoken her name and he had drawn her back.

But Brent knew. Brent had seen her pallor, and he knew.

Knew what? She wondered desperately. This was her wedding. This was the happiest day of her life.

She jumped to her feet, pulling him with her. She tried a radiant smile. "I have to throw my bouquet."

Tina caught her bouquet — naturally, Gayle had tried to throw it to her, but over-the-shoulder aiming had never been one of her talents. By the time it was all accomplished, the eerie feeling of déjà vu had left Gayle, and she laughed easily with the others as they posed Geoff and

Tina together for a picture and then another with Gayle and Brent.

At last it was time to leave. Tears welled up inside of her all over again as she kissed Brent's family and then Tina and Liz and Geoff, but soon she was laughing through the tears because Brent had chosen to change into a pair of stone-washed jeans and a wild Maui T-shirt, and he just looked so very different!

Another shower of rice swept over them, and they raced out to the limousine that would take them to the airport.

Alone in the limo, they engaged in a long, leisurely kiss, until Brent pulled away from her.

"Are you really all right?" he asked her huskily.

"I am really all right," she promised him softly, her eyes aglow as she studied the face she so adored. She stroked his cheek. "I have never been happier."

He slipped his arm around her. "I love you more than anything in this world, more than I had ever imagined it possible to love. More than life . . ."

It was a special moment. One she would cherish all her life. It held at bay the strange fear that plagued her.

Until they were aboard their plane. Then

Gayle drifted into a doze, and again, gray, disjointed pieces of dream and nightmare returned to haunt her.

CHAPTER
10

THE LOVERS

WILLIAMSBURG, VIRGINIA
JULY 1774

Dusk had fallen. He waited for her by the corral, hidden in the dying light by the leaves of an old shade elm. Curiously he fingered the note again and again. He smiled and he brought the fine vellum paper to his face to inhale the violet fragrance that scented her stationery.

Meet me at the corral. At dusk. Katrina.

That simple a message. No kind or tender words, no hesitation. It was almost abrupt. It didn't matter. He didn't know her game, but he would play it. Since he had touched her, he had known that he would move heaven and earth to have her. And though she could run from him, she could never flee from that which simmered and sizzled and

219

flamed between them. A man could not love so quickly, he told himself; but he did. Everything else in his life had been child's play. The dances, the reels, the flirtations, the lessons learned from whores and the chambermaids, and even a refined but lonely widow or two. A touch, a kiss, a flirtation, an affair; nothing compared with this. Nothing had so taken his heart and mind, so distracted him from thought and reason.

James had warned him that it would be a trick. The British already had arrest warrants out for a number of men in Boston. This isn't Massachusetts, Percy argued. If and when the colonies chose the path of separation, Virginia would stand hard and firm — it would be the British who would run, the Tories who would be called traitors.

That time had not yet come, James had told him.

Percy idly crossed his ankles, and leaned back against the bark of the tree. A wistful smile touched his features, and the night breeze blew a lock of ebony-dark hair across his forehead.

None of it mattered, Percy knew. If she brought with her the sure promise of hell and damnation, he would be here still, waiting for her.

There seemed to be a sudden whisper in

the wind, a rustling in the foliage. Percy quickly slipped beyond the tree and waited, his heart pounding. Someone in a dark cape and hood moved about in the darkness.

Katrina had not known that it would be quite so frightening. At night, with the darkness growing and the trees seeming to wave and weave ominously, the town itself seemed very far away. Moving from doorway to doorway, tree to tree, trying to blend with the darkness, she had thought again and again that she should leave. She should run. She should disappear.

There would be nowhere to run. Nowhere far enough away to run. She had wanted to come closer to Percy Ainsworth. She had wanted to touch him. Like a moth, she'd had to kiss the flame, and now she was doomed to pay. It was a bitter irony.

A night bird shrieked suddenly in the darkness, and she nearly cried out. She could barely distinguish the horses in the corral. She could hear the distant strains of conversation and laughter coming from the tavern. Inside, she knew, small bands of men met. They talked and they talked. They toiled, wrote, and planned. Rebellion. They were traitors. They were all traitors. And Percy was one of them. She had to remember that.

She could not see him. The sun had fallen completely; the moon — a half crescent — was making a slow ascent into the night sky. Katrina swallowed briefly, remembering all the old tales she had heard about Indian raids. There were no Indians around here now. They were long gone. She was still afraid of the darkness, of the whisper of the wind, of the skeletal fingers of the trees.

"Percy?"

She whispered his name and stepped into the clearing. A sound came from behind her and a hand clamped over her face. She tried to scream, but the hand was too tight, and she was dizzy and weak with the terror of it.

"Shh! It's me!" She heard his voice, quiet and commanding. He didn't release her though, not until he had taken her back into the shadow of the elms. When they were there, he tossed back the hood of her cape, and he stared down into her eyes.

They were cobalt by night, a tempest of emotion. He mustn't be fooled, he warned himself. "You are alone?" he asked her.

She nodded.

"What are you doing here? You ran rather briskly before, if I recall correctly. You swore that you hated me, and you ran."

She tried to lower her head. He caught her chin and raised her eyes back to his. "I am alone!" she told him. "And — and I do not hate you."

Her heart seemed to hammer and slam against her chest. She could not go through with this. Her brother and his loyalist friends were fools; they did not know him. They had not encountered ebony eyes that could sparkle with laughter and darken like the devil's own with suspicion and mistrust. He was young, with the passion and aggression of youth, yet full grown to power; and through the fascination, the fear remained.

"Why have you come, Katrina?" His voice was harsh, uncompromising. Tonight he was not the man who had whispered so eloquently of love.

"I wished to see you."

"Why?"

She stared at him, then ran from him toward the fence where she stared out into the darkness of the corral. "Mr. Ainsworth," she said softly, "surely you've room for some compassion and mercy in your heart!"

He came beside her. "Don't play the flirtatious little coquette with me anymore, Katrina. I am not one of your brother's fool lackeys in a red coat or high-court macaroni fashion. We have played this game too long. You know that I love you and you know that

I want you. So tell, simply, why are you here?"

He caught her shoulders. He slowly turned her around. He ground his jaw down hard, fiercely reminding himself that she was the sister of Henry Seymour. She was a well-bred young lady from a sheltered home. He had moved too quickly with her. He could not bear her playing the flirt, but neither would he tread anything but gently with her. He would take care when he touched her. He would recall the innocence of her eyes and the angel's pale gold of her hair in order to stem the flow of urgency that came from the seductive feel of a woman's form within his arms. But still, he would have the truth from her now.

He lowered his voice but spoke still with a ruthless command. "Why, Katrina?"

"Because I am sorry!" she whispered.

He looked down at her for several long moments. He smoothed his thumbs over her cheeks tenderly. He thought that her skin was like silk. She was so very young and beautiful.

He looked from her to the darkness of the road beyond them; then he gazed across the corral and pasture to the door of the barn. He looked around them both again and saw nothing but the darkness of the night and the shapes and the forms of the horses and the trees and, in the far distance, the rolling landscape.

"Come on," he told her. He slipped the hood back up about her head and face and set his arm around her shoulders. Quickly, he led her across the open space to the barn. Inside, he closed and bolted the door, then fumbled in the darkness to find the lantern. He lit it and raised it high, setting it into the bracket by the door. He wandered on into the barn. In the center of it he paused, drawing his frock coat from his shoulders, folding it neatly over the gate of a stall. He turned back to Katrina, who still hovered in the doorway.

He bowed to her. "May I take your cloak, milady?"

She shook her head nervously, remaining where she was. Percy did not come to her. He was different tonight. He taunted her, took what he wanted; but always he was eloquent and somehow gentle. Tonight he seemed to prowl with vibrant energy. The air was charged around them and she wondered at herself, incredulous that she had come here with him, alone.

She knew what he wanted of her. Once she had been so haughty, and now she doubted her own ability to resist him. His kisses were a narcotic that robbed her of strength; his touch was a drug that set fire to her very soul.

But he did not touch her then. Perhaps he knew her treachery. She feared him if he did.

He walked on farther, then sat against the high pile of hay stashed in the corner, stretching out his long legs, grinning to her as he selected a piece of the stuff to chew upon.

"The accommodations are not much, I must admit. But do have a seat."

She smiled and he loved her smile. She was shy and nervous here, but it came so quickly to her lips. She stepped into the room, not far yet, but closer. At last she paused where he had done so, and she untied her hooded cloak at the throat. It fell gracefully from her, and she laid it with his coat upon the stall gate. She was so, so beautiful, he thought. Her hair was down, no ties to bind it this night. It was a golden wave that cascaded about her, and he could not help but imagine it spread beneath her or wound around his naked flesh.

Fool, he warned himself, do not think such thoughts. He could imagine himself going to Lord Henry Seymour — and asking for his sister's hand in marriage. Lord

Seymour might well have apoplexy.

He patted the hay beside him. "Come. Sit. I promise, I am no wolf. I will not bite you."

"Ah, but dear sir, I believe that I have been bitten!" She grinned quickly, with a flash of sultry humor touching her eyes, and he wondered fleetingly what she was thinking. He was convinced of her innocence — but maybe all women were born with the ability to seduce.

Or maybe just a few . . .

She set a hand upon the structural pole and swirled around it. "It is dangerous to come too close."

He shrugged, chewing idly on the hay, but watching her more carefully. "Dangerous, Katrina, for which one of us, I wonder?"

She stood silent, and he thought again that she was so beautiful. She was like a young doe that night. It seemed that she would bolt again, when she had only just come.

"Katrina!"

She turned to him.

"It is done," he warned her. "The games are over. The teasing and the flirting — they are done. If you have come to taunt me again, I warn you. Run now. "

She lowered her head. "If I have taunted you, I am sorry. But you, Percy, are as guilty as I, for you were first to drag me here."

"Aye. But you see, I always knew that I loved you."

She looked up, startled at the tenderness in his tone.

Percy stood, pushing himself up from the hay. He came over to her and took her hands in his own. He wanted to tell her that she must choose her side, and that her choice must lie with him, for he did love her. He looked at her, and all he saw was the liquid beauty of her eyes and the shining, rosy moisture of her slightly parted lips.

He kissed her.

He held her fragile chin in his hand, and he kissed her. Her lips were parted and she offered him no protest, and he filled her mouth more fully with the taste and texture of his own, sweeping each sweet crevice with the seduction of his tongue. Her arms were around him too. Hesitantly, she returned the kiss. Her hands fell upon his shoulders; then she grew bolder, and her fingertips raked through his hair. She darted the pink tip of her tongue against his lips and over his teeth.

He swept his arms around her hard, and he brought her to the hay, still kissing her. And when they fell there his lips continued to know her, to seek, to devour, to savor, and taste. He stroked her throat with the brush of his fingers, and he kissed it. Her breasts, high, young, firm, beautiful, were pressed full against her bodice, and he buried his face within their shadowed seduction. He felt her tremble, and he rose above her and saw that her breath came fast and shallow, that her eyes, wide and dilated, were upon him with the cornflower color of a cloudless day, innocent, and beautiful . . .

And trusting.

His own hands trembled.

He set them against her bodice, pulling upon the ribbons there and the ties and the bindings. Her breasts spilled free to him, and his caress upon them was the most tender touch he had ever dealt. And then tenderness was lost because a passion unlike any he had ever known seized hold of him, and he meant to seduce her quickly, and with no mercy.

Tease him, Henry had ordered her. Flirt and cajole, and play the haughty minx, my dear, as you are so very fond of doing. Laugh and smile and bat your lashes, for the fool is falling in love with you. Talk to him, and bring me names and dates and places.

Talk to him . . .

Her brother's words left her mind as quickly as they had come, for Henry was the fool. Percy was different.

And she was the fool, for she was falling in love with him. She could not flirt; she could not cajole. Henry did not understand; this was no boy, but a man. She could do nothing but follow his lead, and where he led, she ached to go.

She moistened her lips, staring up at him. She had to stop this now. "Percy!" Her voice was breathless. "No! We mustn't —"

"Why did you come?" he demanded harshly, his eyes nearly black.

"Because —"

"Why?" The single word was snapped so abruptly she felt as if she had been physically struck.

"Not for this —"

"So you do play the tart, the tease, the whore —"

She slapped him with all her strength. Startled, he brought his hand to his face. Katrina shoved against him, struggling from beneath him. "Don't you ever —"

"No!" She was upon her knees. He caught her wrists. He dragged her back to him, holding her close. "Damn you, Katrina Seymour! It is over, haven't you understood? If you come to me as a woman, then so help me, I will have you as one!"

"Damn you!" She cried out to him.

"Damn you for being a bastard and a traitor!" She was close to tears. Her breasts were bare and forced to his chest, and the air sizzled with the fierce crackling color of his eyes, with the tension in his words.

"Let me go!" She demanded. She could feel him with her bare flesh, and she longed to tear away his shirt. She wanted to run, yet with an ever-growing desire she wanted this to go on, to go on forever and forever. She wanted to discover the path where he would take her. "Let me go!" She pleaded again. "I swear that I hate you!"

"Bitch!" He swore. But his fingers threaded into her hair. Harshly he lowered his face to hers and he kissed her. He kissed her until her lips were swollen, until he and she were both breathless. Until the sizzling tension taken from the air entered into them and began a molten fire that swept through their limbs.

He moved his lips just slightly from hers. "I love you, Katrina Seymour. Deny that you love me too, and I will let you leave."

She opened her mouth. She wanted to deny him. No words came to her. She shook her head desperately.

He pressed her back into the hay. He kissed her lips and her forehead and her throat. Then his mouth fell against her breasts. He laved and suckled and grazed his teeth over her nipples, and the wildfire seized her. She clutched his head against her and she whispered to him and she didn't know what she said herself.

He stared at her then, watching her eyes as he removed her shoes and her stockings. His fingers teased her abdomen as he worked at the drawstrings of her pantalettes and petticoats. She began a tremendous trembling as she felt his fingers against her bare abdomen.

He kissed her again and then manuevered her to free her hooks, to pull her muslin gown over her head. He tossed aside her stays and laces, and she suddenly realized that she lay before him completely naked in the hay.

With a soft cry, she came to him, needing his arms around her to hide that nakedness. "No," he whispered to her, and he laid her back in the hay and spread her hair against it.

Upon his knees he hastily shed his waistcoat and his shirt. Supple muscle rippled in the darkness. He shifted to free himself of his boots and hose and then his breeches. She closed her eyes and then opened them and she shivered, but even as she did so, her eyes widened and she thought that he was beautiful. Truly beautiful.

His hands scorched a path of silk and fire against her flesh. He kissed her and kissed her and was so fevered himself that should she speak, he could probably give no mind to her . . .

He was glorious. As fine and sleek as a puma, as muscled and powerful as a bear, as sure and swift as a hawk. Mindlessly she touched his shoulders and luxuriated in the ripple of sinew and tendon and muscle. His belly was drum-taut, and the ebony hair that crowned his head dusted his chest and created a rich nest for that forbidden part of his body that so fascinated her now. It pulsed; it lived; it was his fire. She shouldn't be there. It was wrong. No decent young woman would dare to do as he said, dare to stretch out her fingers and touch and wind them around him . . .

And no decent woman would let him touch her as he did. But oh, there was no denying him. His kisses were surely depraved, but she could not halt them; she could not force herself to want to halt them; she could not command her own body. She could only feel . . .

"Oh, Percy! This is — not right!" she cried to him once.

But he told her, "Nay, sweet, for when it is love that brings us together, then God has commanded that a man should worship his woman, and, sweet Jesus, I do love you."

She believed him . . . she believed that he loved her. And she believed that anything so intense, so intimate, and so natural between a man and a woman had to be right. Her fingers curled around his, and his lips touched upon hers. His touch . . . Her head began to thrash against the hay. She whimpered as he moved upon her; she gasped, then nearly screamed out as the first, sudden burst of ecstasy exploded within her. Percy caught her cry with a kiss, murmuring against her lips. "Shh! love, take care . . ."

She could not care about the rest of the world. Damp and delirious, she twisted in his arms and her words formed against his cheek. "Oh, Percy . . ."

He chuckled softly, rakishly, and promised her, "We've just begun, love, we've just begun." He went on to fill her with himself, with sweet, burning flames that engulfed and consumed her and brought her again and again to a shuddering awe. Then he kissed her again, held her again . . . and kept her close, close to his heart. She loved that as much, nuzzling against the damp hair on his chest, feeling the protective tenderness in him as he kissed her forehead and smoothed back the curling, wet tendrils of her hair that clung there.

Only then did she feel the hay beneath her back and become aware of the flickering light of the lantern upon her circumstances. She had never meant to give herself completely — even if Henry had not cared how she sought her information. She had cared herself. But this had not been for Henry. None of it had been for Henry. She had been falling in love with Percy since she had first set eyes on him.

And this had been brewing between them since that very first time.

She should be sorry now. She was "ruined" — as people would say — fallen, lost. She should feel the shame and the horror of it, but she did not. She bowed her head against him, and he held her tighter and he whispered to her, "I love you."

"Percy . . . I love you too."

"Come away with me."

"I cannot. My brother would have us followed — and you hanged."

"Your brother be damned."

Feeling troubled, she rolled around, looking deeply into his eyes. She pressed her fingers against his lips. "Don't say that! He has power. He would have no difficulty calling you a traitor."

"Bah!" He was decidedly angry, but perhaps that was part of his charisma, that very boldness and passion, his dead-set belief in his glorious cause. "I swear to you, Katrina, in a year or so it will be Henry Seymour who runs!"

"That may well be so, my love, but now, they are writing out arrest warrants for such men as Hancock and Adams."

"That is Massachusetts. This is Virginia."

"Pardon me! Percy, Percy! Please take care! Do you think that the King's men will care about such distinctions? They will shortly declare the Commonwealth of Massachusetts in rebellion. Blood will flow —"

"Aye," he interrupted softly. "Blood will flow." He leaned upon an elbow then and stroked her cheek. "Trust me, love, the tide will turn my way!" Excitedly, he went on to tell her about the secret liaisons being carried on with important men in Boston.

Men who would soon have nooses strung about their necks, Katrina thought.

"Percy, don't tell me all this —"

He laughed and hugged her, his dark eyes alive and vibrant with youth and determination. "My love, I have to tell you these things; I have to make you see the error of your ways."

His enthusiasm was so great that she could not help but smile. But then there was a soft knock upon the barn door. Katrina let out a soft cry of horror and groped about for what remnants of her clothing she could find.

"Percy?"

The hushed whisper came with another, louder, rapping on the door.

" 'Tis only James," Percy assured Katrina.

"And who is James?" she murmured worriedly, struggling with her corset and chemise and petticoats.

He sensed her panic and helped her with her stays and ties before hurriedly slipping into his own breeches. Tucking his skirt into his pants, he walked quickly to the door. "James?" He glanced back; Katrina was just smoothing her gown over her petticoats. He smiled, thinking of how he loved her. She needed to relax though, he thought with tender amusement — any man would know from the guilty expression on her delicate face exactly what they had been about in the barn. He smiled at her reassuringly.

"Aye, Percy, 'tis James."

Percy opened the door. A handsome young man his own age stepped in, nodded a polite acknowledgment to Katrina, and warned Percy, "It's late. They're saying that Seymour is at Chowning's, looking for his sister."

A knot caught in Katrina's throat. "I — I've got to go."

Percy came to her, agile and quick, running across the barn on his bare feet. He caught her hands. "Run away with me. We'll ignore this ogre of a kinsman. All of them be damned."

Katrina looked at James with horror. "Percy! Cease this foolishness! What of your great and glorious cause? My brother would see that you were hanged."

"Percy." James strode to them and caught Percy's shoulders. "Have you lost your senses, man? She's right. He's her legal guardian; you can do nothing but lose your life!"

"Percy! I must go!"

Aye, she had to leave, and quickly. If she did not, Henry would close in upon them right then. She had to play the game and play it well.

He held her hands, then pulled her close, and kissed her deeply. James cleared his throat. "I'll check the way," he said and disappeared outside. Percy released Katrina at last. "I must see you again soon."

She swallowed. "I'll get word to you soon."

"I love you."

"And I, you."

He smoothed her hair and slipped her cloak back around her shoulders.

" 'Tis clear!" James called to them.

At the door, Percy pulled her back into his arms one more time. "Soon!" he urged against her lips.

"I swear," she promised, and he held her briefly close against him so that she felt his breath against her hair and the pounding of his heart beneath his shirt.

Nearly sobbing, she pulled away from him and ran.

She was able to slip in without Elizabeth's being aware that she had returned. She was relieved. She needed time, moments alone to treasure the night and her love until it had to be marred by Henry's sly intrusion. She washed her face and dressed in a nightgown and lay down in her bed in the darkness, hugging her pillow to her. She relived every beautiful second of the night in her memory, and marveled again and again at the depth of her love for Percy.

Then the door opened.

Henry held a candle high and stepped into her room without so much as a by-your-leave. She closed her eyes and prayed that he would go away, but of course he did not.

"Sit up. I know you are not asleep."

He spoke so confidently she was afraid that he would touch her. She sat up, scowling at him.

He set the candle down and perched at the side of her bed. "You saw him?"

"I did." Her heart pounded with bitterness. Aye, brother, I played your loathsome game, and it is my soul at stake.

"And — ?"

"And what?" she murmured disdainfully.

"I let it be known that I looked for you, a timely intrusion, I hope, if you were in difficulty."

She laughed mirthlessly. "What difficulty? He is a perfect gentleman. And you know full well that his manners mean nothing to you. All you want is to hang him and all his friends."

Henry ignored that. "He is wild and brash. What did he say? Did you learn anything? Did he believe in you?"

She sighed and lowered her head, hoping he would not see the color that flooded her cheeks. "He believed in me. Oh, aye, he believed in me." She looked up, blue fire burning in her eyes. "But there is nothing to learn, Henry. He told me nothing that is not common knowledge."

"What about these secret meetings between the colonies?"

She shook her head. "All that I could discover is common knowledge."

Henry's eyes narrowed. "You will find out more."

She smoothed a ripple in her bed sheet with her fingertips. "Henry, he comes and goes —"

"When he is here, he will come to you."

"I found out nothing!" she cried.

"Nor did you find out anything the last time you saw him, at the ball. You must be more charming. In time he will trust you."

"There is nothing to be found out!" she insisted. "Henry, there are few who can believe now that it will not come to war —"

"Yes." He smiled icily. "It will come to war. And you will be my eyes and my ears when I cannot be there to see and hear. You will do this for me or else I will see you wed immediately to Palmer. Or worse." He smiled. "I am your guardian and I promise you, Katrina, I can find you a truly loathsome husband. Or I can see that Percy is arrested and hanged immediately for some trumped-up charge."

"You are a loathsome creature, Henry."

"Thank you, sister dear. And thank you for your services. I am sure that they will improve."

He smiled again and left her. The door closed. She could no longer relish the sweet

241

memories of her secret love.

She sobbed softly, for in truth, tonight she had lost her innocence.

CHAPTER
11

"You see the tower?"

Gayle craned her neck back, shaded her eyes from the sun, and stared up at the high tower of the Biltmore Hotel. She nodded.

"That's where our room is."

She smiled serenely. It wasn't a room. It was a suite, and one of the most magnificent she had ever seen. It was called the Everglades Suite, and it was a unique and beautiful place in the tower on the thirteenth floor with balconies all around it. There was a central room with high painted ceilings, displaying palm trees and flamingos in painted oval frames. There was a massive coral-rock fireplace and mantel, and a mezzanine that circled all around it. There were two bedrooms and a slim winding staircase that ran from the mezzanine to the living room. There was even a small kitchen. It was vast for two people, but it had tremendous character and Gayle absolutely loved it.

"And," Brent added ominously, "that's where it happened."

"Where what happened?"

"It's where the mobster was shot."

"Oh, really?" she said skeptically.

"Really," Brent swore. "I wouldn't lie."

He rolled around on the giant dragon float they were sharing. It was a beautiful sunny day. The temperature was in the eighties and the sky was a crystal-clear blue. They were there for only one more night; tomorrow they'd be leaving on a specially chartered boat for the Bahamas. Gayle was determined to see Nassau and Paradise Island; Brent was more interested in the Out Islands, but they were both happy to do either. They'd been married for almost twenty-four hours now. An hour ago they had come down to the pool, which was listed as the largest hotel swimming pool in the world. And it was beautiful. From the massive dragon float Gayle could look up and see the tower. "Al Capone?" She said, curious. "Didn't they call it the Al Capone suite when we registered?"

"Yep. It was his suite when he was in residence. He always brought along his own cook, and you know the mezzanine?"

"Yes . . . ?"

"That's where his bodyguards stayed, all

ranged around the place, looking down."

"So Capone did die there."

"Wrong guy. Capone died of syphilis."

"You're awful."

"It's the truth! Capone died of syphilis. And it's true too that a man was shot up there — Tommy 'Fats' Walsh, that was his name. He was a bodyguard, really, for a gangster named Arnold Rothstein. It happened in 1929. The maid showed me the bullet hole in the cupboard."

"Oh, really!" Gayle laughed.

"Hey," Brent protested, indignant at her laughter, "I told you this is supposed to be the largest haunted hotel anywhere."

"I thought it was the hotel with the largest hotel swimming pool?"

"It is." He smiled wickedly. "But it's haunted, too."

"The pool?"

"The hotel," he laughed. He was facing her; they both lay on their stomachs, stretched in toward the dragon's middle. Brent's chin rested on his knuckles. He trailed his fingers through the crystal-clear water, then stroked the coolness over her cheek. "It's the biggest pool; it's the most haunted hotel."

"Just because a gangster was shot?"

He shook his head and carefully rolled

over on his back. Gayle dragged herself up on her elbows to stare down at him.

"This place was originally built by a man named Merrick. He created the city of Coral Gables, which he wanted to be like a Venice. He built the Biltmore and had his friends come down, stay here, and they would look at property. It must have been fabulous in those days. There were waterways that came in from the beach, and passengers were dropped off from gondolas. It was a beautiful, beautiful place — Eden, summertime all the time. Then . . . *whap!*"

"*Whap?*"

"A hurricane. Destroyed half the place. Land values careened straight downward."

"What a shame."

"Then along came the wicked, wanton thirties."

"The Depression."

"Umm, but speakeasies flourished, and gangsters were kings. There were a few wild and willful men playing the part here."

"And then?" Gayle inquired, smiling.

"War."

"War?" Her stomach twisted a little as she realized there were still so many really important things they had yet to discuss.

"World War II. In time, the grand old Lady was taken over as a veterans' hospital.

Men, broken in spirit, broken in body, lying in these corridors. Screaming. Dying."

"Are you making this up?"

"As God is my witness, I'm telling the truth, the whole truth, and nothing but the truth. The Biltmore was in a sad state of disrepair when one of those scientific groups came with all their equipment and tested for ghosts."

"And did they find any?"

Brent grinned.

"Well, did they?"

He laughed. "I don't really know. I got most of this story from one of the bellboys, and he didn't go quite that far."

"You bastard!" Gayle laughed, slipping her hand into the water to splash him.

He caught her hand and tried to roll over and they both went shooting into the water. They emerged, sputtering and laughing still. Gayle jerked Brent back in when he would have crawled back on the float; he retaliated in kind, but finally they were both situated back on the vinyl beast. Panting, with a lock of dripping wet hair plastered to his forehead, Brent tried to finish his story. "I swear to you, all the workmen claim that the place is haunted. Some lady runs around up there — see, on the little balcony? And they all say that it seems a man

247

jumps from the tower window now and then. They can hear him screaming."

"You're trying to scare me."

"I am not!" He smiled. "All right, how's this? Tarzan used to swim here too."

"Tarzan?"

"Well, Johnny Weissmuller. There was a high dive up there, and the pool was much, much deeper and it was even larger. Weissmuller used to swim here, and Esther Williams too. They would do those wonderful water shows and everyone from miles around would come to watch. Is that better?"

"Is it true?"

"Cross my heart."

"Then it's better. The largest haunted hotel, huh?"

"Haunted structure, I believe. I think that's the way that it's been labeled. Are you having a good time?" He grinned.

"Wonderful."

He laughed and closed his eyes serenely. "I thought you'd like it. There's not too much terribly old down here, but this place does have a history — it hasn't been re-opened very long, you know."

"Right." It was a beautiful place, Gayle thought. The lobby was exquisite, with wonderful old Persian rugs and fascinating antiques and a pair of gargoyles to guard twin winding staircases. She leaned down and kissed him suddenly, thinking that he was so very thoughtful. He had carefully chosen this place — just for the two nights — because he was aware that she did love old homes and houses and places with histories.

Her lips touched his; she raised her head. His eyes were alive with sparkling reflections from the water. "Umm," he murmured.

She smiled. "Umm."

"Want to go back up?"

"Whatever you want."

"Can I drink more champagne out of your navel?"

"Shh!" Gayle told him urgently, gazing quickly around them. It was a Sunday afternoon, and though the pool wasn't crowded, there were a number of children about, shrieking with laughter as they struggled with the giant pool toys.

"Well?"

Gayle watched as a waiter came from the building with a silver pushcart laden down with all kinds of trays. The aroma of something good came to her, and she wrinkled her nose.

"Want to eat first? They'll bring us something right to the tables by the shallow end."

"What?" He frowned very seriously.

"I said —"

"I heard what you said and I'm wounded. One day of marriage and you'd already rather eat than —"

She clamped her hand over his mouth. "Brent!" She giggled. "I'm trying to keep up my energy."

"Oh. Well, in that case, all right."

They had lunch by the pool, a cheeseburger for Brent and a salad with little tenderloin medallions in it for Gayle. Brent sat back with a Coors while she finished off two tall glasses of iced tea. He watched her pick at his fries, grinning. "Watch it. What will I paint if we come back with you twenty pounds heavier?"

"Rubens adored plump women," she reminded him. "So did Botticelli and —"

"But you married McCauley," he reminded her.

"For better or worse. For chunky or thin. Right?"

"Right," he agreed lazily. Then, "Are you done yet?"

"Yes!"

Brent signed the bill and they went back into the hotel. Gayle stood and stared from the south balcony down the thirteen floors to the golf course and pool below. It was all so beautiful. The sun was so bright and the breeze so cool, the stretch of lawn so green below. She couldn't imagine being happier. It was as if they had already come to their own little world. The entire floor was theirs. It was an enchanting place, all old-world and very gracious. Gayle paused, aware that Brent stood near her. "It's wonderful," she told him.

"Thank you."

She grinned. "It reminds me of the St. Regis in New York," she told him.

He slipped his arms around her waist. "I thought about the Pink Lady."

"The Pink Lady? What is it?"

"Another hotel. They advertise heart-shaped whirlpools, triple-X–rated movies, and mirrors on the ceiling. And, I might add, rates by the hour."

Gayle started to laugh, twirling around to look up at him. He thought about how much he loved her face in all its moods. She was always so animated. Frowning, laughing, pursing her lips in contemplation, staring up at him now with that siren's smile, all mischief and excitement. "Rates by the hour, huh?"

"That's right."

"Umm . . . you might have been in some

trouble there after all."

"Really?"

"That's right." She led him back inside and closed the door to the balcony. Then she let her towel fall, and stood up on her toes as she placed her palms on his shoulders. It seemed as if she meant to kiss his lips, but she never really touched them with her own at all. She pressed her mouth against his throat and let the tip of her tongue come through. She slowly sank from her toes to her soles, raking her mouth down a path on his chest as she did so, licking him with just the tip of her tongue all the way. He felt each sensation and didn't rush her, even as he began to burn; he barely touched her. She sank, gracefully, ever further, slipping her fingers inside the band of his trunks, running them along the edge again and again until she caught the elastic and dragged it down.

He jumped out to her like a flagpole, and she made a little sound of pleasure in her own prowess. She barely heard the whisper of her name, but tenderly touched him and petted and played and explored all her resources, taking it into her mouth, teasing just the peak with ragged little laps of the tongue. At long last she heard what seemed to be a ferocious roar, and she laughed breathlessly with delight as she found herself supine on the rug, grasped in his arms, nearly caveman-style. "You're going to wreck the suite!" she teased him, but he didn't hear her, or he didn't care, and it was a negligible warning anyway, since the spandex held up very well. With the way he tossed it, though, she was very glad that the windows were closed. She grinned, set her arms around him, and the soft cry that escaped her when he rammed into her was caught sweetly by his mouth in the heat of his kiss.

They climaxed nearly simultaneously, and then they stayed there, on the floor, drowsy, entwined, half awake and half asleep. A while later, Brent rose and left her to go into the small kitchen and to the refrigerator, where he found a bottle of champagne and a wedge of Brie and a square of Camembert and a box of Townhouse crackers. He came back and they set up the sofa pillows on the floor and Gayle leaned against his chest while she fixed crackers and slipped them into his mouth while he struggled with the champagne bottle. It popped with a vengeance, spilling champagne all over them. When they grew tired of the crackers, Brent became more entranced with the champagne, and Gayle giggled and protested and reminded him of what a bottle of the stuff was worth as he fizzed it up to spray more upon her. It ended with her shrieking and escaping from him to the bedroom — and him finding her there and the two of them making love again, with him licking the champagne from her body . . . from all over her body, even from places she was quite sure the champagne could have never gotten to.

At ten they decided to rouse themselves for showers and dinner. They ate in the elegant dining room across a candlelit table and then leisurely strolled around beneath the moonlight and returned to the room once again. Gayle imagined that anyone at all watching them knew they were newlyweds; they had that look about them, that dream quality. There was no hurry to anything; life was sweet and languorous and so all-inclusive of each other.

They made love again, and with their bodies still entwined, they drifted off to sleep. Sleep was dark and sweet, and Gayle would never have imagined that she could dream, but she did.

It started off well, softly, beautifully. She was in a realm she had nearly imagined in her waking hours, that realm she was so convinced belonged only to lovers and newlyweds. The world receded; reality ebbed. There could only be two people in such a world. The mist rolled back all else; it formed barriers and walls, and left only the man and the woman.

And desire — sweet, naked, and stark.

In the dream, she walked on a bed of clouds, she walked and she smiled, just a slow, sultry curve of the lips because she knew . . . she knew she was to meet him, and she knew that they would lie down in the clouds together. And it had been a long time, a long, long time since they had done so. She had been deprived of him, but then she had known that she would see him again, and so the anticipation was heightened, and she knew every sensation. She knew the drift of the mist across her naked flesh, against her breasts; she knew the feel of the clouds against the soles of her feet. She knew the feel of her hair, brushing against her shoulders.

He was ahead.

She could see him, coming out of the mist. Dark and powerful and sleekly masculine, muscular and taut and fine. He came to her, steadily, surely, from out of the mist. Naked as she was, kissed by the silver and gray encompassing clouds, she wanted to run to him. Any moment they would be together; any moment she could touch him.

She started to run gracefully through the gentle mist. She could see him so clearly, the man she loved. Yet even as she neared him, she paused in confusion. Something was not quite right. It was him . . . and yet he was different. How, she couldn't understand.

He was calling to her, shouting her name. His arms were outstretched to her. Still, she hesitated. He called her again, though she could not make out her name, she could hear the sound of his voice, low, deep, reverberating. He came to her, and she forgot what was different because she was in his arms.

Desperate, frantic, they clung together. His mouth on hers, covering it; his hands moved hurriedly, hungrily as he explored her. It had been so long . . . He was almost hurtful, but she didn't care because she understood, and it was so good to feel him, so fine to have his taut, hot body next to hers. She kissed him and kissed him and kissed him.

Suddenly Uncle Hick was there. He was standing beside the two of them, watching them. Gayle knew he was there, and he knew that she and Brent were naked and that they were engaged in an embrace that was highly intimate and personal, and she didn't really care. "War," Uncle Hick said. "There's a lot of tragedy in warfare."

Gayle ignored him. Brent was lowering her down into the clouds. His fevered kisses fell against her breast and his hand was riding along her thigh. Her head fell back and she turned at last to tell Uncle Hick that he was welcome in their home, but he should have the decency to leave them alone in the clouds.

Uncle Hick was gone. Only his voice remained. "War. There's a lot of tragedy in warfare, young woman. Your husband could tell you that. Ask Brent. Ask Brent."

He was suckling her breast. His weight was between her thighs now; his sex was hard and pulsing. She slid her fingers into his hair, pulling his head up so that she might see him and kiss his lips.

She gasped in horror, and started to scream. It wasn't Brent! A corpse was making love to her, a corpse with decaying flesh and an evil, leering smile. His hair came out in handfuls as she touched him, even as she tried to kick away. A chunk of flesh fell away from his face, and she could see the bone. And she could hear the hatred in his voice as he told her, "I have waited for you. I have waited all my life for you."

Then the only sound was that of her own

voice as she kept screaming and screaming and screaming. The mist swirled around her. He was gone and she was gone, and all that remained was the mist and the sheer, horrible terror of her hysterical scream.

"Gayle! Gayle! Dammit to hell, Gayle, wake up!"

The sound stopped; she realized that she was sitting in the darkness, with moonlight drifting in through the draperies. Brent's arms were locked around her and he was shaking her.

She was trembling. She could remember that she had been dreaming and that the dream had been terrifying.

"Gayle!" He sounded so angry.

"I — I'm awake," she told him.

"What the hell was that all about?"

"I — I don't know. I had a nightmare."

"About what?"

"I don't remember."

"You just woke up screaming your head off and you don't remember what it was about?"

"No! I'm sorry. I don't."

He let her go and stood abruptly, padding away on silent feet to the window, where he paused. She could see his naked form in the darkness, tall, powerfully built. She wanted to reach out to him. She wanted him to come back to her and hold her. He didn't. He stayed there, looking out at nothing in the night.

She licked her lips. The question was probably stupid. "What . . . what's the matter?"

He was silent for a moment; then he seemed to explode. "You kicked the hell out of me!"

She was tempted to giggle, except that he wasn't laughing, and the situation didn't seem to be funny at all.

"I'm sorry."

"And I'm amazed that no one is up here; I'm surprised that no one in this hotel called the police. They must think I was strangling you to death."

"Brent, I'm sorry." He was silent, and she was silent — hurt. He didn't seem to care that she had been so upset. What difference did it make what the dream had been about?

She sniffled then, long and loud. Maybe it was a bit of an act — a feminine act at that — but he seemed so far away from her, and she was desperate to have him back.

"Brent, please . . . it was all your fault!"

"My fault!"

"You spent the day telling me that this place is haunted."

Somehow she was certain that her dream

had had nothing to do with the hotel, but saying so might bring him back to her, and she wanted him to hold her so badly. There was a magic that existed between them. Like dozens of silken webs. They were more in love than other people. She didn't want one of those fragile webs broken. She wanted to love him every bit as deeply when she was a wrinkled old lady of eighty and their great-grandchildren crawled around at their knees.

He stayed by the window for a moment longer, then he let out a long sigh of exasperation and returned to sit at the foot of the bed. "You don't remember a thing, huh?"

She shook her head vehemently. "Only that I was very frightened!"

He reached out to her; she threw herself against his chest, hugging him tightly.

"Hey, watch it!" He let out a strangled cry. She pulled away slightly, searching for his eyes in the moonlight. He grimaced. "Injured goods, Mrs. McCauley. You kicked, you bit, you hit, you scratched, but mostly, m'am, you kicked."

"Oh, Brent!" Aghast, she pulled back. She gasped as she saw the scratches on his chest. "I did that?"

"You did."

"Oh, Brent! I am so sorry."

"My chest will survive," he said indignantly. "I'm just hoping the rest of me does as well. This is a honeymoon you know, you mangler."

She laughed at last, aware that he was half serious but teasing her too. "I promise I'll make it up to you."

"You will, huh?" He leaned down upon an elbow expectantly.

"Cross my heart and hope to die!" She did so as she spoke. Then she leaned against him and kissed the scratches on his chest, her silken hair falling over his shoulders.

"I didn't mean that you had to do it this very second," he told her hoarsely.

"I believe in no-nonsense apologies."

He leaned back, lacing his fingers behind his head as she went on to show him how very gentle she could be.

He wanted to forget the incident but he couldn't. He caught her shoulders and pulled her up against him, watching her eyes seriously. "Gayle, remember the other dream you had? At the house?"

"What?" Her eyes clouded. Then she answered a little sulkily, "Oh, yes. That seems like ages ago. Why?"

"I think we may need to get help for these."

"What?" she demanded. "Brent, I had a

lousy nightmare. Everyone has them now and then!"

Not like that, he told himself in silence. "Gayle, you had that awful dream at the house; you passed out at your own wedding; and now you've had this awful dream tonight."

"I told you," she said crossly, "this one was probably your fault, feeding me that bit about ghosts all day."

He sighed and pressed her head down against his chest. She curled her fingers up against him. "Brent?"

"Huh?"

"Honestly, nothing is wrong. I swear to you, I'm well adjusted and I've never been happier in my life, and I don't need a shrink."

He was silent for a moment; then she felt him shrug. "I don't believe in shrinks too much myself. I'm just worried about you, that's all. I love you. I don't like seeing you like that. And," he grinned, fluffing her hair, "I don't like being halfway disemboweled in my sleep by my own wife."

"Oh, you're exaggerating horribly!" She told him.

"Only a little."

"Well, I was trying to make it up to you."

"All right. I guess I'll let you."

"That's very big of you, Mr. McCauley."

"What did you say? Big? That's exactly why I intend to let you get right to it."

She started laughing, but then it turned into one of the most erotic of their experiences together. They touched and laved and licked each other simultaneously, came together, moved together, neared peak after peak, and started all over again. Dawn was breaking when they curled together, fulfilled and comfortably exhausted. Gayle idly stroked his cheek.

"Can it possibly always be like this?" she asked him.

He smoothed back her hair. "I imagine that we will slow down," he told her. She felt him shrug. "But I can't imagine ever not wanting to touch you. To love you."

She smiled, happy in his arms. She whispered how much she loved him.

He was silent for so long that she thought he had fallen asleep. Then he spoke suddenly. "Gayle."

"What?"

"I want you to do me a favor."

"What?"

He rolled toward her and she knew that he was very serious. "If you continue to have these nightmares, you will see someone about them."

"A psychiatrist?"

"Yes. I'll go with you. Gayle — you really frightened me tonight. Even more so than at the wedding."

"At the wedding? Brent, I just passed out! Maybe it was the heat —"

"It wasn't hot."

"The excitement, the crush of people."

"Humor me, okay? I said *if*. Just *if*. Okay?"

"I won't have any more nightmares, I promise," she said. And then she kissed him.

It didn't happen again. Not while they were on their honeymoon. They left on the sailboat that afternoon, the chartered *Cathy Lee*. The captain and his mate were man and wife, a young couple themselves, and though Brent had planned for him and Gayle to be alone, they spent a lot of time with Mike and Sally Cheny, gambling in Freeport and on Paradise Island, snorkeling on the reefs, dining on turtle soup in Nassau, and exploring the coastline along Eleuthera.

Gayle bought souvenirs by the dozens, grass hats and bags and carvings and perfume. They took motorbikes around the islands and visited old forts and churches.

On the Out Islands, silent and empty of tourists, both couples wandered off alone.

Brent and Gayle found their own little stretches of paradise, Edens where the sand was clean and white and no other living soul could be seen. They made love upon that sand and in the clear azure waters. They walked naked hand and hand beneath the sun, like God's first couple.

Gayle did not dream again.

By the time the honeymoon was over she was more deeply in love than ever before. More a part of Brent. And Brent was more a part of her — almost as if a piece of her soul resided in him and she held a section of his heart within her own. It had been perfect and exquisite. Not a single plan had gone awry.

Almost as if God had decreed it all. As if He had looked down from the heavens and determined that everything for them should be like a Shangri-la.

She knew so much more. One day on the beach he had talked about his three years in the service, and she had been relieved to discover that though it had perhaps hardened him and though he remembered the pain of losing his comrades and the horror of jungle fighting, he seemed well adjusted despite it all. She told him that his Uncle Hick had mentioned it to her, and she'd been a little bit distressed to realize then, on the day of her wedding, just how little she knew about him.

"It's all a discovery," he told her then. "We've years and years and years . . ."

But it had felt so good to begin. She had been able to tell him more about Thane, about studying in Paris, about her parents, Geoff, life — everything.

It was wonderful. The freedom was wonderful, the touching, the loving, walking the beach, talking . . .

Sitting together for long, sweet silences.

When it was over, when they sailed back to Miami and flew back to Virginia, Gayle could say that she had touched a piece of heaven, and no woman could be happier.

Neither she nor Brent even remembered the night of her horrible dream. It was as if they had slept right through it.

CHAPTER
12

TILL DEATH DO US PART

WILLIAMSBURG, VIRGINIA
SPRING 1775

Percy pulled his watch fob from his pocket and anxiously looked at the time, straining against the dwindling light. Nearly seven. If she did not come soon, she would not come at all.

He let out a sound of impatience and pushed away from the oak where he had been resting. He came up to Goliath and patted the massive animal on the neck. "Will she come, boy? What do you say?" He grinned, thinking of the cat-and-mouse game they had played over the last year. She had teased, she had flirted, she had tried to see him in public places only; and then she had gambled as desperately as he to find moments alone. It had been a risky venture too, for the relations between the British loyalists and the colonists had rapidly deteriorated. Shots had been fired in Lexington; Massachusetts was in open revolt — and Virginia was following. It was time for the British to depart, for Williamsburg was going to be a rebel town.

Percy's smile faded. She had to come. She had to come to him; he could not believe that she would not. Surely she loved him. He was due in Philadelphia soon to take his place with illustrious men he admired so very much. Men whom these colonies could not turn their backs upon. Great men who had dared to speak out against tyranny. Adams, Hancock, Patrick Henry . . . traitors to the British. Heroes to the colonists.

But even his revolutionary fervor paled when he thought of Katrina. Where was she? When would she come? She was British, he knew. She had lived these years in a nest of Tories. The breaking point was here; what would she do?

He was in love, and so his heart rose and sank with every whisper of the wind. Don't let her know it! he reminded himself. Don't let her know how desperate your heart is, for she can be a minx, eager to see you so humbly crave her favors.

It had gone much, much further than

that, though. She would come with him; surely she would come with him . . .

He started. This time, he heard it. He really heard. The sound of hoof beats against the path.

A horse came charging into view. It reared and snorted as the rider, swathed in a dark, heavy cloak, pulled up hard upon the reins. "Percy!" she called.

It was his love. He strode from the trees, eager to hold her, eager to lift her from her horse. Her hands fell to his shoulders and he brought her down. She tried to speak; his eager kisses silenced her and she clung to him, breathless and weak.

"Oh, Percy!"

"What, my love, what?"

"We're to leave! Henry is to join the British in Boston; I am to be sent back to Kent with Elizabeth."

"No!" He pulled her hard against him, fiercely hard.

"Oh, Percy! This is it, and it cannot be! We'll never see each other again. Never."

"No!" He cried again hoarsely. His heart pounded fiercely. He had known it would come to this. He drew away from her, holding her shoulders and staring demandingly into her eyes. "You cannot go back."

"What?" Her eyes widened. "I must go

back. He is my guardian. He will search for me —"

"But he will not find you. My God, girl!" He shook her suddenly, hard, fiercely, until the hood of her cloak fell away, until her hair tumbled and fell down her back in a golden riot of wild curls. "I love you! I love you! Don't you know that?"

She sobbed out something and threw herself against his chest. "I'm afraid! I'm afraid, Percy. If he were ever to find me —"

"He will not. We will run away, this very night. We will find a priest right away and he will bind us forever. I'll take you home, across the river. Katrina! Marry me! He will never come between us again. Marry me!"

"Marry . . ." she murmured in a daze.

"Yes, tonight, now!"

"Yes, oh, yes! Oh, Percy!" Suddenly vibrant and radiant, she threw her arms around his neck and clung to him and began to murmur little lost words. "I wondered sometimes, I had to wonder, if you would want me for your wife, if it could ever be, and then I dared not wonder, for it could hurt so badly."

"Hush, love, I've always wanted you for my wife. I adore you — you know that. My heart has lain at your feet since the day my eyes first fell upon you."

"Oh, Percy!"

She clung to him again; they kissed passionately. Then Percy jerked away from her, listening. He could hear the pounding sound of hoof beats against the road again. "Hide!" He commanded her, pulling her into the shadows of the foliage as his heart slammed hard, responding to the danger.

The horse came into view. "Percy!"

" 'Tis only James," Percy said with relief.

"Percy, he comes! Henry Seymour with a troup of his lackeys — he comes. He is suspicious. He hopes to take you and bring you to his general in Boston and trump up spy charges against you."

Charges did not need to be trumped up. Percy was a spy. He had infiltrated the British ranks in Boston to provide information to the core of the resisters in Massachusetts. He was quick and nimble with his accents and his manners, and had done very well.

"Thank you, James. He will not find me."

"I will take Katrina back —"

"No, she will come with me, James."

Silence followed his statement. Then the men clasped hands and held for several seconds. "Ride then, my friend," James advised. He smiled at Katrina, waiting anxiously in the shadows, then kissed her cheek. "Good luck."

"Thank you, James."

Percy whistled for Goliath; James helped Katrina onto her horse. Percy waved to James, and then they struck off at high speed into the darkness and dangers of the night.

They rode hard. They dared not stop until they had traveled far inland, far into the west. But Percy knew where they were going, for they came to a churchyard, and beyond it rose a steeple, high in the sky. There was no one about, and so Percy ran to the rectory next door and pounded upon the door until someone answered. An aging priest with flyaway gray hair called out gruffly and appeared at last.

"What, ho! Percy, son, what is it that you're about, waking an old man at this time of night —" He broke off, seeing the woman with him, nay, the beautiful girl with the dazed and frightened eyes.

"Katrina Seymour, Father McCleary. Father, you must make her my bride. Tonight."

"Percy, the hour is late! This is improper. It cannot be done, there are proprieties that must come before a wedding —"

"No, sir, there are not! In truth, we need only God's blessing, sir, and that you can provide."

Father McCleary looked from the young man to the younger woman, and his heart seemed to warm and melt. They were brash and bold and beautiful together, and though he didn't know why they ran, he knew that they were fleeing.

And he knew too, deep in his soul, that they loved each other.

"Come in," he told them. "Come in, come in."

And an hour later, with his wife and his eldest son at his side to witness the ceremony, he led them over to the church. By soft candlelight he performed the rite and the mass. They swore to love and to honor, and she to obey, and he to cherish. There were no rings to exchange and the bride's bouquet was a handful of daisies from the churchyard, yet it was a lovely and solemn ceremony. The priest was proud to pronounce them man and wife, and he asked God's blessing upon them with all the love in his old soul.

They were radiant; they were dazed. They kissed with such tenderness that Father McCleary knew he would never perform the ritual for such a love match again. His wife found some mulberry wine for a toast, and when he asked Percy if he had a place in mind to spend the night, Percy said that he did not.

The priest's wife smiled and nodded to her husband, then led the young couple out to the sexton's cottage, since the sexton had left last week to bury his old mother in Culpeper County. It was drafty and it was cold. The fireplace smelled of stale soot and the blankets were even somewhat moldy.

Yet when they were alone, the bride and groom noticed none of these things. They saw only each other.

It could have been different, Katrina knew. She could have married a British lord, a Tory, and she could have spent her wedding night in the midst of rich luxury.

Yet she did have luxury, the greatest luxury. Percy was all the richness she desired. The bed on which she lay did not matter, the man who lay beside her did. She loved him; she adored him. She was certain that God had never created a finer man, and she was deeply proud to be his wife.

She was so very happy. So deeply in love.

She came to him that night, shedding her clothing with grace and falling before him to kiss his hand, in awe that they could still be together.

"Percy, I love you so. And we are man and wife now. We are one! You have honored me so."

The fire burned nearby, casting golden

light upon the beauty of her flesh and form. Humbly he knelt down to meet her there and kissed her palm in turn.

"No, my love, my wife, you have honored me," he whispered. "You have given up everything to ride at my side. I love you. I will love you with all of my heart, for all of my life — and beyond."

She smiled and their fingers meshed and their kisses were as hot as the fire. And all through the night they lay there, in that hovel that was a palace to them; and when they were not loving each other, they dreamed of a glorious future.

For that one night, no clouds of war rode over them to mar the pure and simple innocence of their love.

CHAPTER
13

"And you said it would never last!" Liz fingered the gold-leafed invitation and smirked over at Tina. "Look at this — an invitation to the McCauleys' six-month anniversary dinner."

"I didn't say it wouldn't last!"

"You did!"

"You said it would never last?" Gayle stared hard at Tina, who lifted her hands, palms up, and screwed her face into a sheepish expression. "You hadn't known each other very long. I think I might have said it at the wedding. There was an awful lot of champagne flowing at that wedding."

Geoff, sitting behind Gayle's desk in the gallery, leaned forward suddenly, fingering his own invitation. He grinned. "Are you two sure that you can keep your hands off each other long enough to have a party?"

"Oh, funny, funny," Gayle retorted, jumping off the corner of her desk. "Neither of us happens to be into public displays."

Geoff lowered his eyes, grinning as he absently doodled on his calendar. "You two have the knack of turning a handshake into an intimate display."

"Geoff!"

"It's not an insult. I envy it," he told her casually. He stood, reaching around to retrieve his jacket from the back of the chair. "Six months, huh? Congratulations, kid. This is Friday night? I'll be there with bells on."

"Will Boobs be coming?" Gayle inquired sweetly, idly tapping a pencil against her chin. She smiled secretively as she noticed that Geoff paused, casting Tina a quick glance before responding in kind. "No, sweetheart, I won't be bringing Boobs. Who else is coming?"

"It's a very small affair. The three of you, Chad, Gary McCauley, and Trish. And his folks might drop by. It depends."

"Sounds good to me," Geoff murmured. "Can we all go home now?"

"Gayle, I can take you," Liz offered. "I'm dropping Tina off. I don't mind the drive."

"Thanks, Liz," Gayle told her friend. "But Geoff wants to see the latest paintings."

Geoff frowned, wondering what Gayle was up to. He didn't really need to see any paintings. Brent had agreed to another showing, but they were going to wait for winter to roll back around, and there was no question as to whether the work would be fine or not.

She wanted something, he figured. In a way, Geoff knew Gayle a lot better than even Brent McCauley could because he had known her for so long and through so many stages of her life.

"Yeah, thanks, Liz," Geoff said, "but I need to take a ride out there anyway."

After Geoff locked up the gallery, he and Gayle started across the street for his car.

He slipped a friendly arm through hers. "So, kid, what's up?"

She shot him a quick glance. They reached his car. He arched a brow, opening the passenger's door for her. Gayle slid in and Geoff walked around. She still hadn't said anything when he had moved into the traffic. He couldn't begin to imagine that there was anything wrong; that probably would have been girl-talk. If she had been having problems in her marriage, it seemed ten times more likely that she would have wanted to discuss them with Liz and Tina than with him.

Once they were on the highway and the traffic had thinned, he glanced her way. She was really one of the world's beautiful people, he thought. She looked as comfortable in fashionable clothing as a *Vogue* model. Her features were fine and delicate and perfect, and to frame that beautiful face was a magnificent mane of golden hair. A little pang touched his heart. Why didn't we ever fall in love with each other? He wondered.

"So how is life in Eden?" He asked her.

"Geoffrey," she said, with a little note of impatience. "Life is fine, and quit teasing me."

"I'm not. I told you — I'm completely envious."

She looked his way. He could see she was worried about something. "Everything is fine, Geoff, really."

"Then why did you want to talk to me privately?"

She hesitated a moment, staring out the window. The autumn breeze picked up her hair and blew it around in sunlit strands. "It's Brent," she said at last. "You know that he finished the set of sketches he was doing of me, and most of the oil work he was doing."

"You mentioned something about it, yes."

"Well, he's been painting something different."

Geoff sighed. "He's an artist, Gayle, and he paints nudes. You knew that when you married him. I can't believe you would be foolish enough to be jealous of a model."

"I'm not jealous of a model, Geoff. He hasn't brought in any new models."

"Oh?"

She shook her head. "He's started working differently."

"Well? Is it good work? Tell me."

She hesitated, lifting her hands slightly from her lap, allowing them to fall again. "Yes," she said softly. "It's very good work. But it's strange."

"Why? Come on, Gayle, for God's sake, what is he doing?"

"War pictures," she said hesitantly.

Geoff frowned. "War pictures? What kind? Oh, you mean like pictures of 'Nam?"

"It started off that way. He did some sketches of GIs running through the jungle. He did one painting. It's wonderful. The soldier is just a kid and there's a bomb exploding behind him, and the expression Brent has caught on the face is heartrending. It's very, very good."

"Then what are you worried about?"

"I —" she started out, caught her breath, expelled it slowly. "I don't know. It just seemed like such a change. And it didn't end there."

"No?"

"He started doing Revolutionary War paintings."

"You mean like George Washington?"

"More than that. Patrick Henry delivering a fiery speech before the House of Burgesses. Battle scenes. Valley Forge."

Geoff hesitated then. "But they're good, right?"

"Wonderful."

"Then I really don't understand what you're worried about."

She smiled. "I guess I'm not really worried. You remember that first painting we were talking about in the gallery. The one in which the lovers are entwined. He's the one who bought it; he bought it for me."

"I know. I'm the one who sold it to him. He insisted on paying the commission on it, even though I told him it wasn't necessary." Geoff glanced her way, then reached across the seat to ruffle her hair. "Can I see the new stuff? Should I mention it, or would you rather that I didn't?"

"Let's see what he says when we get there, okay?"

"Sure."

Not long after that they came to the

house. The gates were open, and they drove right past the foliage to the house. Geoff looked up at the facade of the handsome contemporary home as he slammed the door on his Maserati.

"It's nice, but I would have thought that Brent would have liked your place better."

"There's no room for a big studio in my house," she said briefly. "We spend time there, though. Every other weekend or so." She led the way on into the house, stopping in the foyer to slip out of her coat. "Mary? Brent? I'm home."

The McCauleys' housekeeper — a silver-haired image of apple pie and motherhood — greeted them.

"Hi, dear, Mr. Sable," Mary said. "Brent is in the studio. Mr. Sable, will you be staying to dinner?"

"Uh —"

"Please, Geoff, stay. Brent and I will be glad to have you."

"Sure. Why not?"

After Mary took their coats, Gayle led Geoff up to the studio and knocked on the closed door. Geoff felt like stepping back, suddenly nervous that he was about to intrude on something that was none of his business. But Brent McCauley, handsome and casual in cut-off jeans and paint-smeared T-shirt, opened the door and smiled broadly. He kissed his wife and shook Geoff's hand. Geoff endured the momentary discomfort that always assailed him when he was with the two of them, as if they were politely refraining from jumping on each other's bones because he happened to be there. But they were both so welcoming that he didn't feel uncomfortable for long. He felt jealous then, wishing that he could know what it was like to feel the way the two of them did. To be so damned perfect with someone.

"Come on in, Geoff, I'm glad to see you," Brent told him. "Want to see some weird stuff?"

"You know damned well I want to see McCauley 'stuff' — no matter what it is," Geoff told him.

Gayle went over to perch on one of the tables while Brent led Geoff around the studio, pulling off dust covers to show him his works in their various stages.

Gayle was right: the stuff was good. Damned good. Brilliant, even. As good as his nudes, in a very different way, Geoff thought.

Once he had caught love on canvas; once he had caught beauty. He had expressed in oils the beauty of feeling and emotion that could never be expressed in words.

He had done something powerful here too, but he had captured pain, confusion, horror, and death. And more, of course. He had caught valor, honor — and even cowardice and fear. The things were so real. So damned real. The 'Nam stuff was good. As real as the hell that it had been. Brent had been in 'Nam. He would know. He had been born an artist, Geoffrey was sure; and his artist's mind had clicked away and memorized marvelous and horrible details for future reference, just like a camera.

But the Revolutionary War paintings were just as real too. The people were real. In every little nuance. As if he had known them. As if he had seen the mortar flares and the cannonades, the flaming red coats of the British and the bare and bleeding feet of the Patriots as they wintered at Valley Forge.

"Well?" Brent asked him.

"It's all fabulous."

"You think that the subject matter is okay?"

Geoffrey weighed his answer carefully. "You might have a different market here. No artist remains static, though. You'd wither away and dry up if you did. I think that you had gone the limit with what you were doing — but these are fabulous in a different way. It isn't the subject matter, Brent. Your special gift is . . . emotion. You capture emotion. It could make you go down in history."

"Thanks," Brent said. "That's what Gayle told me." He reached out a hand to his wife. She uncurled herself from the table where she was sitting and walked over to him. He set an arm around her, bringing her in front of him, resting his chin on top of her head. There was nothing especially erotic about the gesture, and damned if they weren't both fully dressed, but as soon as Brent touched her, Geoff felt something constrict deep in his gut and it wasn't so much that he wanted to run out and have sex himself, it was that he wanted to run out and have beautiful sex and be loved like that.

"Would you two please quit!" he begged.

They broke away from each other with guilty looks and Geoff laughed and apologized.

"It's 'cause he broke up with Boobs," Gayle explained to Brent, who laughed and told Geoff that they needed to find him another woman and Geoff said, sure, that was it entirely.

Brent excused himself to clean up for dinner. Downstairs, Gayle left Geoff in the grand living room and went into the kitchen to make them drinks.

She came back out grinning. "Scotch and

soda, one ice cube."

"Perfect. Thanks."

She was a lot more relaxed, and he realized that she seemed relieved that he thought that Brent's pictures were very good, and also that it was probably natural that he had changed subject matter. While they sat and idly talked and waited for Brent to come down, Geoff refreshed in her mind all the different stages of Picasso's work, which seemed to make her even happier.

"In other words, he's still a boy genius?"

"Precisely."

"Good!"

"You knew that all along."

"I knew that the scenes were good," she said, and he didn't know why, but Geoff understood her to mean that it wasn't really the same thing at all.

The phone rang. Gayle rose, calling out, "I've got it!" Brent appeared on the landing, buttoning the cuff of a white dinner shirt, saying the same thing, while Mary echoed them both from the kitchen. Gayle laughed and sat down and Brent grinned down at her and they let Mary get it in the kitchen.

Mary quickly appeared though, looking upstairs to Brent. "It's your father, Brent. And very important, he says."

Brent frowned, excused himself to Geoff and Gayle, and disappeared back into the upstairs hallway. A moment later he came charging down the stairs, his coat in his hand.

"Brent!" Gayle was quickly on her feet.

He stopped, kissing her briefly.

"I've got to get home quickly."

"You are home!"

He shook his head. "Sorry, I mean that I've got to get out to the Tidewater. Down by Yorktown. It's Uncle Hick, honey. He's very sick. Mom asked me to come out. I've got to go."

"Brent! I should go with you." Gayle sounded a bit as if she were strangling. Geoff hurt for her. She probably couldn't imagine being excluded by Brent.

He shook his head. "Gayle, he's not conscious. There's nothing you can do. Stay here, and have some dinner with Geoff. Geoff, I'm glad you're here. I'm sorry —"

"It's fine. I'm sorry, Brent. I hope that your uncle gets better."

"He's so old," Brent murmured. "Maybe I thought he was immortal. Don't worry."

He kissed Gayle again, muttered another good-bye and thank you to Geoff, and left. Gayle watched him, her pretty brow all knit up into a frown. She looked lost and forlorn.

"I should be with him."

"Well," Geoff said. "There's nothing you can do."

"There's nothing he can do — except be there with his parents and family. And I could be there with him."

Geoff shrugged. "He's thinking of you."

"I suppose."

"Make me another drink?"

"Sure." She rose to make him another drink. It didn't help any. Geoff could hear her telling Mary that she should have gone with Brent, and Mary repeated the same things that Geoff had said, that Brent was only thinking of her.

As time wore on, Geoff began to wish fervently that she had gone with her husband. At the dinner table Gayle finally stood up and threw down her napkin. "Geoff, I can't stand this another minute. I know this is an imposition, but would you drive out to the Tidewater with me? I'm so nervous, I'm afraid to be alone."

She was afraid to get there alone, he decided. Gayle didn't want to be rejected again.

"Sure. We'll go whenever you're ready."

She gave him a relieved and radiant smile, one of those smiles that reminded him just how beautiful she was.

"I'll just run up for my purse. And Geoff, thank you."

There would always be regrets. Brent knew that.

He sat in the old estate — really an old farmhouse expanded to elegance — in the upstairs master bedroom at the side of the bed, holding Uncle Hick's hand. He could see the liver spots and the veins, and the flesh he touched was nearly transparent. His own was so tan and strong and healthy beside it that it almost seemed obscene.

Hick was dying. Brent didn't need to be told to know that. His face was already cadaverous. His breath came in and out with a wheeze and a rattle, and his heartbeat had all but stilled.

Brent thought that he should have seen more of this very precious relative. Hick had always been special, unique. Hell, he'd been a damned walking, talking history book. He'd awed Brent when he was a kid; he'd taught him how to fish and hunt and move through the forest just as the Indians had done.

I love you, Hick, he thought, willing the old man to open his eyes. I love you with all of my heart. I did come to see you all the time — until my marriage, that is, and I meant to, even then. Gayle liked you too, you know, I don't know why I stayed away . . .

The old man's eyes opened. They looked rheumy, eerily white. Hick's hand squeezed Brent's. *I love you, too, son.*

Brent didn't know if Hick said the words or if he thought them. But he knew they existed. He knew that Hick squeezed his hand in turn.

Brent's mother, in the back of the room with his father, gave a little sob. He was aware that his father soothed her.

Hick was trying to speak. Brent leaned his head down, next to Hick's mouth, to hear. There was no pretense here anymore, no reason to tell Hick that he should save his breath or his strength. He was dying. He knew it and was ready for it.

"The house . . ." he struggled to say. "The house is yours, boy."

Trying so hard to make out Uncle Hick's words, Brent was barely aware that the door to the bedroom had opened and closed. Hick's hand tightened around his suddenly with extraordinary strength.

"Don't . . . bring . . . her . . . here — don't . . . bring . . . her . . . here — don't . . . bring . . . her . . . here."

There was a soft gasp from the corner of the room. Brent straightened and turned around. Gayle was there.

What the hell was she doing here? She should have been at the house; she should have been with Geoff. She hadn't needed to be a part of this, after all the people she had already lost in life.

But she was there, looking beautiful and stricken in the muted light. She had heard Hick, but Hick was reaching out his free hand to her, and she was coming to take it despite his words.

When she took his hand, he looked at her, and he smiled.

And then he died.

Brent knew the moment that life passed away from Hick. He felt it like a terrible drain upon his energy. He wasn't sure if Gayle realized it right away. It seemed that moments passed, ticking away, before she gasped again, set Hick's hand neatly upon his chest, and turned away, crying.

Brent jumped up and put his arms around her, hugging her close to him. Strange — in touching her, in soothing her, he felt his energy come back to him. He loved her so very much.

"Let's go downstairs, shall we?"

Jonathan McCauley led his wife out and waited for his son and daughter-in-law to follow. They all trod silently down the broad

291

staircase to the old master's den, which had been renovated into a charming contemporary kitchen.

Gayle's hands were shaking. All she could remember were Hick's words. *Don't . . . bring . . . her . . . here — don't . . . bring . . . her . . . here — don't . . . bring . . . her . . . here — don't . . . bring . . . her . . . here.* A glass was suddenly pressed into her hands. Ria McCauley was smiling down at her. She looked worn and ragged herself; her eyes were shiny with unshed tears.

"Drink this, dear. I can't imagine what Hick meant by his last words. He thought so very highly of you."

"He did?" She drank the brandy Ria had given her. Brent nodded to his mother, signaling that Gayle needed a refill.

Ria poured out more brandy, then sank into the chair beside her daughter-in-law.

"Gayle," Ria said firmly, "I don't want you to be upset because of those last few minutes. Hick considered you lovely. In body and soul. He was very impressed with that conversation he and you had at the wedding. He said that you respected the past — he was almost gleeful, he was so happy. He always meant for Brent to have the house because Brent has always loved it so. He was like a little kid after he met you —

he thought that you would love this place too, as he always has."

Don't . . . bring . . . her . . . here — don't . . . bring . . . her . . . here —

Gayle smiled. She didn't know what she felt. Hick had held her hand so warmly. He had gazed at her as if he cared for her, as if he would have wanted to help her. As if he loved her. But he had told Brent not to bring her here . . .

"I'm fine. I'm fine, I really am. He was a marvelous person, and none of us knows what he meant."

Ria smiled. Jonathan called the funeral director. They all sat around the kitchen table, reminiscing. Brent kept his hand firmly upon Gayle's, and she felt his warmth touch her and keep her secure, despite it all.

At midnight, they left to go home.

To what she called home. Brent called *this* place home. Home was wherever he was, wasn't it?

She felt exhausted and dazed. Tomorrow and Thursday would be the wake; Friday would be the funeral. They would have to postpone their six-month anniversary party. As soon as her head hit the pillow, Gayle fell asleep, with Brent's arm securely around her.

But she woke him in the middle of the

night, screaming hysterically with greater terror than ever before. When Brent tried to soothe her, she screamed with greater fervor, fought him desperately, and ran into the corner of the room, where she sank to the floor, still fighting imaginary battles. Desperate, he went to her, picking her up in his arms.

She screamed again, then collapsed against him.

When he woke her up, she didn't remember a thing.

CHAPTER
14

Uncle Hick was buried in Hollywood Cemetery, in the family mausoleum. Service was held at St. Stephen's first, and Gayle could not help but remember that only six months earlier she and Brent had been married in the church, an occasion so much sweeter. The day was overcast. The Ainsworth vault was not far from the gravesites of Jeff Davis and his family, and when dark storm clouds roiled overhead, Gayle keenly felt the solemnity of the place and its beauty, and the haunting knowledge that all of them had but a short span of time to spend on earth. Hick had planned in advance, but perhaps that was something one naturally did after he had lived more than one hundred years. The stone cutters had already inscribed his name on the marble, Andrew Hickson Ainsworth, May 2, 1885 to   . Soon they would come and fill in the date of his death, and Hick would become a memory, a name on a tombstone, and nothing more.

The immediate family would be going back to the Ainsworth house, but Gayle remained at Brent's side while he thanked people who would not be coming to the house for attending the service. There had been a multitude of people there — Uncle Hick had been respected and loved and admired. Gayle knew that Brent was glad to see so many people, and so she was glad too.

Once Brent's parents had left in the mortuary's limo, Brent took Gayle's hand and idly walked with her over to the Davis memorials. He read the inscription on Varina Davis's monument out loud, then sighed softly over the children buried there. Gayle leaned against a funerary angel, waiting, and he looked at her and smiled.

"He lost a child, you know. At the Confederate White House. Jeff Davis, that is. His little boy fell off the porch."

"I know," Gayle told him. She grinned. "I'm from here too, remember."

He kept watching her. "Are you all right?"

"I'm fine."

He turned around and stared at the monuments again. "Gayle, I haven't said much in the last few days because of everything happening, but I want you to see someone about those dreams."

She lowered her head and thought about

fighting him. But the tone of his voice told her it would be a fight that she wouldn't win. "All right."

"All right? That simple?" He was startled. She looked up at him, smiled, and shrugged.

"Sure. Why not? I'm going to go and prove to you that we can spend a fortune for some Freudian fellow to tell me I have strange mental lapses because my mother made me get out of the right side of the bed in the morning."

"Gayle —"

"But you want it, my darling, you've got it." She grinned and he started to laugh and, for a moment, it seemed that the sky around the beautiful old monuments changed from dark to light as the sun peeked out from around a cloud.

"Humor me, right?"

"That's right, Mr. McCauley."

He grew serious again. "What do you feel about the house?"

"The Ainsworth house?" she asked, startled. He nodded. She lifted her hands. "It's fabulous. It should be declared a national treasure."

"It's mine, you know."

"Yes . . ." Gayle said carefully.

"I want to live in it."

She didn't say anything. A week ago she

would have been thrilled with the prospect. The house had everything. Beauty, grace, character, history. But now she didn't know. She understood that Uncle Hick had been very old. But he hadn't been senile, no matter how Ria McCauley might try to convince her that he had been rambling at the end when he told Brent not to bring her there.

But then, she was certain too that Uncle Hick had liked her. He'd been delighted at the wedding.

"I'd like to move into it," he said, watching her closely. He knew what she was feeling — and he wanted her to admit that it was ridiculous. And maybe it was.

"What about your studio?"

"I can make one on the second floor, above the kitchen. For that matter, the property has a number of outbuildings: the old kitchen, the spinning house, the mill —"

"I think the main house should be the place for your studio —"

"So it's okay?"

"What?" She hadn't really meant to agree. She wasn't at all sure why, but she did love the house. Nonetheless she just couldn't help feeling uneasy about it now.

"Will you be all right if we move there? You're not superstitious. After all, you slept in Al Capone's suite at the Biltmore, re-member."

He smiled. He was teasing her. He very badly wanted to move into the house.

"A psychiatrist and the old Ainsworth place, both in one day right after a funeral," she commented dryly.

He came to her, slipping his arms about her so that he pinned her on either side to the angel. He was dressed in a charcoal-gray three-piece suit, with the slight relief of a blue shirt beneath his coat and vest. His cheeks still smelled of shaving cream and his hair was ruffled over his forehead from the breeze. He was so good-looking, she thought, her heart taking a little plunge. A cross today between a devil and a mischievous boy. He wanted to move into the old house so badly. She couldn't blame him. It was unique. It was a treasure and it was his inheritance.

"I love you," he told her.

"You're manipulating me."

"Never," he denied with a grin. "Not in public."

"Be serious. We're in a graveyard."

"I am serious."

The sun disappeared again. Dark clouds seemed to shroud the trees. A flutter of fear surged within her. She had always trusted

Brent; she had always felt completely secure with him.

Now she was afraid.

She placed her palms against his chest and smoothed her fingers over his lapel. "Brent, let's go."

He frowned. "What's the matter?"

She shook her head. "Nothing. I'd just like to leave."

"You never answered me."

She shrugged. "Sure. We'll move. I — I love the place too."

He took her hand and started walking her toward the car. With all the other vehicles gone now, it seemed very far away, down the sloping side of a hill. "If you are unhappy in the least, we can move out again."

Gayle nodded. "I love the house," she repeated.

He kissed her hand. "That's my girl."

They reached his old Mustang. Brent opened the door for Gayle, slammed it, and came around to the driver's side. As they drove away from the cemetery, the sun came out again. It was still shining brightly when, almost an hour later, they came to the main gates of the Ainsworth house.

It was a very beautiful place, Gayle acknowledged. Red brick and whitewash, tall Greek columns, and a massive veranda that circled the house.

"You all right?" Brent asked her.

She started and turned to him and realized that he had been watching her since they had pulled onto the long drive. He parked the car, still watching her. He didn't wait for her answer, but came around to help her out.

She shivered suddenly and then, curiously, when she looked at the house again, it seemed just like home. She was anxious to move in. It would be wonderful. Uncle Hick had kept it up so lovingly, but she could imagine long, lazy Sunday afternoons traveling to distant barn sales and poking through piles of junk to get to the perfect antique for just such and such a room.

"Gayle?"

She looked at the house, then she smiled at Brent broadly. "Can we stay tonight?"

"Well, we haven't any of our things —"

"I'm sure his housekeeper kept extra toothbrushes somewhere. Can we?"

He lifted his shoulders in a deep shrug, grinned broadly, and set an arm about her. "Wonderful. We'll stay."

A month later, Gayle wondered how she could have ever felt the least reservation about moving into the house. She loved everything about it.

There was a colonnade leading from the new kitchen in the house to the old kitchen — originally built as a separate structure in case of fire. Gayle spent three weekends touring around to find copper bedwarmers and kettles, and the like, to decorate the place. It had been unused for years. She set it up with gingham curtains and the copperware and old cast-iron and primitive oak tableware. The windows let in tremendous light, and she loved to come there in the morning. Brent, amused by and pleased with her interest, followed her lead, and by the time they had been there just a week, breakfasting in the old kitchen had become habit.

The main house itself was built around a passage, or large hallway. To the left was the new kitchen, and behind it was what they called the new parlor. There was a music room behind the new parlor, and on the right side of the passage, there was a grand ballroom with a sculpted plaster two-story ceiling. It was big and beautiful, but Gayle found it to be her least favorite room; she didn't know why. She loved the library beyond it, which was small and intimate. Brent ordered a wall unit to be put in there, stereo, disc player, VCR, and a big-screen television. Gayle warned him that his acquisitions weren't "period" at all, and he told her that he'd looked and looked for a "period" TV but just hadn't been able to find one.

Mary and her husband made the move too. They didn't live in the main house — even though it was certainly large enough. Mary liked the small structure across from the rear colonnade — it was small and neat and had once been guest quarters. Gayle was thrilled with the arrangement — she had grown very fond of Mary, but she had never liked someone else actually living in the house with them. She and Brent were too spontaneous — they were simply better off by themselves.

It was all wonderful, really wonderful. They hadn't chosen Uncle Hick's room for their own — they had preferred combining the two rooms across the hall, and adapted them to create a bedroom suite. The bathroom had been put in during the thirties and updated during the fifties; Gayle and Brent renovated again. She found a monstrous claw-footed tub; he wanted a Jacuzzi. So they compromised and had both, and the night the bathroom was complete had her shrieking with laughter because Brent determined that they would go from one to the other, to prove to her that the Jacuzzi had been, in this instance, the better deal. She didn't really disagree with him. They had too much fun.

It was still an hour's drive into Richmond. Gayle kept working for Geoff three days a week.

And on Wednesday afternoons at four-thirty, she went to spend an hour with Dr. Paul Shaffer.

It wasn't that she didn't like him. He was a small man with silver hair and an easy smile. It wasn't even that she didn't enjoy the hour most of the time — it was restful. It was just that she couldn't see how it was going to do her any good. So far she had talked about her childhood: yes, it was pleasant; yes, her folks had been great; yes, it had been devastating when she had lost them. She talked about Thane, and yes, she had felt guilty when he had died. Dr. Shaffer was kindly and sympathetic, but he didn't tell her anything that she didn't already know.

And it just seemed like such a waste of time. She hadn't dreamed since the night Uncle Hick had died. Since they had moved into the Ainsworth house, she'd been completely happy and at ease, and Brent had been happy and relaxed too. He had started asking her to pose for him again, and she had complied. She enjoyed being his model.

If she felt that he was asking her to sit too long, she would complain softly, and he would always apologize. Then she would tell him where she was stiff and he would promise to give her a massage, and one thing would inevitably lead to another. Dr. Shaffer would sometimes ask her about her sex life, and although she was tempted to tell him it was none of his business, she would tell him that it was great. But she resented his prying into something that was very special between just the two of them. She knew that Brent had told Shaffer his version of what happened when she dreamed. Maybe they both thought that there was something Freudian in it all.

She hadn't had the dream in so long, and even when she'd had it, she was able to forget it right away. She didn't understand why Brent was making such a big thing out of it, but since her appointment with Dr. Shaffer was only an hour once a week and made Brent happy, she would comply.

Life, she thought, could not be more perfect.

Or so she was able to believe until the night she and Brent finally gave their belated anniversary party.

She would never forget that night, never, as long as she lived.

It started out so nicely. Gayle came back in from Richmond at six. Brent was still in the studio, Mary was in the kitchen testing out her first batch of coconut shrimp. Their guests weren't due until eight, so Gayle decided to take a glass of wine up to their bedroom, pour bubble bath into the claw-footed tub, and relax.

It felt so good. She would never get over her love of a good bubble bath, she told herself.

There was a knock on the door. "Brent?"

The door opened a crack, and a bouquet of red roses appeared first, and then Brent, sweaty and smeared with paint. Gayle laughed when she saw him and he stepped into their king-sized bathroom.

"They're beautiful!" Gayle exclaimed.

He came and knelt down by the tub, kissing her. She reached for the flowers and soaked Brent, and they both started to laugh.

"Happy anniversary."

"Thank you. It isn't really an anniversary anymore, is it?"

"Sure. It's whatever we want it to be." Gayle held the roses up out of the water. Brent grinned at her like the Cheshire cat, looked at his soaked shirt, stood up, and stepped into the tub, sneakers, jeans, paint-smeared T-shirt and all. Gayle shrieked as the water went sliding onto the floor; then she protested as his toe caught her rear. "Come here!" he told her, and more water went spilling over as he tried to set her in front of him, circling his arms around her.

"You are a fool!" She charged him. "You're too big to be in this tub — with your clothes on and your shoes on and —"

"Would I be too big if I didn't have on my clothes and my shoes?" He wiggled his brows suggestively and plopped his foot up on the side of the tub. "Help, will you?"

"Untie your own wet sneakers!"

"Please?"

Mildly complaining, Gayle untied his sneakers and dropped them over the side, warning him that he was going to clean up the bathroom. He said it was all her fault — the tub was too small for two; they needed to be in the Jacuzzi. With one sneaker on and one sneaker off, he stood up and carried her with him over to the Jacuzzi, and with the jets blasting away against their flesh, they convulsed first into laughter, and then into love, and when it was all over, they were both stretched out in the bedroom over the covers, languorous and worn. Gayle bemoaned the fate of her roses, but at Brent's comical glare, she assured him that the time they had spent together had been worth a few flowers, what the heck.

Brent stroked a finger up and down her spine, circling the dimples he had always known would be there. Gayle halfway roused herself lethargically.

"We have to get up. We've invited people over."

He didn't feel like rising. "Whatever did we do that for?"

"They're our friends. We like them." Gayle made herself get up, smiling down at him. He looked like an indolent lion lying there, something close to a pout knitting his mouth, his body superb in repose. She loved him so much.

"Besides —" She gave him a sharp rap on the buttocks. He caught her hand and she gasped, laughing as he swiftly tugged her back down beside him. "Besides! We want to show off, remember? They've never been out to the house."

"Oh, yeah?"

"Yeah." She kissed him quickly, then struggled free from him. "Mary is down there right now toiling away with the shrimp. I'm supposed to be helping. You have to sop up all that water that's all over the bathroom floor."

"Yes, m'am!" He saluted her, but he

didn't move. He stayed there, watching her dress, and Gayle found herself hoping that life would always be the way it was now, that when she was eighty, he would feel the same way, watching her dress and undress with the same mixture of tenderness and lechery and love.

"Up!"

"I'm up. I'm up. I'm so damned up, I'm standing at attention."

"We're not talking about your anatomy."

"Your mind is in the gutter, my love."

"If it is, Mr. McCauley, you brought it there."

"So I did, and I love it."

She threw a pillow over his head, ran her brush through her hair, warned him one more time about the bathroom, and slipped out, closing the door on him. She ran down the stairs just in time; the doorbell was ringing and she ran to answer it. Tina, Liz, Chad, and Geoff were standing there; apparently they had driven out together.

"Gayle! It's gorgeous!" Liz kissed her, remaining on the step looking around in awe.

Gayle smiled. "Thank you. Thank you — come in!"

She pulled Liz in by the elbow; the others followed. They stood in the passage and looked up at the high ceilings and admired the stairway, and everyone talked at once. The doorbell rang again and it was Gary McCauley and Trish, everyone arriving on time. Gayle was just thinking that she'd like to bat Brent on the head for procrastinating so long when he came down the stairs, smiling.

Greetings went around all over again and Geoff insisted that they needed a tour. Brent led them all into the kitchen first, where everyone greeted Mary, who showed off the size of the kitchen.

Brent let Gayle lead out to the original kitchen, and she showed off her pots and pans and the marble mortar and pestle she had just found. In the main house, Brent brought them through the parlor; Gayle led through the library; and Brent showed them the eighteenth-century harpsichord in the music room.

Gayle arched a cryptic brow to Brent as they went up the stairs — she doubted that he could have taken the time to clean up the bathroom. But when she opened the door to their suite of rooms, everything was clean and neat and perfect, and Brent offered her a smug and self-satisfied smile as she passed him by. Tina gasped delightedly over the size of the bathroom; Liz was in love with the Jacuzzi. Geoff made a strange little *hmmm* sound, smirking at the two of them. Brent laughed in appreciation, then told Geoff the story of the Jacuzzi and the claw-footed tub, and by the time he finished, Gayle was laughingly ready to strangle him. Geoff asked if he could see Brent's latest work. Brent hesitated, then suggested that Gayle take the others downstairs and make drinks. He and Geoff would be right down.

Gayle was a little surprised by Brent's attitude; he'd been using her as the subject of his work again, and she hadn't imagined that he would mind showing their guests his latest sketches.

She glanced at Chad — Brent's agent! — but Chad didn't seem offended. He was teasing Liz about the size of the bathtub.

"Go on, Gayle. Fix me a J&B and soda, will you please? We'll be right down," Brent insisted.

Gayle shrugged and led the others downstairs and remembered that they hadn't gone through the massive ballroom. Liz swept into it with wonder. Gayle smiled, but it was an uneasy smile — she felt more uncomfortable in the room that night than she ever had before.

"Boy, could you party in this room!" Tina said. She looked at Gayle and grimaced.

"This is great! Imagine that stereo system in this room."

Gayle shrugged.

"You don't like it?" Tina asked her intuitively.

Gayle hugged her shoulders and grimaced in return. "It's cold in here, or something. I just don't like the room."

"Seems like a good room to me," Chad said cheerfully.

"When I was real little Uncle Hick had a big shindig here once," Gary told them. "Funny though — I don't think that he liked the room either. The press was here that night — it was a benefit for something or other. But he was like you, Gayle. He just didn't seem to like it very much."

"Foolish, isn't it?" Gayle said. "Oh, well, come on. Let's get back to the kitchen and torture Mary and fix drinks."

When Brent and Geoff rejoined them, they had everything set up in the old kitchen. Gayle didn't know why she felt so anxious, but she watched both men carefully. They were both smiling and apparently casual. Tina mentioned the ballroom to Geoff, and he immediately went with Brent to see it.

"Hey, what about music?" Liz demanded. "Brent! Do something about music!"

Gayle called after the two men.

The sounds of one of the Beatles' greatest hits suddenly blared, then toned down. Gayle grinned and the group of them sat around the antique dinner table. Why, Liz asked Gary, if Gary and Brent were cousins and there were a half-dozen other cousins in the family, had Uncle Hick bequeathed the house to Brent — who certainly didn't need an inheritance? Tina gasped, appalled at the question, but Gary chuckled and said that he had never figured that one out himself. "Brent was always good to Uncle Hick. You know how kids are. They can be cruel. Oh, I don't think that any of us was ever really rude to him. Children can be frightened by age, though. Brent never was. He loved Uncle Hick from the time we were real little. He would listen to the old man's stories over and over again. And he loved this place. Uncle Hick made no bones about it — everyone always knew that Brent would get this house."

"And it is my house."

Startled, Gayle looked from Gary to the doorway to the colonnade. Brent was standing there with Geoff behind him. He was staring at Gary, and his expression was more than hard. It was chilling.

"What's wrong?" Gayle asked him.

He didn't move or twitch, or even seem to breathe, for the longest time. Gayle was about to repeat herself when he looked at her and blinked. "What?"

"I said, what's wrong?"

"Nothing. Hmmm. I smell shrimp." He came up behind Gayle and set his hands on her shoulders. "Which smells better, Gayle or the shrimp?"

"Shrimp, old boy, shrimp — at the moment," Geoff said, laughing. "I'm starving."

"So am I," Brent agreed.

"Oh, you can't be starving. You're always at it," Geoff joked.

"What in God's name do you tell this boy when you go in to work, Gayle?"

"I don't tell him a thing, Brent. He makes things up."

"I've a rich imagination," Geoff said serenely. They all laughed and sat around the table. Pounds and pounds of coconut shrimp were passed around the table, and the Beatles disc gave way to the Police. Gayle caught Brent's eyes across the table and they both smiled; their evening was a wonderful success.

Mary came in to say good night. They all said good night in turn and promised to pick up. Gayle told them it wasn't necessary; she could take care of things in the morning, but in a group action, everything was taken back into the main kitchen. Geoff paused by Gayle at the sink as she rinsed off silverware to set into the dishwasher.

"Have you seen the new stuff Brent is doing?" he asked her casually.

"Sure. I posed for it."

"I mean, have you really seen it?"

She shook her head, confused. "I don't know what you're talking about."

Geoff leaned against the counter, stealing a piece of cheese off the dessert tray. "I don't really know myself."

"Well, what do you mean, then?"

"It's you in that strange costuming. All that froth —"

"What froth?"

He shook his head impatiently. "You haven't seen them. You take a glance at the preliminary sketches, and that's it. He's doing historical paintings now, I think. Turning you into a lady from another period in time." She stared at him blankly. He shrugged, then gave her a wide smile. "Anyway, as usual, they're great. Brent has agreed to do two more shows this year. For one, we'll present the war series of pictures; then we'll go back to these." She still seemed distressed. Geoff tapped her chin with his knuckles. "Hey — I said that his work is great. What's wrong?"

"Um — nothing." She shook her head again. What could be wrong? "Nothing at all. Come on — I'm all set here. Get the cheese plate and the crackers, will you, and I'll grab the coffee pot."

It went on to be a nice, relaxing night. They moved into the main parlor and talked as the music played. Gayle sat on the floor, her head leaned back against Brent's knees. She sipped a Tia Maria and cream and laughed at one of Chad's stories while Brent stroked her hair. Life was more than good; life was delightful.

No one seemed capable of much movement. Geoff was the one to stand finally and thank them for the evening. One by one the others rose. Brent helped Gayle to her feet, and they went back through the passage to the front door together.

Gary and Trish left first, with everyone waving. The others had all come out together — Chad slipped into the back with Liz, while Tina walked around to the front passenger's seat. Gayle smiled, watching her two friends. I can't wait to talk to the two of them in private! she thought. How could they! All this double romance going on, and no one had said a word to her.

Chad said something to Brent; he walked over to the rear of the car. Gayle grinned at Geoff before he could slide behind the wheel.

"Cooling it with Boobs these days, huh?"

"Shush!"

"Well, are you?"

"What is this, Mrs. McCauley, a third degree? A survey?"

She laughed. "Just checking, that's all." Impulsively, she reached up and gave him a kiss on the cheek and a hug. She was certain. Things weren't going on just between Chad and Liz; they were blooming here too. It was perfect! Tina had always thought so highly of Geoff, and now, at last . . .

"Behave, will you?" Geoff groaned. He crawled into the car at last. Brent stepped back behind Gayle. She couldn't help smiling broadly — no laughing! Geoff revved the car and it went into gear. He swerved around and started down the long driveway. Gayle watched until the taillights disappeared at the gate. Then she laughed deliciously, her eyes sparkling with excitement. She swung around, anxious to tell Brent about the new romances that were taking place beneath their very noses.

"Brent!" Laughing, she caught his arms, unaware that he wasn't smiling, unaware that his eyes were deadly dark, darker than the night. "Brent, did you see? Oh, it's wonderful! Things are definitely heating up here. Geoff —"

She broke off, crying out more in startled horror than in pain when the back of his hand cracked against her face.

"Brent!" She backed away from him, aware of his expression at last, aware of the dark tension and strain in his features and the ebony fire in his eyes. "Brent, what in God's name is the matter with you?"

"Get in the house!" He hissed to her.

"Brent —"

"I've had it with you, with him, with your behavior. You won't, you won't do it anymore." He gripped her elbow. Gayle was still stunned by his words, his actions, completely stunned. But when he grabbed her, she felt afraid, and she tried to wrench away from him.

"Brent, let me go! Stop this — it isn't funny, I'm not amused!" She tore from him and turned to run. She didn't know what was the matter with him, only that he was really scaring her. Had he lost his mind? Was he really thinking that she'd had an affair with Geoff? He'd struck her, oh God, he'd struck her —

She screamed. His fingers twined into her

hair and he jerked her back roughly into his arms. Throwing her over his shoulder, he strode hurriedly toward the house.

She swore at him then and she fought him. She screamed — but there was no one to hear her. Mary and her husband would be sound asleep in the guesthouse around the back and down the lane. She didn't even have a dog to come help her, she told herself mournfully.

It was Brent! Brent McCauley, her husband, the man she loved more than life itself! she told herself fiercely.

He would never hurt her.

But he had hurt her and he was dragging her through the house and she didn't know whether to be terrified or furious.

"Brent, stop it. Brent, I mean it. Stop this now. You're frightening me."

"You should be frightened." He entered the passage and strode up the stairs, and again, she became terrifyingly aware of the tension inside of him. His muscles were flexed and she began to panic.

"Brent!" She slammed her fists against his back and struggled wildly. She was no match for her husband; she never had been, but then, she'd never needed to fight him before. "Brent!" Her voice rose shrill and high, and he didn't notice it or her words in the least. He slammed into their bedroom and threw her down on the bed.

Stunned, she gazed up at him. He was methodically taking off his clothes. She rose up on her elbows, watching him in disbelief. "Oh, no! I don't know what this is, but not this time. Brent! What is the matter with you! If this is all over Geoff —"

He paused, his hand still on a cuff. "Geoff?" His voice dripped bitterness. "So now there is a Geoff too? Tell me, my love, what secrets do you whisper to him?"

She inhaled sharply, staring at him. "Brent —"

"Don't call me that!"

He had lost his mind. Or he was losing it fast. Or he was playing a game?

"Stop it!" She screeched, closing her eyes and squeezing her temples between her palms. She opened her eyes as his shirt fell on the floor. In amazement she stared at him. He had stripped naked and was walking toward her, sure, stealthy, like a cat about to strike.

"Brent, leave me alone —" She tried to jump from the bed. He caught her and threw her back and she gasped, stunned, trying to catch her breath. He fell down upon her then, and when she swore at him and struggled, he laughed.

It couldn't be happening.

But it was.

His laughter faded and he crawled over, and when he stared down at her he was no longer amused in the least. He was ruthless.

"Brent — don't!" She whispered.

It didn't mean anything to him at all. He might have hated her, really, truly hated her. Despised her.

He didn't bother much with her clothing. He set his hands upon her lapels and ripped her shirt. She tried to roll from him, and his hands fell upon the hem of her skirt. He shoved it up about her waist, then laid his weight hard against her.

Somewhere, she stopped fighting him. All of her receded into a little world of shock. She felt him touch and she felt him move, but she didn't really register it anymore. Brent. It was Brent. She loved him and she adored him; she was his wife. She would have made love with him any time of the day and anywhere that they could have been alone.

But not . . . this.

He was ruthless. He was nearly brutal. As if he wanted to punish her, as if he had no consideration for her. As if it were not an act of love at all.

But an act of revenge.

She bit into her lower lip and she waited.

And then the sound of another scream pierced through the air. A scream of agony and anguish and betrayal, terrible in the pain that it reflected. Gayle froze, digging her fingers into his shoulders.

It wasn't her scream. It was his.

He went tense above her, dead tense, rigid, as rigid as a dead man.

And then he collapsed, a dead weight against her.

CHAPTER
15

Brent awoke with a fiercely pounding head-ache. He groaned aloud, reached for Gayle, discovered that she wasn't there, and slowly sat up. He opened his eyes carefully.

Gayle was sitting across from the bed on the little Victorian love seat. She was in a white robe and her feet were tucked beneath her. Her arms were hugged about herself and she was staring at him.

He closed his eyes again, wincing. She looked as if she wanted to kill him. What had he done? Damn, he hadn't drunk that much. Two Scotches and a shot of brandy, that was it. But he couldn't remember . . . The last thing he remembered was tell-ing Chad that they would meet soon about the overseas sales on the lovers series. And then . . .

Then . . . he was blank. Somehow, he'd gotten to bed. And now his head was pounding mercilessly, and his wife was staring at him as if he were Attila the Hun.

"Good morning," he murmured to her.

She didn't respond. He looked at her again, more closely. She wasn't just angry, he realized. Her eyes were full of reproach. And fear.

"Jesus, Gayle, I know I must have been drinking, but . . ."

She still didn't say anything.

"Gayle?"

Still no reply.

"What the hell did I do?" he exploded, and then his head hurt so badly all over again that he gripped it between his hands once more, falling back to his pillow. "Hangover," he muttered.

"Hangover!" she said sharply.

"All right, all right, maybe I deserved it! What did I do?"

She just kept staring at him warily with those wide, immense cornflower-blue eyes. "You don't remember?"

Very, very carefully, he set his feet on the floor and balanced his way out of bed. He padded over to her and tried to kiss her.

She pulled away from him. "Don't! Please — don't touch me!"

"What the hell —" he began angrily.

"Brent, you raped me!"

"I *what?*" He pulled back himself. He had been going to sit beside her, but she took him by such surprise that he staggered up instead and headed for the closet, searching for a robe. The words reverberated in his head. *Rape.* His own wife. His own loving wife. What was she saying to him?

"Maybe I was a little rough. I'm sorry."

"You don't remember?"

"No, I don't," he said curtly, his head reeling. "I don't believe it. Why would I rape you?"

"What?"

He smiled at her grimly, sliding his arms into the sleeves of his robe. He needed to be away from her badly. She had almost screamed when he'd touched her. Gayle. His wife. His perfect wife, with whom life had been a fantasy, filled with warmth and laughter. Was this it? The old honeymoon-is-over syndrome? Why did his head hurt so badly?

And why did she look so — scared?

"You're my wife, remember? We spend the majority of our days fooling around in bed. Why would I rape you?"

"You were angry with me. Because I kissed Geoff good night."

"Oh, Gayle, come on!"

She tightened up again, staring at him furiously, as if she were going to burst into tears. "I don't know why — I only know that you did!"

"Gayle —"

"*You* need the shrink, Brent, not me. I mean it — you've got to do something!"

"Over a few too many drinks?"

"Yes! Over whatever it was! So help me, you need the shrink!"

"Are you mad? When a shrink gets hold of an artist, he goes crazy himself. This syndrome and that syndrome. And I love my mother and hate my father and —"

"You're making me go to a psychiatrist! And all I do is scream in the night — I don't hurt people."

"Gayle, I don't even know what you're talking about —" He tried to begin patiently. But she wouldn't have any of it.

"Damn you! Brent, I'm telling you what happened —"

"And I'm telling you — you have to be exaggerating. We're married! You're supposed to love me —"

"I do love you!"

"Then why in God's name would you be fighting me to begin with? Unless you changed overnight, you've always been as much into it as I've been."

"You're getting crude."

"I'm making a point!"

"You need a shrink!"

"Well, I will not go to one."

She was on her feet, hands balled into fists

at her side. "I can, but you can't? No way, Brent."

He straightened stiffly. God, did his head hurt! She had no mercy. He said flatly, "I'm an artist. Brent McCauley. If word ever leaked out, I'd be the laughingstock of the art world." It was a cop-out, he knew. He didn't know why, but he was afraid to see a psychiatrist. He didn't want his mind picked apart.

"Half the world sees analysts these days. And don't you ever, ever pull that super-cool artist stuff on me again, Brent. This is me, Gayle, your wife, remember?"

"Gayle —" He walked toward her. He wanted to touch her; he wanted to pull her against his chest and soothe her, so they could let it all melt away, the bad feelings and the fear. He wanted her back again. He caught her arms and she jerked away from him, tears nearly spilling from her eyes. "Don't touch me! You won't even listen to me now. Don't touch me!"

But he was touching her. He had her wrists, and the sleeves of her robe fell back and he could see little bruises on her arms. "Where did you get those?" he demanded.

She jerked her arms free, glaring at him. "From you! I got them from you." She turned away from him and went into the bathroom and slammed the door. It hurt. The sound of it was a killer. He walked up to the door and raised his hand to tap against it, and then he didn't. He let his hand fall.

The hell with it. He couldn't deal with her in this mood. He was too confused. He couldn't have given her the bruises; he simply couldn't have. She was making matters worse and worse when he already felt sick as a dog to begin with.

"Fine," he muttered. "Fine." He went through his drawers and found some jeans and a T-shirt, then slammed his way out of the bedroom, banging the door as hard as he could. It was a stupid gesture. He was the one with the headache.

Gayle showered slowly, letting the water beat little rays of heat against her. She was afraid to think or feel.

He didn't remember any of it, and he seemed to think that she was making it all up. What was happening to them? She couldn't believe last night; she couldn't believe this morning.

And it hurt so bad because she loved him so much. Was it her fault? Had she imagined things? Had he been drunk? Had he been unaware that he had frightened her, that . . .

He had struck her. Right across the face. And he didn't remember it at all. She brought her hands to her face and whimpered aloud.

"God! What is happening to us. Am I crazy? Or is he?"

Then she started to cry. He hadn't even apologized.

She turned off the jets and came out into the bedroom. Brent was gone.

Despairingly, she dressed in jeans and a sweater, thinking that she had to get out of the house and try to reason it all out.

She came down the stairs to the passage, then turned left and went into the kitchen. It was already spotless, and Mary was sitting at the island table with a cup of coffee.

"Oh, Mary! I'm sorry. I would have picked up from last night."

"There wasn't anything to pick up, Mrs. McCauley. You and your friends did a wonderful job. A few coffee cups about, that was it. Tell me, how did they like the shrimp?"

"They loved them. Everyone loved them," Gayle assured her. She poured herself some coffee and asked, "Have you seen Brent yet this morning?"

"Yes, I did. He just came down, poured himself some coffee, and said that he'd be locked up in his studio for the rest of the day, and he'd just as soon not be disturbed."

Gayle felt as if she had been slapped. She

hadn't wanted to see him — but she had wanted him to have made an effort to come close to her.

She set down her cup, hoping that Mary couldn't see quite how sick she felt. "Well, then, I guess that I'll go out for a while."

"Shopping?"

"Antique hunting, I suppose."

"Try down Mulberry Lane. I went out to a white sale at the mall the other day and saw a sign on my way home. There's nothing like a real barn sale for finding something unique."

"You're right," Gayle said. "Thanks." She picked up an apple off the counter and went out of the house.

There was already a great deal of activity going on. The yard men were there, a crew of ten. Gayle waved and started down the lane toward the road. She drove along the river for a while, then she pulled the car off the road and parked, drawn to it. She stared at the water, but nothing seemed to come to her, nothing to give her reason or peace, or to explain any of what had happened.

She got back into the car and drove again until she saw the sign that Mary had told her about. She drove down the lane until she came to a broad drive that led to a typical large red barn.

There was a pretty young woman in the yard, feeding chickens. She told Gayle to make herself happy nosing around in the barn, and if she needed any help, to let her know.

Gayle picked her way through furniture and farm equipment — scythes, carriage and coach parts, axles, old milk bottles, churns, and the like. There was a beautiful cherrywood desk, though, that cried out for restoration. Gayle decided to buy it; then, when she turned around, she saw the old storage box.

Wondering what it contained, she knelt down beside it, opening it up. There was a stack of papers inside, but it wasn't really paper, she realized, but vellum. She grew excited as she realized how old the things must be. Over two hundred years old, she thought, if she was judging correctly.

Carefully, she studied the contents of the box. At the top, it was all maps. Old maps of the area, she realized. Many things were not listed, but such things as "MacArthur's garden" and "Tinesdale's pasture" were.

Gayle dug more deeply, then gasped when she unrolled the next sheet.

It was a sketch of a battle. There was no color to it; it was a pencil sketch. She peered closer, and she could see cannon and guns and uniforms and she recognized the scene immediately.

Brent had done a sketch and then an oil of the exact same scene just a few months ago. It was a battle that had taken place near Richmond. A Revolutionary War battle.

There were more sketches. Gayle didn't think to look at them yet.

She sat back on her heels. Brent hadn't just sketched the same scene. He had sketched it the exact same way. The expressions on men's faces were the same. Exactly the same. Whatever view this artist had once had of the battle, Brent was seeing through the same eyes.

"Oh, my God," Gayle whispered.

"Can I help you?" The young farmer's wife stepped into the barn. Gayle stood quickly. "Yes, thanks. I'd like to take the desk, and this box here with the maps and sketches. What do you want for them?"

The girl named a ridiculously low price. Gayle smiled and the girl asked her if it was too much. "No — I owe you more," Gayle said, and she insisted on giving the girl twenty dollars over her asking price. The maps belonged in a museum.

They wouldn't go to one yet, though. Gayle intended to keep everything until she decided what she had. She wanted Brent to see the picture of the battle.

No. She wanted Geoff to see it. She wanted to hear what he would have to say.

When she came home, she brought her new purchases into the old kitchen. More than any other room in the house, this one was hers. She took another admiring look at her new desk; then she dragged her box of maps and sketches over to the cupboard. She slid the whole box into the bottom storage compartment, then looked up, startled.

Brent was standing in the doorway.

He had been working — he was covered with bits of paint. But he was watching her, depressed and bleak, his dark eyes anguished. He offered her a dry, crooked smile and reached out his arms to her.

She had to go to him. She let out a little cry and ran into his arms. He wrapped her within them, rubbing his cheek against her hair as she burrowed against him. "Gayle, I don't know what happened, but if I hurt you, then I am so, so sorry. I love you. You know that. I love you so much. You're my life. Please, please, forgive me."

It all seemed to melt away. Clear away, as if a bright, cleansing rain had fallen. All the pain and all the fear and the tempest of the night. When he held her then, she was assured. He loved her. Just as she loved him.

It had to have been a dream. Nothing bad and nothing evil could ever pass between them. There was simply too much love there.

"Say something to me."

She allowed her head to fall back and she smiled at him with the radiance he found so alluring. "I love you. I love you. I love you. I love you."

He pulled her back against him. "I love you. I can never, never tell you how much." He leaned back again. "What did you buy?"

She hesitated just the fraction of a second. "A desk. Do you like it?"

"It's great."

"I have to clean it up."

"Do you have to do it right now?"

"No, it can wait."

"Feel like posing for me? Just for an hour or so. Then we can drive out somewhere and have a long, leisurely lunch. Then we can come back here and have a long, leisurely night. What do you say?"

"Fine." She smiled at him, wondering why she hadn't shown him the maps or the sketches. She brushed past him. "Let me take a quick shower — I'm all cobwebby. Then I'll be in the studio."

He followed her out of the old kitchen and

she nearly sighed with relief. They had no secrets — until now, she thought, feeling a little ashamed of herself. Still, she didn't want him to see the pictures. Not yet.

By that night she had almost forgotten the tempest that had passed between them. She had posed for about half an hour, a comfortable pose, stretched out on a couch and swaddled in some luxurious white fabric. And when Brent had finished, the expression he gave her was so hesitant that she stretched her arms out to him, then came running over to him to press herself against him, naked. He held her tight, admitting he'd been afraid to touch her, and they'd even begun to laugh and tease. They never left the studio, though. They stayed right on the couch.

Later they showered and, as Brent had promised, they went out for a long drive, stopping in a quiet town at a roadside café for a delicious lunch of baked ham and succotash and scalloped potatoes. They sipped coffee out of fragile china cups, and on the way home Brent stopped by a horse farm. They talked about buying a pair of Arabian mares since they had more than enough space for them. Eventually they drove home, and the evening was terribly romantic; Brent built a fire in their bedroom and they just watched the flames and talked, entwined together.

Geoff had tickets to a ball game on Sunday; they all went and their team actually won. Sunday night, when everyone had gone, Brent was as tender and solicitous to Gayle as he had been the night before. She thought about showing him the sketch, and she thought about sharing an even more personal secret, but then she decided that she would wait. She could barely remember the things that had happened Friday night, but she still felt that their relationship was on delicate ground, and she didn't want anything to ruin the new intimacy they were achieving.

On Wednesday after work she went back to Dr. Shaffer for her appointment. It was a miserable hour. She started to tell him about Brent's strange behavior; then she realized that she couldn't tell this little man about all of Brent's behavior, so she hemmed and hawed and made a lot of excuses. Shaffer asked her if she thought that he should suggest to Brent that he come in.

She definitely thought that Brent should, but then she remembered how Brent felt about coming in himself. His attitude was something that she resented, but at that particular time she didn't feel like arguing it out.

Brent couldn't have been any more careful of her feelings than he was in the week that followed. One night when they returned from an antiquing trip, Brent surprised her with a cleaned-out stable — and the pair of Arabian mares they had looked at together. Mary warned them that she wasn't going to be looking after horses, and Brent assured her that he'd hired a foreman for the place. Gayle stroked the smaller mare's neck and said she wasn't sure she wanted anyone else looking after her new baby, and Brent assured her that she wouldn't mind having a few boys around to clean up after her new baby.

Mary told them both good night — she and her husband were going to drive into Richmond for the evening to meet their daughter. Brent stayed with Gayle in the stable until they were gone; then he slipped his arms around her.

"Ever fooled around in the hay?"

"No — and it's amazing, considering how long I've been married to you now."

He laughed. "Well, get ready to ravish."

"To ravish, or to be ravished?"

"Your choice." Brent brought a blanket and laid it over the pile of hay. Laughing, they fell into it. The smell of the hay was sweet and clean, and there was something especially exciting about being out in it. The cool air caressed them as they lay there, feeling very decadent in their naked flesh.

As darkness fell completely Gayle lay against him, feeling languorous and too tired to move. The problem with the stable, she decided, was the lack of a refrigerator or even running water that she trusted. "We'll have to put a refrigerator out here," she murmured; then she rose and stretched, sighing because she would have to dress to go back to the main house. No one should have been on their property then, with the Richardsons being in Richmond, but she was certain that if she decided to sprint like a jay from the stable to the house, a million cars would suddenly come pulling into the drive.

"I'm going to go and get —"

"You're not going anywhere."

Gayle froze. She recognized the tone of voice because she had heard it before. It was Brent speaking, of course, but then again, it wasn't Brent at all.

She backed away from the pile of hay, trying to reason while jumbled thoughts crashed through her mind. It was happening again. She had tried to pretend that it hadn't

338

occurred at all, but it was happening again, and she couldn't begin to understand it.

"I just want a drink of water —"

"No! You can't leave here. Not tonight." He bounded to his feet, sweeping his arms around her and dragging her over to the window. Gayle swallowed sharply and looked up at him. His eyes fell to her.

She expected to find the hatred in them, to feel the loathing he had shown her before.

It wasn't there, or perhaps it never really had been hatred, just anger and terrible pain and reproach. There was torment there and haunted anguish and a fire that burned passionately, but nothing of hatred.

And nothing of evil.

"Brent," she said softly, "I just want water —"

"No!" He screamed out in exquisite agony, and she found herself swirled around again and down beside him in the hay. He was over her, and he stroked the sides of her hair and stared down into her features. "How could you go to him, my love. I'd rather die a thousand times over, don't you know that?"

"Brent, please —"

"Do you know it? Or do you care? Was the temptation too great, or were you ever on their side?"

"Brent —"

"No! By God, I don't want to hear it! They're here now, aren't they? They'll stumble upon us soon, and you'll stand there with them. You were there when I had the fever. You bargained — oh, Jesus — you bargained with them . . ."

"Brent —"

She tried to push away from him. He shook his head almost sadly. "Not tonight, my love. Not tonight. You'll not go running out tonight. You'll remember me. I swear it."

He cupped her chin between his hands, and a glaze of tears shimmered on her eyes. "Brent . . . please . . . not like this, oh not like this! I don't —"

He kissed her, slowly and softly. It wasn't that he hurt her; it was that she was so very afraid. He wasn't hateful; he was in agony, and she was the cause of that pain.

He kissed her forehead and his hand cupped her breast and his whisper came against her ear. "Katrina, how could you betray me so? Oh, my God, all the years and all the love — and all the deceit and the hatred!"

The tears fell from her eyes. She caught his wrist and tried to push him from her. She could not budge him.

"Brent! I'm not Katrina. Oh, God, please

stop this. I don't understand. I want —"

"You'll not leave me again. A kiss, and that kiss is death, my love, but we'll wait it out together. There's no escape, is there? The cordon is around us. You married me; you swore you loved me; and if life ends tomorrow, then tonight at least you are mine." He smoothed her hair from her face. Her tears continued to dampen her cheeks, and she turned in the misty darkness to stare out the door at the moon.

He was gentle and tender, then ardent and fierce. He didn't strive to hurt her, but she felt as if it poured into her, all the tempest that raged in a maddened soul. He whispered a name, over and over. *Katrina.* He railed against her for betraying him, and he told her that she was a slut. And then he made love again, telling her that he loved her anyway. He would never let her go. Never. Until death did them part.

When he was done with her, Gayle was exhausted, physically and emotionally. He collapsed again into a death-like slumber, and nothing that she could do or say awakened him. She had to keep assuring herself that he was alive because even his breathing was shallow. Gayle was startled to touch his cheeks and find them damp. He had been in so much pain . . .

She let out a soft sob, wondering again what in God's name was happening to them. She bit into her lip, and pulled the blanket from the hay to wrap around herself. Feeling as if she were in shock, she crawled into the corner of the barn and watched him as he slept. She felt so lost. Bewildered. She didn't know what to do. Her world was falling apart, drifting through her fingers.

Brent was her world.

She lowered her head and her tears began to fall again and she wondered why. Love was so very hard to come by, and she and Brent had had it all. Maybe she should have expected something bad would happen. She'd learned that life was hard and seldom fair. She had been too happy.

Outside, dawn began to come, arriving with a very soft and gentle pink light. She must have dozed finally because when she opened her eyes Brent was staring at her, and she knew that she had her husband back at last.

"Gayle?"

"I'm here."

"I've got an awful headache. Did we fall asleep in here? God, my mouth feels like rubbish."

Her mouth curled painfully. "You don't remember?"

"What? No, nothing. I must have dozed off early."

It was awful again, the headache that he had. He was going to have to see a doctor about it. Maybe he was getting migraines. He sat up and stretched and then scratched; the hay was itchy against his body.

And then he took a good look at Gayle, and his heart seemed to sink to his feet.

She did not stare at him with anger or even reproach. She seemed ill herself and stricken. Like a wounded doe, wondering why a trusted hand had shot an arrow into her heart.

His own heart thudded hard. She was curled into the corner, with the blanket about her shoulders. Her hair was a wild tangle of golden curls around her shoulders, giving her an air of innocence, while her eyes seemed to have aged with the night.

"Gayle?" He winced as he whispered her name, squeezing his eyes shut. What had he done now? He had no damned memory! He wanted to touch her; he didn't dare try.

"Gayle, what . . . I didn't hurt you, did I?"

She lowered her eyes. "No," she said softly. "You didn't hurt me. And you don't remember anything. Again."

"I don't understand —"

"No," she said wearily. "And you don't want to, do you?"

"What do you mean?" he demanded defensively.

She stood up, dropping the blanket from her shoulders. She was so beautiful with the pink light playing over her body, the firm mounds of her breasts and the peaks of her nipples, the dips and curves and planes of her hips. He felt an instant erection, but knew it was no time to think of sex, or anything else, except for keeping her near him.

"Gayle —"

"You need a psychiatrist, Brent. You are losing your mind. You spent the night calling me Katrina, whispering that I'm a little slut and a traitor — but you love me anyway." She began to dress.

"Maybe I was dreaming —"

"It was demented behavior, Brent."

"Gayle, damn it, I can't see a psychiatrist. Gayle, wait a minute — where are you going?"

She was dressed and headed for the door. He caught her wrist. She stared at his hand coldly.

"Gayle! Where are you going?"

"I'm going up to the house. I'm going to make coffee and then I'm going to shower. And then, Brent, I'm going to leave you."

"What?" he roared, his hold upon her tightening like a vise. He couldn't believe she could even say such a thing.

But she was serious. She nodded sadly, meeting his eyes. "I can't go on like this, Brent. Never knowing what is going to happen. And you don't care. You just don't care."

"What do you mean, I don't care? I love you! Christ, you know that! I love you more than anything —"

"Except for your pride, Brent."

"I — I don't know what I'm doing! I would never hurt you on purpose, you know that. I can't stop what I don't know. I'll try, though, I swear it. I — dammit, Gayle! Marriage is for better or for worse!" He told her bitterly. "I thought that you loved me."

"Brent! I do love you. And you know that —"

"Then you can't leave me!"

"You won't try!"

"Try what?"

"A psychiatrist. I went because you asked me to, remember?" She didn't wait for an answer. She watched him just a moment longer; then she turned and headed for the door again. He watched her. She looked determined.

She really meant to leave him!

"Gayle!"

She was halfway along the lane, heading toward the house, when she heard his voice. She turned around and saw that he was running to her, stark naked, on the lane.

She had to smile. He was as beautiful and graceful as a healthy animal, and he was totally unselfconscious about his nakedness.

He reached her, panting. He set his hands on her shoulders and she didn't fight him. She kept smiling, though tears threatened; and when he held her to his heart, she was glad she felt his warmth and the rapid pounding there.

"Don't go."

"Brent —"

"I'll see Shaffer, I'll call him, and I'll take his earliest appointment. Just don't leave me. Don't ever leave me. I love you so much. You are everything to me."

She kissed him; then she laughed; then she cried. Holding his hands, she pulled back and looked at him. "You are bonkers, you know? It's broad daylight, and you're standing here bare-assed in the breeze, and any moment now —"

She broke off. "Any moment" was happening. There was a truck coming down the lane — the morning paper boy.

"Oh, hell!" Brent swore. He looked toward the house, then toward the barn, and decided they were equally distant. "You, my love, are worth it!" he proclaimed. Then he kissed her quickly and streaked off toward the house.

And Gayle continued to laugh and then she started to cry again. And she sat down, right there, right in the lane, and started to laugh and cry some more.

The paper boy, she was certain, considered her far more dangerous than Brent. He dropped the paper into her lap, asked her if he could help her, and then disappeared before she could reply, as quickly as he had come.

CHAPTER
16

A week later on Tuesday afternoon Gayle sat nervously on the corner of her desk, waiting. Brent was supposed to finish his battery of tests with Dr. Shaffer today, then pick her up at the gallery.

The gallery was filled with bird pictures. Cardinals, hummingbirds, blue jays. Gayle thought they were beautiful. The artist was a woman, a small, spectacled grandmother who had waited most of her life to really put her heart into her work. Geoff and Gayle had both been pleased with the showing — Mrs. Fitzsimmons wasn't a McCauley, but she was very good with her subject, and the paintings and lithographs had sold very well.

At the moment, though, Gayle stared at a red-breasted woodpecker and barely noticed the bird. Geoff came up to her and pressed a glass into her hand; she looked down to see that he had poured her some of his prized brandy.

"Thanks," she told him, smiling. Curiously, Geoff had been the one she had been able to talk to. She didn't know how happy Brent would be about that, but she didn't intend to tell him. Maybe the fact that Geoff had admitted that he and Tina had begun a bit of a temperamental affair had made her break down. Then again, maybe she finally talked to him because she had burst into tears while they were eating a quick lunch in his office earlier that day. Whatever, she was glad that she had talked to him. He had been warm and understanding, and though he couldn't give her any answers he didn't seem to think that either Brent or Gayle had completely gone off their rockers.

"You look like you need that," Geoff told her. He slid into the chair behind her desk. Gayle turned to face him. "You don't have to wait, Geoff. You go on."

"I'll wait. I'm in no hurry."

"What about Tina?"

He squirmed uncomfortably. "Well, we had a spat again last night."

"Whatever do you fight about all the time?"

He grinned. "Other women, other men, where to go for dinner, how to drive through the traffic. The list is longer. Want to hear the whole thing?"

"No!" Gayle laughed, then she frowned, remembering the sketch she had hidden away in the cupboard.

"What's the matter?"

"Oh! I was just thinking. Geoff, do you think you could come out soon? I want to show you something."

"What?"

"A sketch."

"Brent's?"

"No. No, this is old. It's done on vellum. I found it at a barn sale."

"And you think it might be worth something?"

She shook her head. "No. Well, maybe. I don't really know or care. It's just upsetting because . . . because it looks exactly like something Brent has done. I mean, to a T. As if he and this other artist, who probably lived two hundred years ago, had seen the same thing, from the same perspective."

He arched a brow curiously. "Sure, I'll come out. What does Brent say?"

"I haven't shown it to him."

"Oh?"

She shrugged and looked away from him. "I found it after the first night he acted — so strangely. I don't why, but I held off from showing it to him."

The door opened then and Brent stepped

in. Gayle looked at him anxiously, then jumped up to greet him with a kiss, glad to see that he was smiling. "How did everything go?" she asked him eagerly.

"Fine."

"Fine." He looked past her to Geoff and grimaced. "This one has nightmares and screams; I act out Rambo fantasies in my sleep." He looked at her suspiciously, seeming to realize that she had said something to Geoff, then shrugged as if he didn't mind. He smiled at Gayle again. "A clean bill of health. I went through the physical stuff like a Trojan, I swear it. And I stared at ink dots and did the whole bit. I made my life an open book. And I'm clean. There's nothing wrong with me."

"That's great."

"Want to come to dinner, Geoff?" Brent asked.

Geoff lifted his shoulders. "Are you being polite? Would you rather be alone?"

Brent shook his head, pulling Gayle against him and resting his chin on the top of her head while his arms slipped around her waist. "No, we can't be alone in a crowded restaurant anyway. Come on along."

Geoff did come to dinner; curiosity — and that he loved Gayle and really cared for

Brent — decreed that he should do so. They were both still beautiful. Gayle in soft swirling gray silk with padded shoulders, Brent in a casual fawn jacket, tailored shirt, and neatly pressed jeans. She was so light; he was so dark. The fairy-tale prince and his angel-haired princess.

But Gayle was showing the signs of strain. There were shadows beneath her eyes and her face had grown slimmer.

Tonight, Geoff noticed the wear on Brent too. His usual deep bronze complexion seemed faded and the tiny lines about his eyes seemed deeper.

He seemed happy that night, though. He told Geoff about the horses and how he planned to do a series using the mares. "Maybe I'll use Gayle in it too." He smiled at her wickedly. "A Lady-Godiva–type pose."

They ordered champagne and everything from soup to nuts; Brent was in a celebrating mood. But Geoff noticed that Gayle still appeared worried and drawn. She was quiet, while Brent was animated.

It was over coffee that she finally expressed herself, and Geoff wondered if she was even aware that he was there then.

"Brent, if they can't find anything wrong with you, then what is going on?"

"What?" He paused, his spoon halfway to his coffee cup, and frowned.

"You went through a whole series of tests. They don't show anything wrong. So — what *is* wrong?"

He slipped his hand over hers and squeezed it. "Nothing. Nothing's wrong. I must have been having dreams too, and you must have overreacted to them."

"Oh?"

"That's what Shaffer suggested. Of course he's suggested that I come and spend a few more hours with him."

"And?"

He sighed. "I agreed, Gayle. All right? I agreed."

She nodded at him slowly. He grinned encouragingly, then turned his attention back to Geoff.

They parted on the street. Back in the Mustang with Brent, Gayle still felt a little worried about Shaffer's diagnosis. She pressed Brent again.

"You told him everything that happened? Everything?"

He glanced her way quickly. "I told him everything that you told me happened. I didn't remember it myself, you know that."

"Hmmph." Gayle muttered. So Brent was fine — she was the crazy one. Why was it working out that way?

"Oh, stop it with your humphing," Brent laughed, ruffling her hair. Then she started because he drove off the road and parked the car. He took her into his arms and kissed her, and his eyes were bright with excitement and filled with the old self-assurance. "Everything is fine, Mrs. McCauley. And it's all going to be fine. I love you, you know. Till death do us part."

"What?"

He looked at her strangely and laughed. "Till death do us part. I love you."

She squeezed his hand. She still felt uneasy. But he was determined to charm her that night. When they reached home, they went for a long walk around the property, checking the newly planted flower beds and stopping by the stable to see the mares, Sheba and Satima. There was a light on in the old spinning house where the new foreman for the property, Hank Gleason, was being lodged. They stopped by briefly to see him, then went back to the house. Brent put on a recording of soft Viennese waltzes, and they went upstairs with more champagne to sit in the Jacuzzi. It was a good night; he was so happy and so relieved, and although Gayle didn't feel the same way she didn't let him know it. She teased with him and laughed with him and loved him every bit as tenderly as he did her. But when he lay peacefully sleeping, she was still awake, staring at the ceiling.

Maybe that was why she dreamed that night.

She never knew what she dreamed; she knew only that she was in terror. And she never knew where the dream began or where it ended. She knew that she was fighting, that she was struggling and fighting to defend herself; and in her heart she knew she was right. She saw Brent again, and it was Brent and it wasn't Brent, and he was furiously angry with her, throwing things. "That was it!" He shouted. "That was it! Oh, my God! You bought my freedom. My God, I could strangle you. I could tear you to pieces . . ."

She could hear herself denying the charges, denying the things she couldn't even comprehend. But he kept saying things to her, dreadful things, and she didn't want him near her. She was afraid of him, deathly afraid. Then she knew that it was cold and that he was chasing her and that, in the end, he caught her and he held her.

"Gayle! Dammit, please, Gayle! It's me! Gayle, stop, listen!"

She started as a clean slap landed against her cheek. A thousand stars seemed to burst before her, and she suddenly realized that she was standing out on the lawn. Her feet were damp; she could feel the grass. Brent — in his briefs — was standing before her, staring at her with terrible alarm in his eyes. He had just wrapped a robe around her shoulders. She was naked beneath it. Naked, out on the lawn, in the middle of the night. And she'd no idea of how she'd gotten out there.

There was blood dripping down his cheek and long scratches marred his chest. She gasped, then reached out to touch him. She was trembling, shaking so that she could barely reach him.

"Brent?"

"Come on, let's get back in the house," he said grimly.

She tried to walk; she stumbled and fell. He picked her up and carried her quickly into the house. He paused by the kitchen for a bottle of brandy, then came back out into the passage and carried her on up the stairs. He set her down on the bed, wrapping the blankets around her because she was so cold. As cold as death.

"Brent!"

She reached out to touch him again. He smiled and caught her fingers. "You've got to trim those nails, lady. I'll be back. Just let me rinse these off."

She sat there shivering while he went into the bathroom to rinse away the blood. When he came back, the scratches still looked ugly and sore.

"Oh, God!" Gayle gasped miserably.

"It's all right."

"It's not all right!"

"What were you dreaming? That I was an ogre?" He tried to laugh. "That I was attacking you again? I swear, Mrs. McCauley, I've been a perfect gentleman."

"Oh, Brent, don't, don't! I don't remember anything. This is awful. My God, Brent, something horrible is happening to us, and I can't remember anything."

He poured out some brandy, taking a sip himself, then situating himself behind her and bringing the glass to her lips. Gayle sipped it and coughed. "Brent, how did I get out there? What did I do?"

He sighed, leaning back. "You had another nightmare. You woke up screaming. I tried to comfort you. You slugged me in the jaw. You've got one hell of a punch, by the way."

"Oh, God!"

"Sweetheart, I'm teasing."

"You can't! You can't tease! This is too serious."

"Maybe we're taking it too seriously," he said stubbornly.

"Tell me the truth."

"That was the truth. You slugged me and took off. I grabbed my underwear and your robe and tore after you. They were the closest things that I could find."

"Brent —"

"It could have been worse. I could have grabbed your underwear and my robe."

"Brent!"

"Gayle, it's all right!"

"It's not all right. I hit you, I clawed you to pieces and you're telling me —"

"I'll live."

"Brent, oh please! This is getting worse!"

He slid off the bed, and she could see that he was far more tense than he wanted her to know. He ran his fingers through his hair and then paused to snatch the brandy from her, finishing it. He sat down again. "Gayle, I don't know what to do. I went to Shaffer, and you've been going to the man for weeks now." He put an arm around her and pulled her close again. "Maybe the man is no good."

"I don't think that's it," Gayle said dully. "I have an appointment with him tomorrow."

"Are you going to keep it?"

"Yes. I'm going to tell him that I ran out of

my house in the middle of the night, naked, and that I clawed up my husband's face and chest, and I don't even know why."

"Sweetheart —"

"Oh, Brent!"

"Gayle," he asked her, suddenly very serious. "What about Thane?"

"Thane?"

"Thane. The boy you lived with in Paris. The one who — killed himself. You told me why you left him. Do you think that you dream and then fight me, thinking that it's him?"

She shook her head, looking at him pensively. "Brent, it was so long ago! And I never felt for him what I feel for you."

"I believe that, Gayle. I know that. But" — he hesitated — "tonight you were wild. You were terrified of me and you hated me. You kept screaming . . . I'm just looking for answers. Talk to Shaffer about it. See what he says."

"But —"

"But what?"

"Brent, how would that explain — you?"

He sighed and ran his fingers through his hair again. The scratch on his cheek was starting to bleed again. "Oh, Brent!" She whispered, touching it.

She started to cry; she felt wretched. He

couldn't soothe her and he couldn't make her stop. He just held her. And when she had quieted at last, he swung her around to meet his eyes.

"It's going to be all right. It will be all right, Gayle, because I love you. No matter what happens I love you, and I will love you to my dying day."

He stroked her cheek and she kissed him, and at last she laid her head against his chest and slept. She didn't have any more dreams that night.

Gayle never could lie down in Dr. Shaffer's office. Dr. Shaffer didn't mind. He always said that his patients should sit down, lie down, stand straight or even on their heads — whatever made them comfortable.

That day she sat in the wing chair in front of the fireplace and sipped tea. She told him what had happened the night before and he listened, and then he began to question her. It was always Do you think . . . ? Do you think that your husband would hurt you? Do you think that you're harboring jealousies? Do you think that your marriage might have been a mistake? No, no, and no. She told him what Brent had suggested about Thane, that she wanted to make Thane pay;

therefore she was trying to make Brent pay. Brent thought she should take some time and really explore this avenue.

Gayle was certain that she wasn't trying to make Thane pay for anything. He was dead. He'd paid enough.

Then Shaffer asked her if she worried at all that Brent might be trying to make her appear mad or going crazy. There was something in his voice that really irritated her — she had this odd feeling that he was convinced there was nothing at all wrong with Brent, except for his choice of a mate for a lifetime.

She had always liked Shaffer, even if she had believed her sessions with him were worthless, but that day she hated him. In the end, when he kept at her — telling her that he couldn't help her until she chose to help herself — she burst into tears and raced out of the office. Then she got mad again and slammed back in to face him.

"I didn't hate my mother and I had no strange fixations on my father. My folks were great people. I'm sure that I did refuse to eat my peas somewhere along the line, and I'm equally sure that I was furious with them at some point for grounding me. I lost them and, yes, it hurt; it hurt damned badly, but I coped with it very well, thank you. As for Thane, yes, hell, I felt guilty. But I was never stupid, Dr. Shaffer. I know that he was self-destructive, I know that there was nothing that I could have done. I am still friends with the man's family, for God's sake. Dr. Shaffer, we have a real problem. I want help; I'm lost. But if you can't help me, please don't make me really crazy on top of everything else!"

He looked at her and he smiled, and then he looked down at his notes. "Sit down, Mrs. McCauley, please." He spread out his hands with a shrug, undisturbed by her tirade. Gayle hesitated. "Please," he repeated, and she sat down once again. He folded his hands over his notes and leaned toward her.

"I don't think that you are crazy, Mrs. McCauley. Neither is your husband. In fact, for his profession, and especially considering his success, he seems to be an exceptionally well-balanced man, with a wide perspective on the world. I find you to be very bright, and I believe that the two of you are very much in love with each other, and it should be very nice altogether."

Gayle stared at him blankly.

"Of course," he continued, smiling, "there are always things within the human mind and the human heart which are kept secret from others. I could continue to see you and I could continue to see your husband. Something may come out. But quite honestly, Mrs. McCauley, I don't think that I can help either of you."

"You can't?" He was so matter-of-fact.

"I'd like to suggest another approach."

Gayle leaned forward, anxious. "And that is?"

"A parapsychologist."

"*A what!*"

Shaffer repeated himself. Gayle just stared at him. Then she blurted out, "You're talking about a fortune teller! A medium, a Tarot card reader —"

He shook his head. "I'm talking about a parapsychologist. Not a witch doctor."

"Oh, my God! You think that we're possessed!"

Shaffer started to laugh. "I didn't say that at all." He sighed, looked down at his notes, and started to read, quoting her from their last session. " 'He acted as if I had done something to him, something terrible. He kept calling me Katrina. I thought he hated me, but that wasn't it, not entirely. He wanted revenge, but even that wasn't it. He said that he loved me — or Katrina — or whoever he was talking to, but it was so strange, and so awful. Can you hate someone so deeply and love that same person at the same time?' "

Gayle looked down at her lap, fiddling with her purse.

"He called you by another name, Mrs. McCauley. There's something going on here. And your husband is not schizophrenic; I'd stake my career on it."

Gayle exhaled slowly. "You can't believe in any of that type of thing, Doctor; you're a man of science —"

"Many a gastroenterologist would dispute that," he told her with a grin. "I'm a man of the mind. Let's put it that way, shall we? The main thing I learn as I go along is that seeming impossibilities do occur, and life itself is very mysterious." He pulled a pad of paper toward him and began to write on it. "This is the name of a friend of mine. She's associated with the university. She has a medical degree too — she's a psychiatrist, but she doesn't practice psychiatry, per se, anymore. Give her a call. I have a great deal of confidence in her."

Still not quite believing what he had suggested, Gayle realized that she was being dismissed. She stood up and offered him her hand, and he stood too. They shook hands and he smiled. "Mrs. McCauley, now you're staring at me as if I need some analysis. I probably do. We're supposed to be a crazy lot ourselves, you know." He didn't believe it one bit; she could tell by the tone of his voice. "Call Marsha. I think that you'll like her. She's fascinating."

Gayle had the little slip of paper in her hand. She thanked Dr. Shaffer, and told him goodbye.

She was tempted to toss the paper into the trash on the way out. She didn't, though. She stuffed it into her purse.

She expected to find Brent when she came out on the street. He wasn't there waiting for her. Instead, she found Geoff.

He was sitting on the hood of his Ferrari, arms crossed over his chest, waiting. He grinned at her startled frown.

"Brent got held up. He was working and by the time he realized how late it was, he knew that he'd never make it in on time. He caught me in the office and so I promised to meet you and drive you home." He stopped smiling, watching her. "What's wrong?"

"Oh, Geoff!" she murmured miserably. She stepped up and kissed his cheek, then hurried into the car. She thanked him distractedly for coming for her; then, as he pulled out into the traffic, she blurted to him, "He has to be a quack, Geoff! He has to be! He's telling me that I need a — a medium, or something!"

Geoff didn't respond. She had expected him to laugh, to denounce Shaffer dramatically. He didn't do anything of the kind. He looked ahead at the road, and then he shrugged.

"Maybe you do need — something else."

Gayle gasped. "Geoff! Oh, please! I know that you don't believe in — in ghosts."

"I don't believe in ghosts," he told her flatly.

"Oh! You think that we're — oh, please! We are not possessed, or —"

"Gayle, Gayle!" Absently he patted her knee, trying to calm her down while he wound through the rush-hour tangle. "No, I'm not thinking exorcist, Linda Blair, green pea soup all over the place. But . . ." He hesitated again. "Gayle, considering the things you say are happening, it wouldn't hurt to explore a new avenue, would it?"

She thought about that for several moments. "I don't know," she said glumly. "I — I had a bad enough time getting Brent to see Shaffer. He'll never see a medium or a parapsychologist, or whatever this woman is."

"Who is she?"

"What?"

Geoff repeated the question and Gayle

dug into her purse for the name. "Marsha Clark. Dr. Marsha Clark."

Geoff nodded as he drove. "I've met her. She's not what you fear she is."

"You've met her?"

"Yes. At a benefit for the opera. She was telling me about her field of study and I was very impressed. Gayle, face it, there are things that cannot easily be explained. And according to Marsha, they should all be explored."

" 'Marsha'?" Gayle repeated skeptically. "Geoff, this lady isn't another Boobs, is she?"

Geoff made an impatient sound. "No, she isn't. And Boobs' name was Madelaine. It still is."

"How is Tina? Have you two made up yet?"

"We've a date for tomorrow night."

"Good for you."

"Umm. You might want to call Marsha. If only because she's interesting."

Gayle was silent for several seconds. "Maybe I should just get a priest to bless the house."

She thought that he would laugh. "Maybe you should," he told her. "But I don't think that would help."

"Oh? Why?"

367

"Well, it seems to me that this all started long ago."

"It just began —"

"No, it just began so dramatically. But think back. On your wedding day you passed out."

"That was the excitement —"

"And your nightmares began two nights later. And Brent started with the war paintings. All right after you had just met."

Gayle groaned and sank back into the seat. "I don't believe any of this. And even if I did want to meet Marsha Clark, Brent would never do it. He thinks very little of psychiatrists. What is he going to think of a parapsychologist?"

Geoff didn't answer her. They finished the drive in silence.

Brent was outside on the wide veranda, leaning against a column, waiting for them. He smiled and came around to the passenger's side of the car and he kissed Gayle as soon as he helped her out. Then he thanked Geoff for the favor, saying, "Come on in. Let's have a drink."

He led the way into the passage and directed Gayle and Geoff into the parlor. "Gayle, wine? Geoff — a Scotch?"

"Fine," Geoff said.

Brent left and Gayle quickly spun on

Geoff. "Geoff! I think he was late on purpose. I think that he's stalling. It's as if he doesn't want to know what Shaffer had to say."

"Gayle, come on," Geoff murmured unhappily. "I'm sure that's not the case at all."

"It won't be," she said grimly. Arms crossed over her chest, she wandered over to the mantel. Brent came back into the room, balancing a wine glass, a Scotch, and a beer can. Geoff and Gayle both thanked him. Then Gayle accosted him flatly.

"Shaffer says we're both sane. Completely sane."

"Oh?" Brent lifted his beer can to her and sprawled back comfortably on the couch, watching her.

"He did have a suggestion."

"He did?"

Geoff tried to rise. "I think I should probably get back —"

"Geoff, stay!" Gayle pleaded.

He looked at Brent. Brent shrugged. Geoff could already feel the tension rising, and he wanted to leave. Gayle glared at Brent.

"Geoff — stay, please," Brent said with a soft groan. "I think I'm going to want another opinion here, anyway."

Geoff sat.

"Shaffer gave me the name of a woman to see. She's a psychiatrist too."

"Why? Why someone different?"

"She's also a — a —"

"Parapsychologist," Geoff supplied.

"A what!" Brent exploded. He was on his feet in a flash, stalking toward Gayle. *"A what?"*

"I told you!" Gayle said to Geoff, ignoring Brent. Geoff tried to help.

"Brent, she isn't a witch doctor. I don't see how it can hurt."

"And how the hell can it help to have a crone running around here tapping the walls and telling the air to be gone? Uh-uh! No way! This is absurd. We'll work this out ourselves."

"Brent, damn you!" Gayle cried. "We can't work this thing out ourselves!"

"Why not? What has happened? What has really happened?"

"A lot!" Gayle insisted. "Brent —"

He came around to her, catching her hands. "We've acted a little strangely. Chad was telling me once he had an aunt who insisted on singing arias in the grocery store. They didn't waste much sleep on it, though."

"Brent! This is much more serious than that."

"Gayle! I will not see this woman!"

She stared at him pleadingly, then turned to Geoff. "Help me!"

Geoff stood uneasily, shifting his weight from foot to foot. He did want to help them, desperately. "Brent . . ." he began awkwardly. "Ah, hell, Brent, I'm not trying to take her side or anything, but look at the two of you. What you have together is rare; it's the greatest thing in life. It's so very special. Brent, how can you risk that? How can you not grab at any straw, no matter how flimsy it may be, that might help you?"

Brent was very stiff and very straight. Gayle could feel heat waves of anger coming from him, wrapping all around her. But he didn't raise his voice; he just looked at Geoff and apologized softly. "Sorry, Geoff, I just can't do it. Not a parapsychologist." He dropped Gayle's hands and turned on his heel and strode out of the room. A second later, they heard the front door slam and the Mustang revved into action.

Gayle sank down on the couch and started to cry. Geoff set an awkward arm around her shoulder. "He'll come around. You know that he will." He handed her his handkerchief, and she wiped her face and stiffened her shoulders and apologized for falling apart.

"It's — it's okay," he promised her.

She sniffed once, then said, "Geoff!" She jumped to her feet and reached for his hand. "Come with me, please! This is the perfect time, with Brent gone!"

"The perfect time for what?"

"To show you the sketches. You've got to see them."

He followed her through the house and then across the colonnade to the old kitchen. She dug excitedly into a cupboard and came out with a box. She unrolled a vellum scroll and laid it out before him.

He felt his heart thump hard against his chest, and then he felt a queer thrill of fear streak all along his spine.

Gayle was right. The sketch was very, very old. It was probably worth a fortune. It was wonderfully descriptive; it captured emotion.

And it was precisely — down to every last expression — like the one that Brent had done.

"Well?" Gayle whispered.

He tried to smile at her. She was so vulnerable, looking at him anxiously with her wide blue eyes and cascade of golden hair flowing around her shoulders.

How could Brent refuse her anything?

He's afraid, Geoff thought. Brent Mc-

372

Cauley is afraid and doesn't know how to admit it.

"I think, Gayle," Geoff lied, "that Brent must have seen that sketch somewhere when he was a kid. Maybe a copy of it, or something. And it stayed in his memory.

"Do you really think so?"

He grinned. "Sure."

But he didn't really believe that. He reached down for her hand. "Come on, let's go get our drinks. Then I'd better go. I think that you two should be alone when he gets back." He didn't want to look at the sketch anymore. He could still feel that sense of unease scraping against his spine like nails against a blackboard.

Gayle nodded and rerolled the sketch. She slid it back into the cupboard. She tried to be casual as she and Geoff went back to the parlor. It was no good. They were both uncomfortable.

Geoff left, telling her to call if she needed him.

Gayle sat on the couch and waited for Brent. She hoped he wouldn't be late.

She waited and waited and finally cried herself to sleep. He didn't come home late; he didn't come home at all.

CHAPTER
17

Dr. Marsha Clark's office was in a modern high-rise building downtown, not far from the gallery. Gayle didn't know what she had been expecting, but not this pleasant, light and airy place. Long plate-glass windows brought in bright daylight and blue skies. The carpeting and furniture were in earth tones and there was an abundance of plants all about. It might have been any attractively decorated doctor's office, if it weren't for the word *parapsychologist* on the door.

Geoff and Tina were with her. On the phone Dr. Clark had assured Gayle that she wouldn't mind the extra company in the least. While an assistant asked them if they would like coffee or tea and then went off to find the doctor, the three of them looked around.

"Well," Tina murmured, "there are no chickens tied to walls, or anything."

"That's voodoo, I think," Gayle murmured.

"No shrunken skulls," Geoff offered.

"That's cannibalism, I think," Gayle retorted, but their words worked. She laughed and she felt somewhat better. Then Dr. Marsha Clark walked into the room, and things improved even more.

She was a fashionably slim woman, with shoulder-length, permed brown hair. The overall picture was more than very attractive — Marsha Clark was beautiful. She had delicate features and a full mouth, but her greatest attraction was her eyes — they were a very warm dark brown, quick to flash with humor and interest. Her smile was easy and relaxed. Gayle judged her to be in her early to mid-thirties, and she was the farthest thing from an old crone she had ever seen.

Marsha Clark had no trouble identifying Gayle from Tina, and greeted her with a firm handshake. She smiled at Geoff and told him how nice it was to see him again. Geoff introduced Tina; then Dr. Clark urged them all to sit down. Her assistant came in with the tea and the coffee. They chatted about the weather for a moment, all complaining that it was unbearably warm. Then Dr. Clark smiled at Gayle and said simply, "So, Mrs. McCauley, you and your husband have been behaving strangely lately, is that it?"

Taken off guard, Gayle smiled. "Well, yes. In a nutshell, that's it."

"I know you told me a few things on the phone, but let's go over them again. It started with dreams — your dreams. Nightmares, right?"

"Right."

"She passed out the day of her wedding," Geoff said.

"But, oh, you should have seen them!" Tina supplied. "From the moment they saw each other, I think that they were in love. It was so wonderfully romantic."

Gayle cast Tina a quick glare and Dr. Clark laughed. "It sounds lovely. But you passed out at the wedding; then the dreams started. And then, once you moved into your new home — your old home, that is — your husband became affected. Calling you by a different name, behaving as if you had done something terrible to him, being crude and rough and domineering."

Gayle nodded uneasily.

"And then?"

"I — I had some kind of dream again myself. I ran away from him, out to the lawn. When he tried to stop me, I fought him."

"So you've hurt each other?"

Gayle inhaled nervously and looked down at her hands. "Yes."

"And what is the name that he is calling you?"

"Katrina."

Dr. Clark nodded and sipped her coffee. She was silent so long that Gayle grew nervous. "Dr. Shaffer says that we're both sane. So what is it, Dr. Clark? Is my husband possessed? Am I possessed? Are we both possessed?"

Dr. Clark chuckled softly. "I don't think so, but then, there are a number of possibilities."

"Should I have a priest out to the house?" Gayle asked, frowning.

"Maybe. But according to what you've told me, I don't think so. Tell me, where is Mr. McCauley today?"

Gayle stared down at her hands again. "I don't know."

"He was upset with the idea of coming to me?"

She thought about lying, but she needed help desperately. She looked up at Dr. Clark. "Yes."

"Don't be disturbed; I'm not, Mrs. McCauley. A number of people feel that way. If it's necessary, I think that we'll get him in here."

"If it's necessary . . . ?"

"We'll start with you."

"Start — where?"

"Have you ever been hypnotized?"

"No, never."

"Are you willing to let me hypnotize you?"

Gayle stared at Marsha Clark blankly. All of a sudden she was afraid. Deeply afraid, as if a tidal wave were about to wash over her.

Something would come out.

She knew it. Just as suddenly as she knew the fear, she knew that something would come out. A secret inside of her, so deep that Dr. Shaffer couldn't have begun to find it, but there, and brimming on the surface now. "I —"

"Don't be afraid. It's a very simple procedure. What you have heard is true — under hypnosis, you don't do anything that isn't in your normal code of behavior. You're still very much in control."

Gayle looked at Geoff and then at Tina a little desperately. They both nodded at her, and she finally nodded to Dr. Clark. "Good then," the doctor said, rising briskly. "Mrs. McCauley, come over here to the lounge, if you will, please. And there, see the spiral on the wall? Just watch it. Your friends will be fine; they're welcome to stay right there on the chairs, all right?"

Gayle nodded again. She stretched out on

the buff-colored lounge and found that it was very comfortable. Marsha Clark brought her a little pillow, then pointed to the wall, a painted black spiral on it. "Just watch the spiral. And relax. And most important, trust me."

Gayle stared at the spiral and listened as Dr. Clark began to talk. She told her again to relax, to relax her feet and her toes, her fingers, her calves, her hands. She heard the doctor moving about the room, and then she heard the sounds of water running and a breeze rustling through the trees.

It was madness. She could relax from here to eternity, Gayle decided, but she wasn't going to become hypnotized. She was very much wide awake.

Dr. Clark began to describe the stream where the water flowed, and she talked about dusk and about a lazy time of sheer comfort. Gayle kept staring at the spiral; then Dr. Clark told her that she could close her eyes and rest.

"I'm ready to close my eyes and rest," Tina murmured softly to Geoff. He placed his hand over hers and squeezed it. "God, I hope this does something for them," she whispered.

Geoff felt the same. Gayle looked awful. She was so tired. She must have cried most of the night, for it was evident in the pallor of her skin. For a moment Geoff thought that he'd like to strangle Brent McCauley for doing this to her, but then he reminded himself that McCauley was in every bit as much pain.

Dr. Clark told Gayle that she would sleep until she heard three sharp taps. She asked Gayle if she was comfortable, if she could hear her, and Gayle answered yes to each question.

Then Dr. Clark asked her flatly, "You've known your husband before? You've known him very well, before now?"

Geoff wasn't sure what happened then, if his imagination took flight, if fancy claimed him. Perhaps he, too, had fallen under a form of hypnosis. Time seemed to stand still while they waited for Gayle to answer.

"Yes," Gayle said at last.

"Tell me about it."

A smile, a soft and beautiful smile, curled her lips. "I knew him before. Very well."

"When you were Katrina?"

Geoff inhaled sharply. Tina wound her fingers around his tightly.

"Yes," Gayle said.

"You are Katrina. What is his name?"

"Percy. He is Percy."

Geoff swallowed sharply. Tina gasped.

380

Gayle was speaking, but her voice sounded different. There was an accent to it. It sounded . . . British, and yet not like any British accent he'd ever heard.

"You are Katrina; he is Percy. And you are in love with him?"

"Yes. Oh, yes."

Gayle still smiled so sweetly. Yes, Geoff thought, she is deeply in love with him, just as Gayle is deeply in love with Brent.

What was he thinking? It was madness.

"Take me back, Katrina. When did you meet him? Please tell me when you met him."

"The driver was going too fast. The streets were muddy. It had been so rainy . . ."

"Katrina, keep talking to me, please."

Her smile broadened. "The coach fell over. He helped me out. He was so audacious. He said things that a gentleman must not, and yet he was so kind and solicitous. I put him in his place, of course."

"But you were falling in love with him."

She blushed very brightly and prettily on the lounge. Her hands fluttered momentarily in the air, then fell to her sides again. "You don't understand. It wasn't proper. My brother was a lord, a friend to the governor. Percy was . . . backwoods. And more. He was friends with Patrick Henry; he adored the man. He was a traitor, and I wasn't allowed to associate with him."

"But you did?"

She squirmed uncomfortably.

"But you did?" Dr. Clark repeated.

"I will not tell you. I will not."

"You won't tell me anything?"

"No. Yes. I had to see him again. You must understand. I had to see him again. I tried to run into him, and I did. And I knew that he was feeling . . . everything that I was feeling. I wanted him to love me, but I was afraid. I was just sixteen and I had heard so many tales about men. And especially . . . his type of man. A colonist. A Yankee. Ill-bred and ill-kempt. I panicked. I ran home."

"You ran home."

"I was caught."

"Caught?"

"My — brother."

"And what happened?"

"I will not tell you."

"You must tell me."

"I went back to Percy. I went back to him, and I found him in the darkness." She paused, hesitating.

"You went to him. You went to him in the darkness."

"I found him in the shade of the elm and he led me into the barn. You must understand. He was so fine. He had such passion and he was so young and . . ."

"And?"

"I meant to quiz him. I meant to talk and I meant him to fall in love. I wanted flowers at my feet and I wanted to make him humble and adoring."

"But that wasn't his way?"

"No." It was whispered softly. So softly. And with such enduring tenderness, it was nearly painful to hear. "No, it was not his way. He kissed me again and he bore me down to the hay." She seemed distressed again, shifting uneasily on the lounge. "You must understand. It was right . . . it was like the sun bursting down upon us; it was all golden light. They would say it was immoral, but it was not. You must understand —"

"I understand. It was very special. He made love to you, and you consented because it was very special."

"Yes." The smile was back, the awe, the tenderness. "It was right, it was . . . blessed. I loved him. I knew that I loved him when I saw his eyes, when he kissed me. I felt his hands. I felt his touch. He was so very fine . . ."

She went on. She described their first encounter so sweetly and in that soft, strangely accented voice that time and the very air seemed to hang still again. Geoff did not realize until she ceased to speak that he had gone rigid, that beads of sweat had broken out upon his forehead. He couldn't have spoken if he had wanted to, and when he dared to glance at Tina he saw from the awed expression on her face that she was feeling the same thing, that she had been equally touched.

And yet, it couldn't be . . .

He didn't believe in it. They weren't talking about ghosts and they weren't talking about possession. It finally hit him; he finally figured it out.

Reincarnation.

He didn't believe in it. Gayle would not believe in it; she was not overly religious, yet she had her faith; and it had seen her through many ordeals. This could not be. It had to be a trick . . . and yet, what then had he believed? He had urged her to come here; he had known that she had needed a different kind of help from what a psychiatrist could provide.

She had just described a lovers' tryst in startling detail, sweeping her listeners along in the ardency, in the sensuality, of the encounter. And God, which of them could deny it? The love affair between Katrina and

Percy seemed to parallel the affair between Gayle and Brent.

It had happened again. They had fallen in love as swiftly, as completely, in the present as they had more than two hundred years ago. *No! It couldn't be,* the rational part of his mind protested.

"We hid this, of course," Gayle was saying.

No, a woman named Katrina was speaking, Geoff reminded himself.

"And the year passed." She frowned. "It was a terrible year. They wanted to punish Boston, and Boston would not be punished. It came time for the second session in Philadelphia, and Percy had to go. Not that he had stayed with me the whole time, for he had land all over Virginia. His absence was terrible. I was always so afraid that they would arrest him. Then it came time for the British to pull out. He had been right; Percy had been right all along. They were supposed to leave. Henry would be serving with the army, of course, but he meant to send me home. To Kent. I met Percy that night on the outskirts of town. And I never went home, not to Kent. We ran away together and we were married."

"And were you happy?"

"Very happy." A frown clouded her brow again. "Except that there was a war. The war

. . . the war was terrible."

"But you and Percy — you were happy."

"Yes! We were very happy."

"But you have to tell me things —"

"I can't remember."

"What can't you remember?"

"Anything. I can't remember any more. I can't remember. I told you that I was happy. I can't remember any more."

Dr. Clark was silent for several long seconds. Then she told Gayle that she would rap three times, and Gayle would wake up feeling rested and refreshed.

One, two, three . . .

They all heard the rappings. Gayle's eyes opened and she blinked against the sudden light. Then she smiled and gave first the doctor, then Geoff and Tina sheepish smiles. "I suppose I'm not a very good subject. I didn't try to fight it —"

"You did very well," Dr. Clark said.

Tina choked. "Gayle! You don't remember what you said?"

Gayle shook her head ruefully. "No. Was I helpful? Oh, no . . . I let out some deep and dark and dangerous secret. I —"

"Do you believe in reincarnation, Mrs. McCauley," Dr. Clark interrupted her calmly.

"What?"

Dr. Clark smiled. "Coming back to life. The Hindus are great believers in it."

"You mean I was a fly, I got to be an elephant next time around, and now I'm up to being a human?" Gayle asked, confused.

Still giving them that gentle and beautifully determined smile, Dr. Clark said no. "Gayle, first of all, I want you to know that I grew up going to Catholic schools myself."

"That could mean a number of things," Gayle said with a nervous laugh. "I'm Episcopalian, but Geoff went to Catholic schools, and he has lots of funny stories about Sister Paula of Perpetual Pain."

Dr. Clark laughed along with them, in fact much more easily than Gayle did. She looked a little like a drowning child, trying not to believe that the water could cover her over.

"I'm just trying to tell you that I'm not going against any of your religious beliefs. There are answers to all things, in the end. I don't have all the answers, but I do believe, very sincerely, Mrs. McCauley, that both you and your husband lived before. When we meet again, I'll record your answers under hypnotism. For now, you'll have to trust me and your friends. You met and married your husband once before, more than two hundred years ago. It seems that

that lifetime is now intruding on this life-time."

"Oh, please!" Gayle gasped and then she covered her mouth because she didn't want to be rude. But she didn't believe in it; she couldn't believe in reincarnation. "I'm sorry," she murmured hastily. "I didn't mean to be so blunt, I just don't —"

"Gayle, it's true!" Tina interrupted. "It's true, I heard you myself; I heard everything that you said!"

Gayle looked from Tina to the doctor, and Dr. Clark nodded. "That's why your husband calls you Katrina. You told us about meeting and falling in love. Right before the Revolutionary War."

Geoff cleared his throat. "You told us very explicitly about meeting and falling in love."

Her cheeks were burning. Gayle pressed her palms to them. "It can't be."

"You must have had an open mind to have come to me for help to begin with," Dr. Clark said.

Tears were hovering beneath Gayle's lashes and she was trying not to shed them. "I came to you because I was desperate, because my husband didn't come home last night, because . . . I was ready to accept a little spirit, maybe prowling around the house. I was ready to accept a lingering presence in the house maybe, or something like that. Oh, God! I don't know what I was willing to accept, but you're asking me to believe that I lived before, that Brent lived before. So why did we come back together? Why, if we were in love, does he hate me in these dreams or fits of his? Oh, God!" She dropped her face into her hands. Brent was right. She shouldn't have come.

"There are a number of theories," Dr. Clark said calmly. "Some people believe that we live in cycles, that people usually always come back together. A sister becomes a friend, a mother becomes a sister. Roles change, but maybe emotions remain. Others believe that we can come back to do things over. I believe, in your case, that you've come back to achieve happiness."

"We were happy!" Gayle shouted. The room went dead still and she clamped her hand over her mouth. Oh, God, it was true! And she knew it! She couldn't remember what she had said under hypnosis, but that first feeling was back with her. She knew — and she had known — that something would change here today. That something would come out.

She groaned and lay back on the lounge. "Can it be true?" she whispered.

"Yes, I believe it can be," Dr. Clark said.

"And I think that it must be very special, a very special love indeed, to be granted this kind of chance again."

Gayle curled around on the lounge. "But what does this do? What does it help?"

Dr. Clark sighed softly. "I'm not sure. I need to learn more. You blocked me when I tried to go further. All we know now is that the two of you met, fell in love, and married. Katrina insists that you were very happy, then comes up with a memory loss. It's a delicate situation. Maybe just knowing, just accepting the past, will be enough. We can try hypnosis again. Frankly, though, I think that I need to hypnotize your husband too."

Gayle sighed. "That may be impossible."

"Then just you and I will work together, Mrs. McCauley," Dr. Clark said cheerfully. She offered Gayle her hand. "Please, don't look so downcast. We made excellent progress."

Gayle took her hand and stood up. She was wobbly. Geoff and Tina came quickly to her side. "Please, call me anytime you need me, day or night. I'm glad to help."

"Thank you," Gayle whispered again. "What do we do now?"

"Unless you can get your husband to come, I'll see you again in a few days. When you feel that you're ready. Actually, I'd like to come to your home. I think it would provide the better atmosphere since it's where things happen. But we'll go on what we have to go with."

Gayle nodded. "I — I'll try to talk to Brent again." Feeling dazed, she let Tina and Geoff lead her out of the office. They kept staring at her. They touched her as if she were a china doll.

"Stop it, please!" she begged them both.

"I think lunch would be in order," Geoff said. They were right across the street from a steak place. He led them over and he sat down, and he and Tina ordered drinks as if their lives depended on getting them fast. And Gayle discovered that she desperately wanted a drink too. She ordered a double Jack Black and ginger, and when it came she nearly downed it in a single swallow. Then they all looked at each other and laughed nervously, and then Gayle insisted on details and the two of them tried to provide them.

"You really don't remember?" Tina demanded.

"Only vague feelings like I remember from the dreams," Gayle told her.

"Do you believe what just happened?" she asked Geoff.

"No. Yes. I saw it, but I can hardly believe it."

"I can't believe it," Gayle said numbly.

"Well, you really have to believe it, don't you?" Tina said.

"What do you mean?" Gayle asked her.

"Well, what are your alternatives? You've already tried a regular psychiatrist. No help. What if the same kinds of things keep happening? Then what? It must be like living with Jekyll and Hyde. And you! What if you were to have a weapon when you attack him in your dreams? Gayle, the way that I see it, you have to trust this woman. You've got only one other option."

"Which is . . . ?" Gayle asked thickly.

"A divorce, the way I see it. Divorce each other and get as far away from each other as possible. Before one of you kills the other."

"Oh, God!" Gayle groaned.

"Tina!" Geoff said sharply.

"It's the truth," Tina retorted. "What the hell else is she going to do?"

She didn't know what to expect, but as she came home she knew that Brent was there in the house somewhere, and that Mary was not. A Robbie Nevill disc was playing at a high volume, and Brent never played music so loudly when Mary was around because she didn't care for it, and Brent was always courteous to others.

Or at least he always had been, once upon a time.

She entered the passage and closed the door. She wondered if he were in his studio, but once she had climbed the stairs she discovered that he was not. She looked into their bedroom and searched the upstairs, then pensively started down the stairs again. On her way down she realized that the music had stopped.

She stepped into the kitchen, then glanced into the ballroom. It was dark and empty. When she stepped into the parlor it was dark and quiet too. She was about to leave when he spoke from the far corner of the room, startling her so that she almost cried out.

"So you are back," he said softly.

Unease — deep, creeping unease — set into the base of her spine and began to crawl toward her nape. She paused dead still in the doorway and swung around.

She could barely see him. He was no more than a silhouette in the corner of the room, with shadows falling over his features. He was holding a brandy snifter in his hands. He swirled the brandy in his glass while he stared at her.

This is not the man I married, she told herself. His name is Percy, and he has come from another time.

The words were dull and flat in her mind. They were unbelievable.

But as he moved toward her slowly like a stalking tiger, her heart sank, for though it might be incredible, it was true; and every moment of her life was becoming a living hell, for she never knew whether she'd be encountering Brent or Percy.

I am mad, I am mad. I have gone crazy . . . she thought.

"Where have you been?" he demanded harshly.

"Nowhere —"

"God, what a fool you think I am, my love!"

There was a deadly chill to his tone. The afternoon shadows still fell upon his face, which was handsome but cold. He set the brandy snifter down, and in those seconds she thought to run. She turned around, slamming the door on him, and raced down the passage for the front door. She could scream and pray for help, or she could perhaps get to her car and drive away to wait until this regression had passed.

She did not reach the front door. He caught her by the hair and jerked her back, then slammed her hard against the door. She gasped for breath, staring at him desperately, wondering what in God's name she should say or do. Sweet heaven, help me! she thought. If she was Katrina, why in hell didn't she know what to do? Why did the answers elude her? Why couldn't she appease him?

He smiled at her but the smile was nothing more than a hard, bitter, humorless twist of the lips. He planted his hands on either side of her head, pinning her there. Then he asked her again, "Where have you been?"

"Out. Working."

"And what work was that?"

"You're hurting me —"

"Am I?" He brought his hand from the wall to stroke her cheek. His palm and fingers fell to her throat, and when he had caressed the flesh, he tightened his grip. Panic welled inside of her and he saw it . . . and he smiled again bitterly. "Perhaps I should strangle you now. Perhaps it would ease the torment in my soul when I sleep at night. At least I would know where you lie at night."

She could barely breathe. She knew that she could fight, but at the same time, she prayed that even as Percy he could not really hurt her. For if he could, then their marriage might as well end, this way as well as any other.

His hand fell from her neck. For the moment she was free. She shoved him with all of her strength and ducked beneath his arm, desperate enough to run for the ballroom. "Katrina!" He shouted out the strange name and he was behind her. She reached the room and slammed the door shut and bolted it and leaned against it. It was to no avail. He screamed out the strange name again and she heard him slam against the wood. She felt it shudder and she jumped away from it, a scream on her lips. He slammed against the door again, and the old bolt broke. The door opened, screeching on its hinges.

"Percy, please!" She was barely aware that she used the old name, the name so alien to her. And then she swallowed sharply, for he paused, hearing her say it. "Please!" she whispered again.

But he came toward her anyway, reaching out his hand. "I told you . . . I begged you," he whispered, "not to bargain. But you were gone again. Running to him again."

She shook her head. She tried to spin and run again, but this time he lunged at her legs like a football player, and they both fell to the antique Persian rug that stretched the length of the room. He crawled over her and she beat against him frantically. He caught her wrists and stretched them far above her head. She stared at him in the day's pale and dying light, and he whispered to her then, "I loved you so very much."

"I love you."

He lowered his head and kissed her. She squirmed beneath him, struggling. He held her steady with his weight, watching her face, easing his hold on her wrists at last to run his fingers over her face.

"Please let me go," she whispered. "Percy, this is the ballroom."

"Ah, yes, the ballroom. And you are a prim and proper wife now, my love? Tell me, does it matter to you when you go to him? Does it matter if it is a barn or a cornfield, a ballroom or a shabby garret within a tavern? Does it matter then?"

"I don't know what you're talking about!" she shouted.

"You cannot deny it. James was here when the ship came up the river. He was hiding with his troops out in the field. You gave them supplies and quinine, and he met with you here."

"No!"

"Was it in this room, dear wife? Tell me that you did not take him to my very bed. Ah

. . . were you in the kitchen, perhaps, or the little parlor or upon the rug in the music room when you finished with your entertainment?"

"Percy, you are mad! Let me go!"

"I cannot. You are my wife."

"Have pity, then!"

"Did you dance with him? Did you play for him?"

"No. Percy —"

He was on his feet again, dragging her up. To some distant music only he could hear, he began to swirl her around and around the room. She grew dizzy and she held on to him for dear life. Darkness settled heavily upon them. She could almost see it as it would have been, years and years ago, damask on the windows, a player at the spinet . . .

They turned and turned some more, and then she was back in his arms and they had burst out onto the balcony and he took her chin into his hand, lifting her face to his. "By heaven, I love you! Fool that I am, I love you!"

She cried out as his fingers brushed her throat again and he whispered against her earlobe, "Dear God, that you could betray me so!"

"Never!" She assured him, trembling.

"Please, please, don't hurt me again."

"Then love me, my wife. Love me."

Trembling still, she set her palm against his cheek and she kissed him. He caught her hand and kissed it tenderly and swept her into his arms again carefully, as if she wore voluminous skirts. He sank to the floor, holding her.

Her tears mingled with each kiss. He caught her lips again and again, playing with them as he eased his hands beneath her hem and along her thigh. He had seldom been more erotic — his mouth never leaving her lips, his eyes never straying from hers — as he slid his fingers against the lace and elastic of her panties, then swept them away to plunge his fingers inside of her, his breath hot and heavy against her face. She bit her lip and cried out softly in sweet excitement and shame. She shouldn't feel it, she shouldn't want it, she shouldn't have it, this was not right at all . . .

He swept her skirt above and ravished her flesh with his lips and teeth and tongue, and she did nothing but feel the rising pulse of anticipation. When he rose from her at last and stripped, she reached for him eagerly, coming to him on her knees. A merciful blankness filled her mind. The body be-longed to Brent McCauley, and she loved him. Had she loved him before? Was this then the same person? She didn't know. She only knew that he was hers and she was his and that he did not hurt her now, but held her and swept into her with tenderness and love.

Until the end, until the very end. He stroked her hair and he lay beside her, damp and glistening. Then he looked up at the ceiling and then he stared at her in horror. He jumped up. "Oh, my God! It's here! It's right here, witch, that you betrayed me!"

He raised his hand as if he would strike her.

He never did. He fell to the floor, in a cold, dead faint.

CHAPTER
18

It was three A.M. when he woke up. He could tell by the luminous dial on his watch. He was horribly disoriented, having no idea where he was.

He had another headache. It was god-awful, pounding mercilessly against his skull. He tried to roll over, expecting the softness of his bed, but the ground was hard; and he realized that he was lying on a floor, and a blanket had been thrown over him. He winced and blinked, and then the moonlight trickling in through the long windows and sheer curtains began to allow him to see. He looked around the room and saw that he was alone. He was naked and alone beneath a blanket on the ballroom floor. Shaffer was wrong; he *was* losing his mind.

He staggered to his feet, wrapping the blanket around him. He went out of the ballroom and through the passage to the kitchen, desperate for some water and some aspirin. When he had washed down a couple, he came back to the passage and looked up the stairway. A light was on somewhere. He almost dreaded going up those stairs. He had to, though. He had to face her sometime.

He felt old, old and heavy, walking up to the landing. He turned and went toward his bedroom. The door was ajar and the light was coming from there. He pushed it open and entered.

She was dressed in a thin white gown, and her head lay on the pillow. For all the world, she appeared to be the purest, most innocent, and most beautiful of golden goddesses. He bit into his lower lip and walked over to the bed and tried very hard to get into it without waking her. She started, though, as soon as he touched the bed.

"It's just me," he said, trying to sound light. It was probably a dismal attempt anyway. After all, he had no idea why he had been asleep on the floor of the ballroom.

"Brent?" she murmured sleepily, rising.

He slipped beneath the covers and would have set an arm about her to pull her close, except that she seemed to flinch. "Who were you expecting?" he tried to tease.

She stared at him levelly. She didn't demand to know where he had been the night before. She just stared at him so solemnly that fear streaked through him.

"I don't know," she said, and she meant it. "I don't know who to expect anymore."

"What do you mean? What are you talking about?" he demanded defensively.

"You can't slough it off, Brent. Come on, ask me what you were doing downstairs."

He sighed, and he managed to put a measure of impatience into it. "Okay, I tied another one on. It won't happen again, I swear it."

"Oh, will you quit!" she said disgustedly. She threw off the covers and rose, coming down to the foot of the bed to stare at him. "You did it again, Brent. You went Jekyll and Hyde on me."

His heart quickened. "Did I — did I hurt you?"

"No," she said, but it was a word laden with sorrow and bitterness, and he swallowed miserably. He lifted his hands, searching desperately in his mind for something to say. "Where did you sleep last night?" she asked him.

He was able to smile ruefully. "I'm sorry, Gayle. I'm sorry, really. I just slept out in the old spinning house, that's all. In the servants' quarters there. You had me alarmed with all that mumbo jumbo. Really. I just couldn't imagine being part of a séance, you know?"

"I stayed up all night. Waiting for you."

"I'm sorry. I didn't mean to hurt you; I just needed to be alone."

She lowered her head. "I went to see her yesterday, Brent. I went to see the parapsychologist."

"You did *what?*" His tone thickened furiously and he shoved the sheets aside to bound down to the end of the bed and confront her. "You know how I felt about it, and you went anyway?"

She backed away. "Sure, yes, fine! I know how you feel! Don't you care about how *I* feel? I can't take any more of this!"

His jaw tightened. "You were the one trying to claw my eyes out the other night. I didn't hate you for it."

"Brent! You're bigger than I am; you're stronger. You have some kind of defense —"

"I'll remember that when you pick up a knife," he said coolly.

"You son of a bitch!" she flared. "You with your stinking ego and your callousness."

"You just said that I didn't hurt you —"

"I hate it! I hate it. No, I'm not mortally wounded, but I hate being thrown around, and I hate being threatened. And I hate being —"

"Raped?" he said acidly. He rubbed his eyes. "I still don't think I believe all this."

"You saw the bruises you gave me."

"All right, all right. What did the witch doctor say?"

Gayle stared at him a long moment, then took in a deep breath. "She thinks that we — met in a previous life. That we were lovers about two hundred years ago. My name was Katrina, and yours was Percy. Something must have happened then that causes this now."

He looked at her. He just looked at her, then he burst into laughter. "You made me go to the shrink when you're falling for complete rot like that?" He crawled off the bed, laughing so hard that he reached for her. She sidestepped him and continued to glare at him in fury.

"It isn't rot! Good Lord, do you think it was easy for me to believe it? But I think it is true, tonight more than ever. Damn you, Brent, you know you go into total blackouts, but you won't believe what I tell you! If you would just see this woman, you would understand. Tina and Geoff —"

"You took Geoff with you? And Tina? You made idiots out of both of us in front of your dear old friends?"

"They care, Brent. Which is more than I can say for you."

"Gayle, Gayle, Gayle!" He sank down

wearily to sit at the foot of the bed. "Something is wrong, yes. But I wish to hell you wouldn't air our problems in front of everyone else. And I wish you hadn't resorted to a witch doctor. If Shaffer is no good, we can try another reputable doctor. It has to be something in our minds, don't you see?"

"No, I don't see. Dr. Clark wants to see you."

"Dr. Clark?" he said skeptically.

"She's a real doctor. Dr. Marsha Clark. And so help me, Brent, if you love me, you've got to work at this."

"That isn't fair. I love you, and you know it. But I will not see a witch doctor!"

"Please! Just meet her, talk to her."

"Umm. And we can play weird music and rent a fog machine for the house when she comes out. Sure. Haven't you checked into possession and exorcism yet?"

"Stop it! Your sarcasm is way out of line, Brent."

"Gayle! I've never hurt you —"

"Oh, no, it's just great. In fact, I'm having a ball. Let's just live like this forever and ever!" She planted her hands on her hips and whirled away from him, her eyes flashing and her hair flowing. "There is no Percy; that's all in my head. Shaffer is wrong. You have this hidden hang-up. You're Percy, and Percy is you. In fact, you know, Brent, Percy is good. Percy is damned good."

"Gayle, quit this —"

"Maybe I could even prefer him as a lover. Of course, he doesn't exist. He's that thing in your mind that some shrink will find for you. What if you don't like the answer, though, Brent? What if it's sick? What if it's the rough and tough and macho side of you coming out? The side that just has to beat up a little on the old wife before really getting down —"

"Stop it, Gayle."

"But what the hell. I mean, I said Percy is good, didn't I? I should live with it. Really good —"

She broke off with a sharp, startled cry because he had slapped her. The only saving grace to it was that he looked as horrified as she felt, and he was immediately contrite.

"Gayle, I'm sorry. I lost it there, I'm sorry. You wouldn't stop. God, sweetheart, I'm sorry, I didn't mean to — come here, please, Gayle —" He reached out for her, and she screamed at him.

"Leave me alone, just leave me alone!"

"Gayle, please, I'm sorry, I don't know what came over me, sweetheart —"

"No!" She wrenched from his hold. Her

cheeks were damp and she was struggling for breath and she drew the cool side of her hand against her chin where he had hit her. "Maybe I was wrong — maybe I shouldn't have said that. But no, not this time, Brent. Not this time!" She spun away from him and strode for the closet, throwing it open. It took him several seconds to realize what she was doing.

"Gayle!" He walked over to her quickly, locking his arms around her so that she couldn't move. She wouldn't even look at him. "Gayle, please —"

"I'm going, Brent," she said dully. She felt as stiff as a poker in his arms, cold as ice. "I'll be at my house on Monument Avenue if you want me."

"You can't leave me!"

"I have to leave you!"

"Please, God, don't you know how I love you!"

"Let me go, Brent."

He didn't let her go. He swept her up into his arms and he sat at the foot of the bed and he held her and he told her again, desperately and fervently, how much he loved her. Tears glazed her eyes at last, some recognition of all that lay between them. "I love you too," she whispered.

"You can't want to leave me."

"I have to leave you."

"Why?"

"We're . . . we're going to have a baby. And I'm afraid. I'm afraid for our baby." Her eyes focused on his at last. She looked scared and very, very beautiful. His arms tightened.

"We're having a baby," he repeated thickly. "You're sure?"

She nodded. "Yes."

"When?"

"In April."

"You're sure? You're absolutely sure?"

"Yes."

"Why didn't you tell me before?"

"I've been afraid."

"Do you —" he paused, taking a deep breath. It was a painful question. "Do you want my baby?"

The tears flicked off her lashes and her fingers dug into his arms. "Yes," she whispered. "Oh, yes."

"Oh, God," he breathed. "Oh, God, thank you." He pulled her very close to him and he kissed her forehead, and he breathed out another thank you, a thank you to her. Then he shuddered — because he was afraid. He was afraid of the truth in the answers that awaited him. If he didn't look for them, he would not find them. And now he knew that he had to look.

"Don't — don't leave me," he asked her again. And again, he forced himself to take a deep breath. "Please, Gayle, don't walk away from me, from us, from our future. I'll see this witch doctor of yours. I'll do anything if you'll stay."

She looked up at him and she seemed to wilt then against him, exhausted. She touched his cheek, and it seemed that an easy flow of tears would come to her eyes again. She swallowed them back. "I love you, Brent. I just need you to help me."

He caught her hand and kissed it. "I don't — I can't — believe in reincarnation. But I'll see the doctor, Gayle. And I swear, I'll try. I'll do whatever you both want. But we've got to make it together, okay?"

She nodded. She sighed and leaned her head against him, and in a few minutes he knew that she had fallen asleep, worn and exhausted. He picked her up and laid her on the bed, and then he lay down beside her, watching her as she slept.

Loving her.

He touched her cheek and he softly stroked the length of her arm, and he ran just the tips of his fingers, lightly, low over her abdomen. They were going to have a child.

It hadn't really sunk in, but it gave him a thrill of gladness. He had been afraid there that . . . she wouldn't want a baby. Not his baby.

He leaned over and kissed her belly through the flannel fabric. "I'll make it right," he promised her softly. "I swear, I'll make it right."

But when he lay back to sleep, he felt bleak. He didn't know if he could make it right or not. He still couldn't understand what the hell it was that was wrong.

When Gayle wearily opened her eyes in the morning, Brent was fully clothed, sitting down by her side, and wearing a rueful smile.

"Hi," he said softly.

"Hi," she returned.

He kissed her forehead. "You need to get dressed. I called Marsha Clark. She's on her way over."

"What?" Gayle demanded, propping herself up on her elbows.

"I said —"

She didn't let him finish. She threw her arms around him. "Thank you, Brent."

"I love you."

"I love you too. Hurry."

Fifteen minutes later, Gayle came down the stairs. She smiled, seeing that Marsha had arrived already.

She was even more striking on a second meeting, Gayle thought. She was so very finely built, with such delicate features, fair skin, that fashionable mop of hair, and her mammoth dark eyes. She and Brent were down in the ballroom; Gayle heard their voices and quickly found them there.

She was glad that Brent instantly slipped an arm around her shoulders to bring her against him as she greeted Marsha. It would have been easy to have felt a twinge of envy. Marsha was so beautiful, and Brent was at his tall, dark, handsome best in a navy pullover and new jeans. But watching Marsha's warm brown eyes fall over the two of them together, Gayle was glad. She felt that the woman had shrewdly and quickly assessed them, and that the assessment had been a good one.

Marsha believed in them. She seemed to know that Brent still doubted her, but she believed in the two of them. Gayle stretched out her hand to her and told her, "Thank you. Thank you for coming out here, and thank you for coming so quickly."

"It's rare, very rare, to find someone who sees the past as you do, Mrs. McCauley. This is a privilege for me. I'm excited to be here, and I hope very much to help you."

"I've been trying to show her the house."

"That's nice. Do you like it?" Gayle asked.

"It's a wonderful house. I'm amazed that it has stayed in the family so long. Most of these old places wind up in the public domain."

"Well, this one might too, one day. For the time being, I think that we can keep it," Brent told her. "Shall we go? I'll show you the upstairs."

Marsha Clark nodded, but she didn't move. She looked at the ballroom, and then she looked at the two of them. "Strange, I don't like that room very much."

"Gayle doesn't care for it either," Brent said; then he started out, leading the two women along. He paused to show Marsha the library, the new kitchen, the music room, and the parlor. Then they went back to the passage and started up the stairs. "Mr. McCauley," Marsha said, "I had the distinct impression yesterday that you wouldn't be interested in seeing me. Did something happen last night to change that?"

Brent paused, glancing at Gayle. She lowered her head quickly, knowing how he hated others to know the intimate details of the things that passed between them.

But he answered Marsha. "Yes, something happened. I had one of those blackout things I'm sure Gayle told you about."

Gayle still didn't look up. She could feel Marsha's eyes on her with interest. "What happened?"

"Um . . . the usual," she murmured uneasily. Then she looked up, realizing that Brent and Marsha were laughing — obviously, there could be nothing *usual* about any of the happenings. Gayle gazed at Brent with a little apology. "I think that he was Percy from the moment I came home. He accused me of things. He frightened me, but he didn't . . . he didn't really hurt me. We — er — made love and then he passed out." She knew that she was flushing. Brent was staring at her very peculiarly, and he appeared acutely uncomfortable too.

"Our bedroom is to the right," he said flatly on the landing. "Ahead was my great-great-uncle's bedroom. And to the left is my studio."

"I'd love to see your studio," Marsha told him. "May I? I don't mean to pry into your artistic endeavors. I know that artists can be very touchy people."

"Brent's not like that," Gayle said.

Marsha smiled at her quick defense. Brent assured her that he really didn't mind.

Gayle and Brent stood back together as Marsha walked through the room inspecting canvases in their various stages of completion. "You're very, very talented, Mr. McCauley," she murmured.

"Thank you."

Marsha looked up and smiled at last. "Are you ready, Mr. McCauley?"

"Ready?"

"For hypnosis."

"Hypnosis," he repeated blankly.

Marsha laughed. "Ask your wife; it's really not so bad. If I'm going to help you, I have to get to the root of the problem. Are you willing?"

Brent grew so tense that Gayle could feel all his muscles constricting, one by one. "I have to warn you, Dr. Clark, that I don't really believe in all this."

"That's fair," Dr. Clark said amiably. "As long as you give me an open mind and don't fight me."

"I won't fight you," he promised quietly. Gayle wondered if she had ever loved him as much as she did at that moment. It was almost like selling his soul, and he was willing to do it, for her.

"Come on, then, shall we? The parlor will do well, I think."

They went back down to the parlor. Dr.

Clark asked Brent if he would prefer to sit or lie down. He didn't have any preference. Gayle suggested that he stretch out on the couch. She watched as Marsha Clark judged where his vision would fall, then attached her little spiral mechanism to the wall.

"Have you ever been hypnotized, Mr. McCauley?"

"Brent, please. And no, never."

"Then relax. Just relax."

"No watch fob dangling before the eyes, huh?" Brent asked. Gayle smiled. He sounded nervous.

Marsha grinned and sat in the wing chair across from Brent. She drew her tape recorder from her briefcase and set it on the table. Brent looked at it suspiciously.

"A water recording. You'll hear it in a minute," she assured him. "I'm not taping you this session, though I might want to in the future."

"Will Gayle be here?" Brent asked her.

"Not ten feet away from you. Are you ready?"

Brent looked pained one more time, his head and neck stretched up on the sofa. Then he nodded, and lay back down.

Gayle's fingers bit into her chair as Dr. Clark began talking to him. She told him to watch the spiral, and to relax. Relax his fingers, relax his toes. Relax his calves, his thighs, his arms, his back, vertebra by vertebra . . .

The gentle sound of running water filled the room. Relax, relax . . . life is peaceful and life is beautiful. Brent was tired and his eyes and his body were heavy, and he must close his eyes and sleep.

At three sharp raps, Dr. Clark told him, he would awaken and feel refreshed. Did he understand her?

Yes, he did.

"I want you to go back. Far back. Into another life. I want you to become Percy now, Brent. Do you understand me?"

Gayle waited, barely breathing.

"Yes," Brent said.

But it wasn't Brent. It was Percy. And Percy began to talk, obediently answering every question.

CHAPTER
19

PERCY

THE MANOR HOUSE, VIRGINIA,
COUNTRYSIDE
AND VALLEY FORGE
WINTER 1777

Tired, dusty, and worn, he paused, a sudden thrill coming to his heart.

He was home.

He could see down the long, curving path to the manor house; he could see the slaves out in the fields and the rich acres of tobacco and other crops. He could see smoke coming from the chimneys of the curing houses, and he knew that fine Virginia hams were being prepared for the long winter ahead.

Someone must have spotted him. Someone must have given word that he was home, for as he spurred Goliath into a gallop and raced toward the house, she was there.

She appeared first on the veranda. She was dressed in muslin, a gown of white and flowers, the picture of beauty. She saw him and her hands flew to her mouth, and he knew that tears touched her eyes, for they glittered beneath the sun.

Then she began to run, running toward him down the long path. Percy reined in Goliath and slipped from his back, catching his wife as she dashed into his arms, swinging her around and around and then holding her close. She touched his cheeks and she trembled, and then she touched again and he impatiently swept her to him and gave her a deep, heady kiss. It had been so long. So very long since he had held her. He kissed her to taste her; he touched her to savor the softness of her form, to remember . . .

"You're home," she cried excitedly.

"I've a week," he told her.

"A week!"

He shrugged. "It's better than nothing. Come, let's get up to the house."

The slaves greeted him as they walked to the house. He waved to them all, then paused just a moment to speak with the foreman, telling him they could talk in the morning. In the passage, he saw old Ramsay and asked if a bath could be fixed for him, posthaste, up above in the bedroom.

Then his eyes were all for his wife again. He laughed suddenly and swept her up into his arms and ran the length of the stairs. She laughed and protested, clinging tightly to him, swearing that he would kill them both. In their bedroom, old Ramsay had just laid wood in the fireplace, and two of the house-boys were carting in water to the tub. Katrina tried to be sober, since everyone about her seemed to wear knowing grins.

"Percy! We mustn't behave so!" she protested in a whisper.

"Nonsense! My God, my darling, I have been gone so long. I have seen hell, and here I am home, and before God, I have hungered for my wife."

Still, she would stand upon her own feet. She would instruct the boys as to the amount of water. Percy sat upon the bed, watching her contentedly. She was so beautiful. She was spring in endless winter; she was not only his lover but his friend, and during his long absences, she had cared for the estate and earned the respect of his slaves and his freemen and even his foreman and tenant farmers. She was the perfect lady of his house.

When Ramsay and the boys were gone, she stood by the tub, shy and proper. "Oh, your boots!" she cried and she flew to him, falling to her knees to help him off with them.

"You mustn't. I am filthy."

"I care not if you're caked in mud," she swore, and she paused and the shyness was out of her eyes as she met his. "Oh, Percy!" she cried, and she rose to throw herself into his arms. They rolled together on the bed and he kissed her again, feeling the fires in his blood rise, and the longing in his heart.

He sighed though and parted from her, for he felt that he wore the blood of the battlefield and did not want to bring it into their bed. She rose with him in silence, somehow understanding, and she helped him strip down to his skin, then murmured, "I must give this uniform to Anne to be cleaned and mended, and I shall come back."

She was gone. Percy stepped into the tub and he leaned his head back against it, inhaling the steam and savoring the luxury. He closed his eyes. God bless his home! Still so far from the scene of battle. He had changed in the last few years, he knew, changed drastically. Even last year, when the Declaration of Independence had been drafted and accepted, his excitement had still ridden so high. They had been glorious men then, patriots furthering a glorious cause. But since then, Percy had seen battle again and again. He had crossed the British lines in New York, and he had been able to return. But a young man named Nathan Hale had done the same — and he had not returned. He had been hanged by the British, swearing that he regretted he had but one life to give to his country. Glorious cause, glorious death . . . but still life was over, and young Hale lay rotting in the earth. Still he had been executed. It had been a clean, quick death. Percy could not forget the men who did not die cleanly. He had ridden with Washington. He scouted and he spied and he always returned to the scene of the battle. He had shoved his bayonet into the bellies of many young men; he had seen death glaze their eyes, he had seen blood spurt from their bellies. He had ridden over the field after the battle; he had known the despair of the mortally wounded who would take their time to die. He had seen marvelous victory, when Washington had commanded them across the Delaware, and he had known defeat, at the Battle of Brandywine. Freedom was glorious, but in battle lay the pits of hell, and though he would never forget that he fought for God-given rights, he was an older soldier now, battle-worn and battle-weary.

He opened his eyes suddenly, for he felt her touch. Katrina was kneeling down beside the tub, and her ever blue gaze was upon him with worry and tenderness as she moved a cloth over his shoulders, scrubbing and massaging them. He smiled at her lazily, his eyes closing slightly, and she laughed breathlessly, for his thoughts now were so easy to read. She kissed his cheek, then soaped the stubble of beard there. She stroked his chest in circles, swirling cloth and soap there. Then she hesitated, but he caught her hand beneath the water and whispered tensely, "Touch me!" and she did. He sank back, awhirl in the sensation; then his eyes opened again and he reached for her, soaking her. "Percy!" she cried, and then "Percy!" she laughed; and he rose from the wet tub and carried her over to their bed.

He drowned there in the sweet sensations of their love, and he wondered how he had ever lived away from her. He loved her so much. She was so giving. She was a balm poured upon him, a sweet oil that soothed and revived him. Her fingers were magic and her whispers were a gentle stream that washed away pain and sorrow and never failed to bring the pure, radiant beauty of life.

He didn't know how long they lay there. Making love heatedly, then lazily, then beginning all over again, languorously, sweetly. Day became night, and she rose to light a candle. He watched her in the new soft light, recalling every curve and line of her, desperately implanting in his mind every slope and curve, the fullness of her breasts, the dip of her spine, the twin dimples upon the sultry slope of her buttocks. She came back to him and lay beside him and took his head upon her lap, smoothing back his hair. In time, she mentioned that she would see to his supper, and he told her not to leave. She laughed and promised earnestly that she would be back.

He slept then. And when he awoke, she was back. She had his saddlebags with her, and she sat upon the floor in the dim candlelight. She had been cleaning them, he saw, but she was no longer. She had emptied them, and she stared with concern and distress upon the sketches that he had done. And when she lifted her eyes to his, knowing he had wakened, her eyes reflected many of the horrors he had known. "Percy!" she whispered to him. "They are so sad, they are so awful . . ."

He rose from the bed and came to her. He glanced over the sketches he had done and took them from her, rolling them up. "I did not mean for you to see them."

"It is so awful. That young boy —"

"He was just thirteen, with the fife and drum corps."

"My love," she whispered, and she set her arms around him. They stayed there on the floor, holding each other close, then she told him that she had his supper on a tray. He thanked her for the luxury, returning to bed with the tray. He ate and listened while she told him about the affairs of the manor and the farms. Then he urged her back into bed with him and they shared the last of the food upon the tray, and then the food was forgotten as he clung fast to her again.

At last she roused herself to ask him about the army, and he sighed and told her that the British were in Philadelphia.

"Is my brother there?" she asked him.

"So I have heard," Percy told her, and he watched as she shuddered, her eyes lowering. "You need not be afraid of him. If danger comes anywhere near here, I will send James to you. He will take you away. He will take you west, into the Ohio Valley."

"I am not afraid," she said. But he could see that she was, and Percy wondered why.

"I will protect you. I will always protect you. I would die for you, my love, and you know it."

"Oh, Percy! Do not say that! Don't talk of death, please!"

He kissed her and promised her that he would not. "Our army," he told her, "is holing up in a little place called Valley Forge."

She was silent for a moment and then she said, "The General's wife will be there. She will winter with her husband."

Percy frowned. "Yes, probably."

"Then I will come too."

"Katrina, Katrina, you cannot imagine the conditions! The food is horrid and rotten, as often as not; it becomes bitter, bitter cold there. There is terrible disease there and the wounded and —"

"You are there. It will not matter what else. Percy, I will come with you; I will be there too."

He spent the rest of the night arguing with her, but she had her way with an argument. She did not fight him but loved him instead, meeting each cross word with a kiss and each husbandly command with a soft, enticing sweep of her hair against his naked belly. He never remembered saying that she could, but in the end, it was agreed that she would.

First they enjoyed his week at home. They rode over the landscape and they picnicked by the river. Percy met with his foreman, and then he spent long, lazy afternoons with his wife. Here, then, was another world. Here was peace and beauty.

The idyll came to an end, though. Percy knew that he had to get back. There was a battle lull for the winter, but there would be raids and covert activities, and he knew that the Old Man would be depending on him. There was always the desperate need for quinine.

In late November they rode together back to Pennsylvania. Percy was proud of his wife, for she accepted the cold and the rigors without complaint. At night they rested together wherever they could find cover and she would always make him smile, for no matter what the circumstances, they seemed to find a way to make love. In the firelight she would touch his cheek with wonder and ask him if they would always feel the same, and he would realize how very lucky he was. It was no longer an affair; they were man and wife now, yet the sweet, thrilling excitement was still there, the near savage desire to love her each time he saw her.

He was impressed again when they

reached the brutal quarters at Valley Forge. Katrina was quick to help with nursing the sick and wounded, quick to understand their difficulties. He knew that the wounded men thought of her as an angel of mercy, and he was proud.

Perhaps it was inevitable; their first spat came when he told her that he must ride out. She caught him before he could leave their tiny quarters. "Where are you going?"

"Out, Katrina, on a raid. It is all right."

"No! You can't go today; you must get someone else —"

"Katrina, I am an officer in the army. You must understand this; you have known this!"

But today, she was nearly hysterical. "Percy, I am afraid! Please, just today! Claim that you are sick, claim that —"

"Katrina!" Although he was sorry she was distraught, he caught her arms and set her from him. He said, "I must go. Please, Katrina!" He kissed her, but she was inconsolable.

It stayed with him as he mounted up with his men, that feeling of hers, that sense of foreboding. It was a dark day too, frigidly cold and overcast. He and his small party headed east, toward a village outside of Philadelphia. There was supposed to be a cache of British guns and medicines hidden in a farmhouse there.

A two hours' ride brought them to their objective. Percy had his men hold back among the trees. He counted Redcoats about and decided that there were about twenty. His own small band numbered ten, but they were becoming well versed in the ways of Indian warfare.

Percy silently ordered his men about, Welsh and Trelawny in back of the barn, Stern and Hood behind the wagons. In a matter of seconds, the lookouts had been killed, and the men converged to attack the Redcoats in the barn.

It would have been a smooth operation. No more men would have died; Percy would have taken the supplies and left the Redcoats alive.

But at that moment, a force arrived behind them. A Tory force, not of mercenaries, but of British regulars. Percy swore, reloading his musket, as heavy fire broke out around the barn.

He called orders to Hood. Hood and four of his men burst out of the barn, pulling a cart full of the weapons and medicaments behind them. Percy tried valiantly with the rest of his little band to hold off the Redcoats.

Fire was heavy and constant. Black powder and smoke merged with the gray of the sky. In a lull, Percy called to his remaining troops; they would make a run for it.

It was nearly successful. They tore out of the barn on their mounts, and they raced through the powder and the snow. Then Percy screamed, for a musket ball tore into his shoulder. The agony was like raw fire shooting through him. Then another ball caught him in the left rib. The force was so great that he was lifted and thrown from Goliath. He struck the snow-covered ground, hard.

For moments, for long, long moments, he could not remember anything. Then he opened his eyes, and she was there.

Katrina was there. Tears filled her eyes and she held him, and she tried to smooth the dirt and blood from his face. She was so beautiful, with rich fur framing her face. He reached up to touch her.

She did not look at him then. She was staring upward. Dazed and in agony, Percy followed her gaze.

They were surrounded. Surrounded by a band of British regulars.

He wanted to rise; he wanted to protect her. But blackness was all around him as a thick, dark cloud of cannon smoke enveloped him. He was losing consciousness, he knew. Darkness was all around him. He wanted to talk; he wanted to rise; he wanted so desperately to fight . . .

"My, my, my, what have we here?" a voice demanded. "Why, 'tis my Lady Seymour."

Percy dimly heard her cry out, saying that she was his wife and no longer a Seymour.

She knew the man, though. Percy was keenly aware that she knew him.

Then he was aware of nothing, for the absolute blackness claimed him.

CHAPTER
20

He heard a rapping, and he awoke, but he did not awake feeling refreshed. He awoke with such a soaring, splitting headache that he could hardly bear it. He swore, pressing his temples fiercely as he slid his legs to the floor.

"Brent!"

There was the most awful tone of fear in Gayle's voice. She ran to his side, kneeling down beside him, reaching for his hands.

"Dammit!" he swore at her, reeling with the pain. "Can't you leave me alone for a minute?"

She jumped back, startled by his attitude. He could see the hurt in her eyes and he was sorry, but he couldn't even say it — his head hurt so badly.

"Do you remember what happened?" Dr. Clark asked him.

He cast her a murderous glare. "Yeah. I fell asleep and now I'm awake and I think I've got a migraine that could kill. Excuse me, will you?"

He started to the door as fast as he could, wanting only to be alone, wanting to down a dozen aspirin and stick his head beneath an ice-cold spray of water.

"Brent!" Gayle called to him.

"What!"

"Don't you remember anything? You came back as him; you came back as Percy, you —"

"For God's sake, will you lay off, Gayle! Can't you see that I'm in pain?"

He slammed out of the room. Helplessly, and near tears, Gayle raised her hands to Dr. Clark. "What good is it? What good is any of it? Neither of us can remember. He'll never believe any of it. He doesn't want to believe it."

Marsha Clark smoothed her skirts. "Rome wasn't built in a day, Mrs. Mc-Cauley," she murmured unhappily.

"Oh, my God!" Gayle murmured suddenly. She raced from the room and through the passage to the kitchen, and then out through the colonnade to the old kitchen. She sank to the ground by the cupboard and found the rolled sheets of vellum. She ran with them back to the parlor and stretched out the sheets. "Look! Look at these! I bought them because they resembled Brent's work so closely. They *are*

433

his work, aren't they?"

Dr. Clark hesitated for a moment. "I think so," she murmured. She smiled at Gayle. "Just like I think that his recent works, upstairs, are of Katrina."

Gayle sat back, gasping. "They're — they're me. I modeled for him. I sat up there —"

"But the woman he painted is different from you, isn't she? Just a little different."

Gayle sank to the couch in anguish. It had been awful, so awful to watch! She could still recall perfectly the way that he had screamed and jerked and twitched in terrible agony, feeling again the bullets that had torn through him.

"I don't understand," she wailed. "Did he stop because — because he died then? Because he could not go on? And if so, why does he hate me so much? Or Katrina? She must have loved him very much; she followed him into war. Why?"

Marsha sighed softly. "I don't think that Percy died then. I think that maybe whatever went wrong started then. You and Percy both refuse to go any farther. You were willing and talkative until we came to the point of the marriage. Then you insisted that you were happy, but you would go no further. Brent . . . he seems to have the same blocks. Whatever came next is so disturbing that, even under hypnosis, neither of you will speak about it." She rolled up the vellum sheets. "May I take one of these? I'll return it to you soon, I promise." Dr. Clark took the first of the vellum war sketches; she set the others by her feet.

"Yes, yes, of course," Gayle said absently. She looked at the doctor. "So what do we do now?" she whispered desperately.

"I'll tell you what we'll do," Brent said suddenly from the doorway. "We'll just get out of this house."

"What?" Startled, Gayle glanced at him. He was leaning there with a drink in his hand. He looked ravaged and haggard.

He lifted his glass to her. "Drink? Dr. Clark?"

"No, thank you," Marsha murmured.

"Brent —"

"Gayle, I've had it. I've had it with all this."

"Don't you even want to listen?" Gayle demanded.

"No!" He came into the room, and it seemed that he was barely leashing his anger. "No, I want to be done with all this nonsense! Maybe it's the damn house, at this point. Who the hell knows, who the hell cares! Let's get out of here."

"Brent! You came back, I swear it. We were married and we were happy —"

"So tell me why the hell are we so damned miserable now?"

Marsha Clark smiled and repeated her explanation. "You are blocking me. Both of you. Whatever lies there is very painful — I can't make you go back to it. If I could . . ."

"If you could?"

She shrugged. "It could help you understand what happened in the past that's still bothering you now, and it could make you both feel a lot better. But it could be dangerous. It's frightening to play with the past. It's possible to become lost within it."

Brent let out a sound of utter skepticism. Gayle longed to hit him.

Dr. Clark cleared her throat. "Maybe it would be best to stop. Maybe the two of you should get away, take a little vacation."

"Thanks, doc," Brent said crudely. "Thanks a lot. Maybe we'll just do that."

"Brent!" Gayle said with amazement. "Would you please quit being so damned rude!"

Dr. Clark stood up, smiling at Gayle, as serene and unruffled as ever. "It's quite all right; he's not feeling well. Please feel free to call me any time if you should need me."

"Dr. Clark, please —"

"Call me," Marsha Clark assured Gayle.

Gayle walked her to the door. "I'm sorry. I'm so sorry. He's a wonderful man, I've never seen him so rude —"

"Please, don't apologize. I'm sure that the regression experience hurt him terribly." She tapped the sheets she was carrying. "Take care now and call me. Or I'll call you if I come up with anything."

Gayle nodded and waved at Marsha as she drove away. She saw David Gareth, one of the gardeners, out in the field, and she waved and smiled. Then she walked wearily back into the house.

Brent was still in the parlor, stretched out with his drink in his hand, his feet on the coffee table. She had never seen him so morose. He closed his eyes, wincing, then rubbed his temples. She bit her lip; he was obviously in so much physical pain beyond the torment of confusion.

"Brent?" she whispered.

His eyes opened. He reached out a hand to her. "Come here."

"We need to talk."

"Just sit with me for a few minutes, please."

She couldn't refuse him. She curled up beside him and she stroked his nape, pushing hard against the muscles. Then she lay against him and they just sat together in silence while time ticked away and the morning wore on. Gayle felt so tired.

Finally she rose and she still didn't speak. She walked over to the window and she stared out at the beauty of the veranda and the colors of the day.

"You promised me," she said softly at last. "Brent — you were going to try."

He sighed. "I did try, Gayle."

"But you didn't hear yourself. You still don't understand, you don't know —"

"I know that I came out of that thing — whatever it was that she did to me — wanting to die. I can't do it again. And I won't let you do it again."

"Brent —"

His feet fell to the floor and he rose, coming over to her. He took her hands in his. "We can't play around with it anymore. We can't. We're going to have a baby."

"That's precisely why —"

"Marsha Clark said herself that it was dangerous to play with the past."

"Brent! We have to keep trying to work out this problem."

He shook his head, bringing her close to him. "I think that we need to get out of here. I think that we should just go. We should take a trip to the airport and grab the first plane to anywhere that strikes our fancy."

"Can we really run away, do you think?" she whispered.

"Yes." He pulled her more tightly against him. "Do you remember the night that Uncle Hick died? He was crazy about you, Gayle; he didn't tell me not to bring you to this house because he wanted to hurt you. He was afraid. He knew that we shouldn't be here."

"You really think that it's the house?"

"God, I don't know what I really think. But I do think that I want to get away for a while."

She nodded, searching out his eyes. "I'm going to go up and start packing. Are you coming?"

Absently, he nodded. He rubbed the back of his neck and picked up his drink and slumped back to the couch.

"Brent?"

"I just need a minute." He gave her a smile. "I'm trying to get rid of this headache. Go ahead, I'll be right along. Maybe we'll fly down to Paradise. There's nothing — absolutely nothing — old on that island."

She smiled with him, then left him in the dim coolness of the room to head up the passage stairs. Her spirits were lifting already with the idea of leaving, forgetting it all, and just spending time together. Maybe it was the house. Maybe they were all insane, she, Marsha, and Brent.

In their bedroom, though, she paused, sinking down weakly to the bed. No. She hadn't understood what had happened when she'd undergone the hypnosis herself, but she had seen and heard Brent. It might be impossible; it might be against all rhyme and reason, but she believed that it was true. She had lived before, in a life long ago, and she had been a young woman from Kent named Katrina who had fallen in love with a Virginian named Percy.

She smiled a little sadly. Maybe there was a little rhyme and reason to it. She had always felt, from the very beginning, that she had known Brent so well. That she had waited and waited a lifetime for him. She had fallen into his arms so quickly, so ready to love him, so intensely, desperately passionate. Maybe she was destined to love him forever, into eternity; it was a love so deep.

With a little sigh she rose and dragged her suitcase from the closet and began to pack.

An hour later as she threw the last few items in her suitcase, the phone started ringing. She wondered for a moment if Brent would get it downstairs; then she thought that the machine would get it; and then she decided to pick up the bedroom extension on the side of the bed herself.

"Hello?" She caught it on the third ring.

"Gayle? This is Marsha. Dr. Clark."

"Oh! Hello!" Gayle heard the excitement in the woman's voice.

"Gayle, I've got some interesting news for you."

"Yes?"

"Well, I checked into the sketches, and I checked into your property. The sketch is worth a mint, by the way. I had it authenticated. It's an Ainsworth."

Gayle frowned. "An Ainsworth?"

"Yes, yes! I'm at the library now! Ainsworth! Percy and Katrina were Ainsworths, Gayle. He built the house. He wasn't just a revolutionary — he was a very popular artist in his time."

Gayle's fingers tightened around the phone cord. "Then — then, Percy and Katrina were real people, and they did fall in love and get married?"

"Yes! I'm coming back as soon as I can with copies of the documents I've managed to find. I don't have the whole story, but I understand a great deal of it."

"Did he die in Pennsylvania?"

"No. They died on the same day." She hesitated just a moment. "In your house."

Gayle gasped. "Then . . . why, why did he hate her so much?"

"There were a few things that happened over the years. But in the end, he thought that she betrayed him."

"Did she?"

"I don't think so. But what matters is what he believed, isn't it?"

"I — I suppose."

"Listen, I'm on my way over. I hope your husband won't mind. I hope he'll at least hear me out. It's terribly important that he understands."

"He — he'll listen. I'll make him," Gayle promised. "Hurry!"

"I will."

Gayle hung up the phone and sank back to the bed in a daze. It was frightening. It was terrifying. She had lived before and loved before and she had died, right here, in this house.

She jumped up, anxious to tell Brent. She ran down the stairs and hurried to the parlor.

It wasn't until she opened the door that she realized that he should have been upstairs long ago himself.

He was sitting on the floor, looking at the rest of the vellum sketches which she had so carelessly left by the chair. His dark head was bent over them, and his fingers were trembling as he held them.

She should have told him, she thought with a pang of deep regret. She should have told him long ago that they existed.

She cleared her throat, trying to think of something to say now. He heard her and, standing, instantly dropped the pictures.

"Where did you get these?"

"I — found them at a barn sale."

She didn't want to stay there. Suddenly she was frightened, more frightened than she had ever been of him. She backed out of the room murmuring to him, wondering if he understood her or not. "Marsha is on her way back here. She found out —"

"Where the hell do you think you're going now?" He strode across the room and he caught her arm, wrenching it hard. She landed on the floor and struggled to sit up, meeting his eyes as he towered over her. "What did I do?" she asked desperately.

"What did you do?" he whispered the words. He squatted on the balls of his feet again, and he reached out to touch her cheeks. "I didn't want to believe it. All those years . . . and the rumor had been about so long, but had I heard it? Nay, my wife! For love is deaf as well as blind, is it not? You went to him. You went to him! Not only in

Philadelphia, but again when the ship entered into the river. And now. Even now."

He came to his feet, grasping her by her hair, pulling her along with him to the window. "They are out there, aren't they?"

"Who? Brent, who?" He didn't answer her. He stared out the window, his eyes alert and wary. "Percy!" she whispered and he turned to her, dark eyes afire. "Who is out there, Percy, please tell me who?"

"Who! The British, Katrina." He pulled her to him; he pressed his lips against her forehead, and then he laughed. "All these years I have loved you. And all these years you have been betraying me again and again." He gripped her shoulders and he started to shake her. She struggled against him, crying out, trying to force his arms from hers. Then his hands settled against her throat and she went dead still, afraid that any motion would instigate him further. Tears stung her eyes as he stroked her throat and stared down at her, barely seeing her, if he saw her at all.

"They will hang me, you know. You've known it all along. They let me escape before so that you could keep them apprised of my movements. I always said that I loved you so much that I would die for you. And I will do just that, won't I? They are out there, aren't they? When I run, they will take me and they will hang me by the neck until I am dead."

"No!" Gayle whispered, shaking.

"My God!" he exploded. "I would die and die gladly, were it just a part of war." He shoved her from him with a fury, then slapped her so that she fell to the floor again. "Whore! My God, how could you have done such a thing?"

"Stop it! Stop it!" Tears streamed down her cheeks. She tossed back her hair and hugged her knees to her chest, shaking then in a fit of chills. "There's no one there. I swear to you, there's no one there —"

He came beside her, jerking her back up into his arms again, and he smiled with all the haunted, bitter sadness she could imagine, winding his fingers into her hair. "I'll not let you go tonight, love. If it is to be our last, so be it. We will be together, and you will hold me through the night. Come!"

He jerked her along with him, going from window to window, cautiously peering outside. "Stop!" she pleaded with him again and again. She tried to assure herself that he had never really hurt her, never seriously hurt . . .

He had never tried to kill her and surely, please God, he would not do so now. But he was brutally rough, dragging her along with him, checking every window. In the ballroom he pulled her down. He cast a leg over hers and pinned her wrists and held her there, listening.

"You're hurting me!" she told him. His leg was heavy and tense and his weight was hard against her. "Please, Brent, the baby —"

He eased up and stared down at her. He seemed shocked. "Where is the boy?"

"What — what boy?"

"My son! Where is he?"

"He's fine," she lied quickly. "He's fine. I sent him into Richmond for safety."

He touched her cheek. "Have you turned him into a little Redcoat too, my love?"

She shook her head, trying to ease from him. Marsha was due back any second now. What would he do? How would he behave toward Marsha? Was he capable of being really dangerous? No! her heart cried out; this was Brent.

She was wrong, a part of her insisted. It was Percy she was dealing with now, and he was from a different age. He was still fighting a war in which he had been betrayed.

"Percy!" she whispered, and she flung her arms around him and kissed him. "I swear it," she whispered against his lips. "I swear that I have not betrayed you. Hold me. I love you. I love you, for all time. Believe in me, hold me . . ."

His eyes met hers and he kissed her back. She set her arms around him and she rolled with him, until she came atop him. She had to get him to hold on, to wait . . .

"My love, give me a moment," she pleaded and, playfully, she pushed away from him. "Wait for me. Wait . . ."

She brought a finger to her lips, and offered him a secret smile, then rose. He rolled upon an elbow to watch her. She kept smiling at him as she strode slowly toward the door.

But the doorbell rang then, followed by a pounding on the door. He was on his feet in an instant. "Bitch! Whore!" he shouted. She screamed and ran and he caught her, slamming her up against the wall. "You will not go to him! So they are here now!" He pressed against her, glaring into her face. "You'll not go to him now!"

"Percy, please —"

He pushed away, and when she tried to catch his arm he shook her off with vehemence. "Percy!" she screamed again, scrambling up to her feet, chasing after him again. He was already in the passage, reaching for the front door. "Brent, Percy, please!"

He threw it open just as she came pounding against his back. It was Marsha, but she wasn't alone. Geoff was with her. Standing and staring open-mouthed at Brent.

"You!"

Brent reached out and caught Geoff by the lapels, dragging him inside.

Geoff tried to break away from him. "What the hell is the matter with you, McCauley?"

"You Tory son of a bitch!" he swore, swinging his fist into Geoff's jaw. Gayle screamed as she heard the sickening sound of the impact. Geoff stared at them both in astonishment, then slithered to the floor.

"Geoff!" Gayle cried, falling down beside him. She screamed when she was instantly dragged back to her feet by her hair and pressed hard against Brent's chest. His eyes were nearly black now; his brow was knit with fury. "Even now! Even now you would fall at your lover's feet. Whore! Whore!" He drew his arm back as if he would hit her, yet this time he did not. A glistening of tears suddenly glazed his eyes, and one trickled down his cheek. "Whore," he repeated in a soft whisper. "Beloved, beloved whore."

Then his eyes closed and he fell against her. She gasped, trying to catch him lest he hurt himself. She hadn't the strength. She fell, with him atop her.

"Here, here, let me help you," Marsha said quickly, stepping into the passage. She eased Brent's weight from Gayle's body and lifted one of his eyelids. "Dead out," she muttered. "Let's see to this one, shall we?"

Gayle swallowed and nodded and tapped Geoff's cheek, then noticed the swelling of his jaw. "I'll get some ice," she muttered. She ran into the kitchen and in her haste knocked cubes from the tray all over the floor. She wrapped ice into a towel, then she searched beneath the sink for a bottle of brandy and hurried back out to the passage.

Thankfully, Geoff was already coming around. Gayle whispered his name woefully and offered him both the ice and the brandy. Geoff gingerly placed the ice against his jaw.

"What the hell did he do before he went into art? Box?"

Gayle shook her head, and then she burst into tears. Marsha took the brandy from Geoff and gave it to Gayle and told her to take a long swallow. She did so. "Of course, we could just get some glasses, couldn't we?" she offered with a wry smile.

"Let's get Brent to a couch," Geoff said.

Between them, they brought Brent into the parlor and laid him upon the couch.

"He's so cold!" Gayle murmured. "Do you think he's all right?"

She was alarmed when Marsha didn't answer right away, and she repeated the question. "Marsha, do you think he's all right?"

"Yes. Yes, I think so."

"Then — ?" Gayle persisted in mild panic. "Marsha, what are you trying to tell me?"

"Well . . . could I have some brandy too, please?"

Geoff went into the kitchen and came back with glasses. Marsha poured them all a shot and lifted her glass. "Cheers."

"Marsha, please, what are you telling me?" Gayle pleaded.

Marsha sighed. "These spontaneous regressions seem to be getting worse and worse. They're reaching a crescendo. I fear the possibility that — that one time, he won't come back."

"Won't come back?"

Marsha nodded. "Like the hypnosis, Gayle. You have to be very careful." She paused, then tried again. "It's like astral projection, in a way. Dangerous, because the soul haunts two places, two bodies, two lives."

"What can I do?"

Marsha sat down and brushed back a lock

of her hair. "Well, you could leave him. Live separate lives this time."

"No, no! I can't do that." The ever ready tears sprang to her eyes. No. She could never leave him. She could threaten, but she could never leave him. She loved him too much.

More than life itself.

"Marsha, help me! I cannot leave him. I love him." She looked desperately from Geoff to Marsha. "Please!" she said softly in an anguished whisper. "Please! Marsha, we're going to have a baby. Help us! Help us to make it work out right . . . this time!"

Marsha shook her head uneasily. "I don't know, I don't know. Percy and Katrina died — here. He was hanged and she was shot in the back, trying to reach him. He had come home in a fury right before the battle of Yorktown, and that was how he was caught. He discovered something, something about her. She couldn't have warned the British; she was killed by one of them herself."

"Then why —"

"Gayle, maybe it doesn't matter what really happened; what is important is what he believed. Do you understand?"

Gayle looked at her a long time and then nodded. "She didn't betray him, but he thought that she did."

451

"Yes, that's what I believe."

"Then what do I do?"

"Go back. Go back again and face it. Face whatever it was that Katrina did and find Percy in the end. Make him see that no matter what else, she did not betray him to the British."

"Can I do that?" she whispered. "Can I change history?"

"I don't know. We can only try."

Geoff cleared his throat. "Maybe you shouldn't, Gayle. It's dangerous. You heard what Marsha said —"

"I have to!" Gayle said desperately. "I have no choice. Please, Marsha!"

"All right."

"Oh, no! You haven't your spiral or your tape —"

"It's all right. Just sit back. Sit back, and I'll talk you through it. You must relax. Relax your fingers and relax your toes and think back. Relax . . . Think of cool meadows and soft breezes. Relax . . . Feel the cares of the world slip from your body. Feel your eyes grow heavy. Relax, relax . . .

"Go back. Go back to the time when you were Katrina Ainsworth. Go back, go back . . ."

CHAPTER
21

DEATH AND BETRAYAL

PENNSYLVANIA AND VIRGINIA
WINTER 1777 — SPRING 1781

It was bitterly cold. Of all things, she would
remember that it was bitterly cold. Blood was
rapidly staining Percy's coat and spreading
onto her fur, and what she could feel more
than anything else was frigid cold. Snow flur-
ries had begun to fall against the darkness of
the day; they flecked Percy's lashes and his
features and seemed barely paler than his
face.

He was probably dying. No. She would not
let him die. She was determined that he would
not die, even as his life's blood seeped away.

But if he lived — if he survived the bullets
and the surgeon's efforts to remove them —
would he not live only to meet the hangman's noose?

They were alone, for although men rushed around them and she could hear horses' hooves trampling the snow, they were alone. It was a sea of red that surrounded them — British troops. And troops commanded by none other than Lord Charles Palmer, her brother's friend, to whom she had reported ridiculous lies for so many months before the outbreak of war. Lord Palmer, tall and golden and elegant — even in his uniform.

Palmer, smiling with a delighted twist of cruelty to his lips. He had her and he had Percy, and Percy would hang.

Lord Palmer dismounted from his horse and stood over them, slapping the reins idly against his thigh. "Well, well, well. Welcome, my Lady Seymour — ah, alas, 'tis no more Seymour, then, is it? Mrs. Ainsworth. Welcome. Come. Take my hand. Rise. I shall have my surgeon see to your husband's wounds."

Katrina ignored the hand he offered her. She edged back, cradling Percy's head. "Thank you — no," she replied icily. "Your surgeon would just as soon slay him as save him, and he would save him only for the executioner's rope."

"Katrina!" Lord Palmer pretended a wounded reproach. "He is a soldier. Perhaps he could live well and merry, after a few years as a prisoner of war. Who can say?" His pleasant smile faded somewhat. "He will die now if he is not attended to. Surely, my dear, you can see that he bleeds to death."

She hesitated, uncertain. It was true that he was bleeding profusely, but she didn't trust Charles Palmer.

And yet what did it matter? Her mind and heart were numb with the cold and fear. Percy was dying. Now! She had to do something, anything, to save his life.

Then she could worry about a hangman's noose.

"Why should you help him?" she demanded of Palmer.

"For old times' sake, my dear. For old times' sake."

He frightened her even more with his courteous and extravagant bow, but she really had little choice. "I wish to be with him when your man removes the musket balls," she said.

"But of course." Palmer waved a hand and two men came forward with a litter. Katrina stood to help them, fighting tears as they rolled her husband upon the horse-drawn conveyance. He would die, she thought; he would die whatever she did.

Yet she could not cease trying to save his life. Her own would be worthless if his were forfeited.

"May I help you mount your horse, Katrina?"

"No, I will stay beside him."

They came to the British camp. Lord Palmer had taken over a small farm manor for his headquarters, while his men and his surgery were stationed in the outbuildings. Running alongside the litter, Katrina was panting and exhausted when they passed by the guards at the manor. Charles, looking down upon her from the height of his magnificent horse, smiled again. "You may stay with him until the surgery is completed and he is sent to bed. Then, please, I shall expect to see you at the house for supper."

His horse pranced against the snow for a moment; then he was off. "This way, m'am," said one of his young officers and she was quick to follow, for they were lifting Percy again, carrying him into the old spinning house, which now contained quickly put together trestle tables for the surgeon.

" 'Tis Percy Ainsworth!" said the man, working hastily to cut away Percy's clothing from the wounds. He was clad in an apron that was marred with blood, and it seemed that his surgery had already been busy that day. He glanced from his silent patient to Katrina, and perhaps he saw the anguish in her eyes, for he added, "The enemy, m'am, but a respected one. A gallant blade, and an honorable one."

"Yes," she whispered, feeling a little encouraged. "Please, can you save him?"

She knew that he was thinking he would save the man only for a rope, but he smiled at her, and she knew, too, that he would do his best. God had granted her this blessing. The surgeon believed in his oath to save lives, and he was a good man who would not let Percy die upon his table. "You may assist me," he told her. He nodded to his two orderlies. "They will need to hold him down."

She bit into her lower lip and did as the man told her, hurrying behind him to take the metal balls probed from Percy's body, to supply the bandages, sutures, needles, and cloth. Percy rose only once when the surgeon probed and dug; he screamed and fought, and then fell silent. Katrina feared she would faint from the agony of seeing his pain, but she did not. And when it was over, she was rewarded. The kindly surgeon smiled at her and said, "I believe it has been a clean operation. He has lost much blood and will not regain consciousness tonight, but he has a chance to live."

"Thank you," Katrina told him. "Thank you so much."

"His life is out of my hands now," he told her, then paused. "I am Captain Jack Trelawny, Mrs. Ainsworth. If I can ever be of assistance . . ."

She thanked him again for his kindness, then anxiously hurried along at Percy's side, for they were moving him to a bed in one of the storage houses. She tried to enter along with him, then started as her way was barred by a cross of bayonets and a lieutenant stepped from the house to speak to her. "The Major General is expecting you now, Mrs. Ainsworth. If you will please follow me . . . ?"

She squared her shoulders and passed him by, feeling dread begin to take hold of her, to cause her to shiver and quake. She would not let them see it, though; these men respected her husband, and she would not prove his wife a coward. She dipped beneath the crossed bayonets. As she had suspected, the guards were at a loss and did not seek to skewer her through.

"Mrs. Ainsworth!"

She spun with all the dignity she could muster. "Lieutenant, I will see to my husband's comfort, then I will come with you."

Percy was set upon a bed. Jack Trelawny

had indeed attended him well. The bandages were clean and he breathed easily. His arm was set in a sling, but he showed no discomfort. His face had lost the terrible gray pallor.

The soldiers left them. She knelt down by his side and she cried, curling her fingers around his. He did not respond. She whispered to him; she told him that she loved him, and she swore to him that it would be all right. She did not know how, but they would be all right.

Percy never moved. He never gave the slightest indication that he heard her. He was far from being out of the woods. Infection could set in; he could come down with pneumonia; his wounds could reopen . . .

"Mrs. Ainsworth!" It was the lieutenant once again. He cleared his throat. "We've orders to bring you now, m'am, one way or the other."

She did not doubt that Charles Palmer would order her dragged to the house. She kissed Percy's cold lips hastily, then stood as regally as she could manage. She came to the doorway and stepped down into the snow, adjusting her cloak. "I am ready now, Lieutenant," she told him quietly.

They trudged through the snow to the farm manor. It was a fine home, made of brick. The lieutenant brought her up the steps to the porch. He left her once the door had opened.

She was in a narrow hallway. Doors led off to the left and to the right, and a dark wooden stairway led up to the second floor.

She wasn't greeted by Lord Palmer, but by a manservant, small and portly, but beautifully liveried. He bowed deeply to her, courteously asking to take her cloak, very much as if she had come to tea. Then he asked her to follow him up the stairway.

On the upper landing, he threw open a door for her. It was a bedroom, a woman's bedroom, with a beautiful canopied bed and soft lace curtains. A fire burned in the grate and before it sat a high-backed wooden bathtub, with steam rising from it. Katrina's mouth tightened as she saw the gown laid out on the bed and the silver tray set on the desk with a flagon of sherry and two crystal glasses.

"Lord Palmer thought you might want to freshen up, Mrs. Ainsworth," the man began cheerfully, then broke off, for Katrina would have none of it. She marched into the room and took the decanter and threw it against the mantel, and spun on the man. "No, I do not want to freshen up! I do not wish to wash away my husband's blood. I will see Lord Palmer now!"

"Please, please, madam —"

"Why, Jonah, what is the problem here?"

Charles Palmer had come to the doorway, resplendent in his lacy sleeves and satin coat and skintight, white uniform breeches. Had he ever muddied himself upon the battlefield? Katrina wondered.

"Mrs. Ainsworth does not wish to avail herself of the facilities," Jonah said respectfully.

"Well, then?" With grave disapproval, Lord Palmer arched a golden brow at Jonah. "Mrs. Ainsworth is a guest. She needn't do anything that she doesn't wish. Katrina? Please? The salon is right across the hall, if you will."

He extended an arm, indicating she should precede him. Katrina nervously did so. She hated having her back to him for one instant. And the more polite and solicitous he grew, the more she began to dread the coming moments.

She kept her head high, though, and swept into the salon. There was a fine, cherrywood desk there, with plush Chippendale chairs set before it. Charles came in behind her, closing the door, and indicating that she should take a chair.

"I would rather stand. I believe our business will be brief."

"I think not, Katrina. Sit."

He came before her and pressed her down to the chair, after which he smiled again, affable and apologetic. He locked his hands behind his back and idly roamed around the room.

"Life is strange, isn't it, Katrina?"

"If you say so, Lord Palmer."

"Please, why should old friends be so formal?"

"We are not old friends."

"Katrina, I am wounded. All those months before the war you came to us with information. You were a loyal girl then. A fine, loyal girl."

"I never gave you information," she said dully, leaning back in the chair to rub her temples. A thunderous headache had begun. "Even then, I was careful never to give you anything you would not have learned in a day or two, anyway. Things that did not matter."

He made a *tsk*ing sound and came around to the desk where another decanter sat. He poured out two glasses and offered her one. She shook her head suspiciously.

"Fine wine, Katrina, and nothing more. Please — is it so much to ask? Drink with me. Your husband lives down there, and I could have cast his carcass to the vultures long ago." He smiled again. Uneasily, she took the wine.

He watched her for a moment, then murmured, "Good, good." He ambled around behind her once again, pausing at the window. "Are you a spy now too, Katrina?" he asked pleasantly.

"No," she murmured dully.

"Then to what do I owe the pleasure of your company here? It was such a boon, my dear, to find you at your husband's side."

She sighed, wondering if he would believe her or not, wondering if she cared. "Intuition, Lord Palmer. I was afraid. When he rode out, I was afraid. And so I followed him."

"How lucky for us!" Palmer murmured. She flinched; he had come up behind her and his hand rested on her shoulder. "Do you know, my dear, I was quite taken with you. I intended to marry you. I would even have married you after your affair with Ainsworth — except that you ran away with him. I was your friend, Katrina. I cared for you so very much."

Katrina held silent. For a few blessed minutes, she wanted to believe that a miracle could occur. That Charles Palmer was offering her friendship. That he would arrange for her and Percy to disappear behind the rebel lines.

"You were my friend," she whispered. Then she spun around, anxious to meet his eyes. She dared to rest her fingers against his. "Oh, Charles! Are you truly my friend? Can you help us? I know that Percy is wanted, but you've power here yourself. You've given him life already; will you help us?"

He withdrew his hand from hers and walked around to draw out the chair and sit behind his desk. He lifted a glass to her.

"I intend to help you."

"Oh, Charles —" she said eagerly, relief sweeping through her.

"For a price!" he interrupted sharply.

She sank back and lowered her eyes. She didn't want to anger him. She wanted to reason with him. "Charles, I — I can't. I — I — am married to him."

He sat back and laughed, really amused with the statement. "So is many a lady will-fully playing a parlor game, my dear. Truly, Katrina, that is one of your greatest attractions, that innocence you maintain through everything."

She winced painfully. "Please, Charles —"

"No. No, I do not please!" He slammed his glass upon the desk and stood, blond and handsome and striking — and cruel. "We will play no more games, Katrina. We will not fight. I will not drag you anywhere, kicking and screaming. I will make it very simple. Your husband lies under my power. Think of me as God, Katrina. I have given him his life, and I can take it away. It is completely up to you. And you know exactly what I want. I will give you about five minutes to decide. If you wish for your husband to live, you will stand up and walk back to that bedroom, cast away those bloodstained garments and scrub away your Yankee stench. If you choose not to do so, I will go out now, this very night, and have him wrenched from his bed, drawn to the square, and hanged. Do you understand your options, Katrina?"

She stared at him, and she prayed that he would say that he did not mean it; he was a British lord, after all. But he did not smile and he did not blink. And he was not lying, she knew. She began to pray that lightning would strike, that the earth would open up and swallow them all whole, that Armageddon would come.

Nothing happened. Seconds ticked away.

"He would rather die," she whispered.

"Perhaps. If he knew." Charles shrugged. "He would never need to know. For such a little, little thing, you can buy him life. He shall never be the wiser, and in the years to come you will be his wife, and not his widow. Are you so ready to see him hang, then? Is his life so cheap to you?"

"You can never understand such a man, Charles. You don't begin to understand honor, and it means everything to him."

"Oh, really? Dead, Katrina, how shall he ever defend you? When he is hanged I will return you to your brother, and he will deal with you as he sees fit. When I finish with you, that is. I am not a barbarous man, but . . ."

She kept staring at him. The pain in her head became such a buzz that she could not bear it, and then it began to dull. She felt nothing but numb.

He came behind her and leaned down to whisper in her ear. "Your time is nearly up. Get up, Katrina. And be ready for me. I will be with you in twenty minutes."

"I don't trust you," she said emotionlessly. "What will prevent you from having Percy hanged one hour from now?"

He went back to the desk and drew out a sheet of paper. He scrawled upon it, then offered it to her. "It is a pass. Back through the British lines. You will give me two days. He will need those two days for recovery, or he will die anyway when you try to move him. Two days, Katrina. Two days, and you will be free."

She remained silent.

"Am I so loathsome, then?" he asked her.

"Yes," she said. But she stood, and she snatched the pass from him.

He smiled, stretching his legs out on the desk. "Well, my dear Katrina, you will try very hard not to show it. Go. Your time is up."

She swung around and she marched back across the hall and into the bedroom. She slammed the door and sank into despair, giving way to the sobs that welled within her.

There was a tap on the door. "Ten minutes, Katrina."

Thankfully, the numbness fell over her again. Heedlessly she rose. Steam no longer rose from the tub and she was glad; the water had gone as cold as her heart.

It was the only way she could bear it.

When the ten minutes had passed, she was waiting for him. The shadows of dusk fell over the room. She bit her lip as he paused, seeing her there; then she closed her eyes as he began to undress her. He's not ancient, she told herself. He was young and well muscled, and his teeth were his own.

He was fastidiously clean.

It did not help her. When he crawled beside her, when he touched her, a cascade of silent tears ran down her cheeks.

"Don't cry, Katrina," he warned her. "Don't cry."

She forced herself to stop. And inside, she began to shrivel up, and she felt that she was rotting.

Nothing could ever be the same again. Nothing in life. Perhaps Percy would never know, but she would, and that knowledge would lie in her heart forever.

Two days later, she rode away with Percy. He was still barely conscious. Katrina drove a pony cart with a flat attached where he could lie. She was grateful for one thing. He had barely been aware of anything since the moment he had been shot.

An armed guard escorted her part of the way. And after that, she was accosted by rebel lookouts. A riotous cheer went up when she identified herself and Percy, and they were given an escort back into the camp at Valley Forge.

Percy was ill through most of the winter, sometimes desperately ill. But on January 1, 1778 he awoke with clear eyes and a clear mind, and he reached out his arms to her.

And she was certain that any price was well worth his tender smile.

It was not so easy, of course. She had to explain, with her heart beating double time, that the commander of the loyalist troups had been an old friend, who had let them escape, due to past associations.

Percy frowned at first. He had been certain, right before losing consciousness, that someone had been speaking caustically to her. She shook her head, gave him a brilliant smile, and kissed him again, laughing because he had grown such whiskers.

"You have been very, very ill. Feverish and delirious," she told him. "See! It was a friend, for we are here, and we are alive. And Percy — oh, my love! — I could not live without you!"

Sore though he was, he pulled her to him, and a tender kiss became a hungry one. Weak as he was, his hands were suddenly everywhere, and before she knew it the ardent, desperate flames of her own desire had been kindled, and she was with her husband once again. Through it all, she was aware only of him, of the sweet and magical and heady passion that so sweetly raged between them. When it was over, she was grateful. So very grateful, because she had dreaded making love again. She had feared it, until it had happened so naturally. She had been afraid, horribly afraid, that she would burst into tears, that she would shiver or shake, that there would be some telltale sign that he would notice, that he would pull from her horror, that he would discover what she'd done — and despise her.

None of that happened. He whispered how much he loved her, and in the long winter nights that followed he proved it so tenderly that she was nearly able to forget herself.

It wasn't until spring, until Percy was on campaign and she was home again, that she had cause to panic once again. She was pregnant.

She didn't send word to him for the longest time because she was afraid, deathly afraid. So afraid that she was ill with it, and nearly lost the child. In May, she wrote to him because she knew that if she did not send word someone else might do so. In her missive she tried to sound optimistic and cheerful because she figured Percy was feeling downhearted. The war was wearing on and on, and it was going so drearily for the Patriots. The British army was regular and well trained and heavily supported with mercenary troops. The Patriots came from thirteen different colonies, and they were often ill-clad and ill-equipped and ailing, to boot.

He came back to her, though. She would never forget. It was the end of August, and the hot weather was just giving way to lovely cool nights and breezy days. He came riding down the path pell-mell, his horse rearing as he reined it in before the veranda. He leapt down and hurried to her, so handsome in his tight, dove-colored britches, knee boots, and loose white shirt. She felt so heavy! But he lifted her off her feet as if she weighed nothing, and he kissed her and he laughed and he had lamented the fact that she had grown so very big without his being there to see it. She tried to smile and she started to cry because she didn't know how to tell him that she was desperate for her pregnancy to last another month, so that she would know Percy to be the child's father for a certainty.

It did. God must have smiled upon her, for their son — James Percival, after her father and Percy's dear friend and Percy himself — was born on October first, nine months to the day from that first time they had touched after she'd fulfilled her bargain with Lord Palmer.

And again, when she held her son, when she and Percy marveled over him, she was glad again for life. She could forget the horror in the beauty. If there were no war . . .

But there was a war. A never-ending war, it seemed. Percy would come home to her and ride away again. Time helped to ease the painful memories of the past, but the future grew more arduous. With joy Katrina watched her son grow, but with dread she watched her husband ride away again and again. Battles were won, and battles were lost. The British came south, attacking in Georgia and South Carolina. Savannah fell in December of 1778; Charleston was captured in May of the following year.

And in the spring of 1781, the British decided to use Yorktown, Virginia, as their base of operations.

Katrina had heard nothing of this development. One morning she woke to see that there was a British gunboat out in the river. She panicked, for there was no one to help her. James, Percy's old friend, led a militia group which spent much time riding the countryside to protect it, but they would be no match against this kind of force.

Nearly one hundred people lived on the estate, and another hundred lived on the surrounding farms. Katrina wondered if they would burn the house — it was, after all, Percy Ainsworth's house. Then she remembered, with a full and blinding clarity, everything that had happened to her in the winter of 1777, and she nearly became hysterical. She could not lose control; she did not have time.

Quickly she packed a bag for the baby and called a group of the household servants and a young tenant farmer and his wife, entrusting them to bring her son inland, to Percy's cousins in the Valley. She wrote a hasty letter and prayed that it might find its way into Percy's hands, telling him about the ship, and in her haste, telling him that she was afraid. She knew that he was somewhere near. Benedict Arnold, the despised turncoat, had just led troops against Richmond, and Percy had been ordered south to harass and raid the British flank.

She kissed her son, allowing herself the luxury of a few tears; then she watched from the back until he was gone.

By then, the British were coming up the path to her home.

She prayed that this time it might be different. There were many fine officers and men in the enemy army; she knew a number of them.

But when the men drew near to the veranda, her heart sank. There was a naval captain among them, telling her that he needed supplies for his vessel and his troops. She would have gladly supplied their ship and their troops, if that had been all. She wouldn't have had much choice; she didn't have the power to stop them.

But the naval captain wasn't alone. Both her brother, Henry Seymour, and Charles Palmer were with him. Seeing them, Katrina had to grip the column to remain standing.

Henry came straight to her. Katrina ignored him. It had been more than five years since she had seen him. She told the ship's captain that he could take what he wanted, surely. She would be happy to deal with him — that she would have nothing to do with Seymour or Palmer.

"Sweet sister! Sweet, sweet sister! After all these years!"

Henry came up the steps in a fury, pushing her toward the door of the house. "Get back in!" he commanded her. He turned to the naval captain and told him to proceed with supplying his ship.

Henry Seymour drew her into the passage. He and Lord Palmer surveyed the manor with a practiced eye, opening doors to find the salon. With the three of them in the room, Henry closed the door. The silence that held for several seconds was stark and painful. "We should burn it, burn it to the ground," Henry muttered. Then he swung around on Katrina in a sudden fury. "Witch! You turned traitor on me, Katrina. Whore, and then traitor. After all I did for you."

"Henry, you must not be so harsh," Lord Palmer murmured solicitously. Katrina ignored him; she despised even the sound of his voice.

"All that you did for me!" she cried to Henry.

"Still, still, I am your brother, and blood runs thick. When it is over, if Ainsworth is not slain, I will procure an annulment for you. You married without my permission. I will take you home, Katrina, to Kent."

"Spare me your kindness, brother," she said bitterly. "I was never anything more to you than a pawn, Henry. And I will never go back to England. I am well of age now, and I will never leave my husband!"

Lord Palmer paused by her fine Chippendale table, fingering the brandy decanter. "And child?" he queried pleasantly.

"My son is not here; you cannot threaten me with him."

"Threaten you? Why, I'd no intent to threaten you, my dear. I merely wanted to see if he was mine. I'd heard of his birth, of course."

She inhaled sharply, then narrowed her eyes. "You need have no fear. He is not."

"Why the hostility, Katrina? After the disgraceful way you behaved, Charles is still willing to marry you."

"You are both insane!" she hissed. "Now get out of here — your people have taken what they wanted. Go!"

They smiled at each other, as if she had lost her mind. Perhaps she had. There were a few frightened slaves in the house, no one who could come to her defense. She realized with a sinking feeling that they were merely playing with her, that they would do as they so chose.

"Please —" she began. Palmer was walking toward her, still smiling. Henry was ignoring them both, having drawn a knife from his pocket to clean his nails.

Palmer came toward her and she started to scream. He kept smiling and picked her up, laughing when she beat against his shoulders and chest. He kicked the door open and bore her across the hall to the ballroom. She slapped him hard. Then her head reeled, for he returned the blow, and she was breathless and in pain when he dropped her to the floor. He towered above her, staring down at her while he removed his scabbard and sword.

Not again. She could not bear it. If there were a God in heaven, surely He would do something now.

The door to the ballroom burst open. "Charles! Wait, leave her!"

Henry was there, with a dust-covered panting scout standing behind him. "It is imperative!" Henry added.

Scowling, Lord Palmer strode over to the pair. Dismally, Katrina rolled on the floor, praying that they would not take her aboard their ship. She heard a flurry of whispers; then she cringed and stared up dully as Palmer towered over her once again.

"Katrina . . ." He swept off his hat in a gallant gesture. "We thank you for your hospitality."

"Dear sister!" Henry came, knelt upon one knee, and kissed her hand.

And then they were gone.

Miserably, Katrina struggled to her feet. Dazed, she wondered at her good fortune and was actually afraid of it. She hurried through the passage to the door and out to the veranda.

But it was true. The Redcoats were leaving. Leaving her and the manor untouched. Katrina came back into the parlor, and she sank into one of the chairs. Nathan, one of the downstairs servants, came to her. "Miz Katrina, are they gone?"

"Yes, Nathan, they are gone." She could not move. She felt weary. He walked softly into the room and poured her a glass of sherry, bringing it to her. She accepted it in grateful silence.

"I'll see you're not bothered, Miz Katrina," Nathan promised her as he left the room. She sipped the sherry and shuddered because it was all with her again, the shame of those days back in Pennsylvania, the misery. A fly buzzed against the window pane, and she listened lethargically to its drone. The sun began to fall, casting shadows across the room. She could not rise to light a candle.

Then suddenly the door burst open and Nathan was there again. "Miz Katrina, he's coming! The master's coming home."

Katrina leapt to her feet, her heart pounding, and she raced out to the veranda. It was true. Percy was riding down the path to the house. Thunderous hooves brought him at a gallop. He was in uniform — tight white breeches, blue frock coat, dark tricorn. The tail of his frock coat flew out behind him in his wake as he rode, and he was swift and gallant and fine.

She tore down the steps of the veranda to greet him. He had dismounted before she could reach him; he called to Nathan coming from the house behind her. "Take him, Nathan, please. And see that my wife and I are not disturbed."

She should have heard it. She should have heard the stark and hateful tone of his voice. She did not. The day had been too harrowing; she was too joyous to see him. She ran to him and threw her arms around his neck and clung to him.

"We shall go inside," he told her curtly.

"Percy — ?" she said in bewilderment.

"Inside!"

He caught her arm and dragged her up the steps. For the second time that day, she was wrenched into the parlor, and the door was closed. He eyed her as if she were a snake, while he strode for the table to pour himself a drink. He swallowed it down, still damning her with his eyes, eyes darker than the night, darker than any pit of everlasting hell.

"Percy, for the love of God —"

"Aye, for the love of God, Katrina." His glass went down so hard it shattered, and he was across the room, pinning her against the wall with his hands at her sides.

"I ought to kill you. I ought to strangle

you right here, this very second. You beautiful, treacherous slut!"

"Percy, what —"

"Tell me, Katrina, does the name Charles Palmer mean anything to you?"

She was afraid that she would faint. She could barely stand there, and she did not think she could ever speak fast enough to explain herself now.

"He is a British officer. He is —"

"He is running around Virginia, swearing to friend and foe that the toddler son claimed by Percy Ainsworth is his own seed."

She gasped in horror. "It is a lie, I swear it!"

"Is it a lie, Katrina?"

"Yes!"

"Men have claimed — good men — that you struck a bargain with this man. That you went to him willingly, again and again, to buy our freedom in Pennsylvania."

She looked down. She could not answer him.

"Katrina!"

"I did it for our lives!"

He inhaled so sharply that it sounded like a cannon shot. Then his hand flashed out with startling speed, catching her hard across the cheek. She cried out, and twisted past him. "It was for our lives, Percy, my God —"

He was striding toward her, and he looked furious and sick and ravaged. "I would rather die a thousand times over than have my wife bargain for me!" he thundered. She was afraid of him. She turned again to run, but his fingers caught her hair, dragging her back. He pulled her down to her knees, and he lowered himself too.

"And what of this very day, Katrina? Your note reached me. You knew I could not come before they did. They were here again, I know. James and a small band were out in the field. He came again, Katrina. Palmer was here. In my house! Tell me, my wife, what were the stakes this time? Did he have you here? In the ballroom? In the bedroom? Did you bring him there, Katrina? To our very room?" His hands were upon her shoulders; he shook her with a rising fury. She knew that he was heartsick, and yet fury rose within her. "No!" she cried. "No!"

"Liar! Before we were married, before the war ever began, you rode to him straight from me, time and time again!"

She gasped, stunned by his knowledge. He smiled at her slowly and bitterly. "It is true. You married me; you came to me; you lay with me; and you ran back to your Tory lover every time."

"No, no! You're wrong, Percy! I had to

play their game, yes. He could have sent me away! I never gave him anything. I — you fool!" she cried to him. "You and your honor and your manly idiocy! We are alive, Percy. We are alive!" She pushed away from him and got up, hating all the males of the species at that moment.

"They told me," he muttered. "They told me time and time again. I even heard the way he spoke to you . . ."

"Stop it!" she shrieked, and she ran for the door, as heartsick, as miserable, as he. He was after her in a flash, pulling her back, then grabbing her into his arms.

"What is this, Katrina? Even now you would race to your British lover? Supply his ship from my stores? Warm his bed from then on?"

"Stop it! Stop it!"

She tried to fight him. They fell against the ballroom door and rolled together across the Persian carpet and the hardwood floor. She grew hysterical and she kicked him and fought him. He caught her wrists and secured them high above her head, and at last, she saw his eyes, and the emotion within them.

He hated her. Despised her. Abhorred her. She had never seen such reproach or such a glittering, absolute scorn.

"Percy!" She cried out his name in terror.

"You will not!" he told her. "You will not run to your lover, not this night!" Then there was something like a sob that caught in his throat and he stroked her cheek. His fingers trembled and they were hard and taut, yet somehow gentle still.

"God, how I loved you! All these years, all these years you have tricked and deceived me, and still . . . I love you. Love you, desire you, need you . . ."

He kissed her hard. Blood caught in her lip and tears welled up inside of her. "No!" She tried to wrench herself away from him. She had to explain; she had to make him believe her.

"Tonight, Katrina, you will not tell me no."

He didn't understand, she realized bleakly. He thought that she was fighting him; he did not see that it was only his hatred that she battled. "Percy, please —"

"I do not please!"

"I have not betrayed —"

Hot, fevered, and brutal, he was upon her. She could not breathe for his kiss; she could not twist or roll for the weight of him. Fabric tore and was wrenched away, and she struggled with greater ferocity; and then tears washed down her face because he was her husband and she loved him, and it should never, never be like this.

She went still, and she felt then only the softness of his breath against her cheek, and then the feather-light stroke of his fingers on her naked flesh. A strangled sob sounded from him again, and he whispered that he loved her. He rose above her and plunged deep, deep inside of her, and she threaded her fingers through his hair, deliriously glad of him then.

Twilight fell to night. Worn and ragged from the expenditure of emotion, they slept. Dawn came. Katrina became vaguely aware that Percy was up, that he padded silently, agile and naked, to the window.

"My God!" he swore. And he turned and stared at her, even as she struggled to rise and cover herself with her torn clothing. "It was a trick! Betraying whore! It was a trick! They are out there now! The British are out there now!"

"No . . ."

He stumbled into his breeches, watching the window. Then the door to the ballroom burst open, and not just Henry and Charles Palmer stood there, but at least a dozen British regulars in uniform.

Percy looked from the men to Katrina. He smiled, and she would never forget that smile. She screamed; she tried to reach him.

"Whore! Leave me!" he railed, and he

sprang for his sword. Charles Palmer accepted the challenge, leaping into the room.

They clashed again and again. Katrina screamed once more.

Percy had the advantage. He clearly had the advantage. Parry after thrust, thrust after parry. He was the stronger of the two men. In a matter of minutes, Palmer's sword flew high into the air. Percy spun about to meet the next challenger, but he was not to be afforded the opportunity. A pistol shot rang out and he cried out, caught in the shoulder.

"Don't kill him!" Henry flared. "He mustn't die in battle; he must die a spy's death, hanged until dead!"

Men rushed around him to take him. Percy tried to jerk away. "The Patriots hanged Major André," he reminded his captors, "but he died as a gentleman, in full uniform!"

"Take him out!" Henry commanded.

Katrina called Percy's name as she hurried toward him. He turned and saw her, and for a moment, he shook off his captors. He touched her cheek and he smiled and told her softly, "A kiss, and it is death, Katrina. My God, if I could but avenge myself for this betrayal!"

"I did not —" she protested, but they were

dragging him from the room. Outside, a noose already hung over a tree; a horse stood beneath it. They dragged Percy along until he shook them off, and he walked of his own accord, rising to the wagon himself.

"No!" Katrina flew to Charles Palmer's side, wrenching his pistol from its leather holder. She raced toward the boy at the reins of the wagon. "No!" she screamed again.

But it was too late, for the whip had cracked, and the horses bolted and tore.

And Percy fell, hanged by the neck.

She screamed one more time and pain ripped through her. Pain, like a million swords piercing her heart. She grew instantly cold; she turned.

Henry stood behind her, his pistol was raised, and smoke wafted from it in a lazy curl.

He had shot her, she knew. Her own brother had shot her in the back. Death was imminent, and what did it matter, for Percy was gone, swinging from the rope.

Her life was seeping away from her, into the ground with the spill of her blood.

CHAPTER

22

Rap, rap, rap.

Gayle had started to scream. She screamed and screamed, and then the sounds of her voice had cut cleanly away. And she was now silent and deathly pale. Marsha rapped again, trying to bring her back.

"Gayle!" Marsha Clark commanded. "Gayle, wake up now. Wake up, and feel refreshed!"

"What's wrong?" Geoff's voice rang with alarm; he left his chair, running to Gayle's side.

Marsha Clark shook her head in distress, following Geoff to kneel beside Gayle. She searched for a pulse in Gayle's wrist. It was weak, nearly nonexistent.

"Oh, dear Lord," she murmured.

"Dear Lord!" Geoff repeated in alarm. Gayle's breathing was faint and shallow. "Do something! Bring her out of this!"

From the couch, they heard a groan.

Brent McCauley threw his feet down to the floor and tried to sit. "Headache," he muttered to himself. Geoff swung around to look at him. Brent eyed him blearily. "Geoff? What are you doing here? What's going on?"

He broke off, realizing that Gayle was unconscious in the wing chair, that her face was as pale as parchment and that Geoff and Dr. Clark looked alarmed. He tried to rise. He stumbled. "Gayle?" He whispered his wife's name uncertainly, then carefully made his way to her. Geoff moved to allow him room beside her. "Gayle!"

There was no response. She looked dead. So beautiful, almost peaceful. Pale and silent with her eyes closed, her hair about her in a golden halo. Like Sleeping Beauty, she was there but she was gone from him. He touched her fingers, and they were deathly cold.

"What has happened?" Brent demanded hoarsely. Then he swore. "I said no more of it, I said no more —"

"She had to!" Geoff snapped. "She had to, because of you. Because of the violence, because you collapsed, because she didn't know if . . ."

"If what?"

"If one day you would regress to your previous existence as Percy and stay there, stay there embedded in time and in death, and leave her again."

"Leave her again?"

"You son of a bitch! She never betrayed you! She tried and tried to explain. She begged your forgiveness and you —"

"Stop!" Brent clutched his head again, laying it upon his wife's lap. He gasped desperately for breath. Geoff and Marsha both backed away, staring down at Brent's dark bowed head. His fingers wound around hers. "I know!" he whispered.

"What?" Marsha said softly.

"I know. I know, I know what happened!" he groaned. "I've — I've relived it with her. I don't know how. It's vague and the memory fades now, but I know . . ."

He swung around with such passion that Geoff jumped to his feet, wary of violence again. But Brent's only violence was in his desperation. His handsome features were ragged; a pulse ticked furiously in his throat; and his eyes seemed like dark fire. "Take me back to her, Marsha. Take me back now. I have to reach her."

"I — I don't know if I can," Marsha murmured. "You're at the point of death. You're both at the point of death —"

"Then rouse her!"

Marsha shook her head desperately. Tears glazed her eyes. "I can't, Brent. I've tried. Maybe in time —"

"In time! She has no pulse now! She'll die again, in time. I cannot lose her, Marsha. Not again! Take me back there, and if you should lose us to death, so help me God, lose us both! I have to get back there, Marsha! I can't get there on my own! Damn you, help me now!"

He rose, glaring at Marsha. He bent and tenderly swept his wife into his arms and cradled her against him, then sat in the chair, holding her. He kissed her forehead, smoothing back her blond hair, and he whispered, "I love you! Oh, God, Gayle, I love you . . ."

He glared at Marsha again. Geoff stared helplessly. "Damn you . . . please!"

"All right," Marsha murmured, her voice trembling. "Relax," she said, and a sob caught in her voice. "Relax, Brent. Lean back and relax, and think of a peaceful river and a gentle day. Think back to a quieter time. Think back to innocence. Think back to love. Think back to a time when you were Percy Ainsworth, and Katrina was your wife. Think back to a time when you believed that she betrayed you.

"Think back . . .

"Think back to a time when the British dragged you out of this house, humiliated you. Go back, Percy, and see Katrina. Touch her. She loved you. She did not betray you.

"Forgive her, let her know you love her. Touch her, somehow. It is your only chance. . . ."

CHAPTER
23

HANGMAN'S NOOSE

THE MANOR HOUSE,
VIRGINIA COUNTRYSIDE
MAY 1781

The rope was around his neck. It was spring, and even then, he could hear the birds trilling. He could see the fields ready for planting. He smelled the rich, redolent scent of the earth.

He could feel the rope, harsh around his neck. Scratching, tearing at his flesh. Soon that little pain would not matter, for the life was being throttled from his body.

She was running toward him. Running. He could see her in those seconds, in those last seconds. He saw the anguish in her beautiful blue eyes, as lovely as the day, as eternal as the sky. He could see her, and he knew.

He knew . . .

She loved him; she had not sent for him in order to betray him. She loved him, and she had been used. Her eyes, her heart, were pure, as innocent as that long-ago day when she had first come to him, and he had taken her in the hay, fallen in love. For a lifetime. For an eternity.

Katrina!

He thought her name, or did he say it? It didn't matter. He was either dying, or he was dead. But then he screamed it louder. If the voice did not find substance, it was a screech within his head.

He saw it. He saw it all. He saw her rushing toward him, running, racing, hysterical, nearly demented. She shoved past Palmer and she had his pistol in her hands and it was loaded and ready.

But Henry Seymour was behind her. He didn't scream out a warning; he didn't say a word. He shot her. He shot his sister in the back, in cold blood.

But he could do nothing. The rope snapped, and he felt himself leaving. He was departing earth; he had no substance; he had no being. He could not hold her or cradle her. He could not go to her; he could not ease her dying. God in heaven, he could not forgive her, for he was dying himself . . .

Katrina!

Her name reverberated inside his head, and though he saw himself swinging there, swinging from the rope, turning purple and blue and swollen, he also had freedom. He reached for her. He could almost touch her. He started to run. To run and run and run.

Until he fell down beside her. He held her. He turned her into his arms, and he entwined his fingers in hers. *Katrina! Forgive me, forgive me, forgive me . . . Please God, forgive me. Katrina, Katrina, Katrina. Come back to me.*

CHAPTER
24

She felt that she hovered upon a brink, a precipice above a deep, dark pit. There was nothing here, except for that endless darkness, and she floated there, lost.

She was dying, and she knew it.

She would go. She would have to go, for there was no substance; there was nothing to hold her back. There was no light, and there was no sun; there was no beauty, and there was no love . . .

"Come back. Come back to me."

Suddenly, there was sound. There was the whisper of his voice.

And there was love.

"Come back to me. I love you. Oh my God, forgive me. Come back to me. Love me again . . ."

And there was a hand reaching out to hers. She had to catch it; she had to reach out in return.

It was life.

She stretched. She could see their fingers. Just the fingertips.

Touching.

And then he had her. He had her hand and he was pulling her against him and light was flooding back to her. Life and warmth, for where he touched her there was beautiful, wonderful warmth.

She opened her eyes. His face was above hers. Beautiful. His dark eyes glistened and tears dampened his cheeks and, despite those tears, he seemed so strong. Stronger than he had ever been. She reached up and her fingers trembled and she touched his cheek and she felt the moisture there.

"Brent?" she whispered.

"Oh, thank God! Oh, thank God!"

He pulled her tightly against him. He held her so tight that it hurt, but she didn't mind because it made her feel alive.

"Oh . . . goodness!"

They heard a thud, and it distracted them both. "What — ?" Brent began to ask. Geoff rose from behind the wing chair.

"Don't mind us. That was just Marsha. I guess it was her turn to pass out," Geoff answered. "Want a drink? I'm going to pick up Marsha, and then I'm going to have a drink. Hell no, I'm going to have about twenty."

Brent frowned with concern. "Will Marsha be all right? And Geoff, your chin —"

"Marsha will be fine. She's just had a bit too much excitement today. Yeah, my chin. You have one hell of a swing there, McCauley. Don't worry about it." He leaned down and kissed Gayle and patted Brent on the shoulder. "Jesus! Am I glad to see you both here back with us." His voice was husky, and he sounded embarrassed, which was logical, Gayle thought. It was all receding from her already. Something had happened, but she could barely remember what. All she really knew was that she had been lost, and then Brent had been there. He had reached out a hand to her, and she was back.

"But" — Geoff warned with a groan — "in my next life, I sure as hell hope I choose my friends differently. I've probably acquired a head full of gray hair in the last damned hour."

He looked pale. His neat hair was disarrayed and there was a bruise rising on his chin. He smiled weakly. Then he picked up Marsha and stretched her out on the couch that Brent had recently vacated. "Come on, Marsha. It's over. It's all over, and it's all right."

Marsha groaned. She was coming around. Gayle stared up at Brent and touched his cheek. She smiled tentatively and then he pulled her close and then he started to laugh, happily swirling her around and around in circles.

"Don't mind me," Geoff called after them. "Marsha and I will just make ourselves at home here!"

Brent let her fall against him, and she looked past him to where Geoff stood over Marsha, who was now blinking.

"Thank you!" she whispered.

He nodded and she took Brent's hand and he led her out through the passage. "Wait!" she called to him, and he paused. She threw open the door to the ballroom and she ran into the center of it and stood there.

"Brent! It's okay now. It's okay!"

He leaned against the door, and he nodded. He still looked a little pale to her, but he smiled again and reached out his hand. She hurried back to him, taking it and he led her through the passage to the veranda.

The sun was still shining. Just barely. Darkness would fall soon, but in those moments, there was warmth and light.

"God!" he muttered and he lowered his head. And she felt that he was really offering up a prayer. Then he let out a yell that sounded like a rebel war cry, and he swept her into his arms again and they ran down the steps. He swung her around in circles, before lifting her high above and then letting her slide slowly to the ground against the length of his body.

Catching his shoulders, she smiled with the same ecstasy, and then she frowned. "Oh, Brent! What really happened? I thought that I had caught onto something for a moment, but it faded and it was gone. I was so afraid. It was so cold, and then you were there. You were there with me, and it was like walking back into the sunlight again. What happened? I think I know something but it can't be, can it? It must be a dream."

He shook his head. "I don't know," he whispered, never taking his eyes from her face. "I don't know. I only know that, somehow, it's right again."

"It's right!" she repeated before she pressed her lips against his, sweetly and hungrily. In turn he kissed her forehead and her cheeks, the tip of her nose, her chin, and finally her lips again. She fell against his chest. "Brent . . ."

Her head fell back and her eyes, as blue as the sky, and as pure, met his. Nor did shadows haunt the darkness of his. Rakish, languorous, lazy, with the devil's own glitter, but empty of all torment.

"I feel that I have to hold you," he told her.

"Now? Here? We've guests."

"We've a hayloft. And I'm sure our guests will understand and will see themselves out."

She lifted her hands to him happily. He let out a peal of deep, gleeful laughter and swung her into his arms again.

Anyone seeing them together would surely smile: love, young love; it was such a beautiful thing. Honeymooners looked at one another like that, lovers newly met.

Moments later, he had laid a blanket on the hay. Twilight was falling, and the light that filtered in was pink and sweet and fragrant, and it fell gently over their naked bodies when they had shed their clothing.

She walked toward him.

She was glorious, the sleek, rounded curves of her flesh caught in that light. She moved with sensual grace, and yet when she touched him, with sexual pleasure came a curious sense of purity. With her, the most intimate, evocative act would somehow still be innocent.

It was the emotion, of course. So deep, so shattering, it entered into everything. Into the very core of their lovemaking, as if each touch were new . . .

As if it were the very first time . . .

Perhaps, in a way, it was. It was the cleansing, brought by the violence of the storm. It was the spring, come again.

It was a second chance, and if he never understood it in his life, he would still thank God daily for it.

Later he murmured, "Have we been dreaming?"

She smiled beneath him, glistening and damp, and lazily touched his brows, and then his cheeks. "Dreaming. Yes. Surely, we are dreamers. But I love you. I love you so very much. I will love you all of my life."

He touched her lip and grinned. "No, sweetheart. I will love you for far more than a lifetime. I swear, I will love you into all eternity."

"Into all eternity," she agreed, and she kissed him again.